The Body on the Shore

Nick Louth is a best-selling thriller writer and an award-winning financial journalist. A 1979 graduate of the London School of Economics, he went on to become a Reuters foreign correspondent in 1987. He was for many years a *Financial Times* columnist, and a regular contributor to many other financial titles in print and online. *The Body on the Moor* is the eighth book in the DCI Gillard crime series, and his twelfth thriller overall. Nick Louth is married and lives in Lincolnshire.

www.nicklouth.com

Also by Nick Louth

Bite
Heartbreaker
Mirror Mirror
Trapped

DCI Craig Gillard Crime Thrillers

The Body in the Marsh
The Body on the Shore
The Body in the Mist
The Body in the Snow
The Body Under the Bridge
The Body on the Island
The Bodies at Westgrave Hall
The Body on the Moor
The Body Beneath the Willows

NICK LOUTH

THE BODY ON THE SHORE

CANELO

First published in the United Kingdom in 2018 by Canelo

This edition published in the United Kingdom in 2019 by

Canelo
Unit 9, 5th Floor
Cargo Works, 1–2 Hatfields
London, SE1 9PG
United Kingdom

A CIP catalogue record for this book is available from the British Library.

Print ISBN 978 1 78863 546 2
Ebook ISBN 978 1 78863 222 5

Look for more great books at www.canelo.co

Printed and bound in Great Britain by Clays Ltd, Elcograf S.p.A.

3

For Louise, as always

Book 1

Chapter 1

A damp Friday morning in January, and in the south-west London suburb of Kingston upon Thames the rush hour was at its peak. Karen Davies was running a little late. She would normally be at her desk by 8 a.m., but rain had slowed the traffic to a crawl and she was still three miles away from the office in Roosevelt Avenue, between Surbiton and Esher. It was 8.13 a.m. when she nosed her Nissan Micra into the last available slot in the small car park behind the building where she worked. She had only been working as a receptionist in the architectural practice of Hampton, Deedes, Gooding for two weeks, but she already felt that her new life was going well. She had rented an eighth-floor studio flat in Kingston, expensive but manageable, with a glimpse of the Thames. She felt much safer here than in her old home in Cape Town. She had read about a wave of stabbings in the capital, bag- and phone-snatchers on mopeds, but most of that was in inner-city areas, and still a fraction of what occurred in South Africa. Here in the Surrey commuter belt, the worst problems seemed to be traffic congestion, the continually miserable weather, and some Londoners who seemed less friendly than she had hoped.

Fortunately that wasn't true of Hampton, Deedes, Gooding. The office was full of really engaging people, especially Peter Young. He was her favourite of the three junior partners. Always at his desk first, usually by eight o'clock, he always had a pot of coffee ready for others as they arrived. He was a handsome man in his late 20s with a shock of wavy blond hair, which contrasted nicely with his chiselled dark features and big brown eyes. Sadly, for Karen, Peter was firmly taken: a happily married man with two gorgeous children and a beautiful Peruvian wife. The family portrait on his desk looked like something from a fashion magazine. Peter always wore dazzling white shirts without a tie, tight blue jeans and highly polished shoes. Now she felt ready for a boyfriend, she would have to expand her horizons beyond work.

Karen jogged up the stairs to the first floor and let herself in. The smell of coffee filtered into her nostrils as she shrugged off her coat, shook the rain off and hung it in the closet by her desk. As she filled her mug from the still-hot coffee jug, she called out to Peter and asked him if he wanted a refill.

No reply.

It was probably ten minutes later after she'd logged on, checked for any urgent emails and gathered the post that she walked into Peter's office, coffee in hand. What she saw there made her scream loud enough to raise the dead.

–

Craig Gillard was the on-call detective chief inspector for that day, but as the shift didn't begin until 9 a.m. he had taken the opportunity for a pre-work swim at the local leisure centre. He'd had the fast central lane of the pool to himself for the first hour, but now even on front crawl with tumble turns, he knew he wasn't going to be able to

3

finish his second kilometre. Heaving himself out, he went to the communal showers, finding the one reliably hot spigot to stand under as he considered his day. It had been a good week, his second with no boss as DCS 'Radar' Dobbs was still on leave of absence, and the vacancy for assistant chief constable was still unfilled. That had left him free to tackle the spate of moped robberies which had now spread out from Croydon into Surrey's leafier suburbs. An arrest had been made in last Thursday's knifing at Fast Chicken, and two were awaiting sentencing for a door-to-door fraud in Chipstead. That all made it a pretty successful week. As he walked to his locker, towelling his hair dry, he remembered he was taking Sam out for a meal tonight. It was the first anniversary of his marriage proposal, and he'd found a delightful Turkish restaurant in Carshalton, which had got great reviews.

But before he got there, he heard the buzz of his phone. Amplified by the metal of the locker, it sounded like some gigantic angry insect trapped in a cocoa tin. His gut instinct told him, even before he answered, that this wasn't going to be the quiet and easy day he'd wanted, and that the long-planned anniversary was going to be put on ice.

–

An hour later, DCI Craig Gillard stood on the threshold of Peter Young's office. Hampton, Deedes, Gooding, or HDG+ according to the sign outside, was now a scene of carnage. The architect was slumped face down over his drawing desk as if he was asleep, with one arm stretched out. The drawing he'd been working on was creased underneath his body, the tracing paper flecked with blood, and his desktop computer screen was tipped over on its back. The wall behind him, originally white, was sprayed crimson, at first glance like some piece of conceptual art applied with a flick from an over-filled brush. Gory runnels had made their way down to the skirting board.

The young constable who'd been first on the scene looked as sick as a dog. No wonder: even Gillard, with years of experience of murder and assault had never seen anything as heartlessly clinical as this. For PC Niall Weston, who only qualified from police college at Hendon a month ago and lived just round the corner, it was probably overwhelming. Weston had just happened to be walking past HDG+ on his way to get a bus into London for a training session when a hysterical woman burst out of the offices yelling for help.

Looking to his left Gillard could see two neat bullet holes, just over four inches apart, through both panes in the huge double-glazed window, with just an inch-wide circle of frosting around the holes. Young's office looked over Roosevelt Avenue, one of the main roads through the suburb, and traffic noise was now filtering in through those twin fissures.

He'd have to wait for CSI before entering the room. He hadn't let the paramedics in either. When they remonstrated with him he simply pointed to a thumb-sized lump of mauve matter that lay on the edge of the architect's last drawing. 'That's a piece of his brain,' he said. Fortunately, young Weston, having seen the victim was dead, hadn't been in either. He'd remembered his crime scene course and secured the area as best he could until help arrived.

Gillard wouldn't be able to tell for certain for a while, but if Young had been sitting as he was now, the holes in the glass would have been about level with his head, indicating that he couldn't have been shot from street level. However, if he had been standing and then fallen back into his seat, which was unlikely but possible, then perhaps he was. The blood spatters on the wall were low enough to indicate the former trajectory. He couldn't see for certain without entering the room where in that bloodstain the bullets had buried themselves. Establishing that would probably decide the debate very quickly.

The detective steepled his hands on either side of his nose and took several deep breaths to adjust to the enormity of his task. The 'golden hour', that important first hour after a crime is committed, was over. If this was a professional job, the perpetrators would be long gone. The evidence in front of him was safe, so the first priority was to get into the building across the street from which the shots may have been fired. He radioed in for backup and instructed Weston to get some tape to seal off the pavement outside. Gillard exited HDG+, passing a bewildered group of architects on the pavement behind the bus stop who were waiting vainly to begin the day's work. He crossed the broad tree-lined Roosevelt Avenue at the zebra crossing and approached the shops opposite. If the assumed trajectory was correct, the only possible sites for firing the weapon were two first-floor flats, one above a kebab house and the other above a tattoo parlour.

There were two street doorways which looked like they reached the flats. The kebab house was closed, and the tattoo parlour just opening. Gillard bided his time awaiting the uniform backup which would be required to make these buildings two more potential crime scenes. While he waited he looked at the man who was moving about inside the tattoo parlour. He was a thickset fellow in his 40s with a moustache and a complicated razor-cut hairstyle. He had a sleeveless leather jacket which displayed his very large, muscular arms, decorated in an incredibly ornate monochrome. Gillard couldn't help wondering how much, if any, of it he'd been able to do himself.

Sirens heralded the arrival of two carloads of uniformed police and a CSI van. Gillard directed half of them to secure the flats and shops opposite the scene of the killing, locate keyholders and stop anyone entering or leaving. The uniforms were told not to enter either flat. He radioed in and asked for someone to contact the local authority for any CCTV of the area.

The tattooist stood in the doorway of the shop, looking past the female PC who had come to speak to him, and instead asked Gillard: 'What happened?'

'We are investigating a serious incident opposite,' the PC said, speaking to the tattooist's ear. He continued to ignore her.

'She will tell you anything you need to know at this stage,' Gillard responded and turned away. 'But can I ask you, do you know the people who live upstairs?'

'Above me,' he said pointing skyward. 'There's a young couple. I did a butterfly on her shoulder a couple of months ago.'

'What about next door?'

'I think it's family from the kebab place.'

A male PC had rung both the doorbells and got no reply.

Within half an hour the uniforms had located the owner of the kebab shop, the landlord who owned the flat above the tattoo parlour and, by telephone, the couple who lived there. Gillard was joined by Detective Inspector Claire Mulholland and Detective Constable Colin Hodges, who'd already got the Surrey Borough of Elmbridge to put together all of its Roosevelt Avenue CCTV footage for the last 24 hours. The back entrances into both properties had been secured and all that remained was to enter them. 'Do you think there is anyone still in there?' asked Mulholland.

'No,' he replied. 'This looks like a hit. I can't see any chance of the perpetrator still being around.' He looked in at the uniformed police officer, a stocky woman who he thought was called Yvonne. She was sitting in a barber's-style chair opposite the tattooist and taking a statement. Gillard had already established that the tattooist had neither seen nor heard anything suspicious since arriving at the shop half an hour ago. In fact, nobody that the police had so far talked to claimed to have heard a shot. If it was silenced, that would further support the idea of it being a professional hit.

Chapter 2

At 10 a.m. Gillard and Mulholland were in the flat above the kebab house, standing in the doorway of what was said to be the lounge, though it was hard to be sure. Clearly quite a number of people had been living here. There were two mattresses on the floor with dishevelled clothing on them. Damp washing was strung on a cord that zigzagged across the room. Crammed into the room next to a sliding-door wardrobe was a child's cot and a cardboard box of infants' toys. Gillard couldn't see clearly to the window that looked out onto the main road, and wasn't anxious to go further in until CSI got around to checking it over. There was no obvious sign of used cartridges, though if this was a professional job the shooter would almost certainly have retrieved them. The bathroom at the back showed more than a dozen toothbrushes, three or four sets of leather sandals, shower shoes and slippers, in both male and female styles.

Mr Kaban, the Kurdish proprietor, explained that he had many visitors, some from his family which was spread between Kurdistan and eastern Turkey. They would pass through sometimes, working a few days or a few weeks with him at the shop, or at the building firm run by his brother. Unlike others, he said, they didn't mind the noise of traffic or the overcrowding. 'My rent is cheap, very cheap. And if they work for me, is free,' he said. There were three people staying there at the moment, two men who worked with his brother, and the wife of one who did cleaning work in an office nearby. Kaban asked how long before his tenants could return to the flat.

'Not today probably, but we'll be as quick as we can,' Mulholland said.

Gillard meanwhile was using binoculars, trying as best he could to stare through the forest of hanging washing to the architects' practice opposite. This was the view that an assassin would have had. It looked far from perfect, and he couldn't even clearly see the window behind which Peter Young had worked. The only other window on this side of the flat was in the kitchen. Standing at the threshold he surveyed the cramped but clean surfaces, the Baby Belling worktop electric cooker and an old fridge-freezer leaning drunkenly against the window, blocking most of the light. The position of the fridge left only a six-inch strip of glass to the left which gave a view onto Roosevelt Avenue. It was an unlikely place for a hit man to choose, with a restricted position and a sliding sash that was old. The bottom half was clearly painted in, and had not been moved since. The upper sash would perhaps open, but he wasn't going to try until the fingerprint technician had given it the once-over. In any case it would have made for an awkward shooting position.

–

By 10.30 a.m. Gillard had gained access to the other flat, above the tattoo parlour. Angela Dinsmore lived there with her boyfriend Ryan Hardcastle. She had taken a break from her hairdressing job in Richmond after she had got the call to open up for the police. She was a personable and friendly woman in her early 20s, clearly excited more than concerned about the police operation, and full of questions that Gillard was not yet ready to answer. She did confirm, however, that no one had been staying with them, and that no one but the tattooist landlord downstairs had a key to the place. Both she and her boyfriend had left for work shortly after 7.30 a.m. and had not seen anything unusual.

Gillard stood on the threshold of the flat's kitchen-diner and surveyed the large window which overlooked Roosevelt Avenue. Unlike the flat next door, this gave a clear view of Hampton, Deedes, Gooding. While a few branches of a plane tree outside would obscure the sightlines from the left of the room, the remainder gave a clear view, in the right light conditions, towards the desk from which Peter Young worked about 50 yards away.

He descended the stairs and found Angela Dinsmore waiting for him at the threshold. 'Someone outside told me there had been a stabbing across there,' she said, pointing across the street.

'We're not really in a position to confirm the details of this incident,' Gillard said as he watched crime scene technicians in their white plastic suits and gumboots emerging from the building opposite. 'But there has been a death and we have urgent enquiries to make.'

'Well I'm not sure why you're on this side of the road,' she said. 'Like I said, we were gone by 7.30 and didn't see anything.'

Gillard nodded, then explained she wouldn't be able to return to the flat for the rest of the day. He didn't catch her next question, because he was looking at a text on his phone from DC Michelle Tsu.

It seemed that Angela's boyfriend Ryan Hardcastle had a substantial criminal record.

That was interesting. Gillard's reply was brief and to the point: bring him in.

–

Back on the other side of Roosevelt Avenue, PC Niall Weston had been facing something of an insurrection trying to keep everyone out of the building. The senior partner of Hampton, Deedes, Gooding was there, leading the charge. Kelvin Alexander was insistent that there were some designs in Young's office that were needed on-site today. CSI were already in the office where Young had been shot. As Gillard stood at the threshold, he watched two technicians in Tyvek plastic suits and masks bending over the body, while a third was using a laser measuring device on the bloodstained wall.

'Got anything for me, Yaz?'

One of the bending technicians stood up and waved a greeting. Yaz Quoroshi was senior CSI for the forensic service shared between Surrey and Sussex police forces, and the most diligent of crime scene investigators. He stepped gingerly around the desk, picking up a paper evidence bag as he did so.

'Found this on the carpet,' Yaz said, showing him the evidence envelope as if it was a bag of sweets. Using tweezers, he extracted a bloodstained bullet. 'A hollow-point round.' The top end had opened up like a metallic flower whose petals were bent right open and back on themselves.

'Remind me,' Gillard said.

'A hollow-point is designed to spread on impact, causing more tissue damage because of the bullet's broader cross section. They're designed to stop somebody with a single shot.'

'This took two.'

'Not really – the first killed him outright. The second passed through his wrist and ended up in the wall.' Yaz turned and aimed a laser pointer at the wall behind him. 'It's still in there.'

'How do you know which was the first shot?'

'Not too hard. Plaster dust from the wrist shot was deposited on top of the bloodstains from the first.'

Gillard squinted at the wall. 'Any clue on the trajectories?'

'That's tricky. Ideally, with a normal bullet, we would like to be able to line up each hole in the glass with a projectile embedded in the far wall. That would give us a clear line to the origin of each shot. However it seems that the wrist shot was deflected too, so we're going to have to guesstimate.'

Gillard nodded. 'It feels like a hit, to me. What do you reckon, Yaz?'

The Iraqi nodded, his Tyvek suit crackling. 'Definitely.'

'But why would anyone want to kill an architect?'

'Maybe he designs prisons.'

–

It was 2 p.m. by the time Gillard was finished at the crime scene, and his mood was not improved by news from HQ that his team would all be based at the Khazi. The notorious mobile incident room was a glorified Portakabin on the back of an ancient diesel-belching lorry, which was now parked in a side street 100 yards from the architects' office. Gillard's heart sank as he climbed the wooden steps, opened the squeaky plywood door and grimaced at the toilet-like smell and the black mould that proliferated on its institutional off-white paint. DI Claire Mulholland was already there, looking grim, having just come back from breaking the news of Peter Young's death to his wife, Laura.

'Sorry, I'm afraid we're stuck with this,' Gillard said, wiping a runnel of condensation from the wall.

'It's okay so long as you don't lean on the walls,' she replied. 'Black mould is hard to get off a white blouse.'

He nodded. 'So what did you discover?'

'A lot, but nothing that helpful. Peter Young was married with two young children, had been living in Britain for 12 years,' Mulholland said. 'His original name was Pjetër Ardian Cela. He turned up unaccompanied in Canterbury as a 15-year-old, claiming he was orphaned in Kosovo during the conflict in the late 1990s and had run away to Britain to escape persecution by the Serbs.'

'Do we know how he got to be in Kent?'

'He had just got off a French tour bus, and when picked up claimed to have lost his documents. He sought asylum, helped by the children's charity Barnardo's, and was granted it a year later. That was pretty slow by the standards of the time. He changed his name to the maiden name of his foster mother, and seems to have lived an exemplary life. A clever student, a talented artist, Birmingham University, won some prizes. I've left Gabby Underwood with the wife to act as liaison officer.'

Gillard stroked his chin. 'We will need to talk to the foster parents, dig up any original documentation, family connections back home and so on. Any ideas why anyone would want to kill him?'

Mulholland shrugged and ran her fingers through her bob of blond hair. 'Nothing so far. It's too early to start prodding and probing his wife for her ideas. She was distraught, quite inconsolable. We'll need to give it a day or so maybe for her, so let's start with the foster parents. They have agreed to see us tomorrow afternoon.'

—

By the end of the day the CSI team had largely finished with Peter Young's office. Once the body was removed, a laser device on a tripod was set up to try to line up the bullet hole in the glass with the buildings opposite. It certainly looked as if the shots were fired from the apartment occupied by Ryan Hardcastle and Angela Dinsmore, where the fingerprint technician had found plenty of dabs around the lounge window. They matched both Ryan Hardcastle's prints and the elimination prints just taken from Angela, but there was no bullet casing or gunfire residue found.

More progress was being made at the crime scenes than in the Khazi. The printer that Gillard had asked for seemed to be dead, and having waited half an hour for a promised techie to turn up, the DCI squeezed underneath the desk trying to check the connections himself. It was a bad time for his mobile to buzz. Wriggling to get in a position to see the screen, he banged his head, and hadn't quite finished swearing when he pressed the button to take Colin Hodges' call.

'Was it something I said?' the DC asked.

'I'm under a desk trying to fix that bastard printer,' the DCI said. 'I read somewhere that we'll soon be printing 3D components for cars and aircraft, but from my experience anything Surrey Police buys can't even manage two dimensions. This one showed complete bloody bewilderment at a single sheet of paper with a letter on it.'

'My brother's a computer whizz,' Hodges said. 'Looks after some massive technology system for NATO in Brussels, so I always follow his advice.'

'And what's that?'

'Turn it off, then turn it back on again.'

'Thanks,' said Gillard, extricating himself from under the desk, and finding he'd now got a lump of old chewing gum stuck in his hair. 'So what was it that you called to tell me?'

'Ah yes. Ryan Hardcastle is a glazier, and I just rang the yard where he works. His boss said that he took off in a van at lunchtime and hasn't been back since. His phone is switched off. I've alerted everyone to look out for him.'

'Good work,' Gillard said, now back on a seat in front of the one reliably working terminal. He entered the password for the Police National Computer, and then watched Hardcastle's criminal record slowly materialize before him. He had three convictions for affray, one for cannabis dealing and one for actual bodily harm, the latter related to his part-time job as a nightclub bouncer. The photograph showed a thickset man, more fat than muscle, aged 28, with piggy eyes and a wispy dark moustache. Hardcastle obviously thought himself a bit tasty with his fists, and the record showed a man with a temper. The idea that he was also a cool and nerveless assassin didn't quite seem to fit. But on the other hand he may well have met such a man during the six months he spent inside HMP Coldingley two years ago. A category B prison, Coldingley was just west of Woking, about an hour away. He made a mental note to check who he'd shared a cell with.

Just then the door to the Portakabin slammed and DI Claire Mulholland walked in. He greeted her, while continuing to trawl through the notes of interviews on the screen.

'Did you get the printer working?' she asked.

'Not exactly. There's no techie until tomorrow.'

Claire said nothing for a moment, then said: 'That's an original place to keep your gum.'

'Yes, isn't it?' he said acidly. 'Some moron decided that sticking it under the desk was a great idea. Now I'm going to have to cut it out.'

'There are other ways,' she replied. 'But you might not like them. You can soak it in peanut butter for a few minutes, or cooking oil.'

He slowly pivoted around on the chair and scowled at her. 'Peanut butter?'

She began to laugh. 'Okay, I've got some scissors in my bag. Just don't tell Sam that another woman has been running her hands through your hair.'

'I won't. She's upset enough that I've had to cancel our meal out tonight.'

–

Gillard dropped Mulholland off at home in Staines and then in the early evening returned to the offices of HDG+ Architects for one last look at the crime scene. He climbed the stairs and found PC Yvonne Kingsland, the stocky officer who'd interviewed the tattooist, on the door to Peter Young's office.

'Relieving Niall Weston?' he asked.

'Yes, he is absolutely knackered, sir. I think he'll be back for the overnight from nine. Still, shouldn't be too spooky for him. The body's already been taken to the mortuary.'

'Have the architects been giving you a hard time?'

She looked over her shoulder. 'Stuck-up bastard that partner "Mr Kelvin",' she rabbit-eared her fingers. 'Thinks his work is more important than ours. He said Peter Young was working on some vital modification for a construction project that is already underway. Seems he literally died on the job.' She grinned experimentally, only widening her smile when it was clear that Gillard appreciated her dark sense of humour.

'I'll go and have a word with him.' Gillard smiled.

'Actually I'm right here.' A tall man with a dazzling kingfisher-blue shirt had emerged from an office behind them. He had a mane of silvery hair and the kind of weathered tan which has nothing to do with a bottle or a sunbed. He stuck out his hand and introduced himself. 'Kelvin Alexander, senior partner.'

Gillard reciprocated, and then began to explain the importance of crime scenes before being interrupted.

'Look, I know it seems terribly discourteous, but as they've already taken Peter, I just need this tiny little favour.' He circled finger and thumb in front of his eye. 'There is a data stick in or around his PC with his modifications for the roof of one of our clients' buildings in London. They are on my case about it, because they have

18

got three enormous cranes on a daily rental of tens of thousands, not to mention the structural engineers, just waiting for us. Can I just nip in?'

'No.' Gillard held the man's gaze. 'Can't have you shedding your own DNA and fingerprints in there and contaminating the crime scene.'

'This is preposterous,' he said, looking down his aquiline nose. 'I shall speak to the chief constable. We met at the business round table last year. I'm sure your name will come up in conversation.'

'Please feel free,' Gillard responded. He was quite used to this kind of response. 'But I can assure you in this case she will back me up completely. Nobody is to go in there until CSI has finished. Now if I was you, I'd return to your office and get on with your work. It sounds like you have plenty of it.'

The moment that Kelvin Alexander had disappeared Yvonne Kingsland gave a little squeal of glee. 'Well done, sir. That's told him!'

Chapter 3

Saturday

Exactly 24 hours after Peter Young was shot dead, and just over 100 yards away, all the detectives on the case were squeezed into the Khazi. With Gillard, as senior investigating officer, sat DCs Colin Hodges, Carl Hoskins and Michelle Tsu, CSI head Yaz Quoroshi and DI Claire Mulholland. Most were sitting on tables because of the lack of chairs.

'So this is what we know,' Gillard said, raising his voice above the drone of the extractor fan, which struggled to suck the damp from the room. 'Peter Young, successful architect, aged 27, no obvious known enemies, was yesterday killed by two shots fired through the window sometime between 7.45 and 8.15 a.m. when he was found by the receptionist Karen Davies. Next on the scene was one of the partners, Finlay McMullen, and then our own PC Niall Weston who was passing on his way to a training course.' He passed out a pack which included statements from all three.

'As you can see, the most striking piece of evidence is that no one heard anything. Not a gunshot, not the fracture of the glass, no scream nor the sound of the body falling. Now of course there is a fair amount of traffic noise in Roosevelt Avenue at that time on a Friday morning, but it is a little surprising all the same.'

Gillard then invited Yaz Quoroshi to describe the crime scene and ballistics evidence. 'I think we can assume that a suppressor was fitted to the murder weapon, and with the knowledge that hollow-point rounds were used, these do point to a professional hit.'

'I'm no gun expert,' Mulholland said. 'So what's the relevance of hollow-point ammunition?'

'I was hoping someone would ask that,' Yaz said, 'because I had to look it up myself.' He repeated the effect of a hollow-point bullet on the target. 'The curious thing about this kind of ammunition is that it has been illegal for military use since 1899, under the Hague Convention, so it even predates the Geneva Convention of 1949. This was because it would cause unnecessary suffering. However, in the UK and in many other places, it is the only kind of ammunition that can legally be used, apart from shotgun cartridges, for hunting animals.'

'Okay, so it's fine to cause unnecessary suffering to an animal,' Michelle Tsu said.

Yaz laughed. 'It's more the argument that the deformed bullet on exiting the target will not be a danger to anyone else.'

She didn't look impressed by the answer. Yaz continued: 'The obvious places from which the weapon was fired are one of two flats opposite. Early investigations favour the flat above the tattoo parlour because it has better sightlines.'

'Did you get any residues from a weapon there?' Michelle asked.

'No. Nor unexplained fingerprints, but that doesn't preclude it being the location. It's entirely possible that a professional hit man could have broken in while the occupants were at work, made his hit, cleaned up, taken his cartridges with him, and made good his escape.'

'Sounds a bit James Bond,' said Colin Hodges. 'For bumping off an architect.'

There was a general murmur of agreement.

'That leads us neatly into the background. Claire, would you do the honours?'

Mulholland got to her feet and directed everyone to the third and fourth pages of their documents, printed off at police HQ in Guildford as the Khazi printer was still not working. 'The murder victim was married, with two young children, and lived in Surbiton. We know quite a lot about the last 12 or so years of Peter Young's life since his arrival as an orphan from Kosovo. It's a study in determination and achievement, as underlined by the description of him by his former foster parents.'

'Could the missus have ordered it?' asked Hoskins.

'Too early to say,' she replied. 'We're going to take a statement from her later today. She's a speech therapist for the NHS, but seems to have been at home with the children at the time he died. We will have to check on all this, and on the family's financial circumstances. Debts, big insurance policies, that kind of thing.'

'So what do we know about the occupants of the flats?' asked Yaz.

Gillard got to his feet. 'The couple who live above the tattoo parlour are Angela Dinsmore and Ryan Hardcastle. She's clean, but he definitely isn't. Convictions for affray and ABH. Pretty small-time really; on the other hand he left work yesterday at noon and hasn't been seen since. We would very much like to talk to him.'

Saturday afternoon

Eric and Margaret Robinson lived in a large, rambling 1930s council house on the edge of Stevenage, in the commuter belt north of London. Unlike modern-day community housing, these whitewashed homes had large gardens separated by paling fences from their neighbours. When DCI Gillard and DI Mulholland pulled up in an unmarked Ford Focus, they could see three children of various ethnic backgrounds playing in the front garden. They waited a few minutes, hoping that the promised liaison officer from Hertfordshire police would arrive, but then decided to get on with it. When Gillard opened the gate, a black girl with her hair in corn rows said: 'Hello. Have you come to see Mum and Dad?'

'Yes we have,' Gillard responded. 'Are they in?'

'Dad is in the shed at the back, and Mum is doing some cooking,' said a younger Asian-looking girl wearing an anorak.

Five minutes later the two police officers were ensconced on an old and rather sagging settee in an unfashionable lounge, with mugs of coffee and a plate of biscuits on the table in front of them. Mrs Robinson had the robust physique and ruddy complexion of someone who had spent most of her life outdoors. With apple cheeks, pale-blue laughing eyes and a thick ponytail of white hair, she had a passing resemblance to a female Santa. Her husband, wearing old-fashioned trousers with braces over a tartan shirt, came in to join them. He was drying his hands on a tea towel.

'So what is this about Peter?' Eric said as he sat down.

'I'm very sorry to have to give you some bad news,' Mulholland began.

They looked almost paralysed with fear. 'Has something happened to him?' Eric asked. Margaret had her hands over the bottom of her face, in preparation for something horrible.

At that moment a blond boy of about seven burst into the room, breathlessly. 'Mum, Mum. I found a frog under the tree.'

Margaret turned a beaming smile on him. 'That's wonderful, Martin. You go out now, find a bucket to put him in. I'll join you in half an hour. Tell the others to stay outside and not come in. Would you do that?'

'Yes,' he said, only now noticing the two strangers on the sofa, and eyeing them suspiciously. 'Who are you?' he asked.

'We've just come to talk to your mum and dad,' Mulholland said, smiling.

'Run along now,' Eric said, waving the boy away.

When the room had regained its calm, Gillard spoke: 'I'm sorry to have to tell you that Peter Young was yesterday found dead at his place of work.'

'Oh no,' Margaret exclaimed. 'How? What happened?'

'He wasn't even 30,' said Eric, putting a consoling arm around his wife's shoulders.

'We are still examining the circumstances of his death,' Gillard said, 'but we think it only fair to tell you, since you will probably read about it in the papers, that he was shot.'

'He wouldn't have felt a thing,' Mulholland added. She and Gillard waited through the first few minutes of tears from Margaret, and open-mouthed shock on the face of Eric. They embraced without embarrassment, her head against his neck, her tearful shudders stilled by his comforting hand stroking her. Half an hour later, after more coffee, some cake and at least two high-speed visits from excited children with urgent news on frogs, Gillard was able to ask some gentle questions.

'I understand that you looked after Peter as soon as he came to this country. Is that right?'

'Yes,' said Margaret, dabbing at her eyes with a tissue. 'He was just 15. We were only meant to be temporary foster parents. We were normally given the new arrivals, to bed them in, sort of thing.'

'We've looked after so many over the years,' Eric added.

'But Peter stayed with us, on and off, for five years, I think,' she said, turning to her husband. 'Even though the fostering ended when he turned 18. We adored him, and he's done so well for himself. Oh, his poor wife and the two little ones. This is terrible.' She got up and went to a sideboard. There, amongst many portraits, was one of the young Peter Young, fair-haired with big brown eyes and a shy smile. 'That's him – isn't he gorgeous?'

'Beautiful,' Mulholland said, smiling.

'What do you know about his origins?' Gillard asked.

'Nothing really.' Margaret said. 'His own parents, I believe, were dead in the war. There was a grandmother he was in contact with.'

'Have you got any address details for her?' Mulholland asked.

'No. No, we haven't. She couldn't speak English, and was quite old. We're not even sure she would still be alive. There was a phone number, which I think we might have somewhere. But it's abroad, I think it would be terribly expensive to call,' Margaret said.

'Were you aware of him having any brothers or sisters?'

'Oh yes, he did talk about them, but I don't think they were close. Isn't that right, Eric?'

Eric shrugged. 'I don't remember, to be honest.'

Margaret went on to describe how they had fostered nearly 50 children over the last 40 years, and were still in contact with most of them.

'We are very proud of that,' Eric said.

'You should be proud,' Gillard said. There were plenty more questions that he wanted to ask, most of which were too intrusive or sensitive to ask so soon after breaking news of his death. But he settled for one. 'Can I ask you to comb through your diaries, papers, photographs and documents, and just bring together everything that you have that refers to Peter, or gives some clue to his origins? We would like to have a look to try to get some idea of who could possibly be his enemy.'

–

It was nearly eight o'clock on Saturday evening and Gillard was sitting in the Khazi looking at a video screen. He was squeezed between two nondescript, pudgy, mid-30s detectives with similarly shaven heads. DCs Carl Hoskins and Colin Hodges were known as Tweedledum and Tweedledee because of their resemblance to each other.

'Is this all of the CCTV they have?' Gillard asked, watching a long line of vehicles passing a junction.

'This is the road safety camera pointing west at the junction between Roosevelt Avenue and Camberley Road,' Hoskins said. 'The other disc is the east camera. The public order camera outside the Red Lion is defective, and awaiting repair. That's the nearest. Back the other way towards Surbiton there's a pelican crossing camera which was installed after a pedestrian fatality three years ago, but that's a couple of hundred yards away.'

'So there's nothing right outside the architects' office?'

'Nope,' Hoskins replied. 'Not from the local authority anyway.'

'The kebab shop has a camera which shows the door to the street and a little bit of the pavement, but is mainly focused on the till,' said Hodges. 'You can't see across the street, nor can you see anyone coming in via the external door to the upstairs flat.'

'What about the tattoo parlour?'

'No camera,' Hodges replied.

'Where's the nearest ANPR?' Gillard asked. Automatic number-plate recognition cameras were not only used for recording speeding vehicles, but were a great police resource in all sorts of investigations.

'There's one on the A309 at Hampton Court Way and another by Surbiton railway station. If you're in the know, you could easily avoid them. We ran the data on both from six hours before until six hours after the murder. Of course we got dozens of vehicles of interest, mostly the untaxed or those with outstanding fines. We haven't had chance to examine it in any more detail.'

'It's a good start, lads. Let us know if you find anything of interest.'

'I'll tell you what interests me,' said Hodges. 'I've never heard of anyone murdering an architect before.'

'You obviously never grew up in the same council flats I did in Wembley,' Hoskins replied. 'Little purple brick boxes with tiny windows, facing onto more tiny boxes, and nowhere to play. Kitchen window wouldn't open, bathroom window wouldn't close. My mum would have killed the bloke who designed them if she knew who he was.'

'What about CCTV on the buses?' Gillard asked.

'Ah, I looked at that,' Hodges said. 'Transport for London says every bus they run on this route has bus lane cameras, plus one from the driver's compartment covering the entrance and a backward-facing camera behind showing the passenger compartment. It's a bit complicated because there are several private bus companies too, once you get out of Greater London and into Surrey, and I haven't had chance to check all of them.'

Gillard suddenly had an idea. 'Are there any double-deckers on these routes, Colin?'

Hodges flicked through a document in front of him. 'Nope. All single-deckers, the 968 and 969. There's a single-decker night bus too. There are double-deckers on the busier route up Kingston way, but they don't go along here. According to the TfL bible here, there aren't enough passengers to justify them.' He tapped the document.

'Were you thinking of a hit from the top of a bus?' Hoskins asked.

'Just an idea,' Gillard said. 'Just think: there's a bus stop right outside HDG+. It's five yards at most across the pavement, level with Young's office. An easy shot.'

'What about the bus windows, sir?' Hodges asked. 'They've got those funny little pull-in windows, haven't they? Not ideal for shooting out of.'

'Not to mention the other passengers. No bus is going to be empty at that time in the morning, is it? Some great hairy geezer standing up with a sniper's rifle and silencer is gonna be noticed, I would have thought.'

'Fair enough,' Gillard said. He looked around the Khazi. 'Is there a ladder with this thing?'

The two detective constables slowly turned and exchanged a glance, a movement that was almost comical from the mirror image it presented. 'What you want a ladder for, sir?' Hoskins asked.

'I want to look on the roof of the bus shelter.'

The three detectives stepped out of the Portakabin and found a compartment at the back, near where the generator was connected. Inside was a lightweight folding aluminium ladder, intended for access to the air vents on top.

Gillard and Hodges carried it the 100 yards or so to the bus shelter, under which half a dozen youths were laughing and joking. When Gillard propped the ladder against the back of the shelter, they turned and stared.

The corrugated steel roof of the bus shelter was like a time capsule of urban detritus: cans, plastic bottles, burger wrappers, chewing gum and a mulch of leaves from the nearby plane trees. All were covered in a thick layer of metropolitan grime, and in each corrugation a half-inch of dirty water. Gillard was looking for footprints, but saw no evidence that anyone had been standing on there, at least in recent months. He realized that if they really needed to, they could have the whole top unscrewed, removed and examined by CSI. They had already got half of the office furniture from HDG+, so this little lot wouldn't make much difference. He'd make a decision on that tomorrow.

Looking to either side, the plane trees here were too high for anyone to have used as a shooting platform. The lowest boughs would be more like second-floor level than first. Perhaps it was time to get a little bit more information from key witnesses, starting with the woman who discovered the body.

Sunday morning

Gillard was in Kingston upon Thames, sitting in the eighth-floor lounge of Karen Davies, drinking one of her delicious Tanzanian peaberry coffees. HDG+'s receptionist had dressed up to give her statement as if she was attending a job interview, radiating nervousness in all directions. High heels, formal dark skirt, white blouse, smoky eye make-up. But then everything about her seemed an admission that she felt somehow responsible for Peter Young's death. Even before the DCI had sat down, she had apologized a dozen times for imagined failings on the morning of his death. 'I wish I'd gone in his office straight away,' she said. 'Or if I called him out to help restart the printer, then he'd still be alive, wouldn't he?'

'I think from what we have managed to establish about the perpetrator, the person who killed Peter Young was going to kill him anyway,' Gillard responded. 'This is not like an accident, when luck or care plays a part. So I wouldn't give yourself a hard time over it.'

Gillard had taken her personal details. She was 25, single, had been working at the office for just two weeks. 'I don't know if I can stay there, even if they want me,' she said.

'Why would they not want you to stay?' he asked.

'I've brought bad luck,' she said.

'I don't think they would look at it that way.'

Gillard looked down at the details that had been taken before. 'It says here you have dual British–South African nationality.' He looked up. 'And you previously lived in Cape Town?'

She nodded. 'I have patriality through my father, though I was born in South Africa.'

'I thought I detected a bit of an accent,' Gillard said, smiling.

'Really? People tell me it's barely detectable,' she said grinning back. 'A lot of Brits are not keen on South Africans for some reason, so I try to suppress it.'

'So on the morning in question, you say you arrived late and hurried in.'

'Yes. I was very nervous because it's my job to get everything up and running in the morning. And because of the traffic I couldn't even get in on time.'

Gillard asked her whether she had seen anyone at the bus stop, anyone hanging round the car park or on the pavement outside the office.

'I'm sorry, I really can't remember anything like that, I was in such a flap.'

'Here is something you would remember: was there anyone standing on top of the bus stop?'

'Like, on the roof?' She grinned again, revealing an arc of perfect teeth. 'No. Nothing like that.'

'And you didn't hear anything?'

'No. Certainly not a gunshot. I would have recognised that.'

Gillard asked a few more questions, but unearthed no new information. As he was folding up his documents ready to go, he asked: 'So what made you leave a lovely, sunny place like South Africa to come and work here?'

'I didn't have a great life out there,' she said. 'I'm trying to start again. But I'm not off to a very good start, am I? First job, a man gets murdered in the next room.'

'Well, you didn't do it, did you.' Gillard laughed, as he walked to the door. He turned round to face her as he was leaving and saw the most peculiar expression, as if she had held something important back. He turned over his last statement in his mind and added a question mark. *You didn't do it, did you?*

What wasn't she telling him?

Chapter 4

Ryan Hardcastle was arrested on Sunday morning near his mother's house in Bermondsey, south-east London after a short but high-speed police chase in a terraced street in which there were several casualties: a wheelie bin, a roadside bollard and the front wing of Hardcastle's Vauxhall Nova. After being charged by London's Metropolitan Police with dangerous driving and resisting arrest he was then transferred for interview to Staines police station for Surrey Police to have their turn. Gillard took Colin Hodges with him, partly to give him a break from looking at CCTV. The station was one of the most modern in the county, and the interview room looked to Gillard's eye more like a Harley Street waiting room, with a TV, selection of magazines and several healthy-looking pot plants, though not of the smokable type that appealed to Hardcastle.

'So, Ryan, you've given us the runaround today. You must be feeling guilty about something.' He noticed that Hardcastle had shaved off his wispy moustache, though it was no disguise; he still looked like a thug.

'Angie told me the police come round, and I just couldn't handle it. I felt stressed.'

'Why was that?'

Hardcastle shifted uncomfortably, which couldn't have been anything to do with the chair, which was nicely padded and even had armrests. Gillard couldn't remember the last time he'd seen interview room furniture that showed no signs of cigarette burns, knife slashings or other damage.

He shrugged.

'We just want to ask you a few questions.'

He shrugged and leaned back until the chair was on just two legs. 'Go on, then.'

Gillard nodded to Hodges who asked: 'Apart from Angela Dinsmore, has anyone been staying with you at the flat? Specifically on the night of Thursday, the ninth of January, or on the following morning.'

'No. There's no space, for starters.'

'Does anyone else have a key apart from the landlord?'

'Don't think so, unless maybe Angie's mum – she did do some cleaning for us from time to time.'

'What time did you leave to go to work on the tenth of January?'

'Half seven, give or take.'

'Did you see anyone hanging around on the street?'

'Well there are always people at the bus stop at that time of day.'

Gillard interrupted: 'I'm thinking of anyone who was acting suspiciously. Anyone with a large bag, looking nervous.'

Hardcastle shrugged again. 'Not that I noticed.'

'Do you know anyone who works at the architects' office opposite?'

'HDG+? No. I'd sometimes see that guy with the blond hair, the one who got shot. He'd sometimes work quite late. It made me think that I'd like to work in a nice big light office like that.' He laughed. 'Fat chance, of course, I can't even draw a straight line.'

Hodges continued to robotically wheel out the basic questions, which Hardcastle appeared to answer honestly.

'So, Ryan, here is your final opportunity to tell us anything that you think might be of interest,' Gillard said. 'Did Peter Young come to your nightclub? Was he a customer of any of your drug contacts? Did you hear anything about him?'

Hardcastle shrugged, so Gillard decided to put a bit of pressure on. 'Ryan, as far as we can tell, the fatal shot was fired from your flat.'

'No way!'

'Yes. The angle is perfect, the range is fine, it matches the bullet holes in the window opposite. I'll let you go now, but I want you to have a good, hard think about this. You and Angie are in the frame, I'm afraid.'

That wasn't quite true. Gillard returned to the crime scene at noon. A large section of the north side of Roosevelt Avenue was still closed off with police tape, and at its centre the bus shelter, all glass panels now removed, was surrounded by scaffolding. A low loader with a grab was parked adjacent to it. The roof of the bus shelter had been sealed with plastic, and contractors on ladders were using angle grinders to remove it from the uprights.

Sticking his fingers in his ears against the scream of machinery, Gillard climbed up to the first floor of HDG+'s offices. It was as if the movers had been in. Peter Young's desk and chair were gone, and so was much of the carpet. What he did find was Yaz Quoroshi, in civvies, in conversation with a tall, dishevelled man with scuffed shoes, horn-rimmed spectacles and a jacket with leather patches on the elbows. Gillard was delighted that his request to borrow Met Police ballistics expert Neville Tufton had been successful. Despite looking like a super-annuated geography teacher, Tufton was the best in the business. They greeted each other like long-lost friends.

'Take it you finished the CSI, then, Yaz?' Gillard said, trying to make himself heard above the scream of metal against metal.

'Yes. The carpet has gone for analysis, the desk was taken to pieces and we've even given Kelvin Alexander the data stick he wanted.'

'After making a copy, I hope?'

'Naturally. And dusting it for dabs.'

'And any progress on the firearm?' Gillard asked Tufton.

'Some. As Yaz indicated, these are hollow-point rounds – Czech-made point 38s for a handgun, not a rifle. The implication is—'

'That the shots were not fired from across the road?' Gillard interrupted.

'Exactly. That would be way too far for a handgun. I would say they were fired from less than ten yards.'

'So, as they don't do double-decker buses here,' Gillard said, stroking his chin, 'it was either someone on the bus shelter, to which there would surely have been witnesses—'

'Or someone in the cab, or even on top of the cab or the back of a lorry,' Yaz interjected.

'Let me show you something,' Tufton said, leading Gillard towards the double-glazed window through which both bullets had passed. 'Two shots, 116mm apart horizontally at the inner window surface, but 119mm on the street-side glass.' He took two pencils from his breast pocket, poking one through each hole, and they diverged very slightly. 'It's subtle, but the two shots were not fired from precisely the same place.'

'So from a moving vehicle?'

'Quite possibly.'

'Anything else?'

'Yes. Because these bullets have been designed to deform on passage through the human body, we will have a tough time matching them up to the firing weapon. You'll still be able to tell the manufacturer and the type from the base in most cases, but that's it. I'd still like to see the cartridges.'

'That's the least of our worries,' Gillard said. 'I really want a motive for this more than anything.'

–

Peter Young had lived with Laura Diaz in an end-terrace Victorian house near Surbiton station, just a mile east of where he worked. Most of the homes in the tree-lined street were well-to-do, with established, spacious gardens. Young's could charitably be described as a DIY project, right down to the half-full skip of rubble outside. Gillard couldn't help wondering if the considerable amount of work still required would be too much for a grieving wife.

He had arranged with DI Claire Mulholland and the liaison officer Gabby Underwood to meet Young's widow at half past two. He was early. The street was quiet on a

Sunday, and as he sat in the car he swiped through on his iPad a fair amount of the background material that Claire had dug up. The couple had two young children, a very large mortgage and enough additional debt to be a concern. The life insurance coverage, too, had raised Gillard's eyebrows: half a million, in addition to mortgage protection cover. The policy had been taken out seven years ago.

When Claire and Gabby pulled up they went together to the door and rapped sharply with the knocker. A slender woman came to the door. Gillard had been warned that Laura was a beauty, but he still hadn't expected the delicate perfection of her bone structure to eclipse the baggy paint-stained overalls and the dabs of paint in her thick dark hair. Even the smudge of butterscotch-coloured paint on her cheek looked fetching. It made him want to gently wipe it off.

Gillard offered his condolences, and they were all led through a kitchen where half the floorboards were missing and a great harness of electrical cables was revealed by a missing splashback, through to a back room where there were dust sheets on a three-piece suite.

'I'm carrying on on autopilot,' she said, explaining the brush in her hand. 'We were halfway through painting the hall. I don't know what else to do. I had started on the paperwork, official letters to banks and insurers, but it's so upsetting to keep writing "Peter is dead". I'm signed off work for a month, and the kids are with my sister, and it's got to be done.'

The next 20 minutes were spent in some gentle guidance, principally from Gabby, about what would happen next, the role of coroners, the eventual release of the body for burial, and the role of victim support, both officially through the police and via the various charitable organizations. Laura nodded, but appeared to have glazed over.

'Laura, I wonder now if we could ask you a few questions about your husband?' Mulholland said. When she asked how they had met, Laura described a summer evening on the south bank of the Thames where they found themselves among mutual friends after an art exhibition and got talking. Laura had been a student, due to go back to Peru in a year, but she fell for him immediately and just wanted to stay in London.

'It was a fairy tale for me,' she said, her soft brown eyes welling up.

'Tell me what you know about his origins,' Gillard asked.

'In Kosovo? Not much. Terrible things were happening, things he didn't want to be part of. There was always this melancholy about him when I asked him about his family and what happened to them, so in the end I stopped asking.'

'There was a grandmother, I believe,' Gillard said. 'Did you meet her?'

'Only once. I think she wanted him to go back, and they argued. She died several years ago. I offered to go with Peter to her funeral, but he wouldn't go back.'

'Can you think why anyone would like to kill him?'

She sat looking at the floor for a long time, chewing her lips. 'He came here to escape the violence, the tit-for-tat cycle of vendettas that came with the war. He just wanted to live. But there had been family troubles too, that came through very strongly. Blood over there is not only thicker than water, it dries harder than stone. It was a saying he used. The stains can never be washed clean.'

'Are you telling us he might have known he was in danger?' Mulholland asked.

'I think he knew it was possible. He wanted to protect me from all of this, but naturally I worried. The trouble is, I don't know. Or I didn't know, until now.'

'But who would target an orphan?' Mulholland asked.

Laura looked up. 'I actually am not sure he was an orphan.'

–

Gillard and Mulholland continued to try to tease out background facts from Laura Diaz. There was no single revelation that transformed the case, just a series of details that illuminated Peter Young's world view: that one day, quite possibly, he would be killed. He wanted to shield her and his children from that, it was clear. One piece of evidence was the fact that when he and Laura married, she and the children took her maiden name. Another was the size of the life insurance on him, with her as beneficiary. There was also the fact he had moved home half a dozen times in the last six years, renting each time. As Laura described it, the purchase of this house was a result of her pleading, and represented the only time he'd agreed to put down roots.

She took them on a tour of the house, showed them the home office where he sometimes worked, the pictures on the windowsill of Peter and the children, an album of Peter receiving architectural accolades and awards. For all his care, these were high-profile events, at least within the industry. A professional trying to find him had plenty to go on. Peter Young had done everything he could to protect his family. But clearly he could not protect himself.

The one comment she had made that they couldn't get any further detail on was Laura's assertion that he might not be an orphan. When Gillard asked why she felt this, she shrugged and said she wasn't sure, it was just a feeling.

'Did he ever talk about his parents?' Mulholland asked.

'He mentioned his mother from time to time. I don't think he liked his father at all. At first I thought he must've been abused, something like that. In the early years I was curious about his origins but frightened of losing him if I tried to get him to talk.' She looked up at them and said: 'When you love somebody, you don't keep prodding at the one place that gives them pain, you embrace them wholeheartedly to draw them away from the hurt.'

Laura agreed to let the two detectives go through her husband's paperwork. She brought down an old battered suitcase and placed it on the kitchen table. 'You won't find much, believe me – I've been looking too. There's no birth certificate, no passport until his first British one. There are copies of some of the adoption documents that Barnardo's had. That's pretty much it. Not a single family photograph.'

Gillard thought that there must be more, even if Laura was not aware of it. There were two kinds of deception that might have been at play here. His deceiving her and her deceiving them. On balance he expected there to have been more of the former than the latter. Either way, Peter Young remained a man of mystery.

–

The original asylum decision paperwork had shown that the 15-year-old Peter Young had demonstrated to the assessors a genuine and well-founded fear of persecution. It had taken just over a year to come to that decision, which made him eligible to stay in Britain. Exactly what Young had said to the interviewing social workers was not clear, as only a summary of the decision had been retained on the Home Office computer system. Mulholland had a request in to Barnardo's to unseal their full paper case notes but the process, even for officials like the police with privileged access, was not always straightforward.

By the time Gillard got home at eight in the evening, he was exhausted. Sam met him at the door with a long kiss and a glass of chilled white wine. 'I've missed you,' she said. Gillard had met Sam a couple of years previously while working on the Martin Knight murder case. She had originally been a police community support officer, but had now taken a civilian call handler job for the Met Police. Over a meal of crispy belly pork, ratatouille and baked potatoes, he shared his misgivings about the Young murder.

'If we can't find out a bit more about his origins, it leaves us completely in the dark about the motives for the killing. Given that it seems to have been a professional hit, we may not make enough progress with forensics to give us a clue. Despite CCTV all over the place we have no idea what the assailant actually looks like.'

In less than 12 hours he was able to revise that assessment.

Chapter 5

A dark, rain-drenched Monday did nothing for the attractiveness of Roosevelt Avenue. It was 7.15 a.m. and traffic was backed up across Hampton Court Bridge and on the route into Surbiton and Kingston which led, on progressively wider and more congested roads, into south-west London. Craig Gillard was sitting in his unmarked car, illegally parked half on the pavement outside the tattoo parlour opposite HDG+. Temporary ANPR cameras had been set up by pedestrian traffic lights at either end of the avenue to catch the licence plate details of every vehicle that normally traversed the road at this time of day. Tweedledum and Tweedledee were, he hoped, ensconced in the Khazi going through the backlog of CCTV footage. Gillard expected they would be well into the first bacon butty of the day. Nobody liked to use computer terminals after them: the peppering of crumbs, the drops of coffee and the sheen of grease on the keys. During the Martin Knight investigation, Gillard had once poured out a good quarter-cup of coffee from a faulty keyboard into the bin in the incident room where Hoskins and Hodges had pulled a long overnight shift.

The thought of sizzling bacon stuck in Gillard's head. Where on this street of estate agents, opticians, betting shops and travel agencies might there still survive a greasy spoon? The traditional British café, where tea was as dark as coffee and came in chipped mugs, where toast was square and white, where sausages spat and bacon hissed, and condensation fogged the windows. While he was lost in a reverie of breakfasts past, an old-fashioned red double-decker bus rumbled to a halt on the other side of the road.

It took a good few seconds for the penny to drop.

A double-decker! But there aren't any on these routes, that's what Hodges had said.

Gillard grabbed his raincoat from the back seat and leapt from the car, out into the pelting rain. He zigzagged his way through stationary traffic to the bus shelter outside HDG+. The bus was already pulling away and he had to run, dodging pavement puddles, to get level with the doors at the front. Banging on them got him nothing but a mouthed rebuke and angry hand gestures from the driver. It was only 50 yards further on, when the bus was again in a queue and Gillard could press his Surrey Police ID card against the glass, that the doors wheezed open.

'The next one is in less than five minutes,' the driver yelled, indicating with his thumb the bus stop behind. 'Why don't you read the sign? I don't go to the terminus. Last stop is half a mile up here at Fallowfield Library.' He pointed angrily further up the road.

Once Gillard had introduced himself, the tirade stopped. 'What service is this?' he asked.

'Like it says on the signs, it's the 989.' Belligerence had returned to the driver's face.

'I didn't have a chance to read it,' Gillard said. 'Does it run on Fridays?'

'The service is a daily, like it says at the stop.'

'But not with double-deckers. I didn't see any over the weekend.' Gillard saw there were only three or four passengers downstairs.

'No, mate. It's only during the school run, up until 8.30 a.m. weekdays, during term time. Now if you've finished—'

'No, I haven't. Reverse back to the bus stop, please. I want to go upstairs.'

The driver looked as if he just been asked to fly the bus to the moon. 'I can't fucking reverse, because of all the traffic behind me, can I?'

'Yes, you can and you will, unless you want to spend some time down at the station with me. I'll go behind and direct traffic to overtake you.'

With the worst possible grace, the driver complied, cursing under his breath as he reversed towards the kerb, while Gillard walked behind the bus and firmly gestured for traffic to overtake. The 'verbal' that he got from irate drivers who resented this besuited man's apparently self-appointed authority was quite enough to convince Gillard that he never wanted to be involved in traffic policing.

Finally, the bus was right outside HDG+ with two single-deckers behind, blocked from reaching the stop. He got angry glares from the other drivers, the other passengers waiting to get off, and those passengers at the bus shelter who were waiting to board the following buses. 'You wait here,' he told the recalcitrant driver as he climbed the stairs to the upper deck. It was empty of passengers, an oasis of calm compared to the grief he'd been given on the street.

He sat on the left-hand side, next to the inward-folding quarter-light windows. Once he'd wiped off the condensation, he could clearly see the bullet-pierced window at which Peter Young had sat, the holes about level with Gillard's eye. It was a perfect place to shoot from. With his phone, he took a picture of the window at HDG+.

This was it. The killer could have been upstairs on a double-decker bus.

It was a bad-tempered and soaking-wet detective chief inspector who strode into the Khazi, catching Tweedledum and Tweedledee with their feet up and coffee halfway to their lips.

'A bit damp, sir?' Hoskins said, eyeing the dirty black marks on the bottom third of his boss's Burberry raincoat. Hodges, who unlike his colleague had looked first at Gillard's glowering expression, said nothing, but pulled his feet off the desk and straightened the tie which had sagged around his thick neck.

Gillard unbuttoned his soaking coat and tossed it onto a chair between the two detectives. 'I've just taken a short ride on a double-decker bus that stops right outside Peter Young's office. Or perhaps I imagined it, because according to you, Hodges, there are no bloody double-deckers on this route.'

'Ah. That's what it says here,' Hodges said, grabbing a pile of documents and pulling up a Transport for London PDF on his screen.

'That's why detectives occasionally get off their arses and go and check,' Gillard said. 'I just have. There are three reconditioned 1990s double-deckers used by Arriva on this route because there are several schools which have pupils arriving in the morning at about the same time. The school finishing times are staggered, so it's much less of a problem in the afternoon. We didn't see the double-deckers over the weekend for obvious reasons, and we wouldn't see them during school holidays either.'

'That's very impressive, sir.' Hoskins said, trying to put as much psychological distance as possible between himself and his errant colleague.

'There's more to do, Carl. I want you to chase up Arriva for any CCTV they have on those double-deckers. Get CSI to check them over quickly, just upstairs – the three rows of seats on the left underneath the openable windows. That shouldn't take too long.'

Hodges was being a little more truculent. 'With all due respect, I still don't see a bus being empty enough for a hit man to use.'

'Well, we shall see, Colin. Because you and I are going to catch that bus tomorrow morning.'

–

'Who's got my sodding car keys?' DI Claire Mulholland yelled up the stairs of her home. There was no reply. It was almost eight o'clock on a Monday morning, and none of her three kids were up. Tom, 19, should already have left to attend a training course as a chef, but had come in at 3 a.m. What in hell can anyone *do* until 3 a.m. on a Sunday night? Collum, aged 17 going on 6, would by now have been sitting at the breakfast table shovelling in gargantuan amounts of cereal while working his phone and ignoring everyone else. Claire recalled he had a hefty essay to hand in this morning. History? English? She was only sure that it had not yet been written. The only person who was sitting at the table was Kyra, her three-year-old granddaughter, whose yoghurt and banana breakfast, prepared by Claire, seemed mostly to have ended up inside Dexter, the family's ever-hungry Irish wolfhound. Claire's daughter, Mary – or Maz as she insisted on being called – who was Kyra's mother, was still in the main bathroom trying to set the world record for hot-water hogging.

'Maz, did you borrow my car?' Claire yelled again, while pushing the dog's snout off the table. She absolutely had to be out of the house in ten minutes. There was a reply, of sorts, from the shower, but so indistinct as to be incomprehensible. Kyra was singing along to something on the small television which had been squeezed onto the work surface. The big TV in the lounge was also on, but nobody was watching it bar a coterie of Kyra's dolls snuggled up together under a blanket.

Maz eventually thundered downstairs, dripping, her body barely wrapped in one small towel and her hair wrapped, turban-style, in another. 'I didn't take it, Mum. It was probably Tom.'

Claire had just prepared a packed meal for Baz, her plasterer husband who as usual had left at six this morning and would come back at lunchtime to pick it up. For everyone else she had freshened up the leftovers of yesterday's pasta with some fragments of smoked salmon off-cuts that were on special in the Spar shop just round the corner from the Peter Young crime scene. With a dollop of crème fraîche, only one day past the sell-by date, and chopped into it the apple that Kyra hadn't eaten on Friday because Maz had forgotten to pick up her lunch, this would be enough for the kids tonight while she was interviewing Peter Young's widow again.

'Tom, if I have to come up there to look for my car keys, I'm going to Taser you,' she bellowed. A minute later she did run upstairs and knocked on his door. Getting no reply, she burst into his bedroom and flung open the curtains. His whined but wordless complaint was the same tone Dexter used when lobbying for his dinner. Claire noticed there was a girl somewhere under the covers with him, judging by the red toenails, shoulder tattoo and blond head which were partially visible. His bedroom looked, as it always did, like the target of a very hurried but thorough burglary. Some black lacy underwear dangled from the light shade.

'Hello, Tom, hello Miss Elaneous,' she said wickedly as she grabbed the car keys. 'Tom, you'll be late.'

He grunted and turned over.

'Dexter!' she called downstairs. 'Dexter! Doggy wake-up service required, Tom's room. Good boy.' As the dog bounded upstairs she heard the cries of alarm from Tom's room. The dog shot into the room. With a huge grin on her face, Claire closed the door. The cries from inside showed that Dexter's orgy of bad-breath face licking had begun.

–

The incident room meeting was set for 11 a.m., leaving Gillard just enough time to drive to Surrey Police's Mount Browne headquarters in Guildford where, in a locker outside his office, he kept for emergencies a spare suit with a brand-new shirt. Today's drenching was precisely the kind of scenario he had in mind. He was already doing up his trousers and just contemplating what to do about his damp shoes and socks, for which he had no spares, when the door at the end of the corridor opened and the chief constable walked in.

'Ah, Craig,' said Alison Rigby. 'I was hoping to catch you.'

'Yes, ma'am,' he said, easing his feet back into his wet brogues. He stood to face her. Alison was an imposing figure, almost six foot two, with short dark hair and penetrating blue eyes. Colleagues referred to Rigby's stare as the blue screen of death, capable of freezing the mental processors of even the most senior policeman.

'Any progress on the Peter Young case?' she asked, lifting a large earthenware mug of coffee to her lips.

'Some,' he said, surreptitiously checking his flies were done up. 'We think he was shot from fairly close range from the top deck of a bus, not from across the street as we first thought.'

'How extraordinary. And this we think is a professional hit?'

'It has all the hallmarks. We've got nothing from CCTV so far, though there's more to look at.'

'Craig, we really can't have architects being assassinated on the streets of Surrey.'

'Though an estate agent or two wouldn't be missed, I suppose,' Gillard ventured with a smile.

'Very droll,' she said, arching one eyebrow in a way that made it clear the remark was not particularly funny.

Gillard, fresh from a brief shopping foray for dry socks, got back to the Khazi to find the incident room already packed. He recognised the backs of Yaz Quoroshi, Claire Mulholland, Michelle Tsu and Carl Hoskins, all staring at one screen over the shoulder of a seated Colin Hodges. 'What have you got there?' the DCI asked.

'This is from the second of those double-deckers on Friday morning. It might be the gunman,' Hodges replied. Gillard leaned over to the screen. There was a still image of a man in a hooded Puffa jacket, with a bulky shoulder bag, just leaving the bus. The timestamp was 07.57.43. The camera seemed to be from somewhere above the driver's position and focused on the doors, but also covering some of the luggage space.

'Have you got a full sequence?' Gillard asked.

'Yep, for what it's worth.' Hodges rewound, and then hit play. The camera had recorded a series of jerky stills, covering a procession of passengers emerging from the inside of the bus and stepping off the platform into the rain on the pavement outside. The man's hood was already raised, so his face was not visible, but he appeared to be above average height.

'Can you tell whether he was upstairs or not?'

'No, the camera angle is wrong.'

'That's a shame. And why this bus, Colin?'

'Well, the first one was scheduled at the stop outside the architects' at 07.42, which is a bit too early. As you recall Young didn't arrive at work until about ten to, based on when the office burglar alarm was disarmed. We haven't looked at the third bus footage yet, but it's probably too late. It was due at the stop at 08.02 a.m. but according to the supervisor at Arriva it was running about 15 minutes late, so if that's correct it would have been at the stop a little after the receptionist found Young's body.'

'Okay. Is this our stop?'

'No. This is from the following stop, Coulton Road,' Hodges said, looking down to check the documents. 'I figured that it's the moment when the bus is stopped that gives the best shooting opportunity. It would have been amateur to try to shoot the guy and get off at the same stop. A big rush downstairs would have drawn attention to him.'

'Agreed. So why him?' Gillard asked.

'The other passengers are basically female pensioners or schoolkids. No other adult male.'

'Any footage from upstairs?' Gillard asked.

'Nope. These three buses are over 20 years old and only equipped with a single camera, for driver protection.'

'Of course he could have stayed on for later stops,' Gillard said.

Carl Hoskins looked at the DCI. 'Let's hope not. We've got another resource at this stop. There is a road safety camera on the pelican crossing, because there was a pedestrian fatality there two years ago. I've got Friday's footage on disk somewhere here,' he said, holding up a pile of documentation. 'I'll get on to that this afternoon.'

'Whoever he is, he's a cool customer,' Mulholland said, looking up at the skylight, where rain had once again begun to fall, hammering on the perspex.

'So what have you been working on, Michelle?' Gillard asked.

The young detective looked up at him. 'I've been going through the backgrounds of some of the witnesses. Everyone at the architects' is pretty clean, apart from the usual speeding and parking issues. Kelvin Alexander has been visited by us over a report of domestic violence at his home, but that was nine years ago. No charges were ever brought.'

'That might be worth taking an extra look at. Anything else?'

'Yes. One thing seems significant. Karen Davies, the South African-born receptionist, used to be Karen van Zyl. She reverted to her maiden name after the death of her husband in Cape Town.'

'What happened to her husband?' Gillard asked.

'He was murdered two years ago. Shot in the head.'

Chapter 6

Karen Davies had agreed to come into Staines police station straight after work on Monday at 6.30 p.m. Gillard was waiting for her with Michelle Tsu. They couldn't quite return the favour on the Tanzanian Peaberry coffee, but the duty desk sergeant, a pleasant woman by the name of Carswell, had phoned out to have something drinkable delivered.

The South African looked tired but a little less nervous than the first time Gillard had spoken to her. 'We're sorry to have to call you back in at such short notice, but we've got a couple more questions to ask you.'

'It's about Patrick, isn't it?' she said. 'I knew it would be.'

'Patrick van Zyl was your husband, correct?' Tsu asked. 'And he died during a burglary at your home in Cape Town, is that correct?'

'Yes, that is "correct",' she said, acidly.

'So actually, you are a widow, not single.' There was no reply. Tsu looked down at the documents in front of her. 'According to our information no one was ever convicted of the murder of your husband.' She lifted up one of the documents. 'The newspapers say—'

'I think it would be better,' Gillard intervened. 'If Ms Davies gave her own account of what happened.'

Karen smiled icily at him. 'My husband and I were lying in bed, with the windows open. It was that record January when it got to 44 degrees, so even though it was 3 a.m. it was as hot as hell. We were both naked, covered only by a single sheet. I heard a noise downstairs. At first I thought it was Rudi—'

'Who's Rudi?' Gillard asked.

'The guard dog. We had one that roamed in-house and there were two others in the yard. There was also a security guy who patrolled the fence at nights.'

'Sounds like you lived in Fort Knox,' Michelle said.

'Cape Town has quite a crime rate, as you may know. We lived in a gated community with an average level of security. Most of our neighbours wanted more. Anyway, Pat took his Glock and went downstairs to have a look.' She paused and gulped, her brown eyes softening. 'It was quiet for a couple of minutes, then I heard the sound of a door closing. I called out for Pat, but got no reply. Then I heard three shots…' She pulled a tissue from her pocket and blew her nose. The next few words were muffled through her handkerchief: 'When I found him, he was dead.'

Gillard and Tsu waited while Karen composed herself. When she next lifted her face it was twisted with emotion. 'The Cape Town police, bunch of *piel kops*, thought I did it.' Her accent, previously suppressed, flooded out, broad and loud. She seemed a different person.

'Why did they suspect you?'

'Because of my fingerprints on the weapon. But it was just where I moved it from his chest to do CPR because he wasn't breathing. I got covered in his blood. In my panic I left stains on the door handles, the phone, you name it.'

'Was there any other DNA found which would indicate an intruder?' Gillard asked.

'Nothing conclusive. Anyway, why are you asking me this? I was never charged,' she said, stabbing her finger towards him. 'Do you really think I had a reason to kill that cute architect who I had only known two weeks? Christ almighty!'

'We have to eliminate you from the list of suspects, and the best way to do that is by being in possession of all the facts,' Gillard said evenly. 'For example, newspaper coverage of the coroner's hearing—'

'What's this, trial by bloody Google?'

'Ms Davies,' Michelle Tsu said. 'Given more time we can check the official records. What I want to ask you is, do you know how to use a handgun?'

She laughed. 'I was the runner-up in the 2014 SAPSA handgun nationals.'

'SAPSA?' Tsu asked.

'South African Practical Shooting Association. Pat and I were both members. We had two dozen guns in the house, mostly rifles in a gun safe; in the bedroom we had his and hers Glocks. Mine was pink. But I tell you this...' The finger was pointing again. 'From the day he died, I have never again touched a weapon. I came here to start a new life, as a new woman, to forget all the horror. And then look what happens? Two weeks into a job, in good, safe, gun-free Surrey, England, the nicest guy in my office gets blown apart, and once again poor little Karen is in the frame!'

'Did you kill him?' Gillard asked.

She didn't reply, but the look she gave him was venomous. 'Can I go now?' she said eventually.

Gillard nodded and thanked her. After she had left, slamming every door, Michelle said: 'Bit of a chameleon that one.'

'She could have killed him,' Gillard said. 'Easily, if she had the weapon. Park the car in the office car park, three minutes' walk to the previous bus stop. Catch the bus, shoot him through the window, get off at the next stop, go back into the office, discover the body.'

'It's pretty laborious,' Tsu said.

'Not if she is a paid hit woman. Let's face it, she's fully qualified. With her own pink Glock.'

Chapter 7

The same day, 25 miles further south

Sophie Lund stared out of the kitchen window into the pouring rain. It was half past five in the afternoon and Balfour was long overdue for a walk. She wasn't enthusiastic, but the red setter had come rushing into the kitchen, whining, and pushed his snout between her knees while she was playing with her iPad. 'Oh stop it,' she said, pushing the dog away. It was no use denying it: Balfour knew it was time. He had been denied his full run this morning because she had had to drive up to town early, which made him even more anxious to get out now. Balfour may have only been 18 months old, but he knew that after the walk came dinner. The sooner the walk, the sooner the dinner. Dog logic. The trouble was they were no longer in Chelsea, and a walk on the estate meant little chance of shelter and some serious mud.

Sophie stroked the dog's warm head and rubbed him behind his ears. 'Okay, boy, you win,' she said, heading towards the boot room. The dog immediately seemed to know, and started jumping breathlessly, his claws skittering on the kitchen tiles.

'Estela, I'm just taking the dog out. Should be about a half an hour.' Sophie leaned into the lounge where the au pair was building Lego houses with Amber. David, as usual, was on his PlayStation and didn't look up.

'Okay, Sophie.'

'Can you put Amber to bed at six? She had another bad night yesterday, and she'll be tired.'

'I'm not tired, Mummy,' Amber whined, pouting.

'Yes, you are. And you had bad dreams, don't you remember?' Sophie stroked the girl's dark hair and ran her fingers over the strawberry birthmark on her temple.

'So can I watch *Frozen*?' Amber asked.

'No. Maybe tomorrow.' Sophie and Estela exchanged grins. They must have each seen *Frozen* a hundred times. 'I'll get David's dinner when I get back.'

Balfour came bounding into the lounge, whimpering and hurrying her up. 'All right, boy, all right.'

She led the dog into the boot room. She picked her full-length Barbour coat, the broad-brimmed Driza-Bone leather hat, and one of her many pairs of wellies. She grabbed a big heavy torch and stuffed Balfour's lead into her pocket. It was going to be muddy. Very.

She pulled open the door, and the cold wind and driving rain hit her immediately. Normally she would take the long route to Trygg's Foote, four and a half miles, the first and last miles being within their own estate, but this time she would take the shorter loop on the main drive as far as Gibbet Oak. She strode around the east wing, with its ten-foot-high sliding sash windows, and took the steps down, crossing the ha-ha on the footbridge, before joining the main drive. This way there was a half-mile ride lined with mature lime trees, their bare boughs silhouetted against the bilious sky.

Balfour raced away left and then right, following smells. She followed his movements with the torch, trying to spot if he'd done his business. He could never seem to hold it until they'd reached the woods. Dag hated to see it on the lawns.

As she crunched down the gravel drive, she turned back to look at her home: a Grade II listed mock-Tudor masterpiece, as the estate agent had called it. Gables in all directions, a dozen chimneys and magnificent bay windows, casting a warm light over the lawns. It had been fantastic when Dag had agreed to move out of London. The Chelsea townhouse was wonderful, but she had been brought up in the countryside and always missed it. Colsham Manor had come onto the market at just the right time. After Dag had sold a half share in his business, he had been persuadable to buy a country estate. Now she had her own stables, she kept her bay mare Caramelo at home. She might never get back into the British three-day eventing team, but she could still enjoy regular hacks across the estate and beyond.

Dag was a wonderful husband, and so Norwegian. He communicated. He listened. And of course he was wealthy. But most of all he wanted to make her happy. Not only agreeing to move deep into the Surrey country-side, but helping fund her interior designer consultancy. Most of all it was building the family. When she had discovered she was unable to have children, after all the years of trying, and when IVF had failed again and again, he hadn't objected to the idea of adoption. He didn't mind that Sophie had them travel to an orphanage in the farthest corner of Europe to make her dreams come true. David and Amber were the perfect children, and had made them complete as a family.

After ten minutes she and Balfour arrived at Gibbet Oak. The 700-year-old tree, from which a notorious highwayman had been hanged in the early 1600s, dominated a large, rough horse paddock, full of docks and thistles. It now had only one huge bough, which spread laterally from its hollowed trunk. But it was very much alive still, the leaves appearing bright and fresh in late May. Last autumn, their first at Colsham Manor, she and the children had come down and collected handfuls of acorns. David had asked if they were going to feed them to the pigs. She had asked why he thought that when they had no pigs, or indeed any farm animals bar Caramelo.

'I remember with my grandfather, at his house in the mountains, feeding acorns to the pigs,' he said. He was only eight, and this was one of the very few memories that he had shared with her. While Amber was outgoing and chatty, David was much more reserved and self-contained. She wondered what traumas he may have suffered in the troubles in which his parents died. Amber, being only five, obviously didn't remember very much. Her traumas came out in nightmares.

Balfour was off on one of his long jaunts and Sophie had to call for him several times before he returned, his snout muddy. She let him through the kissing gate onto the bridleway going west towards Lacey Dutton, three miles further on. The bridleway was one of several well-used public rights of way across the estate. On Sundays, large groups of walkers with red socks and rucksacks, those silly ski poles and woolly hats would stride across. At other times there would only be the odd dog walker. The estate agent told her that the profusion of footpaths and public rights of way had cut a couple of hundred thousand pounds off the asking price. 'No one likes the hoi polloi trudging across their land,' he had said.

But in fact she didn't mind. Except for Her, of course, the bloody Hinchcliffe woman. And she couldn't do anything about that.

The rain had slackened off a little as she entered Paling Wood. The bridleway narrowed from the broad grass sward, churned up by mountain bike tracks, and went sharply downhill through a brake of sweet chestnut trees, before climbing up to Ewhurst Hill. With the trees closer overhead it was darker here, and the path was very slippery, so she had to turn on the torch to pick her way. The path up the hill led to a popular viewpoint, where picnickers would often sit in the summer. Now, in this weather, it was unimaginable. In the wind at the top you would barely pause to gobble down a Twix.

Balfour stopped, barked and decided to race off into the undergrowth. Sophie called for him and shone her torch into the dark underbrush on the right-hand side of the path. She waited two minutes, calling him to no avail. She put a hand in a pocket for some dog treats and called out. 'Balfour! Balfour! Snacks, boy, snacks!' It normally worked but not this time. Annoyed, she crossed the stile into the dark wood. This path was little-used, and here in the shadow of the hawthorn trees and blackthorn that grew up underneath the sweet chestnuts, brambles had made it almost impenetrable. She forced her way through the snagging briars, impaling a thumb on a thorn, even through her gloves. She took off her glove and sucked at the droplet of blood, then called again for the dog.

Her torch showed the track, dappled with reflections from muddy footprints, which wound down to the stream, whose waters she could already hear gurgling. There was a notoriously slippery footbridge across it, little more than a plank really, which Dag had been meaning to cover with chicken wire for extra grip. The route did lead eventually back to the estate, via the pottery, but was horribly muddy in the winter.

Sophie stepped carefully down towards the bridge, balancing on the protruding roots of a large chestnut, which acted almost like a spiral staircase down to the stream bank. She shone the torch towards the bridge, illuminating the racing waters beneath. The rain had swollen the stream, which in summer was barely more than a trickle. Now it looked to be several feet deep.

'Come on, Balfour, you bad boy! Doggie snacks!' She really was quite annoyed now. Finally getting down to the level of the bridge, she grasped the rotten handrail. Then she looked up, pointing the light across to the other bank.

What she saw there, suspended from a tree, tore an involuntary scream from her. Her wellingtons skidded on the narrow plank, she lost her grip on the handrail and fell into the cold, rushing water.

Chapter 8

Numbing cold water tumbled and roared about her head, and she took a few seconds to re-orientate herself. Pushing hard with hands and feet she levered herself vertical, the water-filled wellingtons dragging like concrete, pulling her downstream as she reached for overhanging bushes at the bank. She grasped at thorny stems, ignoring the pain, just to get herself to her feet again. After a breathless and panicky minute she emerged into near-blackness. The torch was lost somewhere in the water and the branches way above her head were like knotted, gnarled fingers closing out most of the pewter sky, and dripping onto her. Dangling above from a rope was the body of a child: neck broken, face twisted in anguish. It was wearing a woollen hat, similar to the one Amber wore, a green anorak, just like Amber wore, and tiny wellingtons. The last flash of the torch before she fell had burned those wellingtons into her mind. They were the same red and black-spotted ladybird wellies that she had bought Amber a year ago for her first walk around her new home.

Drenched, chilled and terrified, Sophie reached up to the footbridge, grabbing the plank, and hauled herself out of the water. Without looking up she scrambled on hands and knees back up the muddy bank towards the main path. Only when she was safely at the stile did she fumble in her pocket for her soaked phone. She pressed and swiped. Nothing. She barely dared to think about what she had seen, and panicked about what to do next. The corpse could not be Amber, because Amber was safe at home with Estela. So who was this little girl? This little girl who resembled her own precious child?

She turned round to the wood again and bellowed angrily for Balfour. As if by magic, the dog appeared, mud-soaked and with something in its mouth. Sophie didn't even want to know what it was. 'Balfour, drop.' The dog looked up at her, big-eyed and sad, but did not comply. She yelled at him again, and then in her anger and her fear, she struck him across the head. 'I said, drop it, you stupid animal.' The dog whimpered and lay on the ground quivering, paws splayed, ears flat to his head, tail between his legs. He dropped whatever it was, which looked like a dead pigeon.

'Oh, Balfour. I'm sorry.' Suddenly overwhelmed, she knelt by her dog, embraced him and burst into tears. 'You've got to protect me, boy. You've got to protect us all.'

Sophie knew that there was a house down by the road just five minutes away, but her first priority was to get home to check on Amber. Even though she knew Amber must be safe, it was the absolutely essential thing to do. It took half an hour, half running, half walking, fully breathless before she burst into the house shouting for Estela. Only when she had raced upstairs, dripping water, and pulled the little girl out of her bed and into her arms did Sophie dare to think about ringing the police.

–

Despite it being a 999 call, the police took nearly an hour to arrive. A patrol car with blue lights but no siren pulled up at the porticoed main door of the Manor. Estela called to Sophie, who was upstairs in a bathrobe, getting splinters out of her hand, while on the phone to Dag. In expectation of the police's imminent arrival, she had not run the bath she so desperately wanted. She opened the door to two reassuringly solid, uniformed male PCs. She had a brief flash of empathy for those women who found men in uniform attractive. Despite the delay, they were certainly the solidly male reassurance she was hoping for.

She explained where the body was.

'Is there road access, madam?' asked the slightly shorter of the two, who introduced himself as PC Kerrigan.

'No. Well, not this way. You could drive down to Hallam's Brook, and it's only ten minutes up from there. But last time I was there the slurry pit had flooded across the track, so it might be better to go from this end,' she said. 'It's straight on down the bridleway towards Ewhurst Hill.' They visibly wilted at the prospect of having to walk for half an hour in the rain. Police these days spend too much time sitting on their bums in a car, Sophie thought. It was the kind of thing her mother would have said.

'It's no good, you'll never find it. I'll have to show you,' she said. Sophie asked them to wait while she changed upstairs. She emerged, in less than a minute, in a clean pair of moleskin trousers, thick pullover and comfy socks. From the boot room she grabbed a fresh coat, dry wellies and an umbrella, and led them out the way she had come. She was surprised to find that she walked much more rapidly than they did, their unsuitable footwear slipping and sliding on the wet grass. They went to absurd lengths to step gingerly around muddy puddles. The taller of the two walked with a torch, while Kerrigan asked questions. 'Did you touch the body, madam?'

'No, it was quite high off the ground. I probably could have reached it on tiptoe. You'd have no trouble.'

'Did it smell?'

'No. Not to me at least. But it was the dog that led me to it. I hadn't even planned to walk that route.'

'And you are sure that it was your child's actual wellingtons on it?'

'Well, no. They are ladybird boots, so they are not that uncommon. The size was about right.'

'And are your child's boots missing?'

'Well, I haven't really looked. But I didn't see them in the boot room. I've left the dog in there to dry off, so I wasn't keen to go squatting on the floor to check. Of course they could be in the back of the Discovery. I haven't had time to look, you see.'

When they got to the stile that led down to the stream, the two PCs leant over the fence and shone powerful beams towards the bridge 50 yards away. But there was too much undergrowth for them to get a clear view. 'That looks very muddy,' said the tall one, illuminating the churned-up path. 'There might be some useful footprints.'

'Mainly mine, I suppose. And Balfour's.'

They looked at her.

'The dog,' she added.

'I'm going to see if I can get in a different way,' said Kerrigan. He clambered over the fence a few yards downhill, cursing as he got his uniform snagged in brambles and a branch plucked his cap off, revealing a balding pate. He was gone for five minutes, though they could see the glow from his torch.

When he finally returned he was smiling. 'Mrs Lund, someone's been playing a joke on you. I'm glad to say that isn't a child hanging up there. It's a model of some kind, like a penny-for-the-guy for bonfire night. It was dressed up, wearing some kind of wig as well as the clothing.'

The taller PC groaned and looked at his watch.

'But it's been made to look like my daughter!'

'That's as may be,' Kerrigan said. 'Could be some other kids having a joke.'

'This is a bit sophisticated for kids, surely.' Sophie was getting angry now that they thought this was a trivial matter. 'I want to know who did it. I want you to take fingerprints, on the boots.'

'I don't think we can resource that,' he replied. 'I think you would be better off thinking who would want to play such a practical joke on you. If you can work out who it is, we will go round and have a word.'

By the time they left she was fuming. Partly because she felt a fool, but partly because she suddenly realized exactly who it was who had done this.

–

The next morning, as soon as the au pair had driven David and Amber to school, Sophie searched the boot room and her Land-Rover Discovery. There was no sign of Amber's wellies. The boot room was never locked, so it would all have been terribly easy. She would only have had to walk a hundred yards.

Sophie prepared herself for a confrontation. She freshened her make-up with a bright red lipstick, shed her working trousers and slid into her tight new jeans and a figure-hugging blue pullover. Thus girded for battle, she marched across the yard towards the Little Pottery. Right from the moment that she and Dag had moved in, they had had problems with the Hinchcliffe woman. It was only after they had been there for six months that they discovered that Geraldine Hinchcliffe was the first wife of Clive Gashley, the estate's previous owner. That is why a decade or so ago she had been given two cottages, a stable and six acres of paddocks. It was part of her divorce settlement. This was done in a stupid way, to Sophie's mind. A cake slice shape of land cut to the centre of the estate and, because of the established rights of way, the damn woman could go pretty much where she wanted. Naturally having been Lady of the Manor before, she still coveted the entire estate.

If Sophie had known what an irritant the woman was, they might never have bought the place. There had been disputes over parking, over access to the farm buildings at the back, and of course the bloody *leylandii* trees. During the very week they were moving in, the Hinchcliffe woman slid in a planning application to convert her stables into a commercial pottery. She and Dag didn't get the official notice because mail was still being forwarded to the previous owner by the post office, and 'someone' had removed the yellow planning notice from the telegraph pole on the bridleway. So they hadn't known of it and it passed without objection. Of course they might not have objected to it, had they known in advance, except on account of the extra traffic from pottery students going up and down the shared private drive, and parking all over the place on their shared and limited piece of hardstanding. It was two weeks ago when they had had a stand-up row over one of Geraldine's students blocking in the garage which housed Dag's quad bike.

So this was Geraldine Hinchcliffe's revenge. She was an artist, no doubt quite capable of making a mannequin if she could make pots and crockery.

Standing at the door of the Little Pottery, Sophie rapped hard with the knocker, some carved hardwood lump that was presumably supposed to resemble a woodpecker. There was no reply. All she could hear were the stupid earthenware wind chimes that she seemed to breed here and gave an air of melancholy to the place whenever there was a breeze. She looked through the window at the wheels, the kiln and the sacks of clay stacked under the table. The woman didn't seem to be there, though she normally was on a Tuesday. Her car was gone. Sophie would ring up and leave a message. The woman was not going to get away with this.

It was no surprise that Geraldine bloody Hinchcliffe was away, Sophie thought. She probably wanted some kind of alibi for this atrocious behaviour. If she hadn't been so rude, Dag probably would have trimmed their row of *leylandii* that shaded her newly constructed sun lounge-style pottery room. The trees were there first of course, but they did grow very quickly. Then the woman had the nerve to claim that the land on which her former husband had planted them was in fact hers. She had waved some damn piece of legal paper at her, ignoring the fact that the trees were the wrong side of a long-established fence.

Dag, his usual emollient and diplomatic self, had in the first few months urged Sophie to be calm and even suggested that they should cut the *leylandii*, as an act of forbearance. But Sophie had been so furious about the underhand planning application and the parking nonsense that she would have none of it. It was easy for Dag to be forgiving. He was away three weeks in every month, jetting round the world, leasing his oil rigs to giant corporations. She had to live near the damn woman, to watch her exercise her spaniels, which she shouted for in a silly high voice. Pixie and Mixie. They were always off the lead on the footpath through the formal lawns, and she had not once seen the woman stoop to pick up after them.

The whole of Tuesday, her only day off, Sophie stamped about the estate in a bad mood, being short with Estela and blowing up at the plumber on the phone for his failure to get the right taps for the new bath. Tomorrow and for the rest of the week she would be up in London during the day. Dag would not be back until Friday. In the back of her mind, anxiety was crystallising into a nugget of fear. Until Friday, for six hours each day, her children would be alone with just tiny, shy Estela to look after them. Three months ago, even though she hated Geraldine Hinchcliffe, she would never have contemplated that the woman might harm her children. But now this sick mannequin had been hung on the path to terrify her. Thinking about it, it was probably Geraldine Hinchcliffe who threw a dead pigeon into the woods to lure Balfour, knowing that she would follow the dog. It was a campaign of hatred, and the woman was clearly mad.

–

That evening, Sophie decided to play with the children rather than work on the marketing documents that she needed to prepare. At Amber's insistence they played hide and seek. Well, it was better than watching *Frozen* again. With six bedrooms, two lounges, a dining room, a galleried hallway and half a dozen basement rooms, there was no shortage of places to hide. Amber, as always, was just too excited to hide effectively. Her giggling could be heard echoing along the hallway, and she always chose the same two or three places: the linen basket in Sophie and Dag's bedroom, under the back stairs where the vacuum cleaner and brooms were stored, or under the tiny bed in the attic bedroom where Sophie's own antique doll's house and rocking chair were kept. Amber would not go downstairs into the basement. She had had nightmares, claiming that the *shtriga* lived there, and if it was disturbed, she would come for her in the night. Time after time, Amber had awoken screaming about the *shtriga*. Finally, Sophie had looked it up online. Albanian folklore's *shtriga* was a truly horrifying belief, presumably designed to terrify disobedient children: a vampire witch, in the form of an old woman who would suck the blood of sleeping children. This monster could also assume the form of an insect, usually a moth. Not surprisingly, Amber was afraid of moths too.

David by contrast was very inventive at hide and seek. It could take a good 15 minutes to find him, and quite often he would run for home base in the kitchen and get there before Sophie could catch him. He was quite a speedy little runner, though sometimes a little reckless. On one occasion he had tumbled down the staircase and cut his forehead. It was quite a nasty cut, and any normal eight-year-old would have cried. David didn't.

At the end of the game, and after giving it considerable thought, Sophie asked Amber and David to come with her. She led them down the back staircase, in what would have been the old servants' quarters, and into the basement. Amber said she didn't want to go, so Sophie carried her and reassured her that she would be safe. 'I just want to show you something, darling,' she said. She put all the lights on and led them to a very special room. It had originally been the old bakery, but Clive Gashley, who was a precious metals dealer, had turned it into a safe room. There was a thick, shiny metal door of the kind you might imagine for a bank vault, and which was opened by a four-digit combination punched into a keypad. Inside was a comfortable lounge five yards square with a vaulted ceiling. There was no window but a giant TV gave a panoramic view of the main lawns, from a CCTV camera. It had its own air supply, its own independent Wi-Fi network and satellite phone, and originally, access to CCTV cameras both inside and outside the house.

Dag had decided that this room was completely over the top, and had removed the CCTV. But now Sophie was beginning to think the room had its uses. Earlier today she had told Estela that if anything really scary happened, she should go down there with the children. Estela's eyes had widened at the idea that anything that terrifying could happen here.

'Mrs Lund, is there something I should know?'

Sophie had told her about the mannequin, and she had thought it a bit creepy, but not having seen it dangling there from a tree in the pouring rain she had not experienced the full horror. The last thing Sophie wanted to do was to terrify the Portuguese girl, who had been reliable and full of common sense. God knows it was hard enough to find someone she could trust, who could drive the kids to school and who spoke good enough English. But it was only at times like this that the reality of her isolation became apparent. Two women in the middle of a 600-acre estate, without a man in the place at night, and only Michael the estate manager there intermittently during the day at his office, a good five minutes away on foot. If it took the police an hour to arrive, then anything could happen. Especially with a lunatic woman, twisted and embittered, living nearby.

Chapter 9

Detective Chief Inspector Craig Gillard was in full civvies for the Tuesday morning trip on the bus: zip-up leather jacket, jeans and trainers, and a folding umbrella, just in case. He was aiming for the second double-decker which left Surbiton station at 7.15 a.m. while Hodges would get the third, departing at 7.35 a.m. The moment he arrived at the bus stop, he realized what kind of trip this was going to be. The shelter was packed with rowdy teenage girls, sporting only oddments of school uniform, tiny skirts, untucked blouses, and bedecked with jewellery, make-up and smart phones. Pure jailbait. Hanging back a little were some younger boys, who looked to be about eight or nine. From his homework last night he identified their neat royal-blue uniforms as that of St Cuthbert's, the boy's preparatory school in Thames Ditton. The moment the bus arrived the girls charged for it, thundering up the stairs with only the most peremptory flash of their passes to the driver, a man whom Gillard recognised and vice versa.

'No reversing required today,' Gillard said, as he too went upstairs.

'Good job an' all,' came the reply.

The girls had completely taken over the upper deck, standing in the aisle, bellowing insults, swapping gossip, sharing videos. Gillard's 'excuse me' as he tried to find an unoccupied seat brought the surliest of expressions, as if he had gatecrashed the ladies' changing room. One girl, with a rough topknot of jet-black hair, and cheeks powdered to the shade of jaundice, had eyebrows that looked like they had been drawn on in marker pen higher than their natural position, which gave her a look of permanent surprise. She was berating a short stocky teenager, who was blowing gum bubbles while examining her nails. The subject seemed to be text messages sent to someone's boyfriend, and there were threats of significant violence. The detective sat and minded his own business, listening and watching, and appreciating Colin Hodges' astute point that the upper deck of a busy bus was no place for an assassin.

These girls were headed to Hawthorn Road Secondary, as it used to be known before it was taken over by a group called Alpha Academies. It was a world away from the kind of privileged education afforded the boys of St Cuthbert's who had all stayed downstairs. These intimidating girls were on top now, but he didn't suppose it was too snobby to imagine that most of those passing through Hawthorn Road Secondary would become tomorrow's hairdressers, shelf stackers and cleaners. After all, he'd been to an equivalent school himself and fought his way out and up. Nothing was predestined. He was going to rely on their intelligence and cooperation.

It was a good dozen stops before the bus crawled through the traffic to Roosevelt Avenue, and more girls had boarded. Not a single boy came upstairs. Gillard, on the left-hand side, peered down at each stop to see who got on and off. Finally, when the upper deck was full, and three stops before the architects' office, Gillard stood up and tried to make himself heard.

'Girls, can I have your attention for a minute? I'm Detective Chief Inspector Gillard of the Surrey Police, and I'm here to investigate a murder.' As expected, this resulted in almost complete silence, though the activity of thumbs on smart phones and the nodding of heads to earphoned music was harder to extinguish.

'I would like to know if any of you who were travelling on this bus last Friday saw anyone who was acting suspiciously on this upper deck...'

'That was Belinda,' yelled someone.

'It wasn't, you cheeky cow,' came a hissed response.

'Someone who you had not seen before...' Gillard continued, raising his voice further above the hubbub.

'Do you mean a bloke?' asked a young-looking girl with hoop earrings.

'Yes, probably male.'

'Was he good-looking?' someone whispered, to accompanying giggles.

'We don't know what he looked like, that's why we're asking you,' Gillard said. 'If you get any ideas, ask to speak to Mrs Calder, the student welfare officer, who has my business card.'

At that moment the bus lurched to a halt. It was the stop before the architects' office, and the girls piled off. It took a full cacophonous minute for the bus to empty, and as Gillard looked down into the street at the gaggle of them, he saw the short one who had been chewing gum holding her thumbs on imaginary trouser braces, and bending at the knees, as she leaned back and self-importantly announced something to a group of amused friends. It suddenly dawned that she was impersonating him. Confirmation came when a friend pointed to him on the upper deck, and when he waved back, the little actress put her hands over her mouth in embarrassment. He carried on watching until the bus rumbled away, at which point one of the other girls turned around and, with a brief grimace, gave him the finger. He couldn't help but laugh.

Two minutes later the bus arrived once again at the stop beside HDG+.

Gillard was the only person on the upper deck. As the vehicle came to a halt, he stood at the quarter-light window, pulled in the flap and aimed a mock gun of fingers towards the architects' office no more than 15 feet away. No one could see him do this, and the barrel of any weapon would only have protruded a few inches from the bus window. Despite Hodges' misgivings, this really would have been the perfect place from which to murder Peter Young.

Thanks to the persistent bafflement of Colin Hodges, one of the big questions in the investigation remained: who would want to kill an architect? To find the answer, Gillard caught the train to central London to look at the biggest single piece of work in Peter Young's career, the new London offices of Chicago-based agricultural traders Crowgill Mattison. Travelling with the detective was HDG+ architect Finlay McMullen, who had worked closely with Young and had agreed to explain the project.

As they emerged at Southwark Tube station, McMullen pointed out the forest of cranes hard at work converting inspiration into concrete and steel. From this angle it looked like a giant blue-grey turtle squatting above an area of otherwise low-rise buildings. The shell was a shallow dome, still less than half constructed, of pentagonal tiles, while the neck was an open mesh corridor at third-floor level which would ultimately link the building to London Bridge station. 'It's a conceptual breakthrough, in several respects,' McMullen said. 'First, it straddles two existing Crowgill Mattison client sites in a very busy area of south-east London, adding 150,000 square feet of office space, assembled off-site, which will then be effectively suspended over a major road. The road is shielded by an innovative flexible mesh which has allowed the road closures to be minimized.'

'Did Peter design the whole thing?'

McMullen laughed. 'Heavens, no. HDG+ was contracted in for the roof of the main building. The shell, so to speak. It's the most high-profile aspect, using lightweight tensile framing techniques like those pioneered for the Millennium Dome, but on a structure intended to last hundreds of years.'

As they approached the construction site, the vision of the whole was lost in a morass of scaffolding, concrete mixers, hard-hatted construction workers and deafening noise. McMullen flashed his lanyard and led him onto a temporary walkway. This crossed over several large trenches to a complex of Portakabins stacked like Lego bricks. Inside the topmost, he was introduced to several senior engineers and the site manager, Len Starkey, who were all fascinated and horrified in equal measure by the murder of one of the architects.

'I've come here, really, with one question,' Gillard said, trying to make himself heard over the sound of a pile driver ramming a tree-trunk sized metal rod into the excavation behind him. 'I've read up about the many controversies surrounding this building: the overseas finance, the planning process, the objections from local residents and the contractual disputes between firms involved in the project. But perhaps you can tell me: is there any reason why a project like this might be connected with the murder of Peter Young?'

'If anyone was going to be murdered, it would probably be me,' Starkey said. 'Or someone senior at the client's. On a practical level, I'm the public face of this project. I've been to every planning meeting, I attended the coroner's inquest over the death of a cyclist who was squashed by one of our quarry trucks. The thing is, Peter was not really the figurehead of this project. He was an important part of it, but it would be odd to go for him as an individual.'

Gillard nodded. The answer was very much as he expected. 'Are you aware of any personal animosities arising from his work on this or any other project?'

Everyone shook their heads. 'I don't think Peter ever upset anyone,' McMullen said. 'Quite the reverse. He was charming and talented, not a prima donna at all. You might call it something of a rarity in my industry.'

The detective looked around the room, assessing each face in turn. There was nothing in any of them to inspire further enquiry. He turned and looked out of the window at the site, the cranes soaring above him. On the furthest tower of scaffolding, perhaps 15 storeys high, there was a scarecrow figure, in grey hoody and dark trousers, mounted on the protruding top of one of the scaffolding poles.

'Does anyone have a pair of binoculars?' Gillard asked.

A pair was found in the site manager's desk. 'What are you looking at?' Starkey asked.

Gillard trained the lenses on the mannequin. 'Who put that up there?' he asked.

Starkey didn't even know what he was referring to until he taken a look himself. 'Oh, that. It's just a mascot from some of the men. A bit of good luck for the site, I suppose.'

'Some of the East Europeans do them,' one engineer offered.

'How many deaths have there been on this site?' Gillard asked.

'Excluding the cyclist, none,' Starkey said.

'So it's worked,' laughed another engineer.

'Not for Peter Young it hasn't,' Gillard said.

–

On the train back from Waterloo, Gillard asked McMullen a little bit more about Peter Young. 'I got the impression that he got on well with everybody,' the architect said. 'He worked hard, probably longer hours than anyone but Kelvin himself. He would probably have made partner in two or three years.'

'Any office gossip about him?' Gillard asked.

'Well,' McMullen chuckled. 'The secretaries and admin women often had a thing about him. He was a bit of a charmer. There was plenty of speculation, but in all honesty I think he was totally faithful to his wife, if that was your question.'

Gillard nodded, his lips pursed. 'And what about Karen?'

'Excellent receptionist, great references. A good-looking woman, if that's not an un-PC thing to say. She had only been with us two weeks, poor thing. Terrible for that to happen to her. I imagine she will go back to South Africa now.'

'Why? You're not getting rid of her, are you?'

'Quite the contrary. She's getting rid of us. She resigned yesterday.'

Suddenly Gillard realized that he had forgotten to ask Michelle Tsu to request that Karen Davies voluntarily surrender her passport.

Chapter 10

Earlier the same day, 250 miles north

The aged Land Rover coughed and rumbled into the rough, potholed car park and shuddered to a halt, nose-on to the easterly wind howling in from the North Sea. It wasn't yet nine in the morning and, as usual on a weekday, Jim Crowthorne had Theddlethorpe National Nature Reserve all to himself. He turned off the radio, leaned forward over the steering wheel and squinted up at the sky. This was the kind of Lincolnshire winter weather he remembered from his childhood in the 1960s, when parts of the county would regularly be cut off by snow.

There had been a squall of hail earlier, pinging off the windscreen as he drove in. It would probably be like that all day, so he would have to take his chances. He pulled on thick woollen socks and wellington boots, then squeezed himself and his two thick jumpers into an anorak. With his woolly hat pulled well down over his salt-and-pepper hair, and a pair of Zeiss binoculars around his neck, he wrestled open the door into the buffeting gale.

Crowthorne reckoned he was the luckiest man in the world. He was paid, modestly, to look after this stretch of England's east coast. It was certainly one of the most obscure places in the British Isles, yet in its way also one of the grandest. The nature reserve covered an enormous area of tidal flats, salt marsh and dunes 20 miles north of the popular seaside resort of Skegness, and maybe 10 miles south of the depressed former fishing port of Grimsby. To walk right out at low tide took a leisurely 20 minutes. That's a long way with a bucket and spade, so even on a sunny August bank holiday you would be lucky to see half a dozen people on the five square miles that it occupied. On a bitterly cold January morning like this you might see no one at all, just the occasional RAF jet shrieking through the clouds towards the bombing ranges a few miles north.

The beach and the extensive grassy dunes behind hosted a variety of rare habitats, and boasted amphibians, damselflies and a handful of varieties of orchids. At this time of year there was the occasional dead seal washed up, quite often a young pup that had been born just a month or two before at the Donna Nook breeding grounds a few miles away. The reason Crowthorne was here this morning was because someone had phoned in a report of a dead seal close to the waterline.

He strode along the path which ran between thick banks of spiky bushes into the dunes, and climbed onto one which gave a good view of the beach. The sky was painted in gunmetal grey and pewter, the cloud edges limned in pastel shades of mauve, lavender and tangerine. The tide was out and the beach was at its biggest, three quarters of a mile. He lifted the binoculars to his eyes and scanned the horizon. Sure enough, there was something there about two thirds of the way towards the water. The dark, hummocked form might have looked like a seal to the naked eye, but magnified by the lenses he could see that this was no animal.

It was human.

And it wasn't moving.

Crowthorne fingered his mobile phone but decided to make sure before ringing the police. He strode out onto the beach and was hit immediately by the power of the wind; as he marched into its full force, an ankle-high spindrift of fine white sand tore past him in wispy clouds, as if he were tracking across the Antarctic rather than walking on a Lincolnshire beach. The spindrift had already built dart-shaped shadows in the lee of the occasional samphire stem or razor shell fragment which disturbed the relentless horizontal, and crowned even washed-up seaweed, polystyrene and cans in sculptural invention.

It took a good ten minutes to reach the body, which was partially buried. It was stuck in a sandbar, a semi-permanent feature close to low tide, and behind which a shallow but broad creek drained the beach. Protruding from the sand was a pair of hands bound together with plastic ties. The wind had partially covered them but for the curling fingers, from which were sculpted a series of elongated sand shadows. He could see no footprints nearby except his own, which to an amateur sleuth like himself indicated that the body had been dumped before high tide. In a moment of inspiration, and without approaching too closely, he took a series of photographs with his phone. He then rang the police.

Chapter 11

The call that Sophie Lund got on her phone on Wednesday evening justified all her paranoia.

The train from Waterloo hadn't yet reached Clapham Junction, and in the squeal and grind of the carriage moving across points she almost missed the buzz from her bag. It was Estela, and immediately Sophie knew from the sound of her voice that something was wrong.

'I'd just picked up the children from school,' the au pair said. 'Then I was followed all the way back, right through the village, almost to the drive.'

'Was it Geraldine?'

'No. It wasn't her car, and there was a man driving. I turned off on Tithe Lane, and he followed me.'

'No!'

'Yes, he did. All the way until I turned off at the north gate to go in the back way.'

'Did a child get into that other car at the school?'

'Not that I saw.'

Sophie could imagine that many parents with kids at the village school might drive past the estate's front entrance, which was on the busy B-road. But Tithe Lane was hardly used. It was extremely narrow, and served only two farms plus the shared private road which provided back access to the pottery and estate cottages. 'I suppose it could be somebody at one of the farms.'

'No, Sophie. I don't think so. There's something else. He took a photograph on his phone as I was walking out of the playground with the children. Maybe it was not of us, but when he followed me I got nervous.'

'Estela, you did the right thing. With any luck I'll be home by half past seven. Have you seen any sign of that Hinchcliffe woman's car?'

'No not today.'

I wonder where she is, thought Sophie. Something was going to have to be done about her.

—

Sophie now wished she had asked Zerina to stay longer. The children's only surviving close relative, Aunt Zerina, had stayed with them over Christmas for the second year. *Teto* – Auntie – as she liked to be called in front of the children, was a bubbly and rotund lady in her 40s who dressed for a bygone era, with a beehive hairdo, sparkly tops, thick skirts to the mid-calf and, God help us, winged spectacles. She had been brought up in the Albanian countryside, but had married and was these days living in Italy. 'I am from the Accursed Mountains,' she had giggled when she first came to visit them a year ago.

'That's not a real place, is it?' Dag had asked.

'Yes, yes, it's very real.' She had brought up a map on her phone to show them. 'Very tough life, even before the anarchy. Then we moved to fear.'

'Where?' Sophie had asked. 'Is that a real place too?'

'F-I-E-R. A big city, gangsters, bandits, trouble.' She threw up her arms, making her copious jewellery jangle. 'In Albania, everyone has gun. Bang-bang.'

But for Teto Zerina, life improved dramatically in 2003. She was in the flush of youth, as she described it, working as a waitress in the northern town of Shkoder when an Italian on holiday began a romance with her. She got married, left her family and moved to Rome. Her husband Leo was a good 20 years older than her, and previously divorced, which her family did not like. 'But, pfft. Anything is better than staying in Albania,' she laughed.

Sophie and Dag had tried to gently ask about the circumstances in which David and Amber became orphans, but they could never quite pin down the details. Perhaps it was because Teto herself did not know. All they gleaned was that someone with an old grudge had burst into the house in Fier during the night. The mother died from the first bullet; the father took five bullets but did not die for several weeks. Armend was a very tough man, Teto had said so repeatedly. Armend had died in hospital – she had gone to see him before he died. Teto's own parents were much older, and her father still lived in the Accursed Mountains. 'Too tough for me there,' she had said. 'That's why I went to live in Shkoder. And that's how I met a nice Italian tourist.' She made a cash gesture with finger and thumb. 'For me, very nice.'

Sophie had wanted to know why Zerina hadn't wanted to adopt her niece and nephew herself, but couldn't think quite how to phrase the question without making it an accusation. And she was very keen not to give her any ideas. Sophie loved the children; they had become central to her life. She couldn't bear if they were taken away or harmed. Ever since the adoption it had been a tiny, secret fear. And now that fear was growing, like a cancer.

–

Sophie's call to the police about the children being followed didn't elicit any immediate action. PC Kerrigan texted that evening to say he would take a statement from her 'in due course' but by Thursday morning she had convinced herself they weren't planning to do anything else. Then she had an idea. Looking through her old Rolodex she found the business card of a Detective Chief Inspector Craig Gillard. At the country fair last summer she had gone to the police caravan and picked up a series of crime prevention leaflets. She noticed a really very dishy man there, in cycling gear. She had at first assumed he was a member of the public, until she heard one of the uniformed officers called him sir. So she had butted into the conversation and asked about the theft of Dag's quad bike, which had occurred from a locked garage within a few weeks of them moving in. There had been no follow-up to her original report, and she told them she thought it was a bit poor. The two uniformed officers didn't seem to want to take it any further, and pointed out various leaflets on locks and immobilizers, but the detective seemed a little more interested. He took some details, and when a quad bike was recovered, phoned her back. Sadly it wasn't Dag's.

Now seemed a good opportunity to renew the acquaintance.

Sophie wasn't prepared to wait. It was just after eight when she rang the detective's mobile. Judging by the background noise she seemed to have got him in the car. She outlined the details, and he promised that if he was in the area in the next few days he would take a look.

–

Gillard cut the call and let out a hefty sigh. He really didn't have time for anything except the Peter Young case, but as he was sitting in stationary traffic on the Kingston bypass it did no harm to listen to the woman. As he explained to her, he really had no choice but to pass the details back to the original investigating officer, PC Adrian Kerrigan, despite Mrs Lund's lack of confidence in him. Gillard knew well enough that the police could not be everywhere, but he also knew that crime prevention depended on keeping the public onside. There was at least one lesson he could take from this: don't hand your business card out at country shows. He might just be able to fit in a visit on his day off.

When the detective arrived at the Khazi, Hoskins and Hodges were in the usual position, slouched over their respective PC screens, eating and watching CCTV on fast forward. 'How's it going, then?' Gillard asked.

'It's a game of two halves,' said Hodges. 'We've got nothing on where our suspect got on, but we've got him clear as day crossing Roosevelt Avenue and heading up Coulton Road.' Hodges ejected the current disc from his PC and slid another in.

'Any more cameras up there?'

'Not until we get to Esher station. I got the request in.' Hodges was fast-forwarding through the footage, which on the screen looked like chaotic, scurrying ants. As the counter approached the number he had written down, he slowed. 'There, that's him.'

The cameras showed a man in the now familiar hooded Puffa jacket approach the crossing, ease his way between a couple of elderly women and dash across the road before the pedestrian lights had turned green. It was only in the last few yards, as he was crossing to the other side, that he looked back and his face became properly visible.

'So, white British by appearance, bit of a wispy beard. Looks like a nose ring or something,' Hodges said.

'And he's in a bit of a hurry,' Gillard noted.

'It's raining and he doesn't want to get wet,' Hoskins suggested.

'It's not much, is it?' Gillard said. 'We can't even put him upstairs on the bus for sure.'

'That's right,' Hoskins said.

'Get me the best enlargements you can – I'm going to the girls' school this afternoon, see if anyone recognises him.'

Hodges let out a wicked cackle. 'Poor you, sir. All that miniskirted jailbait sitting on your lap.'

Hoskins took up the theme. 'Now now, Colin, I'm sure that DCI Gillard would much prefer to be sitting here with us in the Khazi for the next six hours staring at fuzzy videos of busloads of pensioners crossing the road.'

Gillard sighed. He wasn't going to repeat how intimidating he found these adolescent girls en masse, but he was distinctly nervous about the prospect. These days, there were so many ways to do or say the wrong thing.

–

DI Claire Mulholland joined Gillard for the afternoon follow-up at Hawthorne Academy. She couldn't help noticing how nervous he seemed to be. It was probably down to what he had told her about his experience on the bus yesterday morning. Having grown up at the rougher end of Staines, several miles further north, Mulholland was quite used to rowdy schoolchildren, but from the moment they entered the expensive softwood and steel hallway of the school, she was struck by the level of informality. Teachers laughed and joked with the kids, seeming to adopt more the role of experienced but still sassy older sisters than the stern matrons who had taught her. Mrs Joanne Calder, the student welfare officer, met them and guided them in. She was wearing a purple sweatshirt which carried the slogan 'Hawthorne Rocks!' with a cartoon of a guitar-wielding punk girl on it.

Joanne, as she insisted on being called, guided them into an open-plan coffee-cum-snack bar, lined with vending machines and boasting tall stand-up round tables which wouldn't have looked out of place at a crowded Starbucks. Waiting for them there was a pack of about 70 girls, projecting terminal boredom as only teenagers can. Joanne addressed them in a practised bellow, saying they had been asked to attend as regular users of the bus from Surbiton. She then introduced the police officers simply as Craig and Claire, and invited the girls to listen to what they had to say. The fact that more than half were still working their phones or plugged into earphones brought no remonstration from Joanne.

Gillard repeated a fair amount of what he had said the previous morning, and caught the eye of eyebrow girl, slowly chewing gum, between text messages. He invited the girls to look at the images on his laptop of the man in the Puffa jacket. Only a few bothered to come up to stare at the screen, before shrugging or saying they hadn't seen him. At the end, frustrated by the lack of engagement with his audience, Gillard said: 'Someone must have seen something. And if you see this man,' he pointed to the image, 'please text the police information line.'

The girls gradually filed out, including the short one who had done the impersonation of Gillard at the bus stop. She wouldn't make eye contact with him, but there was a sly smile on her lips as she sidled past, working her phone. 'So are you planning to be an actress, young lady?' he asked.

Something was grunted in reply.

'Melanie, would you be good enough to answer the policeman politely?' Joanne asked.

The girl turned to him and said: 'Nobody but us girls goes upstairs. I've seen that bloke though, he gets off the train at Surbiton, but I think he goes downstairs on the bus.'

'So he's a regular?'

Melanie shrugged. 'Regular, I don't know. But I have seen him on the train.'

'Melanie, why didn't you say something before?' Joanne asked.

'It's none of my business, innit?'

'A man has been killed,' Mulholland said.

The girl ignored her and instead answered a phone call from her mum.

'She's a good girl, really,' Joanne said. 'Chaotic family background, lots of issues.'

As they left, Gillard rang in a request to DC Hoskins to get some CCTV in from Surbiton station. After he'd hung up, Mulholland said: 'Who'd be a teacher, eh?'

'Not me,' said Gillard. 'I did two weeks of riot control in the Met. Couldn't do a lifetime of it.'

–

Sophie had given up hope of a response. But at eleven o'clock on Sunday morning the doorbell rang, and Dag called up to her. 'It's the police.' She came downstairs, followed by David who stared out curiously through the banisters. The man at the door was, as when she had first met him, in cycling gear, and as easy on the eye as she remembered: helmet with visor, skin-tight jersey and leggings, plus pointy green shoes. His mountain bike was leaning against one of the columns of the portico.

'Oh, have you come on your day off?' Sophie asked.

'Well, combining business with pleasure, actually,' he said. 'I've never cycled around here. And the weather is better today.' Gillard spotted the boy on the stairs. 'Hello, young man, what's your name?'

'David. Are you a policeman?'

'I am, yes.'

'Where's your uniform?' The boy slid down to stand next to his mother.

'David, don't be rude,' Sophie said, ruffling his hair and mouthing apologies to Gillard.

'I'm a detective,' Gillard said, crouching down. 'I'm here to help your mummy.'

'Do you catch bad men?'

'Sometimes, yes.'

'So are you a fast runner?'

Gillard chuckled. 'Actually, once, I was. When I was young.'

'I'll race you to the tree,' David said, pointing at a large beech tree about 50 yards away.

'David, the detective hasn't got time for that,' Sophie said. She rolled her eyes at Gillard.

'It's all right,' he replied, turning back to the boy. 'Go on, then.' He adopted a sprinter's pose, but the child was already running. 'Ready, set, go,' he said when he was already five yards ahead. Gillard chased after him, matching his pace to that of the boy, and then letting him win in the final few yards.

David was thrilled, jumping up and down. 'Mummy, I'm faster than a policeman!'

'Yes, you're a very fast runner,' Gillard said.

Sophie smiled at them both as they returned. 'Now David, go upstairs and don't bother the nice man any more.'

Dag re-emerged in combat trousers and rugby shirt, and beckoned for Gillard to follow. Sophie and Dag drove down on the quad bike while Gillard cycled. With the benefit of some watery sunlight and a few dry days the bridleway was much recovered. They stopped at the stile, and Sophie led them over and down towards the bridge. The mannequin was still there, though it was obvious from a few yards away it was not a real person. The hat was gone, the wig had sagged and one wellington had dropped off.

'I suppose I'm a fool to have ever believed it was real,' Sophie said. 'But I can assure you that at night it was very convincing.'

'I don't doubt it,' Gillard said. 'So you say you believe that this was done by your neighbour?'

'Yes. Geraldine Hinchcliffe.'

'Arch-lunatic and potter,' Dag added.

'Have you spoken to her?'

'Not actually spoken,' Sophie said. 'I left a message on her phone, and she left a handwritten note under the windscreen of my car, typical eccentric response, to say she had nothing to do with it.'

Gillard crossed the footbridge, then reached up and with a pocket knife cut through the cord on which the mannequin was suspended. He put it into a large carrier bag. 'We can take a look at this back at the house. Did you ever find Amber's wellingtons?'

'No,' said Sophie. 'I'm sure she stole them.'

'I'll get one of the uniforms to go around and have a quiet word.'

As they returned to the yard there was the sound of a chainsaw starting up. 'Has Michael got some contractors doing some work today?' Dag asked.

'I don't think so. He knows they're not to use machinery near the house on a Sunday. I bet it's that bloody woman,' Sophie said, increasing her pace. From the front lawns she led them to the back of the main house, threading through a series of farm buildings and a small car park. Parked next to a row of *leylandii* there was a Land Rover and trailer, half full of cuttings. A tall figure in a green jacket and orange helmet was wielding a chainsaw on one of the conifers.

'Hey!' yelled Sophie, breaking into a run. 'What the hell are you doing?' Ahead of her, by the Land Rover, a grey-haired woman in a floaty dress and sandals turned to them. It was Geraldine Hinchcliffe.

'We are just doing what you should have done years ago,' Geraldine shouted, pointing the mug in her hand at the three of them.

'You can't do this, it's on our land!' Sophie shouted, trying to make herself heard.

'I've told you, this section is mine,' Geraldine bellowed, brandishing a piece of paper from her pocket and pointing at the base of the trees. 'I've got legal opinion.' She waved it in Sophie's face. 'From a solicitor.'

Dag meanwhile went around the Land Rover and up to the workman, who stopped the chainsaw and turned to him.

'Detective Chief Inspector Gillard, would you please tell this bloody woman…?' Sophie asked.

'I am Geraldine Hinchcliffe and I will not be talked to like this on my own land.'

Sophie looked like she was going to explode. 'It is NOT your land—'

'I think it would be best if everyone just kept calm,' Gillard said in his best public-order boom. 'And you, sir, I would please halt all work until its legality has been verified.'

At that moment, the tall workman took off his helmet. *Oh my God*, thought Gillard. *I don't believe it.*

Chapter 12

The chief constable was quite recognizable once she had removed her orange helmet and safety visor. Alison Rigby, her tall frame bulked out by the thick padded jacket and safety trousers, locked her infamous blue stare on Gillard. 'I think you would agree that this is a civil matter, wouldn't you, Detective Chief Inspector?' she said.

'So long as everyone keeps calm, ma'am,' he said.

Sophie immediately spotted the deference in Gillard's tone and rounded on Rigby. 'I don't know who the hell you are, but you are currently standing on my land, cutting down my trees. That is trespass, and criminal damage.'

Geraldine Hinchcliffe, her long dangling earrings shaking in disagreement, waved the piece of paper under Sophie's nose.

Rigby folded her arms and looked down at Sophie. 'I am Geraldine's partner, and she asked me to help her. We're quite confident the law is on our side.'

'Are you going to arrest this woman or not?' Sophie said to Gillard.

He now thoroughly regretted coming to do a good deed on his day off.

First thing on Monday, as expected, Gillard was called into the chief constable's office. Alison Rigby was sipping coffee from a large brown mug, which Gillard now noticed looked to be home-made. One of Geraldine Hinchcliffe's efforts, no doubt.

'Ah, Craig, take a seat.' She pointed at one of the low chairs that encircled the coffee table, which indicated an informal conversation. Gillard sat, while Rigby continued to go through paperwork for a good five minutes. Eventually she looked up, came around and sat opposite him.

'Unfortunate business yesterday, Craig.'

'Yes, ma'am.'

'So what were you doing there?' she asked.

'I only went along as a favour. Because of the mannequin. Thought I could combine a nice relaxing bike ride with it.'

'Gee told me about the mannequin business and took me along to have a look at it. I have to say I think the Lund woman has blown it out of all proportion. And there is no way that Gee would do anything like that.'

'You know Ms Hinchcliffe better than I do,' Gillard said, not quite indicating that he would take her word for it. He was still waiting for the main subject to arise.

'Look. I'm sorry to have put you in such a difficult situation. I really shouldn't have got involved, but those trees did need to come down.'

'Wasn't it a job for contractors?'

'Poor Gee tried, but when they saw which side of the fence the trees were on, they said they wouldn't be insured. They didn't even want to look at our legal opinion.'

'Are you satisfied over the legality, ma'am?'

Rigby sighed. 'Actually, not entirely. It's arguable, but Gee had been on to me for months about this. I thought if I did it, I'd get a little peace.' She looked up and helped herself to a couple of Maltesers from a jar on her desk. 'You know how it is.'

'Yes, ma'am. If I may suggest, best not to wield the machinery yourself in this case. Saves complications and awkwardness.'

She nodded. 'So I take it we can forget about this little incident?'

'What incident, ma'am?' Craig smiled.

'Yes indeed. And particularly the unintentional insight into my private life.' She flashed the blue stare, long enough for Gillard to realize that this was very important to her.

'Absolutely, ma'am.'

Rigby smiled, having secured the assurance that she needed.

Gillard was aware of the rumours that had filled the vacuum about the personal life of the county's most senior police officer. Rigby was unmarried, nearly 50, and had guarded her privacy meticulously. She had probably missed the opportunity to 'come out' when she was less senior. Though the country as a whole had for a decade or more been relaxed about homosexuality amongst senior public servants, the police itself was infamously stuck in the last century. Male officers' incessant speculation about unmarried female counterparts rarely rose above ribald chuckling about strap-on dildos, muff-diving and bull dykes. What Gillard had seen here, two middle-aged women finding domestic happiness together, was too nuanced to trouble the stereotype.

For Gillard, being the accidental custodian of such a sensitive piece of information was a double-edged sword. He knew enough about the politics of the police to understand that everything he did from now on, every investigation, every mistake would attract the eagle eye of Alison Rigby, and be viewed through the prism of the secret he bore. Firm, fair and married to the job, that was how she described herself. She had a terrific reputation, from her deft handling of the very tricky Girl F child abuse investigation right through to the Knight murder case. Office chatter had her down as a leading candidate for Metropolitan Police Commissioner at some stage, the toughest police job in Britain.

He just hoped now that he wouldn't have to be involved in any further activity in that neck of the woods. Troubles at Colsham Manor could be PC Kerrigan's problem from now on.

He was to be sorely disappointed.

–

Gillard hadn't mentioned to the chief constable the other things that he had been told by Sophie Lund. Her kids being photographed as they left the school and the au pair being followed. In some ways that was more disturbing than this bizarre mannequin. He had made a phone call to PC Kerrigan, and suggested he take an additional statement from her. Kerrigan certainly gave the impression that the case wasn't anywhere near the top of his priorities. Gillard had a suggestion: 'I also think it would be a good idea to take a statement from Geraldine Hinchcliffe, the neighbour. There's a long-running dispute, essentially a civil matter over land boundaries. But I think if you put in an appearance, Mrs Lund will at least consider that Surrey Constabulary has been doing its job.' The additional benefit, which he didn't mention, was that if Sophie Lund was happy, she was much less likely to go to the press, and the chief constable's secret would not be revealed.

'Message received loud and clear,' Kerrigan said.

'Oh, and Constable, make an appointment. Don't just turn up.' He didn't want any other officer tripping over the chief constable.

—

The next call from Sophie Lund came on Monday evening, just as Gillard was putting his keys in his own front door lock. 'I'm really sorry to disturb you again, and only doing so because I would feel silly talking to that PC about this.'

'What's the problem?' he replied as he opened the door and stepped inside, mouthing a hello to Sam, who was in the kitchen.

'Someone has sprayed something onto a doorpost on one of the outbuildings. Some kind of symbol.'

'Is it definitely new?' Gillard replied.

'Oh yes. It's the stables, and I go there every day. It looks like it was done with a stencil. The sort of thing that we used to make in craft lessons when I was a girl. Just the sort of thing that a mischievous potter might make.'

Gillard sighed. There could be so many explanations for this. 'Why don't you take a picture of it, and when you email it to PC Kerrigan, copy me in.'

'Okay.' She sounded disappointed, as if she expected more.

'How are things with the neighbours?'

'The same.' She paused. 'Craig, who is that woman? The one who was hacking at my trees.'

Gillard took a deep breath and lied. 'I've no idea.'

'She certainly seemed to have the measure of you. Treated you like a naughty schoolboy.'

'Mrs Lund, you have to realize that the police hate to be involved in civil disputes of that nature. We always urge people to sit down and negotiate, because that's what will happen in the end. If you can't do it, the court system will do it for you and you will just end up with a massive bill.'

'Oh, so it's just Mrs Lund now,' she said. 'Well, thank you for all your help.' She slammed the phone down.

'Who was that?' Sam asked as she embraced her husband, who was still staring at the phone.

'A real piece of work,' Gillard replied. 'Do someone a favour and you inherit a liability. Someone who expects you to run around at their beck and call.'

'Told you before, Craig. Sometimes you're just too good for the police. You've got enough on your plate with this architect killing. Get someone else to deal with it.'

–

The next call from Sophie Lund was on Thursday morning. 'Look, I'm really sorry to keep calling you, but I have found something else.'

Gillard was at his desk, with a stack of documents about Peter Young in front of him. His eyes rolled backwards in his head in exasperation, though he tried not to sigh too audibly. He cradled his chin in his hand and replied. 'Sophie, I really think it would be better if you dealt with PC Kerrigan.' He didn't want to provoke her into slamming the phone down again.

'Well, he's such an idiot. I emailed the picture to him and I've heard nothing. He didn't return my call, and that's two days ago. I've had nothing from you either.'

'We get hundreds of incidents per day, and you may know we're dealing with a major murder inquiry which is taking most of my time.'

You could almost feel the pout at the other end of the line. 'Craig, I've found some bullets. I'm really scared.'

'In the house? Or outside?'

'Outside. We've got a tenant's cottage, currently unoccupied, in fact in need of renovation. It's about ten minutes' walk from the Manor. I was walking Balfour and, going through the kitchen garden there, which is a bit overgrown, I saw these bullets, about half a dozen lying on the ground.'

'Do you mean bullets, or do you mean spent cartridges? I mean, there must have been quite a lot of shooting of pigeons and rabbits over the years around there.'

'No, I know what a shotgun cartridge looks like. I was brought up in the country, for goodness' sake. These are hollow brassy things, so I suppose they are casings.'

'Look, I've got to go to a meeting in a minute. Take some pictures and, as before, send them to PC Kerrigan and copy me in.' He was about to hang up when he added. 'Oh, Sophie, just a precaution. The chances are that there is an innocent explanation, but just in case: don't touch them. If there is anything suspicious, don't leave your own fingerprints or DNA on them.'

'Oh, I already picked them up and put them in a tin.'

'Okay, too late, then.' As he hung up he realized that she sounded quite excited at the prospect that something might really be happening. What a pain.

The following Tuesday

Sophie was awoken from a deep sleep by a murmuring coming from the baby monitor and then a bang. Instantly awake, she looked at the clock: 3.17 a.m. She looked to her right, seeking the reassuring hummock of her husband's form.

But the bed was flat and undisturbed.

A thread of fear tightened around her as she now recalled he was in Houston, and not back until the weekend, four days away. She flicked on the light, eased her way out of the warm bed and put on a bathrobe and slippers. The baby monitor was connected to Amber's bedroom in case she woke up and was frightened in the night. Quite often Amber called for her after a nightmare, and on several occasions she had awoken screaming. Luckily that wasn't the case tonight. Originally she had had both children sleep in the same bedroom at the front of the house, overlooking the lawns. But Amber's night terrors were disturbing her brother, and he had enough problems at school as it was without going in tired every day, so she moved him to one of the attic rooms looking out over the woods at the back. She didn't want David woken up.

She padded along the 20 feet of corridor that separated the master bedroom from Amber's. She opened the door to discover that the bed was empty and the room was chilly. The little girl was leaning out of the open window.

Somewhere nearby, the piercing hoot of an owl split the night. The girl seemed to be talking to herself and, trying not to disturb her, Sophie came and knelt next to her. 'Hello, Mummy,' Amber said.

'I heard you talking to yourself,' Sophie said.

'I was talking to the angel,' the girl replied.

'Not bad dreams tonight, then, my darling?' She stroked the child's hair.

'No, Mummy. Not a dream angel, a real one. There.' She pointed out onto the moonlit grounds, which swept down to the ha-ha, and the beech trees whose huge boughs overshadowed the formal lawns. At first Sophie didn't see him because of the zebra shadows of branches cast against the trunks of the trees.

And then she did.

A man with a light-coloured raincoat around his shoulders and a halo of wavy hair, standing against the base of the right-hand beech, about 50 yards away. Of course, another scarecrow. Very realistic, this one – super-realistic even.

Then it moved.

Chapter 13

The man walked calmly around the tree, then jumped down into the ha-ha, his raincoat hanging in the air for a split second.

'See, Mummy, angel's wings.'

Terrified out of her wits, Sophie snatched her daughter from the window and slammed the casement closed.

'Stay here, darling,' she said, putting the child back into her bed. She hurried into her own room, picked up the bedside phone and rang Michael, the estate manager. She felt from experience that even if the police took her seriously, they wouldn't be here for ages.

'Michael? It's Sophie, I'm terribly sorry to ring in the middle of the night but we've got an intruder on the lawns. I'm absolutely scared stiff, would you come over, please? Oh, Michael, thank you so much. Apologize to Felicity for me.'

She had barely put the phone down when Estela walked into the bedroom. 'Mrs Lund, I heard noises…'

'Yes, there was a man on the lawn.' The door behind Estela opened and a pyjama-clad David walked through, sucking his thumb, his eyes wide in alarm.

'David, I've told you not to suck your thumb,' Sophie said. 'You are eight years old, for goodness' sake.'

He continued, but reached for the reassuring hand of the au pair.

Sophie went into the en suite to change into outdoor clothes. Before she had finished, Estela called up to say that Michael had arrived.

'I'll be downstairs in a minute,' she said.

Michael was a ruddy-faced, thickset man in his early 50s. Sophie was used to seeing him in a country jacket and wellingtons. Tonight he was wearing a hooded anorak, tracksuit bottoms and training shoes with no socks.

'Mrs Lund, what on earth is the matter?'

She told him all the details, and she was only halfway through when Amber walked into the room, clutching her favourite stuffed panda, Mimi.

'Amber, you're supposed to be back in bed,' Sophie said with exasperation.

Michael crouched down and put his hand out to the child. 'Been having nightmares again, little lady?'

Amber slowly shook her head and held the panda even closer to her face. 'I've been talking to an angel. He said he could take me to see my mummy.'

'But your mummy's here,' said Michael, scooping the little girl up into his arms and turning to Sophie.

'No not this mummy, silly, my real mummy. *Mumje që është në qiell.*'

Michael seemed to stagger for a moment, and his mouth fell open. 'What language is this?'

'Albanian,' Sophie said. 'She was an Albanian orphan. Don't you remember me saying?'

'What did you just say, darling?' Sophie asked, taking Amber from Michael's arms.

David answered for her. 'She said "Mummy who is in heaven".'

'Oh sweet Jesus,' breathed Michael.

'Amber, darling, I won't be cross,' Sophie said. 'But you were imagining what the angel said, weren't you?'

Amber pressed her face into Mimi, a pout forming. Slowly she moved her head backwards and forwards within the panda's embrace.

'The angel spoke to me,' she whispered.

'But how? You were asleep.'

'The owl woke me up, and I went to the window to see if I could see him. Then I saw the angel, down below on the grass.'

'You mean close to the house?'

She nodded, gravely.

'You mean right below your window?'

She nodded. 'He called up to me.'

Sophie's throat dried up almost completely, but she managed to croak out the question: 'What did he say, darling?'

'He said: "*Tregoni atyre. Kam ardhur për hakmarrje.*"'

'He spoke to you in Albanian!' Sophie almost shrieked.

'What does it mean?' Michael asked, looking around the room in bewilderment. Estela shrugged and looked down at the small boy who was still grasping her hand, tears beginning in his eyes.

David spoke. 'It means…' He thought for a moment, his face screwed up in concentration. '"Tell them. I have come for vengeance."'

Chapter 14

Having had enough of the scepticism of the police, Sophie asked Michael to dial 999 for her. The overheard conversation, once he was through to the police incident room, was full of frustrations.

'Yes, it was the child who heard it.' Pause. 'She is five.' Pause. 'No, it wasn't "just a nightmare". It wasn't a dream. There was a witness.' There was a long, frustrated pause as Michael looked heavenwards. 'Yes, that's what I'm saying, a witness who saw the intruder. Yes. On the lawns within sight of the house. It was the child's mother. Well, adoptive mother. Can I pass you over? All right, later.' Michael nodded to Sophie and then continued: 'Well, the man was speaking Albanian. Yes, to the child. No, only the child heard.' Long pause. 'How did she know it was Albanian? Well, she is Albanian. I presume she speaks it. Well, it sounded very convincing to me.' Long pause. 'I'm the estate manager. No, I didn't see the intruder. No, no, we don't have any staff, at least nobody who would be here overnight. The nearest pub? It must be two miles or more. Look, I really don't think it was a drunk. Especially an Albanian-speaking drunk. Look, can I pass you over? She can describe…' Michael rolled his eyes again and shuffled his feet with impatience. 'No, no. I don't think he's been seen since. Yes, it was half an hour ago.' Another pause.

'So you're not going to send anyone? In the morning, all right. Thank you.' He hung up and turned to Sophie. 'I think you got the gist of that.'

'Useless, absolutely useless,' said Sophie, flexing her knuckles and sitting down on the bed. 'Do you have a shotgun, Michael?'

He looked terrified. 'I'm an accountant, not a game-keeper.' Needing more ammunition for his apparently timid stance he said: 'I'm scared of spiders.'

'I have to defend my children when my husband isn't here.' Her face was implacable.

'This is Surrey, Mrs Lund.' He stared at her as if meeting the woman for the first time. 'I'm sure there is some innocent explanation.'

She nodded, but was clearly unconvinced.

'I don't suppose I could trouble you for a brandy, Mrs Lund?' Michael asked.

'Of course, of course. I should have offered.' She knelt down at the glass-fronted cabinet and reached for the Hennessy. With the bottle in one hand she got to her feet and reached on tiptoe to a high display shelf for a crystal balloon. Her fingers somehow lost their grip and the glass fell onto the top of the cabinet, shattering. It was the last of her late mother's glass collection.

'Oh, Mum,' she said. 'I'm sorry.' She sank to her knees to pick up the larger pieces, but before she could even begin, her shoulders began to shudder and an unstoppable wave of tears took hold of her: tears of rage, of frustration and of sheer bloody terror.

Michael crouched by her side and as the crying grew into a wail, gave her a sideways hug. It was a perfect example of the kind of awkward embrace that an employee can in exceptional circumstances offer an employer of the opposite sex: plenty of patting hands on the shoulders, plenty of 'there-theres' but no body-to-body contact. Unable to put up with this for long, Sophie rose to her feet offering a mishmash of thanks and apologies. Michael guided her to the sofa and got them both a brandy in ordinary glasses while Estela cleaned up the broken shards.

As Sophie patted her bathrobe pockets, feeling for a tissue, she saw through her smeared vision her son, David. He was carrying a plastic water pistol, clearly loaded and dripping on the carpet.

'Mummy, I will defend us.' His face looked full of determination.

She pulled the boy to her bosom. 'Oh, David. That's very sweet of you. We need more brave little men like you.'

Wednesday

DCI Gillard took the call from PC Kerrigan on the hands-free as he was waiting at roadworks on the way to work. The constable relayed the bare facts of last night's incident at Colsham Manor in the habitual flat tone of police reportage, while conveying a clear hint that Mrs Lund was a nutcase.

'Thank you for the update,' Gillard said.

'A bit of a fairy story, if you ask me,' Kerrigan said. 'Probably a drunk on the lawn. But it seems like both mother and daughter have a good imagination.'

'And no CCTV,' Gillard replied. 'The husband took it out.' The lights had finally turned green, and he edged the car past a line of diggers and earthworks. 'Okay, as you know, I'm not taking her calls any more, as I'm up to my neck in this murder enquiry. But do copy me in on any significant developments. If I get a moment to myself I'll cast an eye over this. In the meantime you might want to get a colleague to take a look.' He thanked Kerrigan and hung up.

At the next hold-up, Gillard called up his emails. There was a reply from Geoff Meadows, a former detective chief superintendent at the National Crime Agency. Meadows had recently retired and ran a busy security consultancy, but remained one of the few experts on Albanian crime outside academia. He had even taught himself the language, which had proved its value when he sat in on interrogations of Albanian criminals in Britain. In his earlier years, Meadows had mentored Gillard in his first days on the Surrey force. Gillard had immediately thought of Meadows when he heard of the Albanian angle, and had forwarded Sophie's photo of the sprayed graffito on her stable door to him.

He punched in the number and called Meadows.

'So you got something for me, Geoff?' he said when he was finally patched in.

'Can't talk too much now, just about to go into a meeting on a VAT fraud case. But that image reminded me of something I'd seen before, branded on the neck of an informer: a triple-headed eagle with crossed scimitars beneath.'

'A dead informer?'

Meadows laughed. 'Not at the time he was branded. But they killed him, yes. This wasn't in Britain, I hasten to add. I was on a joint operation in Tirana.'

'In Albania?' Gillard asked, fearing that his hunch was right.

Meadows chuckled and then back-pedalled a bit. 'Well, it's only a resemblance. It's hardly likely to turn up in a rural area in Surrey I suppose. Still…'

'Geoff, what are you telling me?'

'Look, Craig, I really hope I'm wrong, because that's the symbol of the Dragusha clan.' He turned away to have a brief conversation with somebody else.

'Who are they?' Gillard asked. It was a couple of minutes before Meadows was able to return to the call.

'Like I said, I really hope I'm wrong. Because the Dragusha are the most murderous mafia family in Albania.'

–

Sophie Lund's interview with PC Adrian Kerrigan on Wednesday morning was every bit as disappointing as she had expected. Scepticism oozed from the man as he sat on her sofa, making intermittent jottings in a small notebook but much larger forays into the plate of biscuits she had provided. It was only with reluctance, and after the plain chocolate digestives had been consumed, that he agreed to follow her to the beech tree where she had seen the man. Sophie had already rooted around thoroughly for cigarette ends, footprints, anything that would prove the existence of what Amber continued to call an angel.

She had kept Amber back from school so that she could recount to the policeman the conversation she had had with the man, but Kerrigan said that wasn't necessary.

'Why isn't it necessary?' Sophie asked.

'Children as young as this are not reliable witnesses, generally speaking. She had just woken up, as you said yourself.'

'Well, I had woken up too. And I can tell you I bloody saw him. Do you want a description of what he looks like or not?'

'Yes, all right,' Kerrigan said with a sigh. 'Fire away.'

'He was slim and quite well-dressed. He had light-coloured hair and a pale beard. And he seemed quite fit. He moved pretty fast when I appeared at the window.'

'Age?'

'Hard to say. Mid–30s? Possibly 40?'

Kerrigan's chorus of noncommittal murmurings in response to Sophie's retelling of last night's events was only interrupted by the approaching figure of Michael. The estate manager was clad in his usual attire of worsted jacket, mustard-coloured corduroys and stout brown lace-up shoes. Kerrigan greeted him with a solid handshake, and a certain matiness, as if sanity had now arrived. As they shared some private joke, Sophie's anger grew. Bloody men, she thought.

Once the constable had waddled back to his car with evident relief, she reflected that there was only one piece of advice he had given her that she was going to follow: to reconnect the CCTV. In fact she was going to go better than that. She was going to expand it.

–

Tweedledum and Tweedledee took the best part of a week to get through all of the CCTV footage from pedestrian crossings, buses and Surbiton railway station, and they were the first to acknowledge they hadn't made as much progress as they'd hoped in identifying their only suspect in the murder of architect Peter Young. DC Carl Hoskins stood in front of the daily incident room meeting and reported: 'We have two seconds of footage from the bus, five seconds of him crossing the road, and a possible brief glimpse at Surbiton station a week earlier. But we don't yet know who he is.'

DC Colin Hodges took up the theme. 'We've got a pretty decent idea of what he looks like. He is about five foot ten tall, medium build, may have a slight wispy beard, and his hair is light-coloured. There may be a nose ring. The bag he's carrying is a leather shoulder bag or satchel made by Next and sold only in their stores. He is wearing canvas high-top baseball shoes, but not, we think, a well-known brand.' He turned to Hoskins to continue.

'Enquiries at the girls' school, as you know, turned up nothing. Only the one girl who thinks she saw him at Surbiton station. I went to St Cuthbert's preparatory school earlier in the week and managed to speak to a number of the boys who are regular travellers on the morning bus. One of them thinks he has seen him. The boy said, unprompted, that the man got off at Coulton Road, which dovetails with the CCTV footage we have on the pedestrian crossing by that stop.'

'But Carl, the boys always sit downstairs, don't they?' interjected Gillard.

'That's right. He saw him downstairs, but he doesn't remember which day.'

'That's going to be a problem for us, isn't it?' Mulholland asked. 'If the only place he's been seen is downstairs on this bus, he's not likely to have been the shooter.'

'Unless he was upstairs on another occasion,' Hodges suggested.

'Let's take a step back,' Gillard said. 'If you want to kill someone, you need to know where they will reliably be at a certain time. Peter Young was clearly visible in that window from quite early each day. If I was a hit man, I would have done my initial reconnaissance by car or on foot. I'd have needed just one prior trip on the bus to make sure the shot was possible, so obviously not downstairs. I would hardly be a regular bus user.'

'But how reliable is the recollection of these kids?' Mulholland asked. 'Maybe he just saw the man coming downstairs and off the bus.'

'Well, they should be astute. St Cuthbert's has over the years produced one former prime minister and half a dozen Cabinet ministers,' Gillard began.

Hodges laughed. 'Nah, sir. What it means is they are in intensive training for a career of lying and evasion, and nothing they say can ever be trusted.'

–

For almost a week there had been no sign of the angel. Dag had returned home from Houston on Friday with a bunch of red roses for Sophie. They had made love passionately all that afternoon, while Estela took the children on a prearranged nature trip to see the newborn fawns at the venison farm at the far end of Tithe Lane. Dag was very worried, and had even offered to postpone his next trip to the Gulf for a week. Feeling a bit pathetic, Sophie had talked him out of it. After all, it was not as if she hadn't made her own arrangements to feel safer at night.

The security company had done a good job. The lawns were now covered by a series of night-vision cameras, directional and sound-activated, including one carefully disguised in the beech tree below which the man had appeared. Michael had agreed to now lock the main gates at night, something that even the previous owner Clive Gashley had not done. She had even broached, with Geraldine Hinchcliffe, the subject of locking the smaller back gates at Tithe Lane. However, Sophie's email of two days ago had not yet been answered.

Even PC Kerrigan had made a return visit, unexpectedly, late on Monday afternoon. Sophie showed him all the new security arrangements, and it was only when they both stood again at the beech tree, looking back at the magnificent manor house, that the constable noticed something.

'Mrs Lund, what are those objects in the gutters?' He pointed out two small bundles, one at either end of the house, below the attic windows.

'I don't know,' Sophie replied. 'I don't have my binoculars with me.' When they walked back close to the house, the angle was too low for them to be able to see, so Sophie led the constable back via the boot room, where she asked him to remove his outdoor shoes, and in stockinged feet they ascended the main staircase to the galleried second floor. There were two front attic bedrooms here, one used as a box room, the other as a toy room. They entered the toy room first, and Sophie fumbled with the keys to the newly installed window locks. She then pulled open the small casement windows and looked out and down to the gutter. Sitting there in a mulch of leaves, wet and bedraggled, was one of the charity shop teddy bears that she had bought for Balfour to run about with a year or so ago.

'Who put that there?' she asked, of no one in particular.

'Perhaps your son, to torment his sister?' the PC replied.

'But it's the dog's teddy, not hers.'

'Who else could have put it there?' he asked. 'The little girl could surely not have reached.'

She dared not think who else. It had to be David.

They went to the other attic room, and below that window was a more fearsome mannequin. One of David's own hooded sports tops, stuffed with dog towels, and with a drawn paper face. The arms were made of sticks, and taped to one was a broken plastic toy pistol, which Sophie thought had been thrown away.

'Kids, eh?' Kerrigan said, lifting the mannequin back into the room. 'I expect you'll find that your son made the other one in the wood too.'

'No, absolutely not. He promised me that it wasn't him.'

The PC shrugged, with a face that said 'case solved'.

Sophie decided that she was going to have a proper talk with David when he got back from school.

–

Sophie took David up to the toy room and asked him whether he had made something to sit in the gutter. 'Did you make a little mannequin out of Balfour's chewing teddy?' she asked.

'It was a monkey,' David said. 'To protect us.'

'What do you mean, a monkey? How can it protect us?'

'Against the *sy të keq*. The evil eye.'

'Do you mean the man that Amber saw?'

David looked down. 'I don't know, I didn't see him. But a monkey helps us all. In Albania, everyone uses monkeys to protect what they have.' David felt for Sophie's hand and pulled her by the fingers to his own room. He opened the window and showed her in the gutter below his own attic window there was a stuffed rabbit, again one of Balfour's, dangling from a wire that went around the window catch. 'Any bad people will see the monkeys, and they will go away.'

Sophie stroked the little boy's dark hair and his warm cheek. 'David. I have to ask you again. Did you make a monkey in the woods? The one of the little girl with Amber's wellies that was hung above the bridge?'

He didn't look at her, but he shook his head emphatically. Sophie hadn't taken either of the children to see the mannequin, in case it gave them nightmares. But she had described it to David. 'You wouldn't lie to me, would you?'

He shook his head, and said solemnly: 'No, Mummy.'

—

That night, after the children had gone to bed, Sophie prowled around the house, listening to the rising wind that bent the leafless trees in the woods at the back and howled down the chimneys. She was feeling anxious and lonely. Dag was in Qatar, and wouldn't be back until Friday. She stopped outside Amber's room, listening carefully. She eased open the door and watched her daughter, asleep in the big bed at the centre of her row of dolls, Mimi the panda clasped to her cheek, and on the other side a cuddly kitten that Teto Zerina had given her which made a noise when you pressed its tummy. The curtains were not fully drawn, and moonlight caressed Amber's delicate forehead and pinkly wet lips. Only her eyelashes moved, traversing some dreamscape, perhaps another country, another life, before this one.

Sophie retreated carefully from the room without waking the child, easing the door closed, and then climbed the final flight of stairs to the attic level. Her hand was poised over the corridor's light switch, but she did not touch it. David's bedroom was the second on the left, and she could see fingers of light from under the ill-fitting door, and the faint sound of his voice. It was well after ten, and he should be asleep. She tiptoed along the edge of the wood-panelled hallway to avoid setting off a well-known creaky floorboard. She pressed her ear to the door of his room, praying that what she heard was not another conversation between the intruder and one of her children.

David was talking in Albanian, but she soon realized that the quality of the sound indicated that the window was closed. She opened the door and walked in. David was sitting on the bed in his pyjamas with a mobile phone to his ear.

'Who on earth are you talking to at this time of night?' she asked, rushing to him. 'You should be asleep.'

'Teto Zerina,' the boy said, putting the phone down. Sophie snatched up the mobile, but saw the call had been ended. The ugly old 'dumb phone' was the one that Zerina had given to the children to share a year ago, so that they could call her cheaply. Sophie didn't approve of the children having their own phone, but Zerina had persuaded her that this would be her lifeline to them.

'Did she ring you?' Sophie asked.

David nodded.

'What did she want?'

He seemed to stumble uncharacteristically over his reply. 'To see if Amber is having nightmares still,' he replied eventually.

'Calling at this time of night is likely to give both of you nightmares. I'm going to call her and tell her not to ring so late.' And it would be nice if she'd rung her first, Sophie thought.

—

DI Claire Mulholland had been digging into Peter Young's background and had repeatedly come up against a brick wall. Beyond the limited documents kept by Barnardo's and a recording of an interview with his grandmother, nothing was known for sure except the fact of a boy being found in Canterbury. Her request for the detailed case notes for the immigration decision makers seemed to have stalled. She fully expected that she would be eventually told that they had been lost.

Peter Young had given his original name as Pjetër Ardian Cela, an Albanian living in Kosovo, a semi-autonomous region of southern Serbia. His birth town was given as Gjakova, and his parents had died in the Kosovan war in 1999 when Serb forces had intervened to end a separatist uprising. Thereafter he was brought up by his grandmother until he was old enough, in her view, to leave in pursuit of a better life. He joined hundreds of other Kosovan child refugees who came to Britain each year from 1999 onwards.

When Claire had emailed the Kosovan authorities in the capital, Pristina, to check the details kept by Barnardo's, the reply came back that records of births in the country were partial, and the only one of that name registered in this town was of a baby who had died in 2002. There was no record of death certificates issued for his parents either, nor of the grandmother. The official advised that as the family name indicated someone of Albanian extraction, which was of course the majority ethnic group within Kosovo, writing to the Albanian authorities in Tirana would be the best course of action.

Claire was gradually coming around to Laura Diaz's theory about her husband. Peter Young might not be an orphan. He could have been sent to Britain with a false identity that was hard to trace to give him a fresh start. By someone, probably family, who had gone to enormous lengths to try to keep Peter Young safe.

But from whom?

The strategy had failed. What would the family do now he was dead?

She had a couple of ideas, but wasn't quite ready to share them with anyone.

Chapter 15

Craig Gillard lifted the glass and peered at the colourless liquid, then held it to his nose before taking a sip. It was a fiery liquor, but with fruity overtones. 'Strong, but tasty. What's it called again?'

'It's raki,' Geoff Meadows replied, before turning his gaze across the table, as he had sporadically all evening, to stare at Gillard's younger and quite glamorous wife. 'Like to try the Albanian national tipple, Sam?'

'All right,' she said.

Madeleine Meadows, cleaning away the dessert plates, gave a little shake of her head, but Sam wasn't going to take the hint. She sniffed the glass and then chugged it in one, before exhaling throatily. 'Whoa,' she gasped. 'Rocket fuel.'

'Good job you're not driving us home tonight,' Gillard said.

'I didn't think you'd like it,' Madeleine said, bringing out a cheeseboard laden with a half-dozen wedges. 'It's far too strong for me.'

'You've got to try it the way the locals do,' Sam said, grinning at her husband.

Craig smiled back, glad to see she hadn't lost her adventurous spirit. They had enjoyed an excellent meal, prepared mainly by Geoff himself, who was a consummate chef. After a ten-year gap in their friendship, Craig was happy that his old mentor had followed up with a dinner party invitation soon after they had talked on the phone about Albanian crime gangs. Geoff had lost most of his hair, now just a fuzz of grey, and his face was lined, but he still appeared to have the upright, athletic build that had made him such a fiendishly tough opponent on the squash court.

'So, Craig,' Geoff said, having topped up Sam's raki glass. 'Any more developments with the gangland symbol?'

'Not really,' Craig said. 'Like you say, the symbol sprayed on the door frame could mean anything. I'm a bit more concerned about an Albanian-speaking intruder wandering about on the lawns when there are two young children in the house.'

'What's this about?' Madeleine asked. Geoff had clearly not mentioned anything, so Gillard explained the basics of the case without identifying Colsham Manor or naming the Lund family. 'So we've got all these Albanian folklore symbols popping up – an effigy of the youngest child hung from a noose, for example – which is frightening the life out of the adoptive parents.'

'How awful. It sounds like a campaign of harassment, rather than an attempt to actually harm the children,' Madeleine said. 'Could it be someone trying to scare them?'

'Well, there is a feud going on with a female neighbour, which rather complicates matters. But I'm pretty sure she doesn't speak Albanian,' Gillard said.

'But poor Craig, he's so bloody diligent,' Sam interrupted 'He's up to his neck in this shooting in Kingston, but this woman keeps ringing him up, doesn't she?'

'Yes, but I'm not taking her calls any more,' Craig replied. 'Much too busy with the Peter Young case.'

'Maybe she's a stalker herself?' Meadows said.

'I wouldn't be surprised,' Sam laughed. 'Women are always making passes at you, aren't they?' She leaned across the table and caressed his cheek.

'I wouldn't say *always*,' Craig muttered. 'The odd one or two.'

'But get this,' Sam said, warming to her theme. 'The ladies' toilet at Mount Browne is full of graffiti about him. Some of it is really explicit!'

'I'm told most of it was painted out some time ago,' Craig said, noting how two glasses of raki, on top of the wine served earlier, had lowered Sam's inhibitions.

'Wasn't there a suspicion that Alison Rigby had written some?' Sam asked, enjoying the discomfort she had caused her husband.

Craig laughed to cover his embarrassment. 'No, I don't think so.'

'I wish someone had written graffiti about me,' Meadows said morosely, passing around the cheese biscuits.

'Well, Geoff, you did get some once,' Madeleine said. 'That little chap you put away for robbing the Co-op found out where we lived and spray-painted "wanker" across the caravan, didn't he?'

'Yes, Maddy, not quite the same.'

–

Sophie sat bolt upright in bed, sure she had heard the sound of breaking glass. The clock showed 2.27 a.m. and Balfour was howling. He was usually a terrible guard dog. He slept on a blanket in the boot room, and it was rare for him to be woken up. But his barking sounded urgent and angry, as if he was face-to-face with an intruder. A Tuesday again, and as before Dag was away. Through the baby monitor she heard Amber calling for her. By the time she had thrown on some clothes, Estela had arrived. 'What's happening?' she asked.

'I think we have another intruder.'

Sophie reached under her bed and pulled out a long wooden box that she'd only put there a few days ago. 'Estela, take the children, go downstairs to the safe room and lock the door. When you are in there, ring Michael, get him to call the police.'

'Why, where are you going?'

Sophie laid the heavy box on the bed and opened the lid to reveal a shotgun and a box of cartridges.

'I'm going after him.'

Estela looked on in horror as Sophie cracked the gun and inserted two cartridges into the barrels. 'Mrs Lund, are you going to shoot him?'

'Only if I have to. I certainly want to scare him, just as he's scared me.' With that, Sophie took the loaded shotgun, strode out of the room and raced downstairs, calling for the dog. She realized that she hadn't heard him for a couple of minutes. She flipped on every light switch she passed before reaching the ground floor, then moving along the panelled grandeur of the hallway, her boots clicking on the polished wooden boards. 'Balfour, I'm coming,' she whispered to herself. She took a short flight of stairs down to the back kitchen, where once again she could hear the dog, whining and whimpering, and the sound of some kind of struggle. With a crack, she closed the gun. 'Whoever is in there, back away! I'm coming in!' she said. She had never fired a gun in her life, and now wished she had done a little training. The sound of struggle intensified. She turned the handle and burst in. The back door to the outside was open, cold air had flooded the room.

Balfour!

The dog had been hung up by his lead, clipped to his collar then looped onto the coat rack. His rear paws, scrabbling wildly, were unable to reach the ground. He was gradually being strangled.

'Oh, Balfour,' she sobbed, as she laid the gun on a table and released the red setter from his torment. The animal was delighted to be freed, whining and yelping with joy.

Nearby there came the sound of a car engine starting, then revving. Balfour began whimpering and barking wildly. Sophie grabbed the gun and a set of keys from the wall, then ran out into the yard. It was a blustery night, chill with the promise of rain. She could clearly see the rear lights of a large car, one she didn't recognise, already a hundred yards away, making its way down the back lane towards Tithe Lane.

Sophie was seething with anger. She knew there would be clues on the CCTV to what had happened, but she couldn't face being patronized again by some male policeman who considered her a hysteric. Thanks to the preparations she had made, the borrowed shotgun, ostensibly for killing rabbits, she was damn well going to get the evidence she needed. Before she hadn't been believed, but now she would be, and vindicated too. 'Come on, Balfour,' she said, and ran with the dog towards the stable block. She flipped on the lights and heard the soft whicker of Caramelo. From the tack room she grabbed the horse's saddle and bridle. She flipped a soft numnah over the animal's back, following it with the saddle which she cinched carefully at the girth. Once the bit was in Caramelo's mouth she eased the bridle over her ears, fastening the throat lash and noseband. She led the horse out into the darkness, slung the shotgun by its strap across her shoulders, then heaved herself up onto the animal's warm back.

She could still hear the car, but where the rough and potholed lane curved right only the faintest red glow of retreating lights filtered through the undergrowth. The intruder may have a three-minute start on her, but that didn't matter. One benefit of the ongoing row with Geraldine Hinchcliffe had been that the mile-long lane had been allowed to deteriorate because they couldn't agree on how to split the cost of repair. Sophie knew a faster, more direct route. It might be 15 years since she had last competed in a three-day event, but with a little luck over the gates she knew she could cut the intruder off before the main road.

Sophie geed the horse up and let her canter across to the south paddock, with Balfour in pursuit. The gate was open and now, with the wind lashing her and fury in her heart, Sophie was ready for pursuit. *No one comes to my home and threatens my children. Whoever you are, I am not afraid of you.* Caramelo lengthened her stride and snorted with joy to be encouraged to race unconstrained. Sophie couldn't remember the last time she had galloped in darkness, and she felt as one with this wonderful animal. The speed felt incredible, far faster than it would have done in daylight. It was only because Caramelo knew the route so well, this being one of their regular hacks, that she had the confidence to let the horse have its head. The first gate, a leaning aluminium affair, she saw glinting a few dozen yards ahead. Caramelo gathered herself, altering stride, ears forward in concentration. The exhilaration of the lift, the soaring stretch and the mud-splattering landing in the field beyond drew a roar of encouragement from Sophie. Caramelo thundered along the edge of a field next to a blackthorn hedge, aimed left for the mown ride through South Meadow thicket and tore up the rise to a stark ash, long dead from a lightning strike. The next jump, a stile oblique to the bridleway, Caramelo took effortlessly after a flying change, while Balfour followed behind, taking it in a single leap.

In the distance, the clouds were basted in the orange light of Haslemere ten miles away and the only sound was a motorbike in the distance. A few hundred yards ahead was Tithe Lane, the lights of a vehicle approaching fast from the right. She had expected to be there long before, but it would actually be touch and go. Sophie urged Caramelo to cross this last field at full pelt, the only remaining barrier a long-ago felled sycamore, put in place to prevent traveller caravans coming onto the field. The mare stretched her limbs and took the tree trunk easily, and Sophie pulled her up short, just before the tarmac of the carriageway. Sophie turned the horse face-on to the car, unslung the shotgun and now, bathed in the headlights of the onrushing vehicle, aimed the gun into the glare.

Chapter 16

The car screeched to a halt 30 yards away. Sophie kept the gun pointing at the windscreen while she dismounted. The passenger-side door was flung open. The person who emerged was familiar.

'Don't you wave that bloody gun at me, Sophie.'

It was Geraldine Hinchcliffe.

'What were you doing breaking into my house?' Sophie said, the gun still levelled at her neighbour.

At this point the driver-side door opened. The tall woman who had savaged Sophie's *leylandii* emerged. She thought her name was Alison something. 'Please put the gun down, Mrs Lund,' Alison Rigby said as if talking to a naughty child. 'Possession of a firearm in a public place with intent to endanger life carries a minimum tariff of five years in jail. I take it you have a licence for it?'

'You can bugger off,' Sophie said, and fired at the front of the car. The blast tore across the night sky, shattering the car's headlamps and throwing them all into darkness. The noise set Balfour off into a torrent of barking, while behind her the horse skittered, and edged backwards towards the hedge.

'Will you calm down!' Alison bellowed, clearly aghast at the damage caused to her vehicle.

'You're a madwoman,' Geraldine said to Sophie. 'We were pursuing an intruder, who smashed a window and got into the pottery. Now he'll have got away.'

'The only car I saw was yours,' Sophie said accusingly as she cracked open the gun and removed the unused cartridge.

'We were in pursuit of an intruder who, after breaking and entering into the pottery, effected his escape on a motorcycle,' Alison said. She raised a mobile phone, tapped out a number, put it to her ear and began to issue orders.

'You're a cop, aren't you?' Sophie said. 'I recognise that bureaucratic way of speaking from PC Kerrigan.'

'Yes I am, and you, madam, are shortly going to be under arrest.'

As if by magic, it was only a minute or two before the blue lights of a police vehicle could be seen approaching on the main road half a mile away.

–

By next morning the police grapevine was abuzz with rumours about what had already been dubbed the Gunfight at the Lesbo Corral. 'I heard that it was the chief constable's ex, trying to bump off her new squeeze,' Carl Hoskins sniggered to Gillard as he helped himself to coffee from a thermos flask in the Khazi. It was probably the last day before the mobile incident room was removed, there no longer being enough local evidence on the Peter Young murder case to justify it. With the investigation being scaled down, the two detective constables were happy to switch their attention to the latest gossip.

The detective chief inspector grinned, but said nothing. He had just received a text from the chief constable herself, asking him to ring her office immediately. Gillard scanned the message dubiously and excused himself. He walked out of the Portakabin and down a residential side street where there was less noise. She picked up the phone on the first ring.

'Craig, good to speak to you. I've no doubt you've heard all about what happened last night.'

'Only the rumours, ma'am.'

'I shan't bother to regale you with my side of the story. I shall be stepping aside in the interests of transparency and bringing in a senior officer from a neighbouring force to investigate whether or not to bring firearm charges against Mrs Lund. For my part, I wouldn't take matters any further, despite the damage to my car, but it is right that it should not be my decision to make.'

'Yes, ma'am.'

'There is, however, an underlying case here which I would like you to look into, as it's got well beyond PC Kerrigan's ability. There certainly was an intruder last night, who seems to have broken into the Manor as well as Geraldine's pottery, so I don't think we can assume that Mrs Lund was imagining things. As there seem to be no fresh developments on the Peter Young case, you can hand that off to DI Mulholland for now.'

'Yes, ma'am.'

'Geraldine will be available for interview at 11 at the Little Pottery.' She hung up.

Gillard was well used to the chief constable's control-freakery, but this was something else. She was again trusting him to investigate matters touching on her relationship, and to keep his own counsel about what he found.

Gillard bumped and crunched his unmarked Ford Focus up the back lane leading to Colsham Manor, working his way around the deep ruts and puddles. He parked by some outbuildings and followed hand-painted tiles which gave directions to the Little Pottery. Geraldine Hinchcliffe saw him before he had knocked, and let him in.

'Hello again, Chief Inspector, good to see you. You come highly recommended.'

'Thank you.' Gillard didn't quite appreciate feeling like a tradesman.

'Where have you parked?' she asked, peering out. Gillard pointed to his car. 'Oh that's all right, then – it's just that her ladyship can get quite upset if you're in "the wrong place".' She whispered the words as if expecting to be overheard.

'I take it a fingerprint technician came earlier?' Gillard asked.

'Yes. He didn't seem very optimistic, he thinks the intruder wore gloves. But there is broken glass.' She led him to a glass-panelled side door which had clearly been forced. 'This is where he came in,' Geraldine said. 'I don't think he meant to break such a large pane of glass. It fell and smashed a vase.' She pointed to the shards. 'I would have been terribly frightened had not Ali been with me. She is so terribly capable, you know. Did you know she is a black belt in karate?'

'No, I didn't. She's very senior to me, so I don't get to hear about that kind of thing.'

'My goodness, she's so terribly impressive. She once smashed a pile of old slates with a single chop from her hand.' Geraldine's face lit up at this display of prowess. 'If the burglar had got into the house itself, I wouldn't have rated his chances.' She made a chopping gesture with her own slim arm.

'I think we should all be glad that it didn't come to that.'

Gillard couldn't help but notice a large amethyst ring on Geraldine's engagement finger and a double-heart locket around her wrist. He couldn't help thinking what his fellow male officers would make of this. But it remained his secret to keep.

Plied with ginger biscuits and a large, somewhat misshapen mug of coffee, the DCI took down the timings and details of the previous night's events. He had to stop Geraldine telling him about the confrontation with Sophie Lund on the lane. 'That has to be dealt with by another officer,' he explained.

'Oh why, for goodness' sake?'

'Precisely because Ms Rigby is so senior in the Surrey force, it could look like she is exerting pressure for a particular outcome. Justice has to be seen to be done, and in this case by a senior officer from another force who doesn't answer to her.'

'Well, I hope they lock the Lund woman up. She is absolutely bonkers. Even worse than my ex-husband, if that were possible.'

Anxious to wrap the interview up, Gillard asked if there was anything else about the break-in that they hadn't covered.

'Oh, there is this,' Geraldine said, leading him back into the pottery itself. 'I meant to mention it to the fingerprint chappie but forgot. But I put my marigolds on then slid it carefully into a paper bag, just like they do on *Silent Witness*.' She giggled and handed him an A2-sized padded envelope. He peered inside and, after donning a latex glove, removed the object so he could look at it. It was a cheap plastic doll, around 15 inches high, missing an eye and dressed in a frilly pink dress. Overall it was a little grubby and a small hole had been punched forcefully right through its torso, while on its forehead was a burn mark about two inches across.

He recognised the mark.

Gillard pulled out his iPad and checked back for the photograph that Sophie Lund had taken of the stencilled graffito on the frame of the stable block. They looked quite similar.

'Where did you find the doll?' Gillard asked.

'It was hanging up here, in the window of the pottery. Suspended by the neck on a piece of wire.'

'Have you mentioned it to Sophie Lund?'

'No. I mean, we're not really on speaking terms.'

'Good. Keep it to yourself – she's got a young daughter and it would terrify her.'

'Don't worry, Detective Chief Inspector. You don't need to have a young child to be terrified by this. We're all bloody terrified.'

Gillard nodded. If Geraldine Hinchcliffe knew that the symbol on the doll was the calling card of the worst mafia in Albania, she would really learn what terror was. The hole through the doll's body he was pretty sure had been made by a bullet.

—

Gillard had hoped to be able to speak to Mrs Lund herself, but she was in London all day. However, Michael Tolling, the estate manager, had agreed to meet him.

'Detective Chief Inspector, so nice to meet you,' he began suavely.

'I've been looking forward to meeting you.' Gillard gave him a meaningful smile. 'I saw your name and it sparked a recollection.'

'Really?' Tolling's eyes narrowed.

'Didn't you stand trial for fraud about 15 years ago? When you were a big commodities trader in the City. If I recall, you were charged with helping create systematic tax losses to minimize tax payable.'

A wry smiled crossed Tolling's face. 'Your memory is a little awry, I'm sorry to say. I've never been convicted of any crime.'

'I didn't say you were convicted. But I did a bit of research. The trial collapsed after the jury had been sitting for two years. The usual thing, I suppose, going googly-eyed over the complex details. Then one juror had a stroke, another had to leave to look after a disabled relative and one of the key witnesses had a heart attack.'

Tolling ran a hand nervously through his hair. 'I was always innocent, Detective Chief Inspector, I merely didn't get the chance to prove it.' His voice had become even more plummy with self-righteousness.

Gillard smiled. 'I'm sure you're right.' He'd not just looked up the case online, he'd followed up with a colleague at the City of London police who described Mick Tolling, as he was then known, as originally a sharp barrow boy type from Dagenham and a prolific trader, before being moved into the creative side of accountancy. He lost his job before the trial, but once the case died down he was quickly given a new position. 'Still, it was handy that a former business contact like Clive Gashley of Colsham Manor was able to give you a job.'

'I think it just shows that my honesty inspired loyalty amongst former clients,' he said smoothly.

Gillard had no reason to believe that an allegedly tax-dodging former City trader would have anything to do with the bizarre goings-on at Colsham Manor. But he was fascinated at the way this working-class boy from an East End council estate, who according to the papers had failed his eleven-plus exams, had now reinvented himself as a bit of a country squire with an accent to match. It was no surprise to Gillard that someone like Tolling would, after Gashley sold Colsham Manor, attach himself like a limpet to a fresh source of wealth, namely Dag Lund.

'Do Dag and Sophie Lund know about your past?'

'You mean I should have confessed to them? Revealing a shocking past which includes not being convicted of any crime?'

Gillard shrugged. 'All right, so they don't. We'll leave it at that.' He then looked down at the documents he had taken from his briefcase. 'Perhaps a little later on we can go through the statement you gave to PC Kerrigan,' Gillard said. 'There is something very fishy going on here, and

I'm not sure we have all the details. But for now I certainly would like to look at the CCTV system.'

'Of course,' Tolling said. 'I should be delighted to show you.'

Over the course of the next half an hour Gillard was shown the new security measures that Sophie had installed, and the safe room where the au pair and the children had hidden during last night's burglary.

Like Geraldine Hinchcliffe, the estate manager was keen to give his view on the shooting incident, and in particular to emphasize that he had not supplied the shotgun. As before, Gillard told him to save it for the investigation which would start in earnest the next day, when a detective chief superintendent from Sussex Police would arrive.

'I'm really as horrified by this as anyone,' Tolling said, as they walked around the safe room. 'I never thought Sophie would do such a thing.'

'So has anyone reviewed the footage from the CCTV last night?'

'Gosh, I really don't know. I haven't, because I haven't even read the instruction manual on how to do it. And of course Sophie won't have had a chance. She only got out of police custody at seven o'clock this morning, and had to go pretty much straight into town for a meeting.' Tolling led Gillard to the master terminal, which sat in a corner of the safe room. It was a standard system, and no password had yet been set, so the detective was able to get straight on. There were a dozen cameras, linked to motion-sensor lights. They didn't quite give full coverage because of the profusion of outbuildings, but there was a fairly sophisticated piece of software which monitored and flagged up suspicious movement in a daily summary report. It was to this that Gillard went first, sorting files by time stamp. The very first file that he opened, stamped 2.19 a.m. showed a man with a longish coat and a torch moving between outbuildings. The image was quite good, and showed a thick head of light-coloured hair, a short beard and moustache. He was carrying a small rucksack. There was some similarity to the man identified on the bus, but he couldn't be sure it was the same individual.

'Can you show me outside where the camera points?' Gillard asked.

'Yes. I think it's just outside the boot room, which is effectively the back door into the Manor through the old servants' quarters.' He showed the detective through the boot room and into the narrow pathway which led between the outbuildings towards the hardstanding shared with the pottery. While he was there by the car Gillard collected a blank disc from the boot to download a copy of the CCTV footage.

Tolling then took Gillard to the kitchen and introduced him to the au pair. Estela d'Souza, a small, dark-haired and shy-looking young woman, couldn't add much to the story. She said she had stayed with the children all night until the mother returned, and then taken them to school.

'Are you aware of any threats having specifically been made to the family or the children?' Gillard asked. It was the same question he had asked Tolling.

'I can't think why anyone would want to hurt these children,' Estela said. 'But I do know that Mrs Lund had been getting quite worried.' It took Gillard less than 20 minutes to realize that the au pair knew little or nothing about Sophie Lund's fears. However, she was able to give some context. She described a happy home environment for the children, with parents who doted on them.

'They are not without problems,' Estela said. 'David is very withdrawn, and he gets bullied and called names at school. The head teacher phoned up a few weeks ago to say that he was found with a knife. He said he brought it into school to defend himself. It was only a little one, but Sophie virtually had to beg for him not to be excluded.'

'What about the little girl?'

Estela sighed. 'Poor Amber gets nightmares, and wakes up screaming. It's very disruptive. Then there was this thing about the angel.' She described what the little girl claimed to have seen on the lawns, also witnessed by Sophie, and the translation of what was said.

The account was more detailed than the summary that Gillard had read in PC Kerrigan's report, and it alarmed him that so many important details had not been recorded. Although he had told Gillard, Kerrigan had made no note in the file of conversations in Albanian, nor indeed the fact that the two children were originally Albanian orphans. With the murder of Peter Young, supposedly a Kosovan orphan, having taken place just 25 miles to the north, it wasn't impossible that there was some link between the two cases. But anyone coming cold to the cases would struggle to make that connection.

'I will speak to Mrs Lund later on, but just to let you know I'm requesting some DNA samples from everyone who was here last night, including your neighbour at the pottery. Once we match up any traces, we will be able by a process of elimination to discover who else may have been prowling around.' Gillard didn't mention that this would also include the chief constable.

Estela looked at her watch. 'I've got to go and collect the children now. We can do it in half an hour if you want.'

Gillard declined the offer. 'I don't have enough DNA sample tubes with me, and I've got a meeting on another case in 40 minutes.' He said his goodbyes, picked up the copied disc and left.

After what happened next, he wished he had stayed.

Chapter 17

Sophie Lund was just wrapping up a meeting with the owner of a fine west London house who was about to spend £2 million renovating the top floors. Gold taps, lava stone worktops, jade fittings, the lot. Sophie had clinched the deal through sheer persistence. The Saudi client kept changing her mind about what she wanted, then flipping between two other competing design firms, before finally coming back to Sophie. The woman had just half an hour ago signed the contract, and arranged for the initial deposit to be paid, when Sophie's phone rang, the third call in five minutes from the au pair, and the first one she decided to answer.

'Estela, what is it? I'm in a meeting. Can't it wait?'

What she heard so shocked her that she wailed in anguish. Her worst fears, her nightmare, had come true.

–

Estela d'Souza had a few absolute priorities in her job as au pair: to feed the children, to keep an eye on them, to take them to the nearby village school on time and to be there to bring them home at the end of the school day. But today, because of the interview with the detective, she was running a bit late. So when she got to the primary school, all the nearby roadside parking slots were taken.

At pick-up time, she normally relied on David finding her car amongst the many, and bringing his little sister along with him. Her snazzy mustard-coloured Fiat 500, with its beautiful alloy wheels, was easily recognised, only two years old and bought for her by Sophie and Dag.

So she sat in the car, with the radio on, waiting as all the other children streamed out to waiting parents. After ten minutes there were only a few cars left, so she nosed up into one of the vacant slots nearer the school gates, and got out to find out where the children were. The lollipop lady, a charming retired woman in her 70s called Irene, was still there, holding her traffic stop sign and shepherding the last gaggles of children across the not-very-busy residential road that bordered the school.

'Forgotten something?' Irene asked.

'No, why?'

'Back a second time, aren't you?'

'I'm sorry, I don't understand. Have you seen David and Amber?'

'You picked them up ten minutes ago,' Irene said. 'Or did Sophie borrow your car?'

'Sophie is in London. Are you saying somebody else picked up the children?'

'If you didn't, I don't know who it was. It was a car just like yours.'

Estela's hands flew up to her face and she covered her mouth in case she screamed. 'Oh my God, oh my God, oh my God! It's all because I was late.'

One of the teachers emerged and asked what the matter was.

'Amber and David have been taken,' Estela said. 'Please, I have to call the police.'

'Whoa, hold on a moment,' the teacher said, a reassuring smile on her face. 'I'm sure there's a logical explanation. A friend of Sophie's, or another parent perhaps?'

Estela fumbled in her bag for her phone, found it, then immediately dropped it on the pavement, beginning to cry.

'It'll be all right, dear,' the lollipop lady said, resting a hand on Estela's trembling shoulder. 'This is a small village, everyone looks out for each other.'

'No, no, you don't understand. You don't begin to understand. If only I had been on time, it's all my fault!' She fumbled again with the phone, swiping pointlessly, all fingers and thumbs. 'They are Albanian orphans, these children. Someone wants to murder them!'

—

Gillard was on his way back to police HQ in Guildford for a meeting on the Peter Young case when the call came through from operations. 'Is she certain that no other parent has taken them? They've only been missing an hour.'

Having heard the details, Gillard conceded that this was not a false alarm. 'All right, I'm going back. Get ports and airports to check for children who match the description of David and Amber Lund – I'll get you some pics. Put out a nationwide alert for that model and colour of Fiat. Find out if anyone at the school got a registration number, and get Rob Townsend to look over the ANPR in the area.' Townsend was the response intelligence officer, an expert at getting the best out of the many police databases and information resources. 'One more thing. Send someone with a full DNA kit to Colsham Manor – I don't think we can wait until tomorrow. We'll also need a liaison officer. PC Gabby Underwood would be ideal if she is available. She'll have her hands full with the mother and the au pair.'

Fifteen minutes later Gillard was back at Colsham Manor. Dealing with a tearful Estela d'Souza kept him from the urgent task of scanning through all the CCTV footage that had been accumulated the previous night. D'Souza was soon joined by Michael Tolling, the estate manager. The next to arrive was Detective Constable Michelle Tsu, who Gillard wanted because she had proved her worth on the notorious Knight murder case a couple of years previously. Walking in behind her was Geraldine Hinchcliffe.

'This lady is a neighbour and says she may have some information,' Tsu said. The group fell silent.

'I heard the terrible news and wondered if I could do anything to help,' Geraldine said, with a smile. Gillard knew exactly who would have given her such up-to-date information.

'Actually, Geraldine, Mrs Lund is expected from London at any time. I don't think she would want to find you here,' Tolling said.

'Well, really! I was only trying to be neighbourly. I would have thought that Sophie would need all the help she could get,' Geraldine said, turning to leave. 'But if you don't need my help, then I shall go.'

'I'll come and see you later on, Ms Hinchcliffe,' Gillard said to her.

The noise of slamming doors marked her departure. She had only been gone five minutes when the echo of quick, hard footsteps and sobbing along the wood-panelled hallway announced the arrival of Sophie Lund.

Ignoring the gathered group, Sophie and the au pair threw themselves into each other's arms.

Five minutes later Gabby Underwood arrived and, after briefing her, Gillard beckoned for Michelle Tsu to follow him. 'We'll leave them to it,' he told her as they ascended the grand staircase to the first floor. 'I want elimination samples of hair from the children's bedrooms – toothbrushes, that kind of thing – and then when they've calmed down, cheek swabs from Sophie Lund and the au pair. Make sure the lab checks familial connections. Don't forget the estate manager. I know this will slow things down a little, but for the children I want mitochondrial DNA analysis too.'

Tsu's perplexed expression did not surprise Gillard. 'Just a little theory I have. It will help clarify family connections,' he said. 'I'll do the swab for the awkward neighbour.'

'Yes, what is it about her?' Tsu asked.

Gillard blew a long sigh. 'It's a bit of a long-running feud. Let's just say it's best not to invite her in again.'

'Okay,' the young detective said. 'Before I left the office I did some Googling on the Lund family.'

'Anything of interest?' Gillard was glad to have Michelle on the team. Her petite, girlish frame and soft features attracted patronizing comments and worse from male officers, but an apparent shyness concealed a keen intelligence and first-rate organizational ability.

'Lots about Dag Lund's oil rig businesses, and quite a bit about his wealth,' she replied. 'He's on the *Sunday Times* rich list, did you know?'

'I didn't.'

'I had wondered whether this could put them in the frame for a conventional kidnapping. There are other indicators too.'

'Very good. Tell me more,' Gillard said.

'The Lunds were a little careless. There was an article about the family in the local newspaper a couple of years ago, something along the lines of "Surrey Mum adopts Albanian orphans". There were pictures of the kids too, in front of this quite palatial home.'

Gillard was impressed. The woman had been on the case less than an hour, and had already managed to open a new and intriguing line of inquiry. He himself had been thinking more about an Albanian family connection, but that might be wrong. It could simply be a good old-fashioned kidnapping, albeit there had to be some Albanian involvement from what the child had heard. Either way, it wasn't going to be easy. According to Meadows, trying to get a joint investigation going in Albania was always a nightmare. The country may have signed an extradition treaty with Britain in 2017, but simply getting your suspect into custody was a major problem. The Albanian judiciary, who were responsible for keeping them there, were 'enormously amenable to inducements', as Meadows had put it.

Bent judges, wary cops and powerful organized crime syndicates. Perfect.

'Okay, Michelle, keep digging on that.'

Gillard's next phone call came from the chief constable. 'Craig, I've just heard,' Rigby said. 'I probably don't need to tell you, but the kidnap of young children is going to generate huge national coverage. I want you to be senior investigating officer and don't want you distracted by anything else, so I'm getting Claire Mulholland to take over as SIO on the Peter Young case. I need you to liaise closely, given the possible links.'

'Yes, ma'am.'

'Another thing, Craig. I've noticed you have just ordered a budget-busting package of express DNA tests. You're very lucky your line manager is off sick. DCS Dobbs would have you write reams of justification for such a comprehensive array, but I want you to know that for this case I share your sense of urgency. I'm happy to trust you and approved them immediately.'

'Thank you, ma'am.' The tone of her voice hinted at a quid pro quo coming down the line.

'Now, Craig. I realize you have to forensically eliminate Geraldine and me following the break-in, but I'd like to emphasize that when our DNA samples and test results come back, they are for your eyes only. They should be marked for removal from the database once the case is concluded.'

'Yes, ma'am, understood.'

'Craig. Find those children quickly, and I will recommend you for promotion.' She hung up.

Gillard stared at his phone. He needed no reminder that Rigby was several levels of political skill above him, but this message was clear: he'd been discreet about the chief constable's private life, and a reward for that was being dangled.

Still, one quite possible scenario would put paid to it.

Two dead kids.

Chapter 18

The first full team meeting for the Lund kidnap investigation took place next morning on a freezing cold February Wednesday in a reassuringly well-equipped incident room at Mount Browne. Gillard's team included DCs Hoskins and Hodges, Michelle Tsu and Rob Townsend. Geoff Meadows was there too, as an independent consultant, and would be joined later, Gillard hoped, by DI Mulholland and someone from the PR department. An abduction of two young children instantly created a news frenzy, as Rigby had predicted. After a hurried news conference the previous evening, most of that day's papers had obliged by publishing family pictures of Amber and David, and CCTV stills of the Colsham Manor intruder. Though the articles quoted a police spokeswoman playing down any connection with the Peter Young shooting, the *Daily Telegraph* and *Guardian* had both linked them. 'The Albanian Connection' was already a live headline.

'Rob, can you summarize where we are with tracing the kids?' Gillard asked.

Townsend was a studious-looking 30-year-old who might have been an accountant had something more interesting not turned up. He went to one of the whiteboards where he had already scrawled some headings. 'There's good news and bad news,' he said. 'We didn't get the registration number of the vehicle the children got into, so ANPR is no help. But I have started by tracing every Fiat 500 of that colour rented within a 100-mile radius. We don't have all the information yet, but it should come in later today.'

'What about stolen vehicles?' Gillard asked.

'I chose the same 100-mile radius. We have 16 stolen Fiat 500s reported within the last week. But my guess is that a professional, if that's what we're dealing with, would only steal the vehicle a day in advance unless they were planning to create a false plate.'

'And the obvious false plate would be a copy of the au pair's car,' Meadows said. He was wearing a surprisingly trendy light grey suit, one which matched his remaining fuzz of stubbly hair.

'Exactly,' Townsend said. 'We've run all the stolen plates through the ANPR database. Excluding vehicles that are accounted for by joyriders or burn-outs, we have a couple of journeys logged, but nothing that would obviously indicate fleeing to an airport or ferry port. I've handed them on to the relevant local forces to pursue.'

'That's a pretty distinctive car,' Hodges said. 'You can't easily steal them to order, or even respray to match without the right type of alloy wheels and all that. You can't even be sure to hire them.'

'That's a fair point. What about the descriptions of the children?' Gillard asked. 'Any positive ID?'

'No,' Hodges said. 'David Lund is fairly unremarkable, but Amber wears spectacles for a lazy eye and has a large birthmark on her forehead which is quite distinctive. I would have hoped that someone might have spotted them following the media coverage.'

'Unless they are already hidden away,' Gillard said. He had two civilian staffers currently manning an enquiry line, but they would need more. Hoskins had been allocated the task of going through all the thousands of mobile phone pictures that had been emailed in of children seen at motorway service stations, airports, ports, cafés and shopping centres who might be either David or Amber. 'Any luck on the pictures, Carl?'

'Nope. It's quite quick work, really, but I'm struggling to keep up,' Hoskins replied. 'I might end up as cross-eyed as the tot herself.'

Michelle Tsu rolled her eyes and exchanged a glance with Gillard.

'So, Michelle, you followed up at the airports and ports. Any luck?'

She stood up and went to a flipchart that she had already populated with extensive details of departures and arrivals. 'I got detailed information on all the direct UK flights to Albania, which isn't very many. There were a few children booked, but judging by the passport pictures they weren't the Lund kids. Indirect flights are a bit more complicated, and I haven't managed to chase all those down yet. The channel ports and Eurostar have sent me some initial information, but there are no obvious matches for their current or original names.'

Meadows shook his head. 'If we are assuming an Albanian angle, they would probably be on false passports. They aren't hard to get in the Balkans.' He shrugged. 'And if this is a professional job, they are almost certainly no longer in the country.'

Shoulders sagged around the room at this assessment from the man most experienced in dealing with Albanian organized crime.

Colin Hodges put his hand up. 'Sir, can I ask your professional opinion on one thing? If it is a bunch of Albanians, why do they want these two kids?'

'It's a very good question,' Meadows said standing up and putting his hands in his pockets, where he began to jangle loose change. 'The way I see it, it is one of two things. One, Dag Lund has upset some very significant organized crime group, perhaps with one of his business deals, and they have kidnapped the children for leverage. In that case the nationality of the children is not that important. Or two, the children themselves are relevant. What the little girl heard in the garden that night, about vengeance, might be true.'

'Revenge against the children?' Michelle asked, incredulously. 'What could they have done to deserve that?'

Meadows gave a grim little chuckle and shook his head. 'It's not what they've done, Michelle, it's who they are. Particularly what family they originally came from.'

—

DI Claire Mulholland wasn't entirely impressed to be handed the Peter Young murder case just when it seemed to be running out of steam. She liked Craig, but if he was being set up by the chief constable to lead the charge to rescue the Lund children, it seemed she had been left with a shovel to deal with what the cavalry always leave behind.

She was at home, on her second glass of Sauvignon blanc, enjoying one of those rare evenings where no one else was in the house, reflecting on what she could find out about the murder that Craig had not. There were tantalising possibilities, but turning them into hard evidence seemed impossible. She had interviewed Laura Diaz a second time, and remained convinced that the victim's wife knew more than she was letting on. There was no doubting the sincerity of her grief. Almost every mention of her husband brought floods of tears. Claire just couldn't see the wife being complicit in the murder, but conversely her expressions of ignorance about his background and what may have befallen him didn't feel quite genuine either.

She had tried to close off all the loose ends. She had re-interviewed all of the Kurdish family members who had stayed above the kebab house in recent months, an exhausting process over the course of a week involving translators, the first of whom was vetoed by the family on the grounds that he was Turkish, and in their view biased against them. All that was uncovered were a few visa irregularities. In the end, the fact the windows of that flat didn't really line up with the bullet trajectories rendered it moot. She also re-interviewed the other staff members at Hampton, Deedes, Gooding. One, with another architect called Derek Prichard, did produce a useful nugget of information.

Prichard recalled that Peter Young had several months ago been involved in an altercation over parking, 'There was this bloke who kept parking his van in our car park overnight,' Prichard had told her. 'We've only got six allocated spaces, and Peter, because he liked to get in early, often found this van still in one of the spaces.'

As Prichard described it, the van man was a bit of a bruiser, and when Peter challenged him on one occasion, there had been a bit of pushing and shoving. The whole thing smouldered on and off for weeks, until one evening, when Peter was about to drive home, he found his car had been vandalized, with scratches down both sides and the wipers broken off.

'Was this ever reported to the police?' Mulholland asked.

'Oh yes,' said Prichard. 'I remember a WPC coming to the office. I think she went and had a word with the bloke.'

Perturbed to have missed this useful piece of background, Mulholland had checked through the records and struck gold. The registered owner of the van, visited by the female officer, was none other than Ryan Hardcastle, the ex-con who lived above the tattoo parlour. To discover he had a motive to hurt Peter Young was a significant breakthrough. It was something she would pursue the next day.

Mulholland's 9 a.m. meeting the next day had been assigned to the small incident room next door to the giant modern one allocated to the Lund kidnap. For now, she was still able to call on the full team that had been on the Peter Young case since the start. That included the familiar overweight figures of Tweedledum and Tweedledee who were going through more CCTV as she arrived.

'Any breakthrough?' she asked. They shook their heads. 'It's just a bit more we got from Surbiton railway station,' Hodges said. 'Haven't found our man on it yet.'

At that moment Craig Gillard walked in, still in his coat, with a coffee in hand. 'You might find him on this,' he said, digging out of his pocket a copy of the CCTV disc he'd made the day before. 'It's the intruder at Colsham Manor.'

'That's brilliant,' Claire said, feeling that she'd just had her thunder stolen. 'How's the search for the Lund children going?'

He shook his head. 'Nothing yet.' He looked exhausted, as if he hadn't slept at all. *That's what happens when Alison Rigby gets on your case.*

Carl Hoskins took the disc from Gillard and slid it into the terminal in front of him. 'Go to 2.19 a.m.' Gillard said.

Hoskins fast-forwarded to the correct time. The image of the intruder was well lit, better than anything they had previously seen of their suspect. 'Aha,' Mulholland said. 'It could be the same guy from the bus, couldn't it?'

On the adjacent terminal, Colin Hodges pulled up the best pictures they had of the man who had been on the bus. All four of them looked from one screen to the other, several times. 'Definitely similar,' Hoskins said. 'Light hair, maybe combed a bit different.'

'No,' Gillard said. 'He looks different to me.'

'No nose ring on the Colsham intruder,' Hodges said.

'True, but the beard's pretty much the same,' Hoskins said.

'The one from the bus looks a bit like a young Bjorn Borg,' Mulholland said. 'This one, I don't know, has a bit more of a delicate face.'

'A bit girlish, you might say,' Hoskins added.

'Amber Lund got it spot on,' Gillard said. 'She called him an angel. He offered to take her to see her mummy in heaven.'

Mulholland turned to him. 'That's a thinly veiled threat to kill her, isn't it?'

'I don't think she understood it, fortunately,' Gillard said.

'She might do by now,' Hodges said. 'I think now he's got them two kids to himself he won't turn out to be so angelic.'

No one said a word for a full minute, then Hoskins piped up. 'Pardon me, ma'am. If we have now officially concluded this geezer at the manor isn't the guy off the bus, then who shot Peter Young?'

Mulholland was horrified to see the three men turn to look at her, as if she was suddenly expected, after less than 12 hours on the case, to magic the answer from thin air.

–

It was just after 10 a.m. on Thursday when the courier arrived with the express DNA test results for Colsham Manor that Gillard had ordered on the Tuesday afternoon. After more than 36 hours with Rigby and the press breathing down his neck it would be a relief to be able to have some fresh facts to work with, and perhaps something to tell the press. He summoned the team together in the large incident room. He then put his head through to the next-door incident room to alert Claire Mulholland, who was talking to Geoff Meadows, and rang up for Christine McCafferty, the PR officer assigned to the case.

'Okay, this is hot off the press,' he said, once they were all assembled. Everyone huddled around as Gillard leafed through the documents until he got to Amber's. He speed-read the summary then gave a little groan of disappointment. 'I was hoping we might find a familial DNA connection between Peter Young and the missing kids. There isn't one, beyond shared ethnicity, which showed up in the mitochondrial tests.'

'You were smart to order both familial and mitochondrial tests,' Meadows said. 'Familial tests rely on paternal linkage through the Y chromosome, while mitochondrial traces the mother's side through the power-generating element of each cell which is passed down the female line. If you put the two together you can be far more sure of the family links.'

'Sorry to be thick,' said Hodges. 'But why might there have been a family connection?'

'I think I can answer that,' says Meadows. 'If Young was a relative of the abducted children, it might indicate a vendetta. Albania is known for them. They have vicious blood feuds that last centuries. I'm not kidding. Tit-for-tat, for decade after decade.'

'You don't have to go to Albania to find a feud,' said Michelle. 'Sophie Lund and her neighbour are apparently at each other's throats the whole time.'

Gillard handed out one DNA report to each officer, to scan through for useful information. He kept two, which he put in a desk to peruse later. They were the results for Alison Rigby and Geraldine Hinchcliffe.

'I've got the residuals report,' said Michelle, who seemed already to be on the third page. 'And it's very interesting. Setting aside those who live or work at Colsham Manor, we've got three non-eliminated DNA samples. Two are from inside the manor, one of which was found quite extensively in a spare bedroom and en-suite bathroom…'

'That's probably an overnight guest,' Gillard said. 'It could be the children's Albanian aunt who stayed with them over Christmas.'

Michelle flipped over a page and then nodded. 'Yes, the familial test does show a family connection: more than 75 per cent of the markers match with the kids. So that's probably her, then.'

'Any others?' Gillard asked.

'Two other unidentified samples on outside door handles, and on the external WC in Colsham Manor's outbuildings,' she said, flipping over another page. 'There are no familial or mitochondrial connections shown.'

'So nothing which proves the existence of our Albanian-speaking intruder,' Gillard said.

'Wow, I don't think we expected this,' Rob Townsend interrupted, waving a bulky sheaf of documents to attract attention. 'There's a familial match of the children against the national DNA database.'

'Really?' Gillard said.

'Yes, there was an unidentified dead body found on the Lincolnshire coast a couple of weeks ago. It's a close familial match to both David and Amber.'

'Lincolnshire? That's got to be 200 miles away. Why didn't we know about this?' Gillard asked.

'Well, sir,' Townsend said. 'I've got a summary report. It seems Lincolnshire Police still have no idea who this person was. There was no ID on the body.'

'Does it give a cause of death?' Gillard asked. 'Did he drown?'

The seconds seemed to extend as Townsend flicked through pages of printout. 'No, not drowning.' He looked up. 'Gunshot to the head. Short range.'

'Front or back?'

'Sir?'

'Front or back, Rob – I'm trying to establish whether they think it's suicide or murder,' Gillard said. 'Gunshot to the back of the head would pretty much eliminate suicide.'

'Yes, sir, it was the back of the head, exit wound at the front.'

'Not a great time to be an Albanian in Britain,' Hodges muttered.

'I bet Lincolnshire Police will be as surprised as us about him being from the same family as the Lund kids,' Townsend said.

'Get on to it, Rob. I want to be copied in on everything Lincolnshire Police have on their investigation.'

'Righto, sir,' Townsend said.

'But what about Peter Young?' Mulholland interrupted. 'Is he connected to this or not?'

'According to this, no,' Gillard replied. 'No familial overlap, although the mitochondrial test does confirm him as being of Albanian origin, like many Kosovans.' He dropped the documents on the table and went to the whiteboard, wiping a space clear with a cloth. With marker pen he drew two boxes, side by side. 'All right, everyone, here's something to get your heads around. Box A,' he said. Inside it he drew four figures, two adults and two children. 'We have one biological family: the Lund kids, their aunt.' He drew a triangular skirt on one figure. 'Plus the guy found on the beach in Lincolnshire. Makes four.' He then drew a second box and sketched in it a single figure. 'Box B, Peter Young, from another family. And no one else, so far.' He then drew a gun beneath the boxes and dotted a line from it into each box, one to the head of Peter Young, the other to the Lincolnshire man. Gillard then looked across the room at each detective there. 'All right, so who's got GCSE or O level maths?'

The lack of replies made him smile. 'Come on, I went to a secondary modern, and even I did Venn diagrams. It's a question of logic.' He saw Michelle Tsu nod her head. 'Come on, then, Michelle.'

She stood up and came to the board. 'If each family is a set, we need to establish if our perpetrator is a member of one or both sets or outside them both.' She drew a small gun with a question mark in both boxes.

'Okay,' Gillard said, as she sat down. 'Anything wrong with that?'

'We could have more than one perpetrator?' Hoskins asked.

'True, and we mustn't forget that possibility. But there's an equally important issue.' He drew a firm line back and forth to wall off the boxes from each other. 'The DNA tests told us that Peter Young has no familial overlap with anyone in Box A, right? Ergo, and that isn't a word you will often hear me say, there is no intersection of sets between Box A and Box B. That is obviously true for the five people on this whiteboard, but it also encompasses the unknown perpetrator. The murderer can have a blood connection to either family, but not to both. Only to one or none.'

'I didn't know you was that brainy, sir,' Hodges said.

'And Colin, I didn't know you were that obsequious,' Gillard replied.

'That's another big word, sir,' Hoskins said, then pointed to the whiteboard. 'So where does all this get us?'

Gillard smiled. 'Nowhere, immediately. Just think of it as a framework that helps to clarify where we stand. Our priority now has to remain quite simple: it's with the living. We have to find those kids and get them home safely. Knowing that someone has shot and killed a close member of their family makes that task even more urgent. And that's why I need to see this Lincolnshire corpse.'

Chapter 19

The Albanian Kanun *or* Canon *of blood feuds was formalized in the fifteenth century as the Code of Leke Dukagjini. It dates back to the Bronze Age, and covers everything from inheritance and the rights of the Church to the treatment of livestock. Leke Dukagjin (1410–81) was one of the leading figures of Albania's resistance against the Ottoman Turks. The two most notorious elements, still applied to this day in the remote northern mountains, are the concepts of blood-taking,* gjakmarrja, *through a feud, and* hakmarrja, *the obligation to take life to right earlier wrongs and to salvage honour. Under the communist government of Enver Hoxha (1944–85), the* Kanun *and its code were suppressed. Participants in blood feuds were executed or sent to labour camps. In later years it has reappeared, though many of the traditional strictures, for example that women and children were exempt from blood feuds, have been ignored. Fear of being killed in blood feuds has been one of the main reasons cited by those seeking asylum abroad. This tendency has become complicated by the emergence of Albanian organized crime in child trafficking, and their growing dominance of the cocaine trade. Blood feud 'certificates' issued by the Albanian police have been used as proof of fear of persecution, though the Home Office believes that many are forged and now refuses to accept them. This leaves British asylum tribunals, faced with hundreds of otherwise undocumented young refugees, unable to distinguish between fact and fiction.*

(Extract from UK parliamentary Home Affairs Committee investigation, June 2014)

Friday

It was a quarter to five in the morning when Craig Gillard slipped out of bed, kissed his wife goodbye, and began the almost 200-mile journey to Lincolnshire. Last night he had looked at the map of the remote place he was going to and realized that he'd never been anywhere near it. The early bits of the journey, on the M25 and A1 (M), were dully familiar, and it was only a long time after he'd left Peterborough and got onto the A16 that the traffic became sparse and the character of the surroundings started to show. A rosy fleck or two on the horizon heralded the sunrise, while the soft grey of the low, mist-wreathed fens was punctured by the steeples of parish churches and the bare limbs of roadside trees. Gillard followed a tractor and muck spreader slowly into the town of Spalding, famed for its Dutch-style canals and unspoiled architecture. The satnav guided him onto a long straight road into Boston, cutting through fields whose rich soil would in a few months' time be green with vegetables and salads. Towns he had never heard of – Spilsby, Alford and Horncastle –

crept onto the satnav map. Gillard was taken by surprise by the rolling hills of the Lincolnshire Wolds, open arable fields, hedgerows, cattle and very little traffic. When he finally pulled into the coastal car park at Theddlethorpe, he felt like he'd been on the road all day, although it was only four hours. Waiting for him there was DCI Trevor Greycoates of Lincolnshire Police and, standing by his battered Land Rover, Jim Crowthorne, the ranger who had found the body.

They had arranged to visit the spot where the body was found at exactly the same position of the tide. Greycoates looked like a 1980s football commentator, with a long grey comb-over, a pepper-and-salt moustache, and even the sheepskin-collared coat. Only the wellingtons spoiled the image.

The moment he got out of the car, Gillard wished he had brought a thicker coat himself. There was a raw, penetrating cold and blustery wind, which got to him even as he put his wellingtons on. The long yomp out, past brambles and dunes to the tidal mudflats, was a revelation to Gillard. 'Why would anyone drag a body this far out?' he yelled to Greycoates, trying to make himself heard above the wind.

'I don't think he was dead when they brought him out,' the detective replied.

Gillard looked around. He'd never seen such a big sky, nor such a featureless beach. It was still another 300 yards out to the shallow surf, marking the start of the North Sea. Another 200 miles beyond that was Holland. Why here? Gillard kept asking himself. His detective brain raced through the limited criminal possibilities of this part of the world: a place for a drug drop or human trafficking?

Maybe. Not too far from the gangs of Grimsby, nor from the bigger players in the port of Hull just 40 miles north, with its ferry links to the Continent. Greycoates pointed to an orange plastic marker in the distance. When they reached it, teeth gritted into the wind, Gillard saw it was attached to a five-foot rod that had been banged into a sandbank.

'This is the place,' Crowthorne bellowed, his back to the wind. 'Of course it's changed shape a little even since I found it two weeks ago. The creek behind meanders back and forth on a weekly basis,' he said.

'And there were no footprints?' Gillard asked.

'Not around the body,' Crowthorne said. 'They would have been washed away by the tide.'

'What about around the car park and above the high-tide level?' he asked Greycoates.

He was met with an expansive shrug. 'As you saw, the path to the beach is concrete, until the last 20 yards before the beach proper begins, and there is loose, windblown sand. We had a look, but we didn't think there was much chance of getting a realistic impression. It wasn't helped that there was a delay of several hours before we marked the entranceway from the car park to the beach as a crime scene.'

'So there had been other visitors?' Gillard asked.

'Not lots, but a few, enough to make tracking foot-prints impossible.'

Gillard looked up, and out to sea. This was a very obscure place. Someone had gone to a lot of trouble to dump a body here. The question was, why would they do that?

He turned back to Greycoates with a couple more questions about the condition of the body.

'I think those answers would be best coming from Dr Javadi. She's agreed to go over her findings with you.'

'I'm looking forward to it,' Gillard said, rubbing his hands. And that was only partially to keep them warm.

–

It took nearly two hours driving west to reach the Leicester Royal Infirmary. Dr Lida Javadi was a very busy woman and kept them waiting nearly half an hour. Finally, the Home Office forensic pathologist came to fetch them from reception. Dressed in a white coat, she was a handsome 50-something woman. After exchanging greetings, she led them into the mortuary. 'We've had a spate of stabbings locally, so I regret that it has taken me longer than expected to put together my full report. At least it makes a change to have a shooting rather than more knife crime.'

'So what did you discover?' Gillard asked.

'First off, the caveats: the body had been at least partially under salt water, presumably the tide, for at least six to eight hours by the time it was recovered. Seagulls and crabs had already made a start on him. Both eyeballs were missing, and there was considerable damage to the mouth and rectum…'

Greycoates winced: 'Is that what seagulls go for?'

'I'm not an expert on scavengers, but my understanding is that bodily orifices are the primary route into a cadaver. Anyway, this inevitably muddies the waters, so to speak.'

Gillard nodded. 'But were you able to get some clues?'

'My full report will be ready by Monday, but in summary we can say this: death was caused by a single bullet wound to the head. Time of death was approximately 12 hours before the discovery of the body. The hypostasis does not indicate bodily disturbance, so there is a strong possibility that he was walked out to the beach and then shot, in the very position he was found.'

'An execution?' Gillard asked.

'That is for you to decide,' the pathologist replied. 'My job is what happened to the body; it finishes at the skin. However, any layman would be able to observe that it is easier to get your victim to walk half a mile to his final resting place than to be carried after death.'

'What else did you discover about the body?'

'Age, perhaps mid-20s, healthy heart, kidneys, liver. Indications that he smoked, nicotine traces both from the lungs and the fingertips. No alcohol in his system, no trace of noteworthy drugs. All perfectly normal, internally. There were a number of contusions, and a parchmented abrasion on the body, on elbows and knees.'

'Almost certainly when they roughed him up,' Greycoates said.

'Professionally, I couldn't possibly speculate. However, common sense dictates that if one was dragged forcibly from a vehicle, one might expect to suffer these types of injuries.'

'What about the burn that you mentioned?' Gillard asked.

'Yes.' The pathologist pulled up an image on her computer screen. It showed the back of the head of a young man with short razor-cut dark hair and an angry-looking circular burn on the nape of his neck, three inches below the bullet entry point. 'This is the type of injury caused by a piece of very hot metal pressed into the skin. A brand, in effect.'

'After he was killed?' he asked.

'I doubt it,' the pathologist said. 'There was time enough for serum to rise to the surface, though nowhere enough time for scabbing.'

'So he was tortured,' Gillard said.

'Quite possibly. It would be hard to conceive of accidental injuries of that kind, particularly in the context of the killing at around the same time.' The pathologist swivelled on her chair to look back at the detective. 'So do you know who he is?'

'Up until yesterday, I would have had to say no,' said Greycoates. 'His DNA didn't match anyone on our database. There was no wallet, phone, nor any papers on him that would give any obvious clue. As you say he is of Mediterranean-looking origin.'

'When the mitochondrial check comes back, we will know more,' Dr Javadi said. 'But I understand you have a connection, Detective Chief Inspector Gillard?'

'That's right. We have a strong familial DNA link with two abducted children.' He reminded them of the details of the case. 'David and Amber Lund are Albanian orphans. Or that's what we thought they were.'

'So this chappie could be their father?' Greycoates asked.

'They are young enough for that to be the case,' Gillard said. 'Or their brother. But until we get the expert analysis we won't know for sure whether they are siblings or children, or some other blood relative.'

'Hmm, fascinating,' the pathologist said. 'I'm afraid the samples I sent for mitochondrial analysis will take another week and a half. Unlike you, at the time I ordered them I didn't think I needed to splash out on the express service.'

'Anything else we should know?' Gillard asked.

'Well, this won't be mentioned on my report because it's not pertinent to the way he died. I did notice that his fingernails have been carefully and probably professionally shaped sometime in the last week. The surface of his nails yielded evidence of a clear varnish, which we should be able to identify. His eyebrows had also been professionally shaped quite recently. I think threading is the term used.'

'Are you hinting he was an uphill gardener?' Greycoates chuckled.

'I don't hint, I give the facts,' Dr Javadi said, raising a well-shaped eyebrow. 'Assumptions about sexual orientation would be quite a leap at this stage. Thirty years ago police officers might have said the same about a man wearing an earring, and it could equally have been a mistake.'

'For all that, it would be an idea to ask the gay community. It could be a real help in the missing persons angle,' Gillard said.

'Well, he doesn't match any of the half-dozen young males missing locally, but if he was brought over here from, say, London, Nottingham or Leicester, we can really cut down the possibilities,' Greycoates said.

'It must be quite a small subset of the population,' Gillard said. 'Well-manicured Albanian males who haven't been seen for a while.'

'So would you like to take a look at him?' Dr Javadi asked.

DCI Greycoates had previously seen the body and made his excuses, but Gillard wanted to see for himself. The pathologist led him into the mortuary, handed him a white coat and some latex gloves. She and a male assistant located the body and pulled it out onto a trolley. A label dangled from the big toe. Gillard leaned over and looked at the man's face. He was dark, hirsute and lightly bearded. While he looked of Mediterranean origin, the absence of eyes made it impossible to say whether he looked like young David Lund or not. The living and the dead, a man and a boy: just a double helix of familial connection.

In this position the body had few visible wounds, apart from the Y-shaped incision from the post-mortem. Dr Javadi showed him each abrasion mentioned on her report. 'Can you show me the neck burn?' Gillard asked.

With the help of the assistant, Javadi turned the corpse over. The burn on the neck was livid, and about three inches across. The discoloured glossy flesh had puckered from the heat, but it was quite easy to recognise the symbol that had been crudely branded on this young man.

The triple-headed eagle of the Dragusha clan.

Chapter 20

DI Claire Mulholland had spent Thursday and Friday chasing two remaining leads in the shooting of Peter Young. The first, Karen Davies, the South African-born receptionist had been easy. The woman had not left Britain, indeed had no immediate plans to do so, and had been happy to be interviewed for a third time. After 40 minutes with her in Staines police station on the Thursday morning, Mulholland was convinced that the woman was innocent. Despite her shooting skills, she didn't fit the profile of an assassin: why get to know the victim before killing him? Why catch a bus and shoot him through the window when she could have done it any morning face-to-face? Most of all, why hang around afterwards to be interviewed three times by the police?

The second lead was a bit more interesting. Ryan Hardcastle, a self-appointed tough guy, lived opposite the murder scene, in a place from which the fatal shot could have been fired. He was the only one with a motive, because of the arguments over the parking place and the vandalizing of Peter Young's car. Although she doubted that Hardcastle himself would have fired the weapon, he might easily have a contact who would do the hit for a fee. Mulholland arranged to interview him, again at Staines on the Friday afternoon, but before that she went to HMP Coldingley, an hour's drive west, to find out what she could about his conduct there. The female governor was very helpful and provided a senior prison liaison officer who had detailed records of Hardcastle's 'known associates' during his time there. Hardcastle was one of the few short-term prisoners in what is generally a lifer's institution, but none of his cellmates over the six months he was there seemed to have the right credentials for a hit. The nearest was a Jamaican gangster called Arthur 'Asbo' Williams, who had worked in the kitchens with him. Williams had years before been a Yardie in Birmingham, and presumably could get a shooter without too much difficulty. He had been discharged from prison just before Christmas. Mulholland started to get quite excited about the connection, and on returning to the office pulled up Asbo Williams's full criminal record. Checking the call records from Hardcastle's own mobile, which she'd got from the service provider last week, flagged up a number which was down as Asbo Williams's landline in Birmingham. Hardcastle had called him three days after Christmas, a perfect set-up time for a hit in January.

So Mulholland was feeling quite optimistic when she walked back into Staines police station with Carl Hoskins that afternoon, ready to interview Ryan Hardcastle. The duty solicitor, a tiny Sikh lady called Mrs Singh, was already waiting.

As before, the interviewee was perfectly polite, with Hardcastle quite readily agreeing that he had fallen out with Peter Young over the parking space.

'There is no parking space anywhere near Roosevelt Road, so what was I to do? It was no bother to him, I'd leave pretty much as soon as he arrived.'

'Why didn't you mention this when you were first interviewed?' Mulholland asked, looking down at Gillard's notes.

'One, I forgot, and two, it was no big deal.'

'But you scratched up his car,' Hoskins said. 'And broke off his wipers.'

'That wasn't me,' Hardcastle said, staring out of the window.

'Please present any evidence you have that Mr Hardcastle was involved in this crime,' Mrs Singh said.

Mulholland shrugged. 'Okay, so tell me about Asbo Williams.'

The abrupt change of tack seemed to surprise Hardcastle, who then gave a rather charitable summary of the Jamaican's criminal CV and his considerable culinary skills, as revealed in HMP Coldingley's kitchen. 'Great jerk chicken, he did. Angie still uses the recipe,' he said. 'Just a bit too fond of the spice.'

'He's good with guns too, isn't he?' she asked.

'Maybe, I don't know,' shrugged Hardcastle. He stared out of the window again.

'Did you get him to do the hit on Peter Young?' she asked.

Hardcastle laughed and looked up at the ceiling ''Course I didn't. I didn't want anyone killed. I'm not like that.'

'You've got plenty of form for violence,' Hoskins said.

'I've never killed anyone, and neither did Asbo. Anyway, Asbo couldn't have done it.'

'Why?'

'Because he died on Christmas Eve. Like I said, he was addicted to spice inside, and got straight back on harder stuff once he was out.'

Mulholland snorted with disbelief and shuffled through her papers, looking for any confirmation of this revelation. There was none.

'Asbo Williams is dead, is he?' she said, having found what she was looking for 'If so, how come you rang him up three days *after* Christmas, on your own mobile, and spent an hour and 45 minutes talking to a corpse?'

'Got a direct line to hell, have you?' Hoskins chuckled.

'I mean, come on, Ryan, don't be stupid, we can check these things,' she added, rolling her eyes. 'If you are going to lie, pick something we can't check.'

Ryan Hardcastle leaned back on his chair, piggy eyes narrowed, and gave Mulholland a level stare. 'Yeah, I rang his missus on the landline as soon as I heard the news. I was giving her me condolences. I liked the bloke. I read the eulogy at his funeral in Sparkbrook.' He got out his phone and started to swipe through pictures. 'There's the picture of him in his coffin.' He showed the police officers the image: a flower-surrounded casket, lid off. Asbo actually looked healthier than in his official mugshot, but it seemed convincing.

Mulholland could feel the colour rising to her cheeks.

'I can get the date off the pic if you want,' Hardcastle said.

'My client is clearly upset,' said Mrs Singh, her head wobbling with indignation. 'I think you should check your facts before making accusations.'

Mulholland terminated the interview, feeling not only foolish but a bully. That Ryan Hardcastle genuinely missed his friend was not in doubt. A friendship is no less valid, she reminded herself, for being forged inside. Perhaps more so, given what jail camaraderie has to get you through. In some ways, she was happy that it seemed unlikely that Hardcastle was their perpetrator. The ballistics evidence indicated a handgun rather than a rifle, which would have been a near-impossible shot from Hardcastle's flat, 50 yards across the road.

Hardcastle hadn't been on the bus; neither had Asbo Williams. Karen Davies hadn't done it. So who had? It had to be the fair-haired man they had seen on CCTV. There was literally nobody else it could be.

–

Gillard arrived at Mount Browne on Saturday ten minutes early for the 9 a.m. briefing he had booked. While he'd been away in Lincolnshire the team had a whole day to establish exactly what had happened to the Lund kids. He stood there at the whiteboard as DCs Hoskins, Hodges, Tsu and Townsend walked in, followed by PR officer Christine McCafferty. He was about to start when a figure in a canary-yellow sweatshirt and tight, fashionably frayed jeans opened the door. Chief Constable Alison Rigby. No one expected to see top brass in at the weekend, particularly not this early. But Rigby, as they were learning, was something else. Every back in the place stiffened, every tie straightened.

'Don't mind me,' Rigby said, pulling up a chair and crossing her legs. 'Just come in to see how things are going.' She was the brightest thing in the room.

Gillard had covered three whiteboards with notes. 'We'll start with the whereabouts of the children. Hoskins, what have you found?'

Hoskins heaved himself out of his seat and lurched towards one of the whiteboards. 'We've had no luck so far with pictures of the children.' He pointed out a series of flight numbers that had been written down. 'We've been through all the direct flights to Albania and most of the indirect ones. We've tracked down bookings for children and we have no matches. None of the cabin crews recall them either. So I think we can rule out aircraft, with or without false passports.'

'What about ferries, Carl?'

'No luck, sir. The catch here is of course that someone can easily drive a couple of undeclared kids either onto the Eurotunnel service or a car ferry, in the boot or hidden some other way, especially if they were drugged. The trouble is we have no description of who was driving the car that went from the school. If we had that, we would have a face that would have appeared in front of an immigration officer.'

'Agreed,' said Gillard. 'Rob, any luck on the car?'

Townsend set up his laptop and projected onto a screen an image of a snazzy mustard-coloured Fiat 500. 'This is a very distinctive vehicle. Countrypolitan yellow, they call it. As far as I can establish, not a single one in this livery has been stolen in the last two months, anywhere in the country.'

There was a stony silence.

'What about hire cars?' Gillard asked.

'There are about a dozen in this colour with the major rental chains. I've got the histories and credit card numbers, and I've run registration numbers through the ANPR. One or two have been flagged up near Colsham Manor, though not on the day in question. I'm still working on tracking down the hirers.'

'Good work, Rob,' said Gillard, and went to a flipchart.

Alison Rigby interrupted. 'All this seems to assume that they have been taken abroad, Craig. Is it not entirely possible they're still in this country? If a ransom was paid the children would have to be returned, and that's more easily done if they haven't gone too far.'

'Well, ma'am, we've been taking the Albanian angle pretty seriously. The children are of Albanian origin, we found Albanian symbols at Colsham Manor and one of the children seems to have had a conversation in Albanian with an intruder. It beggars belief that there is no significance in any of these clues.'

'Unless someone is trying to mislead you, Craig. In which case they have done a fine job.' Even from the back of the room, the blue stare was powerful.

'We'll certainly consider that, ma'am.' Craig turned to Michelle Tsu. 'I believe you are doing some work on the Lund family? Care to run us through it?'

The young detective took over the laptop, and began a professional-looking PowerPoint presentation. 'I looked at this from the other direction,' she said. 'Who would want to kidnap these children and why?' She clicked the mouse and a picture came up showing the company name Drillvest AB. 'This is the company in which Dag Lund has a controlling interest. It specializes in drilling equipment for the oil industry, mainly deepwater rigs.' The next slide showed its billion-dollar revenues and healthy profits.

'Any business in Albania?' Gillard asked. He heard the chief constable clear her throat very loudly at yet another mention of that country.

'Nothing significant that I could find,' Tsu said. 'So that's one theory hit the dust.' She then switched to showing pictures of the children, and the article that appeared in the local newspaper. 'This would certainly have potential kidnappers salivating, because it even mentions the school that the kids go to.'

'I'm interviewing Dag Lund this afternoon,' said Gillard. 'I'd wanted to speak to him weeks ago, but now the children have been kidnapped he's cancelled all his business trips for the time being. Having said that, I'm not expecting any breakthrough.'

'I've also looked in a bit more detail at the adoption background for the children,' Michelle said. 'All the paperwork looks to be in order. The children's original names are Dretim and Albana Goga. I've even found an email address for the orphanage in Shkoder at which they were placed, though at the moment I'm just working through Google Translate, so communications aren't brilliant.'

'I authorized you an Albanian translator,' Rigby interjected. 'Why aren't you using one?'

'Ma'am, we were offered two by the agency we normally use,' Tsu replied. 'But when I asked them to provide visa proof, it turns out their best one, who we have used several times, is actually an asylum seeker with no Right to Remain granted as yet, and while the appeal is in process is barred from working. The second is actually a Serb who only speaks a little Albanian and is the subject of an extradition request from Greece for class B drug offences.'

Rigby's eyes widened, becoming even more blue. 'Well, it's good that someone is checking, Tsu. But is there no one else?'

'There's a shortage, ma'am. The Met has a few, but won't share them.'

'I'll have a word,' Rigby said, making notes. 'Leave it with me.'

'Michelle, have you had any luck contacting the aunt?' Gillard asked.

'Yes. Sophie Lund gave me the number in Italy. This woman is Zerina Moretti. According to Sophie, the children adore her and call her Teto Zerina, which means auntie. She wasn't in, but she rang me back on a mobile to say how desperately worried she was about the children. I asked her the same questions that I've asked the orphanage, and the answers she gave seemed to tally.'

'Is she planning to come over?' Gillard asked. 'We really need to interview her.'

'No, I didn't get that impression. I'll ring her again and ask if she would,' Tsu said.

'Now the wildcard,' Gillard said, taking over the projector. 'Yesterday I drove all the way up to darkest Lincolnshire to look at a body which DNA familial tests show is a close relative of Amber and David Lund.'

He projected side by side the stencil version of the triple-headed eagle symbol and that from the head of the doll. 'Now these, as we know, are what we found around Colsham Manor, one at Mrs Lund's stable block and the other in Ms Hinchcliffe's pottery.' He moved on to the next image. 'And this was what was branded into the back of the neck on the Lincolnshire murder victim.'

There was a gasp from the gathered detectives as they looked at the seared image burned into the young man's neck.

'The Dragusha are sending a message,' Gillard said. 'You don't need to speak Albanian to know they mean business.'

Saturday evening

After pulling 18-hour shifts for the last four days since the kidnap, Gillard had hoped to be home for nine o'clock to spend a little time with Sam, but it wasn't to be. Rob Townsend's ANPR analysis, now cross-checked with every single mustard-coloured Fiat 500, had been ready a little after six that evening. It had shown that every single vehicle in that livery in the UK had been accounted for. Every private and corporate owner had been checked, every car hire firm contacted, every stolen or missing vehicle accounted for. Three had been taken abroad, but in each case the owner had responded to police texts or phone calls and accounted for their movements. The truth, Gillard realized, was that they were dealing with professionals, who had switched the children to another vehicle quite soon after the abduction. More impressively still, the abductors had made the Fiat they had used simply disappear. Neither dumped nor torched. The car had just vanished.

These thoughts had preoccupied Gillard as he had driven home, finally pulling into his drive at 10.15 p.m. The lights of the three-bed semi-detached offered a belated welcome to a house they had bought a few months ago and he'd hardly had any time to really explore. He'd relied on Sam to unpack and decorate because of the extended hours he had been working. Tonight though, as he let himself in, he saw she was stretched out on the sofa watching some slushy film.

'Hello, stranger,' she said, stretching her arms above her languorously. 'Give me a kiss.'

Gillard reached down to embrace her, inhaling her wonderful scent. 'I'm so sorry to be late again.' From behind his back he produced a bunch of mixed carnations, pink and white.

'They're lovely,' she said, ignoring their slightly wilted heads. 'BP or Gulf?'

Gillard laughed. 'Gulf. You got me bang to rights. I wanted a single red rose, but the florist was shut by the time I got out.'

She stood and kissed him slowly. 'Thank you. It's the thought that counts. So, any progress on those poor kids?'

He shook his head and sighed. 'We're still grasping at straws unfortunately.'

She offered him some food, but he just settled for cuddling up with her while she watched the final few minutes of the film. There was, of course, a happy ending. In real life they just seemed harder to come by.

Just after eleven o'clock Sam announced she was off to bed. 'Are you coming, Craig?' She said, holding out her hand to him. He yawned and stretched, then said: 'Just got to do a bit of paperwork. Be up in ten minutes.'

She rolled her eyes and laughed. 'A Gillard ten minutes is normally an hour. I'll probably be asleep by then.'

He kissed her, and watched his wife make her way to the stairs. They had been married less than a year, and he was still surprised that such an attractive younger woman would want to take on a workaholic such as himself. Especially after the business with Liz Knight.

Gillard got his briefcase out and took it into his office, which was in reality an upstairs box room with a view over their small suburban garden. He drew the curtains, logged on to his PC, and then jotted down a few notes.

He had been meaning to research Albanian history as part of the Peter Young case, but with the abduction of the Lund kids he could no longer afford to delay.

The basics he already knew. A small and mountainous Balkan country about the size of Wales, it sat on the Mediterranean coast on the top left-hand corner of Greece, opposite the heel of Italy. A few days ago, when he'd asked Tweedledum and Tweedledee what they knew about Albania, Hoskins gave him some football score from a recent European championship, and the name of some Albanian goalscorer, while Hodges mentioned a local car-washing business which employed lots of Albanians. Asked to summarize their knowledge, they agreed on three words: crime, communism and immigrants.

Wikipedia gave some context. It was true that Albania had laboured under the Maoist dictatorship of Enver Hoxha from 1944 to 1985, but in the brief flourishing of democracy afterwards, something even more damaging happened. The savings of an entire generation had been lost through a series of government-backed pyramid savings scams. Tens of thousands who had scrimped and saved for a better life lost everything they had. Violent demonstrations from 1997 led to the overthrow of the government and a civil war in which 2,000 people died. This had hardly died down before the conflict in Kosovo, Albania's immediate northern neighbour, caused further instability from 1998 to 1999. A million ethnic Albanians fled under Serbian threat, and there was a NATO intervention to protect them.

The country had enjoyed a less 'interesting' history in the last 20 years. Under democratic civilian rule it adopted broader European standards of government and legislation towards a hoped-for entry into the EU, which still looked years away. But it still retained a few unhelpful legacies of wilder times: the highest road accident rate in Europe; enduring mistrust of the police and judiciary; well-entrenched mafia gangs, powerful enough to rival even those in Italy; and the world's highest per capita possession of guns after the US.

Finally, Gillard homed in on the essential research: who or what were the Dragusha gang? There was plenty of information in Albanian, but much less, at least in public forums, in English. The Dragusha family, based, appropriately enough, in the city of Fier, had a fearsome reputation and an unmatched arsenal that included some sophisticated weaponry looted from military stores during the civil war.

The head of the clan was serving a life sentence in a special cell in the high-security prison of Tarduz. Vjosa Dragusha, aged 66, had boasted of personally killing more than a hundred adversaries. His nickname was the Butcher of Fier and he had a personal emblem.

Gillard clicked on the image to enlarge it: a three-headed eagle in black and gold on a crimson background, poised over a pair of golden scimitars. He then clicked on the photograph that he had been sent by Sophie Lund of the graffito sprayed onto her stable doorpost. The stencil was only an outline. But there was no mistaking the resemblance.

Three hours later the detective chief inspector lay awake, in the embrace of his sleeping wife, unable to turn off the anxiety that was bubbling in his brain. It seemed very likely that the man on the Colsham Manor lawns, a man who seemingly spoke Albanian, was the same man who had sprayed the stencil and who abducted Sophie Lund's children. Whether or not he was a genuine member of the Dragusha clan, the outlook for David and Amber Lund was very grim indeed.

Sunday

The Lund family certainly believed in closing the stable door. When Gillard had first visited Colsham Manor a few weeks ago, he was able to cycle in through the main gates and up the grand drive to the Georgian portico. Now, when he and Michelle Tsu took the same route, they found the gates were locked and there were at least two CCTV cameras covering the pedestrian gate adjacent to it. 'I had intended to show you what a grand place this is,' Gillard said. 'But I'll have to go round the back way instead.'

'It's okay,' Tsu said. 'I've seen it all on Google Earth and Street View. I downloaded the floor plan, which is still on the estate agent's website from when it was on sale a few years ago. I also know what the Lunds paid for it, thanks to the Land Registry. Did you know, the vendor knocked almost half a million off the asking price?'

'I'm impressed with what you can do without leaving the office,' Gillard said as they made their way up Tithe Lane. The car juddered as it negotiated the bumpy track that led past Geraldine Hinchcliffe's little empire and to the outbuildings. A white BMW seven series was parked there, which he presumed belonged to Dag Lund, the man they had come to see. Gillard and Tsu made their way around to the imposing portico and rang the bell.

The au pair came to the door and wordlessly let them in. She cut a diminished figure compared with the lively youngster that Gillard had seen previously. Her large dolorous eyes were dark-rimmed, and it was possible to imagine what she would look like in late middle age. She showed them into a large reception room where both Dag and Sophie were waiting, on their feet, for their arrival. Dag was a well-proportioned man with iron-grey hair and a dark, well-trimmed beard. He looked every inch the successful entrepreneur.

'Have you heard anything?' Sophie asked eagerly.

'We've made some progress,' Gillard said. 'But we don't know yet where the children are.'

Sophie closed her eyes and sighed, and Dag put an arm around her shoulders to comfort her.

'I know you are doing everything you can, but if there's anything more that we can do to help you've got to let us know,' Dag said.

'I take it you haven't had a ransom demand?' Gillard asked.

They both shook their heads. 'Nothing, nothing at all.'

'No letters, emails, texts or any more of those curious symbols appearing anywhere?'

Sophie shook her head. 'I've walked all the bridleways and footpaths, with a camera in hand, looking for anything that has changed.'

'What about you, Mr Lund? Has anyone been in contact? A ransom demand may not always be obvious – it can sometimes be a taunting message on your company's website, an insult on Twitter even.'

'Checking this was one of the first things I did,' Dag said. 'Anyone who has been in business at the level I have will have made enemies. I've been taken to court, of course I have, but I really can't think of anybody so upset with me that they would do anything like this.' He held out his hands expansively, as if the kidnap had taken place there in the room.

Gillard decided to reveal a little of his own researches. 'Five years ago your company was involved in dismantling one of your own rigs in the North Sea. You were accused of dumping bits of rig into the water.'

Dag groaned at the rehearsing of a well-known complaint. 'Jesus, we followed all the rules, I can assure you. Greenpeace and others have been hounding us about this for years. But-we-exactly-followed-the-official-guidelines.' He chopped one hand into the palm of the other.

'So those accusations are untrue?'

'Detective Chief Inspector, I really can't believe I'm in a conversation about this when my children are missing. But to answer your question, some heavy concrete elements and corroded structures cannot cost-effectively be retrieved. We make sure they are cleansed of pollutants before—'

'The only reason I'm asking,' Gillard said, 'is that this is a possible motive from some on the fringes of the environmental movement.'

'But I'm so green,' Dag said emphatically. 'My company is *the* most environmentally conscious in the industry. How can these people target us?'

Michelle Tsu interjected. 'Somebody has, Mr Lund, and they haven't found it very difficult. Anyone reading the local newspaper could see what your children looked like, where they went to school, and the name and location of your home.'

'Could this really be environmentalists?' Sophie asked.

Dag Lund steepled his hands on either side of his nose and closed his eyes as if having difficulty breathing. After a few moments he looked up. 'You know, with all my years in the oil industry, I've lived in Angola and Nigeria, and we even lived together in Venezuela.' Sophie nodded as Dag continued: 'I took all of the precautions for my and Sophie's safety that you would expect of places with their kind of reputation. But this is Britain. This is Surrey,' he said opening his hands. 'It's supposed to be safe.'

'Sadly, there is no such thing as absolute safety,' Gillard said.

'Look, what about this Albanian who was on my lawn, talking to my daughter?' Sophie asked.

'We haven't made any clear progress on that. We only had that one brief statement from you about what was said between them,' Gillard said. 'But it is one of our major lines of enquiry.'

'Well, we're not waiting for you,' Sophie said. 'We've just taken on a private detective.' She held up a letter.

'Sophie,' Dag said, rubbing his forehead in exasperation. 'I told you not to mention that.'

'Well actually I'm glad you did,' Gillard replied. 'In truth having two people chasing around trying to talk to the same witnesses only complicates matters. Particularly in the case of the kidnap, where the lives of your children are clearly in danger.' Gillard asked the name of the firm they were using.

'It's GM Associates,' Sophie said, reading from the letter. 'A chap called Geoff Meadows. He says he knows you.'

'He does indeed. I have no trouble working with Geoff.' In fact he was secretly relieved to have such an experienced hand involved. Just as they were about to leave, Gillard said. 'One more thing, Mrs Lund. You sent me a photograph of some bullets, said you'd kept the actual objects somewhere?'

'Oh yes,' she said. 'Hang on.' She came back with a tin and showed it to Gillard. 'Sorry about handling them and everything, I didn't think about fingerprints.'

They were indeed casings for pistol bullets, not shotgun cartridges. Someone had been firing a handgun.

'Can you show me where you found them?' Gillard asked. She nodded and led them into the boot room where she began to get changed into outdoor gear. The earlier rain had stopped, but it was half past three and the light was already getting low. Gillard went back to the car and got out a powerful LED inspection light from the boot and rejoined Michelle, Sophie and Dag at the back of the stables. Sophie led them on a slightly overgrown path which wound down through a copse on a footbridge over a stream, and then joined a larger but muddy track bearing right. There were a number of disused farm buildings at the top of the rise, and beyond them a windowless cottage.

'We keep meaning to renovate all these,' Sophie said. 'But the Manor is such a money pit we never seem to get round to it.' She led them into what would have been the back garden of the cottage, walled in what was once whitewashed brick, only a few flecks of paint remaining. The brickwork was overrun by ivy, nettles and brambles. Only the flag-stoned patio immediately behind the house was entirely clear of weeds, although a pavement path to the exterior gate could still be discerned.

'It was right here that I found most of them,' Sophie said, indicating the patio. 'There's a lot of broken glass down by the bottom wall, but it's so overrun I didn't feel like tackling it.'

'It looks to me that someone has been doing a bit of target practice against the wall,' Gillard said, illuminating the brickwork with the torch. 'I'll get someone to dig through this in daylight in the next couple of days. I'm sure we'll find some bullets.'

But even as he said it, Gillard was doubting that this could be connected to the abduction. A professional would never do their target practice in what was effectively the backyard of the victim. It just made no sense. On the way back to the house he shared his misgivings with Michelle Tsu. 'This doesn't add up,' he whispered.

'Maybe the eccentric neighbour likes to fire off a few rounds from time to time,' she replied. 'And maybe she's a radical environmental activist.'

'Christ, I hadn't considered Geraldine Hinchcliffe at all,' Gillard said. He now recalled that Geraldine Hinch-cliffe had a Greenpeace sticker in the rear window of her car. And in her kitchen there was a calendar from some other environmentalist group – Sea Shepherd, he thought. 'I do hope you're wrong about there being a Hinchcliffe connection.'

'Because she is the chief constable's girlfriend?'

News really does travel fast, Gillard thought. This investigation is getting more uncomfortable all the time.

–

Gillard dropped Tsu at Godalming railway station, just over five minutes from the village where the Lund children went to school. Driving out of the station car park, something occurred to him. On the edge of the town they had passed a Fiat dealership, still seemingly open late on a Sunday afternoon. He now turned around to go back to the place. The moment he set foot inside the showroom, a smartly dressed young man approached him with the usual sales patter. Before he'd got too far, Gillard identified himself and then showed him a photo of the au pair's car. 'Do you have any Fiat 500s in this livery?'

'Yes, just the one.' He led Gillard over to the car, near the front of the window of the dealership. 'It's pretty sporty for such an economical model, with three years warranty of course.'

'Yes, thank you, but actually I don't want to buy it. I'm on an investigation.'

The young man pushed his hand through his dark hair. 'Sorry, force of habit. Is this about those two abducted children? Seen that on the television. Terrible business.'

'Indeed it is. So if I wanted to take it for a test drive, would I need to book it in advance?'

The salesman now look confused 'So you *are* interested?'

'No, I mean if a customer wanted to take a test drive. A punter.'

'Not necessarily. It depends.'

'And you would go with the potential customer?'

'Normally, unless we know them.'

'Do you keep a record of the test drives?'

'Well, we're supposed to.' He gave a conspiratorial look. 'But in practice not always.' The salesman led Gillard into the office and opened a ring binder. 'They're in here.'

'Was this particular car taken on a test drive on Tuesday last week?'

The salesman smiled. 'Oh yes, I've no need to look that one up. It was, but it was returned within 25 minutes. I had thought about that when I saw the appeal on TV.'

'You're sure it was back that quickly?'

'Yes.'

Gillard shrugged and thanked the man. Still, it had been worth a try. He returned to his car and sat inside, and was just about to start the engine when he changed his mind. The salesman smiled to see him return. 'Decided to buy after all, sir?'

Gillard smiled indulgently. 'Do you remember who took it for a spin?'

'Yes, a charming Italian woman. She had been shopping for a Fiat for some time. Said her father used to make them. It was her third test drive in a week.'

'No one else?'

He checked the ledger. 'Nope, that was it for that day.'

'Did you or one of your colleagues go with her?'

'No. As I say she had been a couple of times before. We trusted her not to drive off with it. We took an imprint of her credit card.'

'No children in the car when she got back?'

'No. Just her.'

'I'd still like a record of her details, if you have them,' Gillard said.

The salesman flicked through a filing cabinet. 'We don't keep the credit card imprint, but I do recall a passport. Let me have a look. It might take a while.' He began searching through screenshots on the PC.

A little light bulb went off in Gillard's head. 'Bear with me one minute.' He went back to the car and returned with his laptop which he powered up. Searching through the pictures connected with the case, he selected an image of Amber and David provided by the family. The two children were by a Christmas tree, surrounded with unopened presents. Sitting on the sofa behind them was a middle-aged woman in shiny tights, overly tight puce woollen dress and gold-framed spectacles. Teto Zerina.

Gillard turned the screen so the salesman could see it. 'Is this her?'

'Yes,' he said. 'Without a shadow of a doubt.'

'Okay,' said Gillard. 'We need that car pushed out of the showroom and kept somewhere safe until we come to collect it…'

'Pushed?'

'Yes, ideally by fingertip with gloves on. No one is to go inside or touch the door handles. That car is a crime scene. Get one of your grease monkeys to disconnect the handbrake from underneath so it can be moved.'

Gillard pulled out his phone and rang Rob Townsend to make arrangements. Auntie Zerina was one clever woman. She had taken the Lund children. But taken them where? And why?

-

Gillard drove straight back to Colsham Manor with the good news. Sophie Lund almost fell into his arms when she heard that the children were in all likelihood taken by their aunt. After waiting through a brief bout of tears, Gillard listened as she gradually moved from relief to indignation and from indignation to anger.

'I don't get it,' Sophie said. 'Why didn't she ask? We've encouraged Amber and David to keep in contact with her, and they both enjoy her company. Why on earth would she do something like this without speaking to me first?'

'It's possible that she no longer feels that they are safe at Colsham Manor,' he said. 'Maybe she knows something about the nature of the threats and hasn't told you.'

'But this is ridiculous. I've spoken to her most days since the abduction, and she seemed to be as worried about their safety as I was. In fact she was beside herself when I first told her. It just seems ridiculous that it was she who took them.'

Gillard had to broach the trickiest matter. 'From the point of view of Surrey Police, Mrs Lund, this matter may now be taken out of our hands.'

'What? Are you really saying that she hasn't broken the law?'

'I'm sure she has, because you and your husband have parental responsibility and didn't give her permission to take them. It's more the fact that this becomes a child protection issue, in which social services would be in the driving seat. I've put in some calls to them but, seeing as it's Sunday, not yet got any firm answers. My understanding is that there would be an emergency Family Court hearing to make the legal case watertight. In the meantime we have to tread a little carefully, but there are still numerous grounds for us to pursue the case, particularly if we have reason to believe that she might harm the children. Do you believe that might be the case?'

Gillard watched Sophie Lund's expression tighten as she calculated whether or not to lie in order to keep the police involved. Finally she said: 'No, I don't believe she would harm them. So where are they?'

'We don't know yet. They could be with her in Italy, but possibly still in the UK. We're still checking her whereabouts. I've left a number of messages on Zerina Moretti's mobile phone, but she hasn't returned them. Perhaps if you were to try we might get a better result.'

'Absolutely, I'll ring her right now.'

Gillard waited while Sophie made the call. 'It went to voicemail,' she said.

'Surprise, surprise, she doesn't want to speak to us,' Gillard said.

Monday morning

Eventide Funeralcare in Thames Ditton was sandwiched between a Tesco Express and an independent financial adviser, and hid behind the blandest of shop frontages, with the signage in swirls of lilac. As instructed, Claire drove her unmarked Vauxhall up the shared access with the convenience store to parking bays around the back.

She was met by Charles Anderson, the manager, a pleasant young man with short gingery hair and, for a man who listened to the last wishes of clients all day, the tiniest of ears. Claire had been notified yesterday morning that the coroner was satisfied to release Peter Young's body to his family. Though there was much still to do in the investigation, the coroner's initial report said that given that the cause of death was firmly established, the tissue, blood and organ samples being retained would be sufficient for any foreseeable further enquiry.

That would be good news for Peter's widow Laura, who appeared not to be coping very well. The first few days, as so often, seemed to be spent in denial. She had carried on renovating the house which she and Peter had bought together. According to liaison officer Gabby Underwood, Laura was well into the anger stage of grief. Being left with two young girls, a house in a barely liveable condition and all the mind-numbing probate paperwork had produced alternate bouts of inconsolable tears and a tendency to blame anyone who happened to be about. Gabby was used to being an emotional punchbag: none did it better. But even she struggled to find new ways to say that there had been little progress in finding the culprit. Claire knew that didn't augur well for this evening's interview.

Her first task this morning, though, was one that required a small piece of subterfuge. She had asked to be present at the funeral home as Peter Young's body was being prepared. She explained it as natural curiosity, and indeed she had never seen it done, but she had an ulterior motive.

Anderson introduced her to the embalmer, Tina, who was hidden under green scrubs, cap, face mask and over-boots. They led Claire past the chapel of rest and along the corridor to the mortuary, a much smaller version of what she had seen at hospitals. 'This is where we embalm the deceased,' Anderson said.

'The gentleman came in late yesterday, so we placed him in the fridge overnight,' Tina said. She led Claire into another workshop-type room, where there was a floor-to-ceiling industrial refrigerator. Tina opened the door, letting a huge gust of cold air into the room. Claire's ankles and feet were immediately chilled. The body, still zipped into the disposable body bag, was slid out onto a wheeled trolley and Tina pushed it through to the mortuary room. She and Anderson slid the bag onto an examination table. On a counter beside it was a cylinder like an office water cooler, with thick translucent rubber pipes, and next to it a tray of wicked-looking instruments.

Tina unzipped the bag and a gust of foetid air wafted into the room. Claire felt her stomach twitch a little as the taint of death slid up her nostrils. The body was still inside the paper shroud provided after the post-mortem, and through it she could make out identity tags on both wrist and ankle. Tina slit the shroud with a scalpel, revealing Peter Young's body as a pale, waxy mauve, with a huge, roughly sewn scar from pubis to clavicles and a matching scar across his scalp. 'Because the gentleman has had a post-mortem, some of the messiest part of our work with the viscera has been done for us,' Tina said. She used a spray disinfectant to cleanse him all over, particularly mouth, nose and ears, and carefully wiped the stains that disfigured the left-hand side of his head. The entry wound on the right side was by contrast small and unobtrusive. 'I'll rebuild the left-hand side of the skull with a wire frame and wax and cover the hair over later. Thankfully, he had a good head of hair. I'm still surprised they went for an open casket though,' she said turning to Charles Anderson.

'I tried everything I could to talk her out of it,' Anderson shrugged.

She turned back to the corpse. 'The major task is to give him a quick shot of body vodka, or embalming fluid, to give it its more formal title.' From the tray she picked up a terrifying hook-ended instrument. 'This is an aneurysm hook, which we use to find ourselves a nice fat artery,' she said. She took a scalpel and cut half an inch of the previous incision near the right collarbone. 'I'm looking for the carotid,' she said. It was like cutting raw fish; there was almost no blood. It was only when she pressed the aneurysm hook in and snagged a pale-blue blood vessel that the wound began to weep. She pulled the reluctant artery until it emerged from his neck like a pale slug and slid the hook fully under so it could not retreat into its hole. Tina cut into the artery with a scalpel and connected one of the rubber pipes with a cannula. A gout of dark blood emerged. She then cut another blood vessel, which she explained was the jugular vein, and fitted a drain tube into it. 'Blood out, glutaraldehyde in.'

'What's that?' Mulholland asked, pointing to a tubular dagger on the tray.

'That's called a trocar, used to aspirate organs, to let out foul air from small intestines, pancreas and stomach,' she said. 'We don't need it in this case, because it was done when the post-mortem took place.'

It took a few more minutes to set up the embalming machine, and once it was running Tina took some cotton wadding and popped it into the corpse's throat. 'That stops him purging any fluids or vomit while he's being moved. I've already done the anus.' She took two small plastic cups about an inch across and slid them under the eyelids. 'His eyes have dehydrated a lot in the week since he died, so that makes them look normal. We also use a kind of mouth guard to give his cheeks some shape.' From her tray she took an already threaded needle and with practised hands reached into his mouth, put a suture behind the front teeth, under them and up in front, then through the upper jaw into the nose, and via the septum down again. She tightened the thread, closing the knot and tying it, before poking it back in his mouth. 'There, no one can see that.'

'What's it for?' Claire asked.

'We can't have his gob drifting open as if waiting for the communion wafer, can we?'

Once finished, she took a small jar of moisturizer and delicately worked it into the face, and particularly the eyelids and cheeks. Even to Claire Mulholland's amateur eye, it was clear that Peter Young looked a bit livelier, a bit rosier in the flesh than he had before. The body was then moved to a specialist body hoist which facilitated dressing. 'This means we never have to turn the deceased over,' Tina said, as she slid a pair of trousers onto Young's body and fastened them at the waist. 'That's important because we can get purging of the stomach contents or damage to his face.' She and Charles deftly lifted the shoulders and slid on the suit jacket that he was to wear. 'A lot of people these days go for T-shirt and shorts, or jeans. Whatever the deceased was comfortable wearing.'

Tina laughed. 'My boyfriend complains that I'm a bit too practised stripping him at bedtime. He knows where I do my rehearsals.' This was a woman who clearly loved her job.

Finally, there were socks and shoes and a tie to put on.

His tasks over, Anderson left to make a phone call. While Tina stepped out of the room to get some equipment, Claire was left for a moment alone with the corpse of Peter Young. This was the moment she had been waiting for. She had set everything up in advance, and it had been ready since the first moment she walked in. She unzipped the murder victim's flies, then slid an object into the newspaper wadding that bulked out the crotch of his trousers. She withdrew her hand and zipped him up again.

'Goodbye, Peter,' she said. 'It's been nice knowing you. If I'm ever passing I'll let you know,' she said.

By the time Tina came back into the room, DI Claire Mulholland was ready to leave.

She emerged into the reception room of the funeral director's just as Charles Anderson was greeting a family. His tiny ears seemed to waggle in sympathy as he nodded his head at the tale of grief he was told. The sombre mood was shattered by the vibration of Mulholland's phone. She apologized and made her exit onto the street.

'Got something nice for you,' said DC Colin Hodges. 'We've found the man on the bus.'

-

Oleg Sikorsky sat in the interview room at Surbiton police station, wearing the same fashionable Puffa jacket and high-top canvas shoes that had been seen on the CCTV. Claire peered through the window at a man who seemed to fit not only the description of the man on the bus, but in the flesh slightly resembled the Albanian-speaking intruder at Colsham Manor too. He was about five foot ten, had nearly shoulder-length sandy hair, a thin wispy beard and a nose ring. The only problem with all of this, as the desk sergeant explained, is that he had come in voluntarily.

'He's Polish, was back in London on business, said he saw himself on the TV and was really worried.'

Hodges banged his way backwards through a series of doors from the street with three coffees clutched to his chest. He handed one to Claire, another to the desk sergeant and took a tentative sip at his own. Before they went in, they ran over the details that Sikorsky had given. He was a self-employed graphic artist, based in Milan, who had been visiting Britain on and off for two years and had a girlfriend in Hersham. Every time he came to London, which was perhaps three or four times a year, he would go and see her.

'So why wasn't he on the train from Waterloo?' Claire asked. 'Hersham is the next stop after Esher, isn't it?'

'He says he was, as far as Surbiton, but the service was suspended on that day, so he caught the bus most of the rest of the way.'

'Did we know that there were problems with the trains on the day Peter Young was killed?'

'I might have seen it,' Hodges admitted. 'It would have been hard to predict that it was relevant.'

Mulholland sighed. 'It sounds plausible. Shall we go in?'

—

The Pole was a model of cooperation. Yes, he said he had been on the train, but got off at Surbiton when it was clear the service was not going any further because of signal failure. He decided to try his luck by bus, but stayed downstairs.

'I like going upstairs on London buses, but this one was crazy busy with mad girls,' he said. 'I stayed downstairs with the old folks and the posh boys. I got off, I can't remember which stop, and then walked to Esher.'

Sikorsky spoke German, English and now Italian, as well as Polish. But he claimed not to know a word of Albanian. Asked about Colsham Manor he looked mystified. After half an hour Claire was convinced that this young man had absolutely nothing to do with either case. She would take a cheek swab anyway. She had one final question for him.

'You said you did go upstairs?'

'Only when I first got on the bus at Surbiton.'

'Did you see anybody on the bus who looked suspicious? I mean, we're looking for a male, carrying some kind of bag.'

'I don't remember anything like that. I only stayed at the top of the stairs for a moment or two.'

After another half an hour, and after taking a cheek swab, they released him. 'So what do you think?' Hodges asked.

'We'll have to check his story in detail, but it all sounds plausible enough. The infrequency of his journeys explains why only one person recalled seeing him.'

'But he's got to be lying,' Hodges said.

'Why?'

'Because without him, ma'am, we've got nobody in the frame for the murder of Peter Young. Somebody fired that gun and murdered that poor bloke. If it's not the Pole, who is it?'

Tuesday evening, 5.30 p.m.

Craig Gillard sat with Claire Mulholland in the Fat Friar café in Guildford. It was a hurried meal, of the deep-fried variety, grabbed between respective meetings, primarily to get away from Mount Browne for a while.

'So it was the aunt who snatched the kids?' Mulholland said, spearing a chip with her fork.

'It looks that way,' Gillard said. 'She flies over, stays in a hotel nearby and keeps her head down. Sophie Lund presumably has no idea she is there. Auntie knows what car the au pair uses from her previous visit at Christmas. It's a tricky problem for Auntie, because with the obsession over paedophiles there is no end of teachers and parents keeping an eye out at the school gates. So she needs an identical car. She softens up the garage by going to test drive a different car every day for three days. By the third day she's an old friend, and she's had plenty of practice going the route to the school and back. So on day three, they let her drive the car on her own. She nips up to the school early, the kids see the car and are presumably delighted to see Auntie Zerina.'

'So there's nothing that would make the lollipop lady suspicious.'

'Nope. She then drives the car to some secluded spot where she's parked her own car, not at the garage but nearby. She moves the kids into that car while she returns the Fiat. The car's away less than half an hour. She then walks back and drives off, presumably to the Continent, in some grey Hyundai whose number we don't know.'

'It's brilliant.'

'It's bloody frustrating, that is what it is,' Gillard said, chewing on a sausage. 'Being family, she could easily claim to have had permission to take them. We're chasing up her passport details with ports and airports. But at least on the bigger picture we have much less reason to worry about the safety of the kids.'

'That's a relief, then,' Mulholland said.

For a few moments there was no conversation, then she spoke.

'They're burying Peter Young tomorrow. Widow Laura wanted an open casket.'

'What, with bullet holes in his head?'

She nodded. 'I watched them prepare him for the hereafter.'

'Spare me the details,' Gillard said with a grin as he smeared some more mustard on the remains of his sausage.

'I've got a cunning plan,' she said. 'I've done my research. It's a good way to test if there really is an Albanian angle. I'll let you know if it works out.'

Gillard grunted. 'Have you seen any sign of a Dragusha symbol – you know, that three-headed eagle job – in Young's house?'

'No. I had a look when you sent it to me. Nothing like that.'

Gillard scooped up the last of his chips onto his fork. 'The way this is going it looks like all roads lead to Albania. It might be the only way we get the answers we are looking for.'

Chapter 21

By Wednesday's incident room meeting, many of the blanks in Zerina Moretti's movements had been filled in. The whiteboards were filled with notes, and Rob Townsend had set up a laptop projector.

'Okay,' said Gillard. 'First the good news as regards Amber and David Lund.' He described the identification of the children's aunt from the test drive of the Fiat 500. 'She boarded a car ferry from Dover to Calais later on the same day, driving a grey Hyundai hatchback. There was no record of the children as passengers, but they could easily have been hidden. I've got the details of her mobile, and with the help of the French police we've been able to track it. Though it has been off a good deal of the time, it does appear she drove down through France and across into Italy.'

'Why did she do all this in secret?' Michelle Tsu asked.

'We don't know. The upshot is that this may well now become a more complicated case. Surrey Social Services have got a Family Court order to go after her, and a couple of senior social workers who are liaising with the Italian police.'

'But the big picture is that the children are in Italy and safe,' Mulholland said.

'We think so. We've also asked the Italian police to help, starting with an interview with her. But we've been warned that this may take a while.' Gillard sighed. 'All right, Colin, what have you discovered?'

DC Colin Hodges stood up and went to one of the whiteboards. 'I went round with CSI yesterday afternoon to the back of Colsham Manor where the handgun casings were found. It's nearly half a mile from the Manor, but it is their land. As the DCI suggested, someone had been doing target practice in the walled garden. It was a good two hours' work to clear enough weeds to find and be able to retrieve any bullets. But we got two. They're going off for analysis, but one thing that was obvious immediately, because of the deformed flower shape of the projectile, is that they are hollow-point.'

'So the same as the ammunition used to dispatch Peter Young,' said Michelle Tsu.

'Precisely,' responded Hodges.

'So whoever killed the architect was practising near Colsham Manor,' she said.

'I don't think we can be sure of that,' Gillard said.

'To me,' Mulholland said, 'everything seems to be professional except doing target practice so close to where the children lived. And this strange night-time appearance where someone speaks Albanian to the little girl.'

'I'm not sure we can give any weight to that,' Hoskins said. 'She is only five.'

'Well, we have Sophie Lund as witness to a man appearing on the lawn,' Mulholland said.

'But not to the Albanian speech,' Hoskins added.

'And let's not forget,' Gillard said, 'that on another occasion both Sophie Lund and separately Geraldine

Hinchcliffe and our own chief constable witnessed and gave chase to an intruder…'

Hodges sniggered. 'Well we know how that turned out.'

'…which is an important piece of corroboration to a CCTV image. We do know there were a series of intrusions on the grounds of Colsham Manor in the last month.'

'Can we have another look at our intruder?' Mulholland asked.

'I was just coming to that,' Gillard said. He gestured to Townsend who clicked his mouse and projected an image onto the screen. It was the same picture that Gillard had already examined from the Lunds' CCTV. It showed a man in a long, light-coloured coat, with fair or possibly grey hair, and a small rucksack.

'He still looks quite a lot like that Pole, doesn't he?' Hoskins said.

'He does a little. There's one small problem with that,' Gillard said. 'Sikorsky wasn't in the country on the day this footage was taken, according to passport records.'

'So who is he?' Michelle Tsu asked.

'I'll tell you who he is,' Hodges said. 'He's an Albanian assassin, with multiple passports and a disguise kit, who has killed twice already, and may be about to murder two kids. Case solved!'

Hoskins laughed and shook his head. 'That's cobblers.'

'Lots of little things are niggling me,' Gillard said.

'Like what?' Hodges said.

'It would be neat to have just the one guy, obviously. But they don't look alike, we have this weird target practice at Colsham Manor which would be so amateur, and then there's something that's just come up via ballistics.'

They all looked to him expectantly.

'A different kind of ammunition was used to kill the Lincolnshire victim.'

'Have they found the bullet, then?' Mulholland asked.

'No, but ballistics think the exit hole in the guy's skull is too small for it to have been a hollow-point round. Rob, could you do the honours?'

Townsend turned off the lights and clicked the mouse next to the laptop. A series of images were displayed on the pull-down screen. Gillard continued: 'On the left is Peter Young's skull, where you can see that there is extensive damage to the skull on exit. On the right is that of Mr X, our mysterious body in Lincolnshire. By contrast the exit hole is only big enough to accommodate a pencil.'

'Could the difference have been accounted for by the difference in range at which the shot was fired?' Mulholland asked.

'It's a good question. Ballistics sent off the images to Sheffield University to analyse the differences. They would need to examine both bodies to be sure, and Young's has been released for burial, but their initial conclusion is that we are talking about different ammunition.'

'I'm no expert,' Michelle Tsu interrupted, 'but you can use different types of ammunition in the same gun, can't you?'

'Yes, generally,' Gillard replied. 'Trouble is, Lincolnshire Police are still trying to find the bullet that killed Mr X,' Gillard said. 'They've dug up all the sand within a five-yard radius of the body, and they haven't found it. Nor the casing, for that matter. If the perpetrators were professionals, they would have dragged the body 10 or 20 yards after shooting him, and with the action of the tide and the shifting of the sand, the bullet would be lost for ever.'

'But whatever the result of that, surely one gunman can have more than one gun?' Michelle asked. 'So the crucial question, of whether it was the same finger on the trigger, still isn't answered, is it?'

'Absolutely,' Gillard responded. 'We mustn't make assumptions.'

Colin Hodges shook his head. 'Look, it seems obvious to me that we've got two gangland-style executions, admittedly more than 200 miles apart, with the same modus operandi, and the same ethnic target, an Albanian. I would have thought that it's common sense that we're talking about the same perpetrator or group of perpetrators.'

'Yeah,' added Carl Hoskins. 'Especially when you think there's a third Albanian angle, in the abduction of the two orphans, at the site of which we just happened to find some more hollow-point ammunition. That kind of ammunition is rare. This cannot be a coincidence.'

Gillard raised his hand. 'We're in the realms of conjecture here. The only way I think for us to get to the root of it is to investigate exactly who Peter Young, and David and Amber Lund actually are.'

'I thought we had already tried that,' Hodges said.

'This time I'm looking for answers in Albania,' Gillard said. 'I'm flying out on Tuesday.'

–

News that it was Zerina Moretti who had abducted the Lund children rather than some deadly Albanian mafia changed the nature of the enquiry. Gillard rang Geoff Meadows, who had already heard the news directly from Sophie Lund. 'That's a great relief,' he said. 'It's so much easier now that we're sure the kids aren't in danger, and that they are in Italy instead of Albania. Hopefully we can have this wrapped up within the week.'

'Do you know where she lives?'

'Moretti's husband comes from quite a wealthy family. He has an estate down in the south, near Bari, sort of on the ankle of Italy's boot, but there's also a flat in Rome. I got the details from Dag and Sophie, so I'll fly off tomorrow. I've got good contacts in the Italian police, which should help. However, it's the social workers who will have the court order, while for me as a PI it will be a matter of persuasion. I must have left 25 messages on the woman's phone, so it's not going to be easy.'

Gillard laughed. 'Well, good luck with that.'

'One thing, Craig, as you're going to Albania, I'd appreciate you checking in at the orphanage where Sophie first met the kids. I'll need all the original documents they can let us have.'

'It's already on my list,' he replied. 'Let's keep in contact.' He hung up.

Chapter 22

Thursday

Peter Young's funeral took place at St Nicholas's Church, Thames Ditton on a still but bitterly cold mid-February morning. Several hundred mourners shuffled into the twelfth-century flint-built church, far more than the narrow pews could contain. Claire Mulholland, playing the role of a miscellaneous mourner, was in plain black trouser suit and modest heels. She stayed towards the back, leaving Gabby Underwood in uniform as the official presence, soaking up the many pointed questions about the lack of progress in the case. Claire's role was more subtle. Though she didn't really expect to find a professional hit man turning up in a tuxedo, she wouldn't have been surprised if the assailant had wanted to see the last few moments of his target's earthly existence.

The entire practice of Hampton, Deedes, Gooding seemed to be there, and some of Laura Diaz's Peruvian family too. The two daughters, pretty honey-skinned creatures of seven and eight, wept inconsolably as the coffin, a pure white casket with golden handles, was borne into the church. Six identically dressed male pallbearers carried him solemnly by.

Around her she heard whispered comments by elderly ladies about the tragedy for the family and the anguish of the children. And each conversation ended with the same question: 'They haven't caught him, have they?'

Mulholland recognised Peter's foster parents near the front, supporting each other in an embrace. In the eulogy it was noted that Eric and Margaret Robinson had Peter baptized, and instilled in him the regular habit of church attendance. The priest made much of Peter's escape from the war in Kosovo, and noted that he appeared not to have any living relatives who could attend the funeral. Claire watched carefully to see if heads turned to look at anyone who could be a relative.

After moving tributes from work colleagues, the coffin was carried out into the churchyard. Though there were no buds to be seen on the many trees that surrounded the almost rural-looking graveyard, there were plenty of snowdrops and winter flowering shrubs.

She was too far back to see the burial itself, only the sashes and the white surplice of the priest breaking through the mass of dark clothing. Peter Young had come from mystery. Now he was being returned to the soil. A sharp gust of wind brought flurries of snow which flecked the grass.

Mulholland wished now she had brought an overcoat and, beginning to shiver, hurried away from the mourners towards the lich-gate. As she did so she passed two tall, shaven-headed men in leather jackets watching the funeral. Their dark eyes, sallow complexions and sharp cheekbones gave them a Mediterranean look. They spoke softly enough to each other, but it was still obvious to Claire that the language was not English.

Albanian perhaps?

Gillard had promised Sam that he would cook her Sunday lunch. When he left her asleep at 6.30 a.m. that morning he had stolen downstairs in his dressing gown and slippers, quietly extricated their largest casserole dish from a stack of cookware, placed in it the half shoulder of lamb he had bought on Friday from the farm shop in Colsham village, then padded outside onto the patio to tear off three bay leaves from a shrub in a pot. It was almost the only thing in the garden that still had leaves. He dug out a bottle of what he called Millwall fighting wine and emptied the whole thing into the dish, tossing in an entire bulb of garlic and a stock cube. He gently sliced up half of an aubergine, two onions and a large potato, before adding them too. He set the oven on low, put in the casserole and gently closed the door. It should easily be done by two o'clock, when he hoped he'd be finished at the incident room.

Now washed, shaved and showered, he was just towelling himself dry, congratulating himself on not waking Sam in all of the kitchen activity, when the landline rang. Five shrill rings later it was a sleepy Sam who wandered naked into the bathroom with the cordless handset. 'DCI Greycoates for you, all the way from sunny Lincolnshire,' she smiled, beautifully dishevelled hair cascading around her shoulders.

'Trevor, what can I do for you?' Gillard asked, watching Sam's rear as she shuffled back towards the bedroom.

'Sorry to get you up so early on a Sunday,' Greycoates said, not sounding sorry at all. 'But we now know who our dead body on the beach is.'

'I'm all ears,' said Gillard as he dried his testicles.

'We think his name is Jetmire Kogan, 22, a Starbucks barista of Albanian nationality who lived in east London. He's been missing for two weeks.' Greycoates permitted himself a small laugh. 'And as I thought, he was gay.'

'Who have you spoken to so far?'

'His employer and his landlord yesterday and now, finally, his flatmate. I'm heading down to Ilford now to interview her. I'm sure you'll have plenty of questions for her. So fancy meeting me there, 10.30?'

'Okay,' Gillard sighed. That would put paid to lunch, then. He took the details and hung up, then went in to break the news to Sam, who was now snuggled under the covers again. 'Best make it dinner, love,' he said.

She smiled up at him and gently slid the covers from her body. 'What time do you have to be there?'

He told her. 'Traffic across London shouldn't be too bad on a Sunday.'

'Good. I fancy a meaty breakfast,' she said, reaching under the towel.

–

Avril Lennox had shared a studio flat with Jetmire Kogan. The place, though tidy, bright and modern, barely looked big enough for one person. An open-plan kitchen, a tiny bathroom and a bed-sitting room. Gillard and Greycoates sat side by side on one of the two settees and wondered how the arrangement worked.

'It's simple,' said Avril, a short 20-something woman with blonde hair and a lip ring. 'Both beds are fold-down. You're sitting on his, and that one is mine,' she said, pointing to one on the other side of a bookcase. 'It only works because I work nights in the warehouse at Tesco and he worked days at Starbucks. We'd often share meals – breakfast for me, supper for him, and vice versa. It worked really well. He didn't mind curry for breakfast or Weetabix for supper.'

The logistics of Jetmire Kogan's life sorted, Gillard wanted to know about the man himself. 'He was kind and gentle, a real darling,' she said. 'I can't imagine why anyone would want to kill him.'

'You mentioned that he was gay,' Greycoates said, apparently unable to stay off the subject. 'Did he have a boyfriend?'

'I don't think so. He wasn't into the scene as such. He never brought anyone home. To be honest I think he was nursing a broken heart from some time before he even came here. The man he loved died, and I don't think he was ready for anything else.'

A slight sneer slid across Greycoates's face. Gillard turned away and flicked through the meagre collection of documents that Kogan had left behind. An Albanian passport, a British residency document, a UK driving licence and a bundle of envelopes and photographs in a shoebox.

'Did you know anything about his parents or family?' Gillard asked.

'He didn't talk about his family. I think his parents were dead; there may have been some distant relatives perhaps. He used to say that he hated his country and wished he had been born somewhere else. It was his dream to come and live in London, and he didn't mind that he had no money and lived squashed in a box with a wee Scottish lassie like me. He was just happy to be who he wanted to be. And, boy, he could make good coffee!'

'So we're not sure who the next of kin is?' Greycoates asked.

'No.'

Gillard looked through the shoebox. There were dozens of letters, presumably in Albanian, with neat handwriting and the kind of flourishes that would only be used between the closest of friends. He had no doubt that they were love letters. He found several photographs of two young men, perhaps in their late teens, with their arms around each other's shoulders. One undoubtedly was Jetmire.

While Ms Lennox went into the kitchen to make them her version of a good coffee, Gillard turned to Greycoates. 'I'll leave you to sort out a DNA match from personal items here. I know it's your case but I'd like copies of the personal correspondence and photographs, to see if they can shed any light on the connection with the missing Lund children.'

Greycoates nodded. 'I hear that you're off to Albania on Tuesday.' He gave a wry smile as he got up to leave. 'Fucking dump of a country by all accounts. Gangsters, drug dealers and car thieves. I hope I don't read about you lying dead in a ditch.'

'Thanks for the encouragement,' said Gillard. 'One more thing. You haven't found his phone, have you?'

'No, but the landlord and his employer both gave me the same number. I'll get on to the service provider tomorrow.'

'Can you copy me in on any text messages and emails, and all the metadata? I'd particularly like to know any Albanian numbers that he contacted.'

'I'll also be looking at the location data,' Greycoates said.

'I don't think you'll get much. Assuming the guy that murdered him was a professional, he'd either have ditched the phone before dragging the victim off to Lincolnshire or at least kept it turned off.'

Greycoates nodded. Avril came in with the coffee. Proper wide cups, foaming cappuccino and a little sad face in the froth.

'That's for Jetmire,' she said. 'I didn't know him for long, but it was long enough to know that he didn't deserve what happened to him.'

Book 2

DCI Gillard's early-morning flight from Heathrow arrived promptly in Tirana. As the jet descended through a thick layer of cloud, snow-strewn mountains came into view, partially encircling the city. The sprawling Albanian capital was veiled in haze, but patches of snow could be seen in the thousands of narrow strip fields around it.

Detective Sergeant Besin Tokaj was there to meet him in arrivals. An upright grey-haired man in his 60s, Tokaj gripped Gillard's hands in both of his. 'So good to meet you,' he said, in heavily accented English.

The Albanian told Gillard that he didn't need to stay in the hotel that had been booked for him. 'Stay with me and my wife Leila,' he said. 'You are my guest.' This was the first but not the last example of what Gillard later learned was called *besa*, Albania's medieval code of honour that pledges hospitality to strangers. Tokaj led him through a slushy car park to his aged white Renault and told him they were heading south of the city. 'Now, Craig,' said Tokaj, looking across at his passenger. 'If I understand correctly, the children who were abducted are now in Italy. But you still have a murder to solve?'

'Two murders, actually.' He explained about the Lincolnshire murder, and then reminded the Albanian about the murder of Peter Young, the details of which he had sent to him the previous week. 'We have two ethnic Albanians, both executed in Britain within a couple of weeks of each other. They are not related, from the DNA tests we have done. However, the man killed in Lincolnshire does seem to be a close relative of the abducted children. It seems to me that the answer to why all this happened must lie in Albania.'

'Perhaps,' Tokaj said. 'However, Albania's police force is still constructing a DNA database. The project began in 2014 with the help of the Polish police, and still continues. The taking of DNA samples from suspects is still haphazard and irregular, and not everyone is well trained. We have had a few embarrassments, so must rely on more traditional investigatory methods.'

'I feared that may be the case,' Gillard said gloomily.

They were still on the outskirts of Tirana when Gillard noticed a half-built four-storey building. At the top were three mannequins hanging by the neck from concrete reinforcing rods. 'Whoa! Please stop the car,' Gillard asked. Tokaj did so, and the British detective jumped out to take a closer look. 'Why are these here?' he asked.

'Ah. This is an old Albanian custom,' Tokaj replied as Gillard got back in the car. 'You will see this on every new property, on many farms and gardens. It is just a little piece of superstition, from the time when Albania was a simple rural economy. We call them monkeys, and they are talismans of good luck.'

'Good luck? The mother of the missing children was terrified to discover one near her home in the UK.'

'Different cultures,' Tokaj shrugged. 'Trust me, many rational and educated people still believe in the evil eye, and this is seen as a protection.'

Gillard didn't hide his scepticism.

'Do you walk under ladders?' Tokaj asked.

'Not if someone's balanced on top with a pot of paint,' he chuckled.

'Well, most Albanians will not go underneath a ladder at all, and I think this is also common in your country.

Listen, my wife broke a mirror a year ago. That is seven years' bad luck, a belief going back to Roman times.'

'I hadn't realized it was that old.'

'Yes, and so is the antidote.'

'There is an antidote to the bad luck?'

'Yes. You must take all the pieces of the mirror, every last little sliver, and bury them under moonlight. Leila did this.'

'Is it working?'

'I'll let you know after the end of the seven years,' Tokaj said with a chuckle. 'But this little piece of witchcraft was very important to my wife.' As he drove along he then pointed up at a newly constructed apartment block. 'Look, another monkey. You see, we all believe.'

It was true. On the journey he spotted dozens of scarecrows and mannequins. These so-called monkeys were on construction sites, allotments, porches, fence posts and even petrol stations and car wash businesses. He realized what he had seen in the woods around Colsham Manor and in Geraldine Hinchcliffe's conservatory was an everyday part of Albanian culture.

As Tokaj drove out of the capital into a small town, Gillard's attempts to talk about the case were met with smiles and polite evasions. 'There is no hurry,' Tokaj replied. 'For best results we do things the Albanian way. First we eat *drekë*, lunch.' The detective's home was 20 miles south of Tirana, a charming and partially renovated cottage with an attached smallholding, still buried under a blanket of snow. He trundled Gillard's wheeled suitcase up the icy path and in through the front door, then called out for his wife. Leila Tokaj was a tiny woman who greeted them wearing a headscarf and soon retired into the kitchen, from which delicious smells emanated.

Gillard got out his briefcase and passed across copies of all the passport, nationality and residence documents of the two murder victims. 'This is all I have. Peter Young arrived in the UK as a 15-year-old without any documentation, and a year later was given official Right to Remain as a child refugee from Kosovo. His original name was Pjetër Ardian Cela. However, the authorities in Pristina have no record of him, so he may be from Albania.'

Tokaj shrugged. 'Maybe, there were many such cases.'

'In the case of Jetmire Kogan, we have an Albanian passport and a date of entry on a tourist visa with an address in Pogradec. He overstayed on the visa, but had managed to get a flat share and work in London without too much difficulty.'

'What are the other papers?' Tokaj asked, pointing to the remaining stack.

'These are the adoption papers for the Lund children, from a Roman Catholic orphanage in Shkoder. At some stage I would like to check them.'

'Then this is what I suggest,' Tokaj said. 'Pogradec is a long way to the east on bad roads, even by Albanian standards.' He laughed. 'So if it's just to check the given address of Jetmire Kogan, it seems easier for me to just phone a colleague there. The orphanage is much closer, we can visit this afternoon.' He went to a cupboard and brought out a crystal bottle from which he poured healthy measures of a clear liquid into shot glasses. 'You must join me in a glass of raki,' he said. 'I am afraid I may be judged a very bad Muslim, but in Albania we say better that than be judged an inhospitable man.'

Unwilling to appear rude, Gillard sipped at the liquid, which seemed even fiercer than the one Meadows had given him. Tokaj drained his in one, then emitted a happy sigh.

'That is strong,' Gillard said.

'Strong enough to do the job,' Tokaj said.

Or stop you doing the job, Gillard thought. 'Speaking of the job, I would also like to interview Vjosa Dragusha, who I understand is in Tarduz prison,' he said.

Tokaj laughed and shook his head as if Gillard just requested the impossible. 'The Butcher of Fier is a sick man. He is also not someone we can just demand to see without going through the proper channels and formalities,' he said.

'I thought that was something you would do for me,' Gillard said. He had already made the formal request, via Alison Rigby and her counterpart in Tirana. This was perhaps an example of the difficulties that Geoff Meadows had described in dealing with Albanian officialdom.

'Why do you want to interview him?'

Gillard explained about the Dragusha symbol branded into the neck of the Lincolnshire murder victim, the forehead of the doll found at the pottery and sprayed onto Sophie Lund's stable. 'He would know whether any of his underlings were involved in this.'

Tokaj nodded. 'I'm sure of it.' At that moment Leila Tokaj came in bearing a large pie and a generous salad. After serving up slices of the lamb and cheese pastry to the two men, Mrs Tokaj withdrew. 'I have, of course, put in the requests. But there is no certainty,' he said, bending to eat.

'Perhaps then you can answer a more general question for me, Besin,' Craig said. 'I have read much about the Dragusha family, their links with the 'Ndrangheta mafia group in Italy and so on. What mystifies me is why so many of the prominent members of this crime family still appear to be at large.'

The Albanian detective smiled as he chewed. 'In Britain, as I understand, no one stands in the way of the police doing their duty. Criminals are caught, convicted and go to jail, yes? A B C.'

Now it was Gillard's turn to smile. 'If only it were that simple. Yes, you describe the process, but there are all sorts of checks and balances on police power, on prosecutors and even on the judiciary. Evidence found by prosecutors must be shared with the defence, even if that evidence might undermine the prosecution case. Forensic advances mean it is rarer now for innocent men to go to prison, but lapses in procedures mean it is still very common for guilty men to walk free.'

Tokaj nodded. 'Albania is very different. There are centres of power which must be respected. This was the lesson of the anarchy. The government has power, yes. But the people have power too, and powerful families cannot be ignored. The police and the judiciary are careful about what they can and cannot do, if you understand me.'

Gillard mopped up the last of the gravy with a piece of bread, something he had just watched his host do on his own plate. 'So the Dragusha clan are one of the powerful families, I presume?'

Tokaj shrugged. 'No one is above the law, they understand that. They know what is expected of them: stay subtle, don't brag about your power, don't kill the innocent, make your trouble abroad or at least within your illicit business rivalries.'

Gillard nodded. 'Okay, I see where you are coming from.' He thought for a moment. 'If the Dragusha clan was trying to kill two innocent orphans, then for the authorities that is surely overstepping the line.'

'For sure,' Tokaj said, wiping his mouth with a napkin and standing up. 'If that is all they are. Now, we have to visit the orphanage to find out.'

–

The drive north to Shkoder was on busy but poorly maintained roads, with potholes the size of washbasins. While Tokaj drove cautiously, they were constantly overtaken at high speed by daredevils, most of them for some reason driving black Mercedes. Yet they also passed donkey carts and saw ancient agricultural machinery still in use. 'In Albania there is only one rule for the road,' Tokaj laughed. 'Everywhere, you always have right of way.'

After two hours they reached the medieval town of Shkoder, perched in the foothills of the Albanian Alps and overlooking a lake which formed the country's northern border with Montenegro. 'There are the Accursed Mountains,' Tokaj said, pointing to the peaks ahead of them, the snowfields glinting in the watery sun.

'That is where Teto Zerina's family comes from, according to Sophie Lund,' Gillard said. 'So maybe that is where Amber and David grew up.'

'Ah, up there they are very tough people,' Tokaj said. 'That is the land of the blood feud, where old scores are never settled but carry on, generation after generation.'

'Why there?'

'It is tribal land, jealously guarded. They have never trusted the police to deliver justice.'

Gillard had expected the Orphanage of the Blessed Saints to be some crumbling medieval building surrounded by gardens in which wimpled nuns would smilingly watch children at play. In fact it was in the basement of a high-rise block hemmed in by busy roads near the centre of Shkoder. The orphanage was modern though quite small, with only three or four children visible. An even bigger surprise was that the Sister Giulia they had arranged to meet was an attractive young woman in jeans and an Oxford University sweatshirt who had a tattoo of Christ on the cross visible on her forearm. She greeted them in accented English. 'I am happy to meet you both,' she said, offering them coffee and pastries.

Gillard reminded her of the details of the case.

She nodded. 'I wasn't here when the two children came to us. I was still training. However, we have the full records in the church offices across the way.' She led them out of the building and across a murderously busy dual carriageway to a much more traditional ecclesiastical building. 'The original orphanage was demolished to make way for a wider road,' she said.

Sister Giulia led them through the nave of the Roman Catholic church and into a cramped office at the back occupied by an elderly but upright nun in a plain brown habit. They exchanged words in Albanian, and Tokaj joined in. The young woman unlocked an ancient wooden cupboard and drew out a hefty leather-bound ledger. She and the older nun pored over it and located the entry they were looking for. 'See. This is the formal record for Dretim and Albana Goga. It means that the signatory has seen their birth and baptismal records, and the death certificate for both parents.' She pointed to the four columns in which ticks had been made as the other nun nodded her head.

'Do you keep copies of those documents?' Gillard asked.

Sister Giulia spoke briefly to the other nun, and got a reply which from her nodding head appeared to be in the affirmative. The older woman walked over to a bookshelf and selected a modern file folder, which she laid down on the desk. She looked through the ring binder, unclipped the rings and then brandished two photocopies. 'Birth certificates,' she said.

Gillard and Tokaj looked at them. To Gillard's eye they looked not dissimilar to a British birth certificate, with a signatory and in this case a counter-signatory which gave it an official imprimatur. From other ring binders Sister Julia produced copies of the certificates of baptism and the death certificate of the father. Tokaj nodded, indicating that everything appeared to be in order. Gillard was not so convinced.

'This only proves the relationship between the various pieces of paperwork. It doesn't prove David and Amber Lund are Dretim and Albana Goga.'

Tokaj looked bemused. 'You think these children were presented as orphans with false paperwork?'

'It's possible, surely. There have been many cases in the UK of children being trafficked from abroad with false paperwork.'

'Of course that is very common, but in this case you said that the adopting family came here to Albania, and the paperwork shows that.'

Sister Giulia nodded her agreement. 'It is all quite clear.'

'Yes,' Gillard said. 'The motivation of Sophie and Dag Lund is I think above suspicion. What I'm saying is that if it is true they were orphaned because of the murder of their parents, David and Amber may have been sent away for their own safety and presented here already with false identities.'

'We know nothing of this,' said Sister Giulia, handing them photocopies of all the documents they had seen. Gillard and Tokaj expressed their thanks and returned to the car.

'Regrettably, what you describe was a very common occurrence, especially in the time of chaos,' Tokaj said. 'In Albania it is not uncommon for children to be passed within the extended family, perhaps if the mother is working or if the parents travel abroad. The ties of kinship are very broad, more so I think than in your country.'

'Maybe we will get an answer to this in the next day or two,' Gillard responded. 'The children are with their aunt, or a woman who claims to be their aunt, in Italy.'

'This is the Zerina Moretti you mentioned?'

'Yes. For many days after the abduction she claimed to be frantically worried about the children, but then we discovered that it was she who picked them up from school, took them on the ferry to France and drove down into Italy.'

'So the children are safe.'

'We are assuming so. After all, she has spent weeks with them over Christmas, and they know her well. We really need to talk to her, because if anyone knows the whole story, she does.'

On the way back from Shkoder, Tokaj took Gillard to meet his senior officers at the Tirana police headquarters. This was a modern glass and steel building which could have been in any European city. The British detective shook hands with at least 20 different officers, male and female, most of them dressed in smart blue shirts and trousers with a red shield on their shoulders. Many seemed genuinely delighted to meet Gillard, and had questions about Britain and policing in the UK. One or two expressed themselves to be devotees of British crime authors from Agatha Christie through to Ian Rankin. After a bewildering hour and numerous cups of strong black coffee Gillard was taken into an office decked with memorabilia and the flags of the police and Albania itself. Behind a large desk sat a dapper middle-aged man with a full head of dark hair and a worried, hangdog expression. Tokaj introduced him as the Director for Serious and Organized Crime. He had an impossible name, but urged Gillard to call him Mr Zok, an acronym built from his initials.

Mr Zok spoke no English, but was eager to show the progress that had been made against gang violence and organized crime in his country. There were books of cuttings, photographs and reports, all of which were laboriously summarized for Gillard first in Mr Zok's Albanian, and then in Tokaj's translation. Pride of place was given to a photograph of half a dozen officers in combat gear and balaclavas standing over the restrained body of a large middle-aged man. Only the smiles visible through the mouth vents of their face masks showed that this was a moment of triumph.

'The arrest of the Butcher of Fier,' Tokaj translated, 'ninth of April 2014. A proud day.'

Gillard looked at the officer, who positively beamed. 'That's great,' he said. 'Do you have DNA samples for most of your prominent gangsters?'

After hearing the translation, Zok insisted on arranging a visit to the adjacent forensic unit, which had been modernised with the help of the Polish police service. 'This is just one of the improvements we have made in order to be ready, one day, to join the European Union,' Tokaj said, summarizing his host. 'We now exceed all required standards.' Certainly the units looked modern, well staffed and appeared to be under the direct control of the police themselves.

'I would like, if I may, to interview this man,' Gillard said tapping the photograph of the Butcher of Fier. 'We are trying to make connections to murders in the UK.'

Zok permitted himself a brief smile and spoke to Tokaj who translated: 'He says he can't promise anything.'

Gillard opened his briefcase and brought out some stills captured from the CCTV at Colsham Manor, showing the fair-haired man that Amber had spoken with. 'Do you know this man?' he asked Mr Zok.

The Albanian policeman gave a nervous laugh and then turned to talk to Tokaj. 'He says he cannot be sure, but there is a marked resemblance. But it would of course be very unlikely.'

'Sorry, unlikely to be whom?' Gillard asked.

'The Angel of Death.'

–

Gillard had many more questions, but his phone rang. It was a call from Geoff Meadows, so he excused himself to the corridor to answer it.

'Craig, we've got a bit of a snag,' Meadows said. 'I'm here at the Moretti estate in Italy with two social workers from Surrey and an Italian policeman, and it's pretty much deserted. The husband is in Rome, and the gardener, who seems to be the only person here, thinks Zerina Moretti left yesterday. He was happy to show us around, but there is no sign of her car or the kids.'

'That's unfortunate.'

'The social workers are off to Rome to interview the husband, but I think that is likely to be a waste of time. Look, as a private investigator I can't officially request the phone tracking data from the Italian police,' Meadows said. 'You would have to do that. I've left a message with Claire Mulholland, but I thought I'd just let you know where we stood.'

'Claire will be on top of this, I'm sure,' Gillard replied. 'I'm happy to pass on any location data that we get.' He thanked him and hung up.

Mr Zok's office door was now closed and there seemed to be some meeting taking place. Gillard tracked Tokaj down in reception, where he too was on the phone. The British detective had to wait ten minutes for him to hang up.

'So what do we know?' Gillard said, hoping to hear more about the Angel of Death.

'That was the local police in Pogradec. The address given on the passport is a derelict apartment in the south of the town, not fit for habitation. It is unclear whether anyone has been living there in the last few years. The name Kogan is not a common Albanian name, and my colleagues in Pogradec could not find any trace of a Jetmire Kogan in their records, nor through the regional registrar of births and deaths.'

'So another set of false documents?'

'It looks that way.' Tokaj led him back to the car.

As they pulled out of the police car park Gillard asked: 'Now, about this Angel of Death.'

Tokaj blew a loud raspberry. 'I think Mr Zok was joking.'

'He doesn't look like a comedian.' Gillard recalled Mr Zok's anxiety-creased face. He would make a perfect sad clown, especially with that name. 'So why do you think he was joking?'

'Well, for one, it wasn't a very good image. But more importantly it doesn't seem very likely that such a man, the Butcher's right hand and probably the most wanted man in Albania, would be interested in going to Britain to frighten some children.'

'All the same, I'd like a DNA sample of him, if you have one,' Gillard asked. 'We're hopeful that one of the murder weapons will turn up, or some fresh evidence at Colsham Manor, to try to get a match.'

'I'm glad you didn't ask Mr Zok that,' Tokaj said.

'Why?'

'It's a sensitive subject with him. Soon after the arrest of the Butcher of Fier, we took a DNA sample from him and raided some of the properties of the Dragusha family to get as full as possible a sample of DNA from the family.'

'That was an enterprising act.'

'Yes. It was in the early days of the new forensic lab. Mr Zok's predecessor believed we could crack organized crime completely by sidestepping what had been the major problem, which is that nobody had the courage to stand up and testify against them. Instead we would use the very latest forensics to put these criminals at the scene of the crime without needing witnesses.'

'I'm getting the impression that something went wrong,' Gillard said.

'Yes. It was at the first major prosecution when the new DNA evidence was to be used. The prosecutors had all the test paperwork which connected several leading members of the Dragusha to the slaying of a rival in Elbasan. The Dragusha's defence lawyer demanded an independent retest of the samples, and because of the newness of the forensic service, the judge granted it. The samples were couriered under high security to a laboratory in Switzerland. Its conclusion was simple: it wasn't human DNA. The case collapsed, of course, and the credibility of the new forensic system was dramatically undermined.'

'So the Dragusha have the power to infiltrate the forensic service?'

'Yes. But they were even cleverer than that. I didn't tell you what type of animal the Swiss found the samples were from.'

'Pigs, donkeys?'

'No. That might have reflected badly on the Dragusha. No, the DNA samples were from an imperial eagle.'

Gillard blew a sigh. 'That's amazing. Straight from the Dragusha calling card, the triple-eagle emblem.'

'Exactly. What this said to the world was: "Yes, of course we committed this crime. The mark of the eagle is on it. But you cannot catch us."'

'So where did they get eagle DNA?'

'From Tirana zoo. It was a terrible place anyway, no one cared properly for the animals, and it has been closed down since 2015.'

'This is all highly depressing,' Gillard said.

Once they returned to Tokaj's house there followed another large meal, with copious raki. Gillard, never much of a drinker, wondered what his alcohol unit count for the day had been. Over dinner, after Leila had joined them, the British detective once again tried to chivvy some detail about the Angel of Death from Tokaj. But he shook his head. 'I will not discuss such things in my house.'

Leila picked up on her husband's discomfort and asked him something in Albanian. He replied briefly and her eyes widened in alarm.

Gillard was quick to apologize. 'I'm really sorry, I didn't mean to cause upset.'

Tokaj waved away his concern. 'You weren't to know. Just another of our superstitions. Name something and you give it power. Discuss it enough, and the ghost becomes real.' He took a big draught of the raki and wiped his mouth with the back of his hand.

'So, Craig, tomorrow I take you to meet a real Dragusha and you can see for yourself.'

Eventually the British detective was shown into a tidy little room in the eaves of the house, with a traditional carved wooden bed, blankets and freshly starched gingham sheets. He dreamt of fierce, sharp-eyed eagles circling over his body.

Wednesday

The next day dawned bright and cold, with a hard easterly wind. Detective Sergeant Besin Tokaj drove Gillard south to the town of Fier for a planned meeting with one of the members of the Dragusha clan. He said he had been working on this rendezvous for over a week, and it was clearly something that required considerable diplomacy. The Albanian was quiet on the drive, and seemed a little nervous. It was only in the last few minutes before their arrival that he turned to the British detective and spoke. 'Now, Craig, I caution you, that this may not come off. In Albania you must have low expectations and then be pleasantly surprised, not the other way around. He is not obliged to turn up, and there is nothing I can do to make him.'

'What is the guy's name that we are meeting?'

'My contact couldn't tell me. He will probably be a *kryetar*, a mid-level boss. It was the best I could do.'

'I'm in your hands, Besin,' Gillard said. He felt his frustrations grow as it became clearer that the relationship between the police and organized crime in Albania was as awkward as that between brothers in a broken family.

By noon they were approaching Fier, a busy city choked with traffic. The Albanian detective drove them to the southern suburbs. They slid past a series of tired grey blocks of flats, similar to those built all over Britain in the 1960s, their slab concrete dark with water stains. Here the balconies were stacked with firewood, and tattered awnings projected out over the sunward side. Washing lines dangled between adjacent windows, and headscarved women called down to children playing beneath. The land between the blocks was litter-strewn waste ground, dotted with abandoned cars, fridges and builders' rubble, through which gangs of ragged kids roamed. Despite this evidence of poverty and neglect, most of the cars that Gillard saw being driven were new, top-of-the-range models: BMWs, Range Rovers, Porsches and, overwhelmingly, Mercedes. He didn't want to fall into the prejudice that Greycoates had shown, but equally it didn't seem possible that the average Albanian could afford the average Albanian car. He'd read the National Crime Agency reports: Albania was the destination for thousands of Europe's prestige cars, stolen to order in highly sophisticated operations and shipped out in containers. As he had often explained to victims of car theft across Surrey, your stolen Jag, Merc or BMW is, as likely as not, heading for a small mountainous country of which most of us know nothing.

As they moved further into the estate, there were two or three car wash joints, with black four-wheel drives and luxury saloons being given very careful pressure-washer treatment by groups of fit-looking young men in tracksuits. These youths all sported identical number two shaven hairstyles, and seemed immune to the bitter cold. One young man was on his hands and knees, under the watchful eye of a big man in a dark suit. Amid a sea of litter and broken glass, he was vacuuming out with forensic care the inside of an almost-new black Porsche Cayenne. Funny how some types of cleanliness matter and some don't, Gillard thought.

One tough-looking youth eyed them as they approached, his hand absentmindedly straying to an ominous bulge at the back of his waistband.

'One of the lads there is packing a handgun,' Gillard said.

Tokaj nodded as they cruised slowly past him. 'It's normal. All these people are Dragusha, and most are armed. Don't worry, we are expected.'

Towards the end of the street they passed what looked like scrap yards, fenced in with vertical planks, old bedsprings and sheet metal. Mildewed caravans, roving dogs and ragged children brought to mind the worst of the traveller sites Gillard had seen. But what he had not seen before was a wizened old lady in a headscarf shepherding a gaggle of turkeys with a stick. Finally, at the end of a long, straight, unpaved road they arrived at a two-storey industrial building. It was painted entirely black, including the window panes, as if it was some Mancunian nightclub. As the car pulled up, two large leather-jacketed figures in sunglasses detached themselves from the shadows and strode over to the driver's side where they barked some kind of instruction. Tokaj obligingly lowered the window, showed them his police card and spoke to them briefly. 'We go in now,' he said to Gillard.

As one of the toughs turned to direct them, Gillard noticed an intricate circular razor cut in the hair on the back of his head. It was the triple-headed eagle of the Dragusha clan, beautifully rendered.

The two cops emerged from the car and were escorted into the building. Faint red bulbs lit their path into its stygian depths. They were shown to a table in a large but deserted bar. There were plastic flowers in a vase on the table. One of their escorts brought over a clear bottle with some liquid inside and two shot glasses. 'Raki,' he said to Gillard with a grin.

Looking around, Gillard reckoned that this was indeed some kind of nightclub. There was lighting equipment and a false ceiling, and a stage at the far end with a steel pole in it. He could guess the kind of entertainment that might be offered here. His own flesh and that of Tokaj had taken on a lobster sunburn hue under the lighting.

'Now we wait,' Tokaj said, sinking his first raki.

–

It was an hour later and the raki was almost gone when Gillard began to lose patience.

'I think we've been stood up,' he said, getting to his feet. 'I think it's time to leave.'

There had been no activity in the building, and only the distant booming sound of rock music from a vehicle outside to break the monotony.

'I don't know if we can go yet,' Tokaj said.

'We need their permission to leave?' Gillard asked. It was 1.15 p.m.

'Having asked for an audience, it would be an insult, and if you want their cooperation you had better not insult them. Trust me on this.'

'Besin, you have to understand that I have two murders to solve and only a limited time here. I need to show that I am making some progress.'

The Albanian detective hauled himself to his feet. 'Have it your way,' he said with a shrug.

Gillard felt his way out of the darkened bar into the afternoon sunshine. The two sunglassed henchmen they had seen earlier were leaning proprietorially against Tokaj's car, their arms folded. As the British detective marched towards them, Tokaj called out something in Albanian, which even to Gillard's untrained ear had a pleading intonation. He got a fierce barked response from one of the men, while the other flipped up the flap of his jacket pocket and rested his fingers on the clearly visible butt of a pistol. 'They say we have to stay,' Tokaj said.

The stand-off was broken by the ringing of Gillard's phone. The display showed that it was Mulholland.

'Hi, Claire, how are you doing? Better than I am, I hope.'

'Maybe. We've had the results of the DNA analysis for Jetmire Kogan. He's the older brother of David and Amber, not their father.'

'Pretty much as we expected,' he said.

'Well, I've won my own bet too.'

'Ah, is this the hunch you wouldn't tell me about?'

'Yes. Peter Young has disappeared.'

'But he's dead and buried!'

'Dead, yes, but no longer buried. The grave is empty.'

Chapter 23

Gillard turned away from the two henchmen and steadied himself against the wall of the nightclub. 'What are you telling me? Wasn't he buried just three days ago?'

'Yes, and sometime last night he was dug up from his grave. The coffin is missing.'

'I don't believe it.'

'You'd better, because he has definitely left Surrey. In fact, as far as I can work out Peter is on his way to you.' She gave a small laugh.

Gillard eyed the two Albanians who were staring at him, then walked a few paces away to be doubly sure he could not be overheard. He couldn't guarantee they didn't understand English. 'I really don't get this, Claire.'

'You may recall that I told you Peter's widow requested an open coffin. That's a fair amount of extra work for the funeral home people, with embalming and so forth. That got me thinking, so I went along to see the process, which was fascinating.'

'I'm sorry, Claire, I still don't see where all this is leading. Why would anybody want to steal Peter Young's body?'

'I spent a long time with Laura Diaz, Peter's widow. Both Gabby Underwood and myself felt that she was under some kind of extra pressure, something in addition to the grief she was feeling. We were also pretty sure that she knew something about Peter's background that she wouldn't tell us. My guess is that he is part of an important Albanian family.'

'A crime family?'

'That would be my guess. Anyway, the reason I had to keep all this to myself is because I have rather broken the rules and permitted a small indignity to take place with Peter Young's body.'

'I can see you're enjoying this, but go on.'

'When the funeral home technicians briefly stepped out of the room, I took the opportunity to secrete a smartphone into the crotch of his trousers. That phone is linked to mine with an app originally designed to track cheating spouses. But the upshot is that his GPS location is copied to me, and I can see him on a Google map. Peter Young was flown out of Gatwick first thing this morning and arrived in Tirana around ten, local time. Judging by the speed, he was then taken in a vehicle on the highway heading south from Tirana. I've texted you the latest coordinates from an hour ago, before the signal went dead.'

'That was an absolutely brilliant piece of intuition, Claire. Were you tempted to ring the phone?'

She laughed. 'Yes, that might have been hilarious. But I've taken enough liberties as it is. I just thought that as we were having such trouble working out who he really was, the easiest way to be sure is to see who claims him as their own. So on that score I now pass the baton to you, Craig.'

'I have my own troubles at this end,' Gillard said. 'I arranged to see a member of the Dragusha clan, but nobody of any significance has turned up and we are basically being kept here at their pleasure. I've never experienced anything like it.' He ended the call and checked his watch.

Tokaj came up to him. 'You're looking worried,' he said. 'What's happened?'

That was the moment when Gillard realized that he might not be able to fully trust his Albanian liaison officer. 'It was a lead we were working on that just led to a dead end.'

Tokaj shrugged. 'In Albania that is the fate of most leads.'

They were kept kicking their heels for another three hours until finally, in the cold February dusk, they saw a pair of headlamps in the distance coming towards them at sufficient speed to create a dust trail. The two henchmen turned to watch and their bearing stiffened, proof that they were finally about to meet their contact. A black Mercedes-Benz S-Class coasted to a halt and three men emerged. Two were stone-jawed henchmen, fresh from Hollywood central casting, with the same uniform of black leather jacket, dark trousers, cropped dark hair, sunglasses and white Nike trainers. The third was more slightly built, bespectacled and neatly bearded. He was formally dressed in a black trench coat, black tie and white shirt. His shoes were highly polished. He could have been an after-dinner speaker for some provincial British dinner club.

'Gentlemen, I apologize for keeping you waiting,' the man said in American-accented English. 'You can call me Qendrim.'

Tokaj introduced Gillard, and there followed a short conversation in Albanian.

'I told him that you have some questions about a matter in Britain. He says he will help if he can. We are to go with him.' Tokaj and Gillard were ushered into the rear of the car, while Qendrim took the front passenger seat. The driver had the same triple-eagle design shaved into his suede-like hair at the back. The two toughs followed in another car, which had been parked around the corner. Black and highly polished, of course.

Once the car pulled away and there was a rumble of noise inside, Tokaj inclined his head towards Gillard's. 'This man is quite senior,' he whispered. 'We have done well. He is the numbers man, connected by marriage to the upper levels of the Dragusha clan.'

'That's good,' Gillard responded. He had thought carefully about what to ask, and then leaned forward between the two front seats. 'Qendrim, I'm not here to interfere in your business operations,' he said. 'But I have some questions about two murders in the UK. If you can shed any light on these I will be grateful.'

Qendrim turned in his seat as the car increased speed and left the squalid estate behind. 'In Albania we don't like questions. But you are from abroad and you are our guest, so we will indulge you. What are these murders?'

'Last month a young architect of Albanian origin called Peter Young, originally Pjetër Ardian Cela, was shot dead in his office. Just a few days later, on a beach 200 miles away, a second body was found. Jetmire Kogan, who was also Albanian, was executed at point-blank range, and had a brand on his neck that matched your own Dragusha emblem. That same coat of arms was found on what you would call "a monkey" at a place called Colsham Manor, about 30 miles from where the architect was murdered, and where two Albanian orphans were later abducted. We also found near Colsham Manor hollow-point ammunition that matched that used to kill Peter Young.'

Gillard waited for a response, but there was none forthcoming. Qendrim directed the driver and they took a turning onto another road going through the suburbs of Fier.

'Qendrim, if your family is not involved, then you should know that your family's coat of arms is being used by someone else.'

'So what is your question?'

'Was your family involved in the murders of Peter Young or Jetmire Kogan?'

'I do not recognise these names,' Qendrim said, reaching into the glove compartment. Gillard felt Tokaj stiffen in the seat next to him, but when Qendrim turned back to them he had in his hand a bag of boiled sweets, not a gun.

'Have one,' Qendrim said, helping himself to a sweet, which he rattled around in his mouth. The cloying scent of artificial lemon filled the car.

Gillard tried variations on the same questions for the next ten minutes as the car was driven sedately through the town. As they approached a roundabout, the traffic already circulating gave way to let them on, and a few minutes later the driver exchanged greetings with a traffic policeman who gave them priority at a junction. Ten minutes later they pulled up outside a hotel in the centre of town. Black cars and people carriers were already parked two deep outside, and on the pavement dozens of fit, sharply dressed men with Dragusha haircuts, sunglasses, black suits and ties acted as doormen, parking valets and security guards. The only women, also in black, were handling large wreaths. Two of the doormen walked out to their car and escorted them to the hotel.

'What's all this about?' Gillard asked Tokaj. 'This looks like a wake. Why have we been brought here?'

'I think he's trying to make a point,' the Albanian policeman replied. They were shepherded into a crowded ground-floor restaurant, where more than a hundred men of all ages were seated at six long tables, filled with food and drink. There was a separate salon to one side where a group of about 20 women were taking their places at an oval table.

Though the meal was clearly underway, Qendrim found places for the two policemen near the top table. Waitresses were summoned, and extra plates of salad, meat, fish and bread were brought to them. Qendrim made some kind of introduction of his police guests to those on either side, and Gillard found himself shaking hands right across the table, as well as with those on either side. No one spoke any English, though one man, whom Tokaj described as a senior local police officer, spoke some Italian which Gillard could vaguely understand.

'*Il fratello morto è vissuto a Londra*,' the officer said. 'The brother who died lived in London. *Povero Pjetër*,' the officer added.

Gillard turned to Tokaj. 'Pjetër, that's Peter Young's original name.'

The Albanian policeman nodded. 'He also said that he was a good boy, never in any trouble, unlike some of his brothers.'

Gillard finally realized. 'We're at Peter Young's wake,' he said. 'They stole his body from his grieving widow to bring it home.'

'Albanian blood is thick,' Tokaj answered.

'They have the nerve to bring us here to participate.' Gillard shook his head in incredulity. 'These guys really think they can do anything, don't they?'

Tokaj gave him a knowing smile. 'They can, and they do.'

The cogs were turning inside Craig Gillard's brain. If Peter Young was Pjetër Dragusha, then his murder was almost certainly intended as a blow *against* the Albanian mafia, not a crime *by* them. The only alternative explanation, that he had in some way crossed his own family and been rubbed out by them, didn't square with the Dragusha going to so much trouble to retrieve his body.

Either way, Peter had clearly known for a number of years that he was on the death list. *Povero Pjetër*, poor Peter. Abroad, unprotected, the black sheep of the Dragusha clan. Claire Mulholland had been spot on when she reckoned that Laura Diaz knew that her husband was living on borrowed time.

But who would have the nerve to kill a member of the Dragusha? A carefully planned professional hit with hollow-point bullets surely signified some other mafia gang. If so, then the Lund children and Jetmire Kogan might also be members of that rival clan, and like Peter Young, the soft unprotected underbelly. If this was indeed a bitter historic feud, it seemed clear that instead of targeting the mafia bosses, the victims were those most defenceless in each of the warring families.

Finally, with a glass of raki in his hand, Gillard looked to the top table, where the 16 most senior Dragusha men were seated. 'Who are they?' he asked Tokaj.

Gillard was shushed as a burly moustachioed man at the top table rose to speak. The detective considered trying to take photographs with his phone, but realized that this might enrage the attendees, even though some were themselves taking pictures. It is one thing for family to take a picture, quite another for a police officer from another country, here on official business.

The man gave a short speech, with pauses during which heads nodded among the assembled throng. Glasses of raki were raised and they all stood to toast those at the top table. Tokaj warned Gillard not to clink glasses with his neighbours, as that was not appropriate at a funeral. Taller than most of those around him, the British detective now had an unrestricted view of the top table.

Someone had just in the last few minutes arrived to fill the final vacant chair. It was someone he recognised. A slender, almost androgynous man with a halo of fine blond hair and a neatly trimmed beard and moustache. He was wearing a very well-tailored suit and had numerous rings on his fingers. Gillard could not be absolutely sure, but it looked to him like the so-called angel that Amber Lund had talked to on the lawn of Colsham Manor. It was the same face that had been caught on CCTV a few days later on the night that Sophie Lund had chased an intruder on horseback and ended up face-to-face with the chief constable.

This was the man who had told the little girl: 'Tell them. I have come for vengeance.'

This man was almost certainly a murderer.

The Angel of Death.

—

After what Tokaj had said, Gillard assumed the Albanian police had no DNA sample from this man. Perhaps it would be a good idea to try to get one for himself. As the meal came to an end he tried to make his way towards the top table. He didn't tell Tokaj what he was doing, and the Albanian policeman trailed after him. Such was the crush of guests, and the hearty backslapping and embracing amongst the big men at the top table, that he couldn't make much progress. The Angel slipped from his view. That still left the cutlery and glassware that he had used on the table, and Gillard kept it in focus. He was just three feet away, within reaching distance, when a young waitress gathered up the plates and cutlery from dessert. He cursed inwardly, now focusing on the chair that the man had used. The top table had leatherette chairs, rather grander than the cloth-covered seats which filled the rest of the restaurant, and somewhat worse for the retention of hairs. Nevertheless, Gillard was able to take an unused paper napkin, dip it in a water jug, and then wipe the backrest of the chair that the man had sat on. Having done so, he folded it and put it in his pocket, ready to send back to the UK for DNA testing.

It was late evening when Gillard and Tokaj took a taxi back to their car outside the nightclub. As they drove back to his home, the Albanian policeman became a little more open about the Dragusha family. 'I couldn't tell you anything at the restaurant. That policeman sitting opposite you, you remember? He works for them. He may understand English even though he claims he cannot speak it.'

The Surrey policeman found he was struggling to adapt to a world in which even the most minor of police procedures needed to be checked against the sensibilities of a powerful mafia. Tokaj in turn admitted that he had been very circumspect early on with Gillard's investigation because it had often happened that foreign policemen caused problems by behaving as if they were at home.

Besin Tokaj said that some of his superiors, having heard what Gillard's intentions were, would have been happiest to have him taken on various minor and irrelevant excursions to waste his time, until he realized that the case could not be solved. This was not Tokaj's way. 'I may be a realist, but I'm not without ideals. I want to see justice done. I want to see these animals behind bars. If you can get it done, I will try to help.'

Gillard thanked him, and returned to an earlier question which Tokaj had previously ignored: 'who hates the Dragusha family? And who is powerful enough to strike against them by murdering their one innocent and vulnerable brother, living a blameless life in a faraway country?'

It took half an hour for the Albanian detective to list all of the enemies who would want to destroy one of Albania's most powerful mafias. 'But wanting to do it and having the capability are not the same thing. The Xhakja clan from Shkoder, the Bregus and the Allushi, and of course the Banda e Lushnjës, all have rivalries with the Dragusha. There are low-level skirmishes, the occasional murder but not outright war. It may be about blood but it is also about business, and fixing the boundaries between the two. Things have not always been so diplomatic. The

Dragusha wiped out one of their biggest rivals, the Banda Kreshnik, three years ago. The Kreshniki had a lucrative trade in car theft from Germany, Holland and Britain. They have lost all that now. Almost the entire family are dead.'

Gillard's head was spinning at the prospect of delving into the intricacies of internecine mafia politics. 'In the end, this may all be beyond the scope of my investigation. But I would have thought that the Dragusha would want to help find out who killed their youngest brother.'

Tokaj demurred. 'They would prefer to do it themselves. It undermines their honour and machismo to seek the help of the police. I think in inviting us to join the funeral meal the Dragusha wanted to show the pain they have suffered. But they are too proud to put it into words for you.'

Gillard guessed that Peter Young, or Pjetër Dragusha as he now knew him, had wanted to escape the violence, the rivalries and gang criminality of Albania, to come to Britain for a new life. Despite the fact his family was already 'in blood', undergoing a murderous vendetta with the Kreshniki, they had reluctantly accepted his decision. They may perhaps have helped him establish a new identity, knowing that there was still a chance he would be targeted. In life they granted him some freedom, but in death he was pulled back firmly within the enfolding family. Gillard had one further conclusion.

'We already suspected it was the Dragusha who were skulking around Colsham Manor, advertising with their symbols and night-time conversations that they knew who the Lund kids really were. That message was lost on the adoptive parents, but someone else in that rival family must have known. Could it have been Jetmire Kogan? He was a member of the same family.'

'Or maybe it was somebody else,' Tokaj said. 'Someone senior.'

'So once we solve the mystery of who Kogan and the Lund children really are, then we know which family is involved in a feud with the Dragusha.'

Tokaj smiled. 'Dear Craig, you make it sound so straightforward. Finding out will only be half the battle. Tomorrow morning, I will show you some of those battle-fields and some of the fallen. And only then I will tell you about the Angel of Death.'

–

Even though they arrived back at Tokaj's home at midnight, there was another substantial meal awaiting them. Gillard was too polite not to finish the fish dish that Leila Tokaj set in front of him, and was happy enough with the thick crusty bread and astringent white wine that she served with it. Besin Tokaj translated Gillard's many compliments and Leila grinned with pleasure, fiddling with curls of her hair under her hijab. After the wine came more raki, but Gillard really did demur this time.

A little while later, as he sat in bed with his phone, ready to email Mulholland, he heard the sound of springs from next door and Leila Tokaj's muffled moans of plea-sure as her husband made love to her. He thought what a tough calling it was to be an Albanian policeman. The temptations of bribery ensured the easy life were always there. But to do it right, to single-mindedly pursue justice, was dangerous.

He looked down again at his phone. In the last few minutes of the restaurant meal, he had managed to take a selfie of himself with the bent Italian-speaking cop, by then much the worse for drink. He'd taken three pictures, and in only one of them achieved his goal, which was to capture in the background between them the blond man, Amber's angel.

He attached the picture to the email and pinged it off to Mulholland with a short message. Britain was an hour behind Albania, but he was still surprised to get a quick response. He read it twice but still couldn't believe it. Gillard had stopped worrying about the Lund children because he assumed they were still safely with their aunt in Italy. But Claire Mulholland had upset all his assumptions.

Italian immigration confirms Zerina Moretti left the country with two children yesterday. They took the ferry from Brindisi to Vlorë, Albania, arriving 11.55 a.m.

He couldn't believe this turn of events. What possible reason was there for an aunt who claimed to be protecting the children to bring them back into the heart of danger? It crossed his mind that perhaps this woman was not who she claimed to be, though the familial DNA links between her, David and Amber seemed clear enough. Those poor children could have no idea what danger they were being exposed to.

Gillard forwarded the text to Geoff Meadows, then turned over in bed, unable to sleep. There was something wrong here, something he couldn't understand. This just didn't make any sense. If the woman was being forced to bring the children back, surely she would have been able to leave some message with Sophie Lund or even to have returned one of the many calls that he himself had made. Sleep evaded him, and he got up and went to the window. He slid up the sash and let the cold night air pour into the room. The Dragusha gang seemed to have a massive gravitational pull: not only able to retrieve their own dead from exile, but to draw their enemies to them, even the children of their enemies. Their reach was prodigious.

Surely it was not possible that Zerina Moretti was a member of the Dragusha. But what other explanation could there be? If it was dangerous for them in Surrey, it was surely deadlier here.

Gillard thought back to what Sophie Lund had told him about Amber's nightmares. The *shtriga*, the female vampire who feasted on the blood of children. Albania was such a male-dominated society, the women always consigned to the shadows. In Albania's *Kanun*, a woman was dismissively described as 'a sack, made to endure', worth 'half a man, or a dog'. Underestimating women was ingrained into Albanian society, but he realized he and his fellow detectives had fallen into the same trap with Teto Zerina. She'd already shown she was ingenious and determined in the way she had kidnapped the children. But what if this woman, this kindly aunt, was actually a killer too?

Chapter 24

The main cemetery in Fier is draped over a wooded hill south-west of the city. It is surrounded by a high stone wall as if the many thousands of the departed might otherwise escape into the world of the living. With an early start for the long drive, Detective Sergeant Besin Tokaj and DCI Craig Gillard were there at 9.45 a.m. They parked on the street and entered at the main eastern gate. The flower sellers' displays were fresh and bright, droplets of moisture standing out on the petals. There were huge bunches of chrysanthemums and lilies, roses and carnations, and there were also wreaths of laurel and holly. As Gillard gazed at the fragrant display, a stocky, ruddy-faced woman waddled out to encourage him to buy. Much to Tokaj's surprise, he did: a big bunch of mixed chrysanthemums and lilies. He also wrote a note on the label he was provided.

The two men strode purposefully along the main avenue which divided the cemetery into two, heading towards the crest of the hill. The British detective was surprised to see Roman Catholic, Eastern Orthodox and Muslim graves side by side, a seemingly random cohabitation that might perhaps have proved elusive in life, and in many countries even in death. The Muslim graves, each with a crescent moon engraved on the headstone, were generally aligned to the east. They tended not to have images of the dead, while the Catholics and Orthodox had not only photographic inserts but, on some of the grander tombs, inlaid mosaic images of the interred. As they ascended the hill, the headstones and graves became more elaborate, glossy granite plinths, with delicate marble angels and crosses of every type and size. The lack of moss, mildew and grime proclaimed not only the care with which the deceased were attended to, but the relative recency of their departing. Deaths from the 1980s and 1990s, especially of the youthful, seemed to dominate. The grief of riven families was writ large and often across that hallowed hill.

Towards the top, family mausoleums dominated, and Tokaj stopped to point out the resting place of one particular crime family. 'This is the resting place of the Kreshniki,' he said. It was a sizeable basalt monolith, with a huge crescent moon above. Beneath it, engraved in gold, were the names of the many deceased listed in columns like First World War battle casualties. Gillard looked, but could find no reference to anyone called Jetmire.

Underneath was a quote.

> *Vdekja do të të gjejë edhe sikur të fshihesh në kështjellat e ndërtuara të forta dhe të larta. Kur'ani 04/78*

'What does it say?' Gillard asked.

Tokaj sighed. 'It is from the Koran. "Death will find you even if you hide in fortresses built up strong and high."'

'That's a bit depressing.'

'What do you expect? Almost every Kreshniki man is dead from Dragusha bullets. An entire bloodline eradicated. And, actually, I do not mourn a single one of them.' He pointed to the list of names and dates.

'This is where it really started: 1997.' Tokaj read out an unpronounceable name. 'This man set up a pyramid scheme, which made the Kreshniki rich. He promised a 15 per cent return each year from investing in new hotels that were supposedly being built for tourists along the Mediterranean coast. The middle classes loved the idea, and piled in their life savings, hoping to see Albania open to the world. Some hotels were built, and the first investors got their payments, but without knowing the money came solely from the new deposits. Word spread, more people bought in, and there were more new deposits to fund the interest on the old ones. The news always seemed good, even though none of us ever seemed to meet the foreign tourists who were supposedly flocking in. Of course, like all such things, it collapsed when there were no new suckers like me to put in their savings.'

'You were affected?'

'Yes. Leila and I had a smart flat in Tirana once. But we lost it in the pyramid scandal. You would probably say that we were naive to trust such a scam, but we had just emerged from decades of dictatorship under Enver Hoxha, and we were blinking like trusting rabbits in the bright, optimistic light of democracy. So when the government said these schemes were fine, Albania will join the world, we believed them.'

Gillard stared at the policeman. 'That must have been terrible.'

'We are Albanian, we know how to suffer.' He turned back to the list of the fallen. 'The wife of one of the senior Dragusha crime lords lost a million when the pyramid collapsed. This man,' he tapped the same golden letters. 'He fled to Switzerland. The Dragusha poisoned him, and he died in slow agony.'

'That was the start of the feud?' Gillard asked.

'Yes and no. It had been low-level before, but this marked an intensification. The Kreshniki retaliated within a month, killing a *krye*, a boss. Two of them rode past his car on a motorcycle, and the pillion passenger shot him through the window. The man who died was the brother of the Butcher of Fier, and in the time of anarchy the Butcher was able to flex his muscles without restraint. Look at all the victims: 1996, 1997 three times, 1998. It goes on.'

Gillard stared at the list of the dead. 'There's a little cluster of deaths just three years ago. And isn't that a female name?'

'Yes. That was a notorious incident, even by Albanian standards. And this is where I tell you about the Angel of Death. At the funeral dinner last night you may have noticed one man with a crown of blond hair at the top table.'

'I did,' Gillard said. 'I recognised him from the CCTV in Surrey. So that really is him?'

'Yes. I didn't expect him to be there. He came late, with his personal bodyguard, and he left early. That is his way. His name is Nikolai Dragusha. He is the third son of the Butcher, but he is known as the Angel of Death. He is a very cruel man, even by the standards of the Albanian mafia. He enjoys killing, not just because it is a family duty. It gives him pleasure. He made it his duty to kill every Kreshniki.'

Gillard felt his blood run cold as a realization came to him. Could Amber and David Lund turn out to be part of the Kreshniki? Is that why they were targeted?

Tokaj continued. 'He had already killed many Kreshniki, but eventually tracked down a cousin of the instigator of the pyramid scheme. This cousin, Armend Kreshnik, may well have been involved in the gang's car theft operations, but he was not a major player.'

'Armend?' Gillard said. 'I think Sophie had said the children's father was called Armend.'

'It's a common name in Albania,' Tokaj said. 'Anyway, the Angel left symbols as a warning for the family, to terrify them, because that is what he likes to do.'

'That fits with what we found at Colsham Manor too.'

'The family got guard dogs, but they were poisoned. They hired an armed guard, a former policeman, but he turned out to be an informer working for their enemies. One night, when the family were asleep, Nikolai and his men slipped into the house using a key supplied by the security guard. They tied up Armend and made him watch as they did unspeakable things to his wife and teenage daughter, before slitting their throats and leaving them to die like beasts in a slaughterhouse. He would have done even worse to Armend Kreshnik, had it not been for the sound of sirens.'

'The police came?'

'The Kreshniki were not without power and, yes, the police were on their way. But fearing the Dragusha, the police in Fier were neither so fast nor so stealthy that they might prevent the crime or catch the perpetrator.

That is the nature of their compromise with evil. So, hearing sirens, the Angel of Death settled for firing five bullets into Armend Kreshnik and left him for dead. Amazingly, he survived for several weeks. He was in the hospital under guard, but in the end succumbed to his injuries.'

Gillard's mind was racing. 'Were there any other children in that family?'

'I do not think so, which is why I doubt that the abducted children are Kreshniki. There was a rumour that one male Kreshniki escaped. If so he must have fled abroad, because they are just women now, that family. A few old women, hiding in the Accursed Mountains. No men, no fighters. But the Dragusha are merciless. They do not have the honour of their ancestors. That is what new money does to ancient peasant virtue. It corrupts, it cheapens. Blood survives but honour is washed away.' He made a noise of disgust in his throat and turned away to spit.

The Albanian policeman led Gillard further up to the very apex of the hill, and the grandest mausoleum of them all. This was a rococo Catholic edifice, each memorial slab adorned with weeping cherubs and grieving angels, each gilded in gold and silver. But above it was a jet-black basalt carving, 15 feet high, growing from the roof of the mausoleum. From the back it could simply have been an enormous squat angel, but from the front the figure was much clearer: the triple-headed eagle, wings outspread. At this early hour its shadow fell long and dark over many of the surrounding graves. Chiselled into its breast was the single word: Dragusha.

'This is the empire of blood,' Tokaj said, spreading his hands. 'Built on violence, extended through marriage, cemented by corruption and bulwarked by fear.'

Gillard walked around the corner. There was a new grave within the Dragusha complex, still buried under fresh flowers, the notes and the labels neither smeared by rain nor yellowed by sun and time. He moved a vase of sunflowers so that he could see clearly the headstone, fresh and new.

Pjetër Dragusha.
1990–2018

The photograph embossed into the stone was one Gillard recognised. It was one half of a picture of Peter Young and Laura Diaz standing side by side that he had seen on the widow's sideboard. She had been carefully excised from the picture, just as she had been excised from his life.

Gillard added his flowers to those already on the grave. The card he had written on one bunch read: 'On behalf of your grieving widow, Laura, and your children.' On the other he had written simply: 'We never give up. We will catch them.' He signed it on behalf of Surrey Police.

'Do you have any idea who actually killed him?' Tokaj asked.

'We've been through a long list of suspects. One of the strongest remaining theories is that Jetmire Kogan, or perhaps I might venture, Jetmire Kreshnik, killed him and was in turn executed himself.' What he didn't say was that it wasn't clear how Jetmire could have done this. He was pretty sure there were no males on the bus. 'Perhaps the Dragusha have their own idea who fired the gun?'

'Maybe they do, or maybe they don't care so long as they can keep killing Kreshniki,' Tokaj responded.

'I'd like to ask them,' Gillard said.

'Well, if that is your wish you may even be able to meet the Butcher himself.'

Friday

Tarduz prison squats on the side of an ancient mountain in the east of the country, a thirteenth-century Islamic fortress famed for its deep dungeons and the bitter cold that killed so many imprisoned there. Tokaj drove the aged Renault up a steep mountain road in its shadow, towards a tennis court-sized crimson flag bearing in black the Albanian double-headed eagle. Only on the final turn did any element of modernity intrude: the mobile phone mast on the highest tower, the thick coils of razor wire glittering like knives along the battlements, the security Portakabins outside the main doors.

A bitter breeze blew as they emerged from the car, scattering last year's leaves and flurries of litter, while the flag above snapped and roared in the wind. Uniformed guards stamped backwards and forwards within granite alcoves while Gillard's papers were exhaustively checked by bundled bureaucrats within wooden kiosks which boasted their own braziers and aluminium chimneys. Tokaj translated the various questions and finally they were shown through to a cavernous hall, which might once have been the stables of a mighty cavalry regiment. Blackened torch holders still clung to the walls more emphatically than the strip lights which replaced them.

A female guard of Soviet appearance, with hewn cheek-bones and wearing a greatcoat, arrived with a clipboard, torch and, ominously, a single surgical glove. She guided Gillard to yet another wooden shed. Once inside, and under her basilisk gaze, he was ordered to undress, each hesitation on his part met with the reply: 'Continue.' The final indignity, committed brutally with one cold finger within the glove, was the only thing that brought a smile to her face, though not to his. She ticked a box on a clipboard and left Gillard to regain his dignity.

Five minutes later, after Tokaj had emerged from the same shed, they were led through a long stone corridor, along which dozens of rusting iron doors glowered under the dim wattage of bilious rectangular strip lights. Finally they emerged into a courtyard containing a kitchen garden, and thence followed more medieval byways along the inside of a battlement, finally descending a flight of broad stone stairs. There the female guard, now in grey kidskin gloves, pressed a bell. After three or four minutes the door opened and she spoke with apparent submissiveness to an unseen man. Gillard and Tokaj were ushered into an antechamber where two more guards, with Albanian flag epaulettes on their greatcoats, led them through a sliding steel gate where two large unsmiling men in medical coats stood to meet them. One of the medics explained something in Albanian. 'We are now going to the recuperation lounge for the prison hospital,' Tokaj translated. 'He says we are not to tire out the prisoner.'

Finally they were led into a modern-looking apartment with a roaring fire in a grate, a large TV, a leather-covered three-piece suite and a picture window with views stretching miles into the valleys.

'Very nice too,' said Gillard.

On a wing chair in front of the fire, between a wheezing oxygen machine and a portable drip stand sat a bull-chested slab of a man dressed in prison fatigues. He had Slavic features, steel-grey hair and pale, deep-set eyes. In his glowering presence everyone in the room seemed somehow smaller and less substantial.

'My name is Craig Gillard, I am a detective chief inspector in Surrey Police—'

The man interrupted him, growling something from beneath his oxygen mask.

'He says he knows who you are,' Tokaj said.

The man hauled himself to his feet and stepped forward, a meaty paw extended. The IV lines tautened and the oxygen tube stretched until he pulled the mask from his face. 'I am Vjosa,' he rasped in guttural English. He swallowed Gillard's right hand in his own and shook it with surprising vigour. 'You look who kill my son?'

'Yes, but I hope you might be able to help me.' He explained about the murder of Jetmire Kogan on a beach in Lincolnshire, and how the police thought this was linked to the feud between the Dragusha and the Kreshniki.

He hadn't finished when Vjosa began to laugh, a deep belly laugh that soon dissolved into a bout of coughing that required him to sit and take a deep draught of oxygen from the mask. Eventually he quietened, and his pale eyes narrowed.

'There is no feud between Dragusha and Kreshniki. Because there are no Kreshniki.' He turned his baleful stare upon Tokaj and ordered: 'Explain him.'

Tokaj replied in Albanian, and then turned to Gillard. 'I told him that I already explained to you about the erasure of the Kreshniki crime family and the loss of their businesses to Mr Vjosa Dragusha and his family.'

'So you had nothing to do with the killing of Mr Kogan?' Gillard asked.

Tokaj translated, and the crime boss merely shook his head as he was dragged into another bout of coughing. Eventually it subsided. 'You work for me? You find killer, you are my friend. You are friend of all Dragusha.' He took a deep suck of oxygen. 'You get nosy, you ask too many questions about my business, then I am not your friend.' The eyes locked on to Gillard's. 'Not friend to you, not friend to your wife Samantha, not friend to her parents.' He broke off as if concentrating. 'In Kes-wick in Lake District, with nice dog, Boris. You understand?'

Gillard's throat dried up. This dying man, barely able to breathe, had the nerve to casually threaten his family and the power to know he would get away with it. Anger flared in the detective's heart, stronger now than fear. For a moment he didn't trust himself to speak, but an important question still needed to be asked.

'Have you or your family had anything to do with the threats made against Dag and Sophie Lund, and their two young children?'

'No.'

'Really? Your personal emblem was sprayed onto their home, and a man who appears to be your son Nikolai broke into their home.'

The big man's face darkened behind the oxygen mask, from pink to purple, and his eyes narrowed. He tore the mask off and leapt to his feet, shouting. The IV machine was jerked from its moorings and tipped onto the floor where it emitted an electronic shriek. One medic steadied the prisoner while the other turned to Gillard and said in English. 'Go, quickly.'

The crime boss's mottled, porcine face had threads of drool dripping from his thick dark lips. He said something slowly and emphatically in Albanian, and then suffered another bout of coughing. Tokaj, who had shrunk into the corner, guided Gillard out, translating the Butcher's words as he left. 'He said "If you haven't learnt to be afraid, we do free lessons for beginners."'

—

They drove back in silence on roads slick with sleet, flecks peppering the windscreen, accompanied by the rhythmic lament of the wipers. At Tokaj's house, Gillard was fed a hearty home-made soup, full of chunks of lamb and root vegetables. Leila seemed to pick up the gloomy atmosphere and quickly withdrew, leaving the two detectives, the remains of a bottle of wine and two glasses of raki between them.

'I'm shocked that he was able to find out so much about my family,' Gillard said.

'The Dragusha have money. They can get anything done. That is what you have to understand.'

Gillard's phone rang. It was Geoff Meadows. After a brief greeting Meadows said: 'I'm in Vlorë, just off the ferry from Italy, but a day and a half behind Zerina Moretti. She left her Hyundai in the ferry terminal car park at Brindisi, and boarded as a foot passenger with two children who, according to the passports presented, were her own. I don't have time or the contacts to try to find out whether she hired a car here or not.'

'Okay. We've got the details of her bank cards from the Italian police. If she has hired a car it should flag up at the credit card-issuing bank in Italy, but it may take a day or two to show.'

'That's too slow,' Meadows said. 'From what I remember there is no ANPR system in Albania, so even if we get the registration number we'd be struggling. Besides, someone may have come and given her a lift.'

'Any idea where she might be heading?' Gillard asked.

'Well, I tried to squeeze every bit of information out of Sophie Lund that I could about the aunt's background. She claims to have grown up in the Accursed Mountains in the far north, which is a day-long drive from here. Mrs Lund can't remember if any town or village was ever mentioned. It would help if we had the aunt's maiden name, which locals might remember. Without some kind of pointers we are going to be stuck. She could be staying in any kind of rural dwelling, and the area involved is enormous – hundreds of square miles of snow-covered mountains and barely passable roads.'

'Look,' said Gillard. 'I'll see if I can persuade the Albanian police to get to work on this, even though Mount Browne hasn't yet managed to file a European Arrest Warrant.'

'Well, that wouldn't be much help here anyway. Although Albania has an extradition treaty with the UK, they are not signatories to the European Arrest Warrant,' Meadows said. 'In the meantime I'm going to tap my own sources. I've hired a car and I'll be up in Shkoder for a couple of days, which is the nearest big city to the mountains. I'll let you know if I make any progress.'

'Okay,' Gillard said. 'Look after yourself.'

'Speak soon,' Meadows said and hung up.

He was wrong. They would never speak again.

Chapter 25

Late that evening Gillard sat in the tiny attic bedroom of Tokaj's home, watching the snow settling gradually in the garden. Something about his experience in the prison at Tarduz had made him miss his wife very much. They hadn't yet been married for a year, but their bond was deep. He didn't want to terrify her by mentioning the threats that the Butcher of Fier had made, but he realized he could hardly avoid the subject either. He rang her, and spent the first few minutes telling her how much she meant to him.

'That's very sweet, Craig,' Sam responded warily. 'Has something happened? Are you okay?'

Only a year, and he realized how well she could read him. 'I'm fine.'

'So have you found the missing kids? The TV news said they were in Italy.'

'They were, but now we think they're here in Albania.'

'Albania? Oh my God, their mother must be desperately worried.'

'I'm sure she is,' Gillard responded. 'And she doesn't know the half of it. I have to say that we are getting into some very deep water here, with a very nasty organized crime syndicate.'

'Oh, Craig. I knew something was up the moment I heard your voice. Please, please look after yourself.'

'I will. I'm big enough and ugly enough to take care of myself. But I'd just like you to take some basic precautions too.'

'Craig, what are you telling me?'

'I can't go into details, but I think it might be a good idea if you took a few days away, perhaps with your parents.'

She laughed. 'They wouldn't want to go. The weather is crap here. Besides, I'm not even sure I could get the time off at such short notice.'

'I don't know, a city break somewhere? It's just an idea. I'm going to get some of the uniforms to swing by every day or two, just to check you're okay.'

'Now you're really scaring me, Craig. Trust me with the truth, okay?'

So he did. He told her about his meeting with the Butcher of Fier, and the mention of Sam and her parents, even the dog. Full credit to Sam, she'd worked around the police for long enough to keep her cool. There was no panicked shrieking, just a sharp intake of breath at the other end of the line.

'But the guy, the one who made the threat, is in jail?' she asked, in a small voice. She was grasping at straws.

'Technically, yes. He's dying of lung cancer, but is not dead yet. So he is a patient in the prison hospital, but I think he has everything he needs to continue running his illicit businesses. When you're as powerful as him, in jail, out of jail, it makes no difference. He's too sick to come and go as he pleases anyway, but he has every other freedom. Look, don't tell your mother…'

Sam laughed. 'Well, obviously. She would have hysterics.'

'If you have any worries, ring Claire. She's got the clout she needs.' As he hung up he had a horrible premonition. Something was about to go very wrong. He could hear Tokaj snoring in the other room. Like the slow, deliberate sawing of wood.

Saturday

Craig was awakened by the deafening ring of Tokaj's land-line from the other room. It was still dark, just after three in the morning. His heart was already beating hard when the Albanian policeman rapped twice on his door and came in with a grim expression on his face. 'You need to get up,' he said. 'I have some bad news.' Tokaj was already wearing a shirt and trousers, rapidly buttoning them up as he talked.

'What happened?' Gillard asked, throwing off the covers. Please don't let it be Sam, he thought. Please, not Sam.

'There has been an accident involving your colleague Mr Meadows. We should go.'

'Oh Christ. Is he okay?'

Tokaj shook his head. 'From what I heard, I would expect the worst. It looks to have been a head-on collision with a truck on the main road between Berat and Fier.'

That was several hours away to the south. Gillard persuaded the Albanian cop, whose breath still smelt of raki, to let him drive the first stint. The old Renault wasn't a four-wheel-drive but had snow tyres, which proved essential in making their way onto the main road.

Tokaj gave directions, but spent most of the time on the phone to headquarters, while Gillard squinted through the driving snow and the wailing wipers to pick out a path in the beam of the headlights.

After a 20-minute call, Tokaj hung up and turned to the British detective, who was waiting in a line of cars to pass a snowbound lorry. 'The car fell down an embankment and almost slid into a reservoir. They can now confirm your colleague was found dead inside the vehicle,' Tokaj said. 'I'm sorry, Craig. I know that you knew him well.'

'I did. And his wife, Maddy, and their three grown-up kids. He was one of the good ones. Smart, fearless when necessary, but also cautious. A very good brain, and lots and lots of experience. Experience we need.'

'Only God knows why these things happen,' Tokaj said.

'I only hope we can put it down to God,' Gillard said, wrestling with a wheel to get traction on a particularly slippery slope. He had no idea if these roads were gritted. He had only seen one snowplough, half off the road in a particularly deep drift, its crew standing around a glowing brazier in their high-vis jackets, toasting with raised plastic cups every vehicle that passed.

It took three hours of careful driving to reach the site of the crash. Gillard was surprised that this particular piece of road had been where Meadows met his end. It was a relatively modern carriageway, a fast sweeping curve with good visibility. On the generous hard shoulder, which overlooked an enormous U-shaped reservoir, there were three police vehicles, a recovery truck and a badly damaged fuel tanker.

Tokaj got out and went to speak to one of the officers. Gillard, scarecrow-like in borrowed woolly hat and wellingtons, was introduced to them, and then ignored. Seeing how badly stoved-in the front of the lorry was, it looked to Gillard to have been a high-speed impact. Meadows's car was on its roof, a hundred yards down the slope towards the water, and from the path carved through the snow seemed to have made most of that journey upside down. His stomach turned over when he contemplated what Meadows would have felt in those last few desperate moments. The British detective felt for his torch and made his way down carefully through partially flattened weeds, mud and slush to Meadows's vehicle, a Citroën C4. The roof had been squashed on one side and the windscreen smashed. The driver-side door was gone, presumably cut away some time earlier to get him out. Snow had already begun to accumulate on the underside of the roof, stained pink from the blood it had absorbed. Gillard squatted and shone the torch around the crumpled interior. The remnants of the airbag, cut to allow the body to be removed, hung down like a shroud and the seat, upside down and above him, was ripped. On it there was hair and blood and burn marks, the latter presumably from the emergency service's cutting equipment. But it was the other side of the car that interested him. In the passenger-side window, on the lowest part, there was a neat, round hole with a margin of impact frosting around it.

A bullet hole.

Mentally setting the car back on its wheels, Gillard realized this hole would have been through the highest part of the window, the bullet fired from a level somewhat higher than the car. Perhaps from a motorcycle. Lying sideways in the snow so as to shine the torch right round the squashed interior, he looked for other bullet holes. He could see none. He was just getting back to his feet when Tokaj and one of the uniformed policeman, a tall man with a high-vis cap, came up to him.

'Did they notice the bullet hole?' he asked Tokaj.

They hadn't. The three of them went round to the other side of the vehicle to look at the passenger window from the outside. The tall officer waved his arms around and said something. 'He says that is not a bullet hole,' Tokaj said. 'He thinks it is a fragment of metal coming from the inside of the car during the crash.'

Gillard crouched by the hole, removed his glove, and carefully inserted his little finger into the hole. 'This is too smooth – it indicates a higher velocity than accident splinters,' he said. 'Besin, are they treating this as a crime scene?'

The Albanian liaison officer shrugged. 'I don't think so.'

Gillard stood and brushed the slush and snow from his freezing hands. 'Where is the door they removed to get him out?' He looked up towards the recovery truck on the hard shoulder.

After a brief conversation the tall officer pointed the other way. The door was about 20 yards away, down by the lake edge. Gillard made his way down. The bent and scorched metal, barely recognisable as from a vehicle, had been tossed here, shattering the ice which fringed the reservoir. The British detective gingerly made his way to the water's edge, and in doing so almost trod on a pair of broken sunglasses. He picked them up by the tip of one arm. They could have been Geoff's. Nearby was a notebook, its pages already stiffened by ice, which probably had also fallen out of the driver-side door pocket. Gillard picked it up and slid it into his coat pocket.

He carefully flipped over the door so he could see the inside. Although the entire window frame was twisted, the plastic moulding which formed the armrest assembly inside had simply folded in two, forming a white stress line in the plastic cast. Holding the torch close, Gillard could see a bullet hole through the plastic. Tipping the door back again, there was no exit hole through the exterior metal panel. A metal rattle indicated the bullet might still be trapped inside. With freezing fingers he prised off the interior moulding in its entirety. There, rolling around in a metal well above the door sill, was a bullet. The only plastic bag he could find to put it in was one which contained the spare button on his coat. That would have to do for now.

As he stood to retrace his steps the snow came in harder, driven by an icy wind that tore across the lake. Making his way up to the road, he saw that the police were now crowded around some kind of mobile food van, from the inside of which a sleepy-looking man with a moustache was dispensing hotdogs and coffee. Having persuaded this poor man to get up for them, the uniformed police were now cheerful, laughing and joking as they sipped their scalding drinks.

'What have you found?' Tokaj asked.

For a moment Gillard was unsure what to say. What he had done was a complete crime scene disaster, breaking almost every rule about contamination. Clearly the local police had no intention of pursuing this as a crime, but at least he had satisfied himself that Geoff Meadows didn't die in an accident. He was targeted. If he gave up the bullet to the local police, then he would have no evidence. On the other hand without the entry and exit points he had seen in the vehicle, possession of a bullet would prove nothing. He would have to trust them.

'I've got proof that somebody tried to kill him,' Gillard said. He lifted up the plastic bag. 'I found this inside the driver-side door.'

The tall policeman held out his hand and Gillard handed it over. They locked eyes for a moment before the cop scrutinized the find. The British detective was beginning to feel that he was regarded as little more than a nuisance.

'From the angle, and the fissure in the seat fabric, I expect we will find the bullet passed through the victim's leg,' Gillard said. 'May I see the body?'

Tokaj translated the request, which had the expected effect of dampening the spirits of the police officers. 'I don't think they're enthusiastic about pursuing your theories at this time of night and in this weather,' Tokaj said. 'I will make a phone call in the morning and see if I can get my boss to talk to theirs. But for the rest of tonight, we should sleep. I have booked us a room in a hotel in Elbasan, and we can see Mr Meadows in the mortuary tomorrow morning.'

Gillard nodded and thanked him. The snow had stopped by the time they reached the ancient fortress city, and the hotel, opposite a floodlit medieval tower in the tourist district, turned out to be modern and comfortable. A long hot shower soon thawed him out. He had mentioned nothing about discovering Meadows's notebook. He was too exhausted now to pursue it, but he was looking forward to seeing what leads his old colleague was pursuing.

Too late for Meadows though. Dying here on a lakeside in Albania, he was merely another body on a shore.

Chapter 26

Saturday morning dawned bright and sunny. Gillard and Tokaj drove the short distance from the hotel to Elbasan hospital. The British detective had already emailed PC Gabby Underwood, his most trusted family liaison officer, and asked her to break the sad news to Meadows's family. He would follow up with a personal phone call to them later in the day. But for now, Gillard had to inspect the body.

The mortuary was a clean and modern facility. A female technician led them into the examination room where a body bag was already lying on a stainless-steel table. She unzipped the bag, and Gillard was able to confirm the formal identification. There were significant head injuries, bruises all over the body and, as he had expected, a long, shallow and bloody puncture wound through the right thigh.

'You were right,' Tokaj said. He got out his phone and took a series of photographs of the injury. They thanked the technician and made their way out.

'My guess is that the gunmen knew his car and were waiting on a motorcycle at the roadside for it to pass,' Gillard said. 'They went after it, and presumably would have tried to overtake to get the easier driver-side shot. But my guess is that Geoff spotted them and accelerated hard. They only got one shot off, and that from the passenger side. But they were lucky. It hit him in the right thigh, and at that moment he lost control and strayed into the path of the oncoming truck.'

'Not the most professional hit job,' Tokaj said as they sat together in the car. 'They usually strike in traffic jams in towns, when the target is a sitting duck.'

'But who did it? Who, apart from you and me, knew he was coming?'

Tokaj shrugged 'I don't know. I didn't even know what hire car he had.'

'Somebody did. Besin, I think this can only mean one thing.'

Tokaj looked puzzled.

'It's simple if you think about it. Geoff must already have met a source or contact with connections to Zerina Moretti and learnt something important about her whereabouts. Someone must've been observing that meeting to make a note of the car and the direction he was travelling in. So it's either the contact himself or somebody who had the contact under surveillance.

Tokaj shook his head with admiration. 'Craig, that's a very impressive piece of deduction. Yes, it would make sense. They needed to kill him before he rang you with whatever information he had found.'

'Which means that where he was killed must have been not too far from where he met his source.' Gillard opened the glove compartment and took out his map of central Albania. 'Well, the obvious location would be Fier. That's only 20 minutes away.'

'Home of the Dragusha,' Tokaj said.

Gillard nodded. 'I need access to Geoff's phone. Can you lean on the local cops?'

'I spoke to Mr Zok this morning,' Tokaj said. 'He's happy to incorporate this incident into his broader Dragusha enquiry. The local police will hand over the evidence to him. You can rest assured that this is now in the hands of dedicated professionals.'

In the meantime Gillard realized he had a very sensitive matter to attend to, and asked Tokaj to excuse him for a few minutes. He walked back from the car park into a quiet corridor of the hospital and rang a number in Surrey. The phone rang out 10 or 15 times, and Gillard imagined it echoing in the grand drawing room of Colsham Hall. Eventually, he heard the cultured tones of Sophie Lund.

'Hello Mrs Lund, it's DCI Gillard—'

'Oh, Craig, do you have any news?'

'Not about the children, I'm afraid. I'm in Albania, as you may have been told.'

'So are you with Geoff?'

Gillard looked over his shoulder towards the mortuary. 'Er, no. But it's about him that I'm calling.' He deliberately left a pause. 'I'm afraid I have some rather sad news.'

'Oh my God, what are you going to say?'

'Late yesterday afternoon Geoff's hire car was involved in quite a serious road accident here. I'm afraid that he did not survive it.'

'God, I don't believe it.'

'Albania has an exceptionally high rate of road traffic accidents,' Gillard said. He felt pathetic trotting out this irrelevant factoid, but he knew that it was way too early to tell her the truth, that Geoff had been murdered.

'Oh no. What about his poor wife and children?'

'They've already been told,' Gillard said, impressed that Sophie still had the breadth of humanity in her heart to think beyond the fate of her own children.

'I can assure you, Sophie, that I will take on Geoff's work as best I can. Now that we know that Zerina Moretti has ignored all attempts at contact from the police, the European Arrest Warrant will be served. It's not valid in Albania, but it will be effective if she ever returns to Italy. You can be assured of our best efforts to keep your children safe.' Craig knew that this was the right time for that assurance, even though he was far from confident that he would be able to deliver a successful outcome.

'Thank you so much, Craig,' she said.

'It's the least I can do. Now I have a question to ask you: when did you last hear from Geoff? And had he told you where he was going to be yesterday afternoon?'

Sophie paused and then said: 'We had an email from him when he was on the ferry from Italy. He said he was on his way to Shkoder, which is the part of the country where Teto Zerina came from. But he also mentioned meeting a new contact who might know of her where-abouts.'

'He didn't say where?'

'No, I'm sorry.'

'Okay.'

'Craig, one more thing. Do be careful on the roads. I couldn't bear to hear about another fatality.'

He thanked her and hung up.

–

Trying to work out what Geoff Meadows had been inves-tigating when he was killed was proving difficult. Gillard had combed through the notebook he found at the site of the accident, but most of the information scrawled there was a rehash of what was already known. The biggest mystery was an Albanian mobile phone number, twice underlined, but with no indication as to whose it was. Meadows's mobile phone had already been recovered, but the Elbasan police were sitting on it, together with the satnav from the hire car. Although Mr Zok had promised him that the organized crime directorate would be in charge, the local police seemed to be dragging their feet to show they could not be ordered about. Being mired in local politics was very frustrating. Gillard needed to know exactly where in Fier his late colleague had been, and the satnav would have given vital clues.

The organized crime directorate seemed to be too busy to return his or Tokaj's calls. Something was going on and neither of them knew what it was. The two police officers sat in a busy restaurant in the centre of Elbasan, trying to work out what to do next.

'Should we ring the number?' Gillard said, tucking into a grilled fish and chunky chips that bore comparison with the best of British.

'I could get it traced but it would take time,' Tokaj said, popping a prawn in his mouth, shell and all, and crunching it noisily.

'With those two kids, I'm not sure we even have time,' Gillard said. The restaurant was too busy and noisy to make the call, so after they finished and paid for the meal they returned to the car.

'Best use my mobile,' Tokaj said. 'If the caller shows up as a domestic number it is more likely to be answered.' The Albanian tapped out the number and held the phone to his ear. The number rang several times then went to messages. 'It doesn't tell us whose number this is.' Tokaj said, slipping the phone back into his pocket.

They sat for a few minutes in the car, then tried again with the same result. 'I have an idea,' Tokaj said. He rang it a third time, then after the message kicked in he tapped out a few digits, then hit zero on the keypad four times. Gillard watched him as he listened carefully. A smile crept up on the Albanian policeman's face. Eventually he hung up.

'What have you discovered?'

'From the style of automated message, I guessed I was ringing a dumb phone. There's an option for message retrieval. I opted for it and guessed that the owner of the phone might not have changed the default code from the factory settings.'

'So you tapped in four zeros? We have a name for that. Phone hacking. It was a big scandal in Britain about ten years ago, journalists digging for celebrity news.'

'I like to think we are doing this in a higher cause,' Tokaj said haughtily.

'So were there any messages?'

'Yes, a couple of days ago.' He played the message again, and pressed the phone to Gillard's ear. He couldn't understand it, but the woman's voice was cheerful and full of life. Tokaj translated for him: 'What she said is: "Hi. It's me. I'm on the ferry, we get in at 11.55. We'll wait by the taxi rank. Text me back. So looking forward to seeing you. Bye."'

'It must be her,' Gillard said. 'It sounds like she is talking to a relative or close friend. How on earth did Geoff Meadows manage to get this number?'

'Maybe it was from whoever he met in Fier?' Tokaj said.

'Can we get your colleagues in the organized crime directorate to dig out the location data?' Gillard asked.

'I don't think they'll get round to it quickly,' Tokaj said. 'Something big is going on, and I'm not being kept in the loop.'

'The way I see it we've got two options,' Gillard said. 'We can either do it the old-fashioned way and go up to Shkoder and start passing around photographs of Zerina Moretti to see if anyone recognises her. Or we do it the modern, underhand way.'

'Which is?'

'We go to Elbasan police headquarters this evening and steal Geoff's mobile phone and satnav.'

Tokaj grinned. 'I like your style.'

Chapter 27

Saturday evening

Elbasan's police headquarters was on an aged industrial estate west of the historic city centre. Not as grim as many of the surrounding buildings, which were mainly concrete barracks from the days of Enver Hoxha, but a dull, low-rise piece of architecture nonetheless. Gillard and Tokaj picked their time very carefully. It helped that it was a Saturday. The Albanian football team was playing away against Croatia, a match that started at seven o'clock. At a nearby bar on the main road dozens of men, many of them no doubt policemen, were glued to a giant screen. Gillard and Tokaj drove past the bar and parked outside the police HQ 15 minutes before the match was due to end. As they expected, the place was almost deserted and the reception desk was staffed by a young female constable who looked barely beyond school age. Tokaj slapped down several sheets of paper, topped by a letter written by Mr Zok which bore the impressive crest of the Directorate of Serious and Organized Crime. Beneath it was Gillard's own request for assistance, in English, signed by the chief constable of Surrey. It all looked very impressive, especially if you couldn't or didn't read it, as none of it pertained to the road accident in which Geoff Meadows died.

While she flicked through the paperwork, Tokaj said that the directorate had sent them because they urgently needed a quick look at two pieces of evidence retrieved during the accident. He cited the reference numbers. Both Gillard and Tokaj displayed the full array of male impatience, from drumming fingers to watch-checking and tutting. The woman, clearly intimidated, left them at the desk while she hurried off to the evidence room. She was back in five minutes with two brown paper packages, on which were pasted white labels.

She said something in a plaintive voice which Tokaj translated: 'According to the labels, she's not supposed to sign these pieces out without the counter-signatory of the inspector. He's watching the football, and she is clearly afraid to disturb him. So I said I would ring him.'

Tokaj made a short phone call, and after some apparently shared laughter and male bonding hung up triumphantly. He then spoke to the desk officer. She shrugged and then signed out the two pieces of evidence, which Tokaj countersigned.

As they walked out, Tokaj said: 'I didn't actually ring him. That was the speaking clock. I didn't want to take the chance of him saying no.'

'That's very naughty,' Gillard said. 'The poor woman will probably get into trouble.'

'Maybe, but it's not her fault but theirs. It's what happens when you think football is more important than your job.'

-

Later that evening the two detectives sat in their hotel room eating a takeaway pizza. Under Gillard's expert manipulation, the satnav device revealed the details of Meadows's journey on his first and last fateful day in Albania. There were two locations of interest. One, as Gillard had anticipated, was in Fier and the other in Shkoder. The phone, too, yielded secrets. The call log showed Meadows had indeed rung the mysterious number in his notebook, the same mobile phone number on which Zerina Moretti had left a message. Geoff had called it on half a dozen occasions, the first call being at 2 p.m. on the day he died, less than half an hour after the satnav recorded the start of his second journey from Fier to Shkoder. It did sound like this was the crucial number gleaned from the meeting in Fier.

With no better way of doing it, Gillard simply emailed from Meadows's phone to his own every piece of potentially useful data. That included every non-police number called, the last three days of his email inbox and sent box, plus copying every outgoing and incoming text and their times. It was fiddly, and took nearly an hour.

'You know, Besin, we have a machine in Surrey called the Accesso Kiosk. You just stick the SIM card in and it retrieves not only the metadata, but most of the actual data sent or received. Wish we had one here.'

Tokaj smiled and took another bite of his pizza. 'First thing tomorrow we should go back to Fier.'

'But we still don't have the exact address,' Gillard responded.

'Maybe not, but Meadows called four phone numbers before that first journey to Fier was complete, and not afterwards,' Tokaj said. 'So whoever he met in Fier should correspond to one of those.'

Gillard shrugged. 'We still don't know who we're trying to meet or why. If it's a long-standing contact of Geoff's, they may not even want to speak to us. They may be too afraid.'

Tokaj grinned, helping himself to the last slice of pizza. 'Or too dead.'

–

Sunday morning dawned with the sound of church bells. Gillard showered and prepared himself for the drive back to the home turf of the Dragusha. While shaving, a phrase kept circling in his head. *I have nothing to fear but Fier itself.* He thought of Geoff, and his family. His reverie was broken by an exclamation from the bedroom. He guessed that what he was hearing was Albanian swearing.

He popped his head through from the bathroom: 'Banged your head?'

'No.' Tokaj put down the phone. 'I don't believe this. Vjosa Dragusha had a stroke on the night after we visited, then his kidneys failed on Friday. The Butcher of Fier is dead.'

'So that's the secret that Mr Zok and his crew have been sitting on for the last couple of days,' Gillard said. 'No wonder we can't get anything done.'

'The funeral will be tomorrow. In Fier.'

'Monday? So soon?'

'Yes, this is the Albanian way.'

'The Angel of Death will be there?'

'Of course. Everybody will be there: the entire family, those who do business with them, those who work for them, and those who wish to show respect. Which is all of the above. You will never have seen anything like this.'

'It's a great opportunity. I need to speak to him. I need to question him.'

Tokaj stared at Gillard as if the British detective seemed incapable of learning. 'I know we have other reasons to go to Fier. But from this event, Craig, I would stay away, honestly. You would not be welcome. There will be those who blame you for his death, even though he was dying anyway. They will remember your face, believe me.'

By mid-morning they were in Fier. Following the satnav they parked in the same road where Geoff Meadows had parked three days earlier. They had expected a residential street, but in fact it was adjacent to a high wall on one side and a park on the other. The trees were bare, and patches of snow obscured much of the ground. No doubt in summer it was a beautiful place to spend time. At the centre of the park was a circular wooden café. Gillard approached. There were half a dozen people inside, well wrapped up and enjoying the benefits of two big portable heaters. Outside, stacks of chairs and tables leaned against a wall, awaiting warmer days.

Returning to the car, Gillard worked his phone, looking again through each of the emails that he had copied from Meadows's phone. Several were to Albanian police contacts, some of whom Tokaj knew of. One was to the same orphanage in Shkoder they had already visited. But none of these referred to a visit in Fier, nor directly to any presumed location of Zerina Moretti or the children. Tokaj meanwhile rang each of the numbers that Meadows had called on the last morning of his life. He left messages on two of the numbers and got answered on two. One of those turned out to be a garage and the other an elderly man who seemed to be hard of hearing. He had not heard of Geoff Meadows, and seemed alarmed when Tokaj identified himself as being from the police.

'We are getting nowhere,' Tokaj said.

'I just wonder,' Gillard said. Working his phone, he found on Google a photograph of Geoff Meadows from a news item about his death. 'Come with me.' He walked back into the café and up to the slender middle-aged woman serving at the counter. Tokaj translated Gillard's question: 'Do you work here every day?' She nodded. 'Did you see this man in here last Thursday?' She looked at the photograph and smiled. '*Ah! Anglisht.*' Even Gillard could understand that: English. The woman said that the Englishman had sat with one of her regular customers, a middle-aged local lady. He had left a large tip, which still apparently made the waitress smile.

Gillard could feel the excitement bubbling up inside him. He flicked through his phone until he found a picture of Zerina Moretti. 'Was it her?'

The waitress looked for a long time, inclining her head left and right as if to indicate doubt. 'Maybe, maybe not,' was Tokaj's translated answer.

'Were there children with her?'

'She says no.'

Further questioning of the waitress, and the purchase of some pastries, produced more information. The woman whom Meadows had met had come in once or twice a month since the waitress had started working there six months ago. Gillard left her with his phone number in case the woman should come in again, and deposited an obscenely large tip, prompting a gasp from the waitress. He promised her twice that amount if she rang him when the woman arrived. She beamed like it was Christmas.

When they were outside Tokaj said: 'Craig, that was a mistake. That tip was too big. It may not be so much in Britain but it is a month's money here. For certain, she will be too excited to keep her mouth closed. If the woman does come in, this waitress will think she has won the lottery. I wouldn't be surprised if she does a little jig.'

Craig acknowledged his error. If someone with the experience of Geoff Meadows, someone who spoke the language, had come unstuck here in Albania, it was no surprise that he was having difficulties.

Chapter 28

Monday

It was snowing the morning that they buried the Butcher of Fier. The ceremony was taking place at the Catholic cathedral in the centre of the city, but as Tokaj had predicted, the police had been warned to stay away. So Gillard and Tokaj were parked on the road opposite the cemetery where so many Dragusha were already interred, awaiting the arrival of the cortège.

At 11.22 a.m. they spotted a black Mercedes saloon leading a procession of dark vehicles along the slushy main road from the centre of Fier. On its radiator grille was a black-framed portrait of the Butcher, and from its rear window fluttered a triangular pennant bearing the Dragusha insignia. As the car drew level, the two policemen were eyed suspiciously by the four shaven-headed men inside. This car was merely the first in an endless procession of black, highly polished vehicles, each carrying four or five intimidating-looking men, many of them wearing sunglasses. Some of the cars had full-size Dragusha flags tucked into their bonnets, others had smaller pennants or flags stuck against the windows. The eleventh was a hearse, laden with flowers, and with a large, black-framed portrait of Vjosa Dragusha along the side.

Another three hearses were behind it, the middle one bearing the coffin of the head of the family. For half an hour cars passed, each of them full of the foot soldiers of surely one of the largest crime organizations in Europe. Gillard stopped counting at 89 vehicles, but still they kept coming.

'Where will they all park?' Gillard asked.

'They'll just take over the street,' Tokaj said. 'No one will complain, I can assure you. They will probably use the south gate where there is more space.'

The cortège passed the main gates of the graveyard and continued down the road south of it. Towards the tail end, there were buses, draped in flags from the windows. Most of the red velvet curtains inside were drawn but, where Gillard could see inside, he spotted the first female faces. There were three more buses, several people carriers, taxis and a collection of older vehicles, not all of them black. Gillard roughly calculated that there must be 1,200 to 1,500 people who had come to pay their respects. This wasn't a family, it was an army. When the final vehicle had passed, Tokaj looked at his passenger and asked: 'Are you ready?'

'I certainly am.'

Gillard had borrowed a dark tie from Tokaj. Both policeman, now formally dressed in black, with heavy overcoats, crossed over to the far side of the road, where a gaggle of pedestrian mourners were walking along to the south gate. These people were generally middle-aged or elderly, less well-dressed and less affluent than those who had passed in the vehicles. As Tokaj had explained, every business owner, every neighbour, anyone who paid dues to the Dragusha was expected to be there.

As they arrived at the south gate, they saw a very large crowd, umbrellas braced against the snow and wind, queuing to be let in. Beefy-looking men in overcoats, their shoulders dusted with snowflakes, were checking clipboards and directing entry with the same kind of speed and efficiency that could be expected at an open-air rock concert. Many of them had walkie-talkies, while a more elite group of sunglassed heavies inside the gates had earpieces.

'They're taking no chances,' Tokaj said. 'I'd thought we might be able to mingle with the crowd, but it's clear this event has been planned for a long time, and is being carefully supervised.'

Policed to keep out the police, Gillard thought. 'What about going back to the main entrance?' he asked.

'No, they will have that covered.'

As they watched, the crowd parted for a group of pallbearers, all at least six feet tall, bearing an enormous white casket draped in the black, red and gold flag of the Dragusha. Mounted on top of the coffin was a golden figurine, fully 18 inches high and three feet across, depicting the clan's triple-headed eagle. It was surrounded by wreaths of red and yellow roses, and dark tulips. No expense had been spared. A group of black-clad women trailed behind, wailing and crying. The double gates of the cemetery were swung fully open and, on the broad shoulders of eight big men, the coffin began to ascend the steps which led up to the crown of the hill. So steep did these steps become that the pallbearers struggled to keep the giant coffin stable and the wreaths of roses had to be removed from the coffin top.

'I've got an idea,' Tokaj said.

They skirted the crowd, moving further along the fat end of the teardrop-shaped cemetery. They arrived at the far west end, where an elderly woman in a narrow wooden kiosk, surrounded by flowers and wreaths for sale, kept watch over a pedestrian gate. The ornate iron gate was locked, and almost as high as the ten-foot stone walls that girded the graveyard.

Tokaj had a word with the woman, and after two minutes' conversation produced something from the inside of his coat pocket and passed it through the window to her. She shuffled out, bent and bowlegged, and pulled her grey knitted shawl tightly around her head and body. She produced a key and unlocked the padlock which held the gate, and ushered them in. The door was closed and padlocked behind them.

'How much did that cost?' Gillard asked.

'Not much to you or me. But a week's pay to her. It is enough.'

'I hope she's going to let us out if we need to escape in a hurry. I don't think I could squeeze underneath.'

Tokaj smiled enigmatically. Ahead of them was a steep and overgrown path climbing through an older and congested part of the graveyard, where headstones had begun to tilt and the moss and lichen had begun to reclaim the memories of man for nature. They moved gradually up the slope, past tall and untrimmed cypress trees, whose branches were now beginning to gather snow. A crowd had begun to assemble around the Dragusha mausoleum at the apex of the hill. The two policemen stayed 30 yards back and watched as families, with black-clad children in tow, joined the throng. A lot of the younger mourners had their smartphones out, either for selfies or to video the growing congregation. There was one gaggle of primary-school-age children where two little girls had Dragusha-patterned helium balloons, emblazoned with the triple eagle. A girl of perhaps 16 stood nearby, with her dark hair carefully plaited, wearing a severe dark dress and a woollen shawl, as if she was preparing to be a grandmother. Holding her hand was a boy, half her age, neatly suited and hugging a large teddy bear. He had a Dragusha symbol razor-cut into his severely shaven hair. Poor kid, Gillard thought, already on the mafia ladder.

From their vantage point behind an obelisk the two detectives had a partial view of the mausoleum, and could see a bishop standing above the crowd with a gold-embroidered mitre and a full, dark beard. His billowing white robes were held in place by a gold and purple chasuble, and he held in his hand an enormous bible, its gilt-edged pages fluttering in the breeze. He began to address the crowd over a public address system. The tannoy echoed around the gravestones, and though Gillard could understand not a word, the emphatic proclamations and the responses from the crowd made it feel more like a 1930s political rally than a eulogy.

Creeping forward, he hoped to spot Nikolai Dragusha, the most murderous of the Butcher's sons. Where better to find the Angel of Death than at the burial of a mass murderer? With all eyes now on the bishop, Gillard and Tokaj were able to gradually ease their way through the crowd. They passed one of the earpieced henchmen without incident while he was photographing the casket on a smartphone. Gillard could now see clearly to where the priest was directing his impassioned and fiery speech. To his left, staring down, were three or four men that he recognised from the wake last week. One of them, wearing small round sunglasses, his wavy hair anointed with snowflakes, was Nikolai. The British detective was now within three rows of the front of the crowd. The only way to get a better view was to climb on the plinth of a neighbouring monument. But to do so would risk attracting attention. While he considered this, he sensed in his peripheral vision that he was being scrutinized. A man to his left was whispering in the ear of one of the security guards and pointing in his direction. Gillard had hoped to get close enough to Nikolai Dragusha to ask him some questions once the formalities had finished, but this was now looking to be a very high-risk enterprise.

The bishop was clearly rounding off his eulogy, and must have called on the congregation to pray, because every head dipped. As the ecclesiastical voice softened, intoning requests for a blessed passage into the afterlife, the snow began in earnest. Big fat flakes fell in hair and eyelashes as the deep grinding sound of the opening of the mausoleum began, picked up by the priest's microphone and magnified to a thunderous roar across the snowscape. Gillard picked his moment to move onto the adjacent plinth, out of sight of the two men who had been looking at him. It also gave him a tremendous view of the casket, lying on an ornate metal trestle, and the two men hard at work on metal handles, winding open the slabs that covered the maw of the tomb. Half a dozen coffins were visible, stacked either side of a dark sepulchre and a wooden ladder, carefully manoeuvred by the pallbearers so they could get inside to receive the body of the Butcher.

What evil lies in that pit, Gillard thought. I hope he goes straight to hell.

At that moment the prayer finished. The Angel of Death, standing opposite Gillard, raised his gilded, snow-dusted head and locked eyes with him. Nikolai Dragusha had a pale, feminine face and almost colourless eyes, but his crimson rosebud of a mouth was twisted, as if unsure whether to express pain or pleasure. Gillard could see why Amber Lund thought she was looking at an angel. Recognition bloomed in Nikolai, a slight, cruel smile and a single raised eyebrow.

Gillard realized his predicament. At least 200 armed gangsters surrounded him. He had nothing to defend himself with.

Nikolai turned his head to talk to an associate, but kept his gaze sideways on Gillard.

What happened in the next two seconds would be burned into Gillard's memory for the rest of his life.

There was a 'pop' sound like a bottle top being removed from a beer, and Nikolai's coat, jacket and chest erupted, gore flying in all directions. A gasp from the crowd was cut by a second identical sound, then a ricochet of metal on stone. The Angel of Death twisted and fell, tumbling onto his father's coffin and then into the open mausoleum. The bishop, his vestments spattered with blood, wailed into his microphone, a bellowing ululation that seemed to tear open the sky. The crowd panicked, pushing back from the open grave. Gillard dived down behind the granite crucifix of the grave where he stood, and realizing that he too was spattered with blood. He couldn't see Tokaj, but he could see some of the Dragusha security detail, guns drawn, looking wildly for suitable targets, then pointing away down the hill to the entrance they had entered by.

Gunshots rang out, which seemed to Gillard excuse enough to dive for cover, then crawl away from trouble down the narrow gap between these elaborate tombs, towards the cemetery's main entrance. He had barely a chance to process what he had just seen, but he was now clear that the Angel of Death had been shot, and by a silenced weapon. Only the ricochet had given it away. First Peter Young, now Nikolai Dragusha. Perhaps the Kreshniki were not as dead as they had assumed.

The one question on Gillard's mind was: had Tokaj fired the shots? He didn't think his Albanian colleague was armed, but he might have concealed a weapon as well as the grudge to go with it. In Albania anything is possible.

Chapter 29

Gillard hid between two very large tombs, squeezed against the freezing stone. As an obvious foreigner he couldn't afford the attention the bloodstains would bring. He took a tissue and tried to wipe the blood off his face, using the mirror setting on his smartphone to guide him. His shirt collar was peppered too, and there was a coin-sized spatter by the knot of his tie, though you would have to get close to see it, crimson on black. Nonetheless, this was a crime scene he didn't want to put himself anywhere near. After a few minutes the sirens of approaching ambulances could be heard, and the shouts and cries of the mourners diminished to an angry buzz. Eventually, after a good 40 minutes and with fingers and toes numb, he stood up and walked out of the graveyard's main gate as naturally as he could. He was among the stragglers leaving the place, and though there were two of the Dragusha henchmen at the gate, they were in a heated conversation with each other and not looking at him. He tried to ring Tokaj, but with no reply had to settle for leaving a message.

Gillard could not get out of his head the idea that Tokaj was the assassin. The Albanian had played at being reluctant to take the risk of being here. It was Gillard who had insisted. They had crashed the party, but everyone else, surely, was family and vouched for.

It was too dangerous to wait for the Albanian policeman by the car, which must certainly have been identified by some of the Dragusha henchmen who had so venomously stared at them. So instead Gillard took shelter in the outdoor seating area of a restaurant in a small botanical garden. Though the restaurant was closed given the season, he was able to keep an eye on the street where Tokaj's car was parked.

Unable to reach the Albanian policeman, and a little worried about his safety, Gillard felt like hearing a friendly voice. He rang Claire Mulholland and told her what had happened. She was astonished at the turn of events, and expressed fears for his safety.

'I'm all right, but am a bit concerned about my liaison officer. He's not replying to calls. I was hoping to get to speak to our main suspect, the Angel of Death as he is known, but of course I'll never be able to do that now.'

'So is that going to be another Albanian dead end?'

'Well, not completely. I'd been trying to get a DNA sample of this guy for days. Now one has been blasted all over me. All I need to do is take off my tie, stick it in an evidence bag and send it back home, and we will be able to find out if he was ever at Colsham Manor.'

'Every cloud has a silver lining,' she said. 'So have you seen any sign of Zerina Moretti or the two children?'

'We have some clues, courtesy of Geoff, that she at least passed through Fier. Things are getting very dangerous now. I can look after myself, but I don't much rate the chances of an overweight middle-aged aunt with two helpless children against this lot.'

–

301

It was another half an hour before Tokaj emerged, walking boldly along the street towards his car. As the Albanian policeman bent to open the driver's door, Gillard tapped him on the shoulder and made him jump. 'Oh shit. Don't do that, you crazy man. Get in, let's get out of here.'

Tokaj drove off at speed. 'I don't want to be seen anywhere around here,' Tokaj said.

'Why didn't you answer my call?' Gillard asked.

'I lost my phone in the crowd. There was a stampede, and it was knocked from my hand. Lots of mourners were crushed in the panic, women and children were screaming.'

'Then let's go back for it.'

'No, it's too dangerous. The Dragusha will make sure that their own police inspector will be in charge of this crime scene. It will be that guy who spoke Italian, the one I told you about.'

'Oh, him.' Gillard looked out of the window for a few moments before asking: 'Did you shoot the Angel of Death?'

'Are you crazy? Of course not.'

'So who did shoot him? Did you see anything?'

'No. May I use your phone? I have to call my boss.'

Gillard passed his phone across. Tokaj drove like a maniac while conducting an animated conversation with his head of department in Tirana. Finally he finished, passed the phone back and let out a long sigh.

'We have to go to Tirana, now. Big meeting.'

'But what if the waitress calls?' Gillard asked. 'It may be our only chance.'

Tokaj shrugged. They were now back in the centre of Fier, stuck in a traffic jam in which angry honking horns made conversation difficult. Gillard's imagination kept replaying the same scene over and over again. The blood erupting from Nikolai Dragusha, the body twisting and falling.

Tokaj kept looking in the mirror. 'Motorcycle! Get down!'

Gillard shrank himself down into the seat as best he could as a trail bike with a pillion passenger threaded its way between the lines of traffic, past them to the head of the queue. He didn't see a weapon in the passenger's hands. Nonetheless, visions of Geoff Meadows's death flitted through his mind.

'False alarm,' Tokaj said, risking a smile.

'Is this the normal method of assassination?' Gillard asked.

'Yes, especially once they know your vehicle. And by now they will know ours.'

It took half an hour to get past the roadworks which had caused the snarl-up, and it was only once they were on the open highway heading north towards Tirana that Tokaj began to explain what he had seen at the funeral.

'This was a shot from behind, and seemed quite low, which would indicate someone fairly close behind in the crowd. If it was a sniper's rifle from some distance it would have been a headshot.'

'I'm no ballistics expert,' Gillard said. 'But the size of the exit holes torn in Nikolai Dragusha makes me think that, just like with Peter Young, we are dealing in hollow-point ammunition.'

'Maybe you're right. But how he was killed is secondary.' Tokaj shook his head. 'What matters is that this is the most brazen assault on the Dragusha clan since the time of chaos. It must be one of the big crime families. No one else could have organized this.'

'What about a squabble within the Dragusha? A fight to take over the clan, isn't that possible?'

Tokaj shook his head emphatically. 'It's the timing that makes that impossible. Can you imagine, I mean can you even consider, that any one of the Dragusha gang would choose the moment of burial of the head of the family to settle a personal score? I can't think of a better way to make sure that every single member of the clan will round on you.' Tokaj continued to shake his head. 'No, it cannot be family. It must be external. It is designed to humiliate the Dragusha, to show that they cannot even control the burial of their own dead, to show that their enemies can reach them anywhere.'

'Kreshniki?'

'No. This is surely beyond the resources of a bunch of old widows. But we will learn more at headquarters. Apparently we had a spy at the funeral. I didn't know that, but apparently there is new information.'

Monday afternoon

Tokaj and Gillard sat with Mr Zok in the main incident room at the Tirana police headquarters. An urgent meeting was taking place with several senior detectives. Though Gillard could not understand what was being said, the frowning expressions and the urgency of the discussion seemed to indicate a high level of worry. They were all waiting for a conference call with their undercover officer, apparently female, who Mr Zok called their most precious asset in the fight against the Dragusha. It was almost an hour later when the more junior officers were asked to leave, and with only four of them present, a battered TV screen on the wall crackled into life.

This was a Skype call, but the camera was angled so that it only caught the keyboard, desk and hands of the woman. She was, from those bare details, middle-aged with silver nail varnish. Gillard could tell from the slight shine on indentations on her fingers that she had removed her rings, presumably to protect her identity.

Again Gillard didn't understand what was being said, but after the call was finished Tokaj translated for him. 'She said she didn't see the shots, but she did see two of the Dragusha's henchmen running down towards the west entrance.'

'That was the entrance that we came in by,' Gillard said. 'It was locked.'

'Yes, when she got there she said the toughs were trying to climb over the wall.'

'So someone had escaped that way?'

'Maybe, and maybe with the help of the flower seller.'

'A locked gate. That's the best way to make sure you couldn't be quickly followed. For a clean getaway,' Gillard said.

'There is something else. She returned to her family group and overheard quite a lot of what was said. The Dragusha already think they know who the killer is.'

'Did they name names?'

'No. In fact they're keeping this completely secret, which is significant in itself. All she knows is what the wife of one of the leading gangsters let slip in the coach on the way home. She said: "Even when you think you have slain the monster, and cut off all its heads, there is always one poisonous serpent left.'"

–

The conversation was interrupted by Gillard's phone ringing. When he answered it, all he heard was a breathless female babbling in Albanian. He passed it over to Tokaj, who listened and tried to interject his own comments. Eventually the monologue became a dialogue, and after five minutes Tokaj thanked her and ended the call. 'As you probably guessed, that was the waitress from the café in Fier. She said the woman came back half an hour ago and asked for the radio news to be turned on. She listened with a big smile on her face.'

'That doesn't mean anything. Everyone who'd ever had to pay protection money to a mafia would delight in hearing about them being taken down.'

'Well, yes, but you haven't heard the rest. Your over-generous tip has transformed our waitress into a veritable Sherlock Holmes. She engaged the woman in conversation; her name is Bella Lalic and she lives locally, in the same block as the waitress's brother-in-law. She works in a pharmacy, but has no children because, and I quote, her husband's pi-pi doesn't work. She even sneaked a photograph which she emailed you.'

'Not of the offending organ, I hope.'

'No.' Tokaj smiled and handed Gillard's phone back. He swiped to his emails and pulled up the picture. Bella Lalic was in her late 40s, with masses of dyed coppery hair, tortoiseshell spectacles, wearing a smart grey trouser suit and rather a lot of jewellery. In the picture she was smoking something rather ostentatious in a holder. It wasn't Zerina Moretti, though there was a vague resemblance in her dated B-movie dress sense.

'It looks like another dead end,' Gillard said.

'I think not. I've kept the best till last. This woman told the waitress that her younger sister Zerina and her beautiful niece and nephew had come over from Italy to stay with her for a few days, but they left this morning to go back to the Accursed Mountains.'

'Fantastic! She is worth every penny.'

'She thinks so too. She wants $1,000 in cash, used notes no bigger than fifties, to give you the name of the village where they are going.'

Gillard laughed. 'We've thoroughly corrupted the woman, haven't we?'

Late Monday afternoon

Both policeman knew it was going to be dangerous to go back to Fier, but the waitress's insistence on cash for the details of Zerina Moretti's location made it unavoidable. While Gillard rushed to a bank to get the money together before they closed at five, Tokaj went down to the police car park to look for a new unmarked vehicle less well known to the Dragusha.

They rendezvoused an hour later, in the gathering dusk, in front of the entrance to the police HQ. When Gillard saw that Tokaj had swapped his white Renault for an even older black Golf GTI, he couldn't help but laugh. The vehicle had been lowered, boy racer-style, and had rusting sills and what looked like a couple of amateurishly filled bullet holes. 'Well, Besin, this is deep cover,' he said.

'Appropriate for junior gangsters. Still, at least it's the right colour.'

Tokaj shrugged. 'This is the trouble for us poorly resourced police,' he said. 'This car was seized as part of a prosecution, which is how we get a lot of our undercover vehicles.'

'I just hope it will get us there.'

'Don't worry. Our mechanics have spruced up the engine. It's also got snow tyres, and a full tank of fuel.'

As they drove south, on the busy and now familiar road to Fier, Gillard's mind was again drawn back to the ghastly vision of Nikolai Dragusha's chest erupting, and the warm bloody rain that spattered the congregation. Whoever had been the assailant, it was clear that the Dragusha would now be mad with fury. Hundreds of young men, armed to the teeth, desperate to make an impression and fill the leadership vacuum. He couldn't imagine a more potent recipe for violence.

As if reading his mind, Tokaj said: 'We have to be very, very careful.'

It took less than two hours to reach Fier, and they made their way through the centre of the city without encountering traffic jams. They spotted a number of black Mercedes saloons, each packed with shaven-headed young men, but there were no suspicious motorcyclists. The waitress had agreed to meet them at eight o'clock at a church round the corner from the café, which was now closed for the evening. They were a few minutes early and there was no sign of her. The Eastern Orthodox church was set back from the road on a tree-lined but grubby plaza, strewn with litter. The building itself was grand, with a high square tower at one corner topped by a shiny cupola, and a frontage galleried by arches. Gillard's attention was drawn to two benches on the plaza occupied by vagrants. One on the left seemed asleep under a blanket, with a bottle visible under the seat. Opposite him, 50 yards away on the right, another man, moustachioed and dark-featured, was wrapped up against the cold with his possessions in a shopping trolley.

Tokaj was looking at them too. It was a perfect set-up for an ambush. If they were Dragusha men, they could cover every angle to the church.

'What are the chances that we're being set up?' Gillard asked.

'About 75 per cent. I don't like these two.'

'Look. We're only here for two things. One is the name of a town, which might turn out to be nonsense. And the other is to give her the cash.'

Tokaj nodded. 'She's clearly been talking to somebody in the know because of her demands for the cash. Otherwise we could have wired it to her.'

At that moment a female figure came into view from around the back of the church. She was nearly 100 yards away, but it could well have been the waitress, overdressed in high heels, dark bulky fur coat and fur hat.

'Let's ring her. Get her to walk to the café, and we'll see if these guys move,' Gillard said.

'Good idea,' Tokaj replied. He rang her, and they saw the woman lift a phone to her ear. The vagrant lying sideways on the bench levered himself to a sitting position and stretched with an ostentatious yawn.

Gillard let out a long deep breath. 'Doesn't look good. He's looking around.'

They continued to watch as the waitress walked steadily left across the plaza and onto a footpath which went through the trees to an adjacent road. Once the woman had crossed that road and walked through some more dimly lit parkland, she would be back at the café where she worked. Neither of the two men on the benches followed, which reassured Gillard. 'Besin, I think it's okay. The Dragusha wouldn't yet be organized enough to have more than two operatives on this, given what's happened to them today.'

'Agreed. Let's drive over and park by the café.'

The two policeman left the car 200 yards further down the road and walked back to the café from the far side. The waitress didn't see them until they were just 10 yards away. Tokaj called out a greeting and she turned to him. Her face lit up, and she began a long discussion in Albanian, before Tokaj cut her off. He took the money out of his pocket, rapidly counted it out for her and got a slip of paper in return. The two policeman thanked her, then beat a hasty retreat.

'She gives receipts?' Gillard asked as they walked away.

'It's the address of the woman she saw in the café, Bella Lalic.'

'Zerina Moretti's sister,' Gillard said.

'Yes, and she's also written the name of the village where Moretti has headed to.'

'Great stuff.'

'If it's accurate, yes,' Tokaj said. 'But she could also be taking us for an expensive ride. Anyhow, we'll know soon enough. Mrs Lalic lives just around the corner.' Tokaj quickly led him to one of four stained concrete high-rises. Mrs Lalic's apartment was on the 11th floor, facing inwards over a patch of well-kept gardens and allotments. A few children were playing in the corridor. Gillard pressed the doorbell and waited. No one came. Tokaj asked the children, who ranged in age from 7 to about 12, if they had seen the woman who lives there recently. They shook their heads.

Gillard and Tokaj exchanged a knowing glance. 'Let's do it,' the British detective said. Keeping his back to the children, he used a gloved fingertip to press gently down on the door lever. It opened.

The moment the door swung open it was obvious. The Dragusha had got there ahead of them.

Chapter 30

Gillard only took a few steps into the hallway of the flat. The doorway into the lounge was open, and a woman's clothed body lay partially in view, a discarded shoe on its side stained with blood. He pointed to another door off the hallway on which some graffiti had been written in marker pen.

Kreshniki −2

'Minus two Kreshniki,' he said. Gillard stepped a little further into the room, pulled out his phone and photographed the woman, who had been shot in the chest. She was not Zerina Moretti, but could have been her sister. He carefully opened the door into a bedroom, on whose bed a man lay, also shot dead.

'Poor guy. He's never going to need his pi-pi again,' Gillard said. He photographed him, then quickly checked the other two rooms, a kitchen and a bathroom. The children were not there.

'If this investigation falls to the Dragusha-owned detective, the gang will never be called to account for it,' Tokaj said.

Gillard shrugged. 'It's in his patch, there's nothing we can do. Our priority now is to find Zerina Moretti and the two kids in the Accursed Mountains before the Dragusha do.'

They then slipped out of the flat and carefully closed the door behind them. Snow was just beginning to fall, thick flakes drifting down in the orange sodium-light glare which whitened the darkness, muted the traffic and softened the edges of urban Fier.

Before they had got back to the car, Tokaj took a phone call from his wife. His face became grave as he listened to what she had to say.

'Leila says the Dragusha have sprayed their symbol over our front door,' he said as they got into the VW. 'And someone keeps ringing the landline but not saying anything. It's freaking her out, obviously.'

'Do you think the Dragusha would really come for you there?'

'For me? No, they would come for us, but especially for you. As an outsider, seen sneaking around at the Butcher's funeral, you have a pretty big bull's-eye on your back, my friend. You were insolent and disrespectful to him at the prison, and they probably think you need to be taught a lesson. They have their spies. They will know that I am hosting you. That is why my wife and I are in danger.'

Gillard let the reproach sit between them for a moment. 'I really wouldn't want to put you in danger.'

'Too late for that, eh?' Tokaj said with a savage grin, gunning the engine and pulling out into traffic. 'Never mind, we'll be okay. A bit of stiff British lip, eh?' He slapped the British detective's thigh.

'Upper lip. You're allowed to wobble the lower one,' Gillard corrected.

'Whatever.'

'So what are you going to do?'

'For a start we're not staying at my home tonight. We're taking Leila and going to my older brother's farm in the hills, which will be safer. His wife died a few years ago and he will be glad of the company.'

They stuck to the coast road heading north out of Fier, but even on this lower route snow was soon lying thickly on fields and walls, and beginning to settle even on gritted roads. They arrived at Tokaj's house just before 11 that evening. The moment he opened the door Leila flung herself into his arms. Behind her were several suitcases which the Albanian detective quickly packed in the boot of the Golf.

'I hope you do not mind, but Leila has packed your things too, in the red case,' Tokaj said. 'It saves time.'

The journey to the farm took only half an hour, mainly on narrow roads, where theirs were often the only tyre tracks. They pulled into a parking area where the snow was already three or four inches deep, next to a snow-capped red tractor which looked at least 60 years old. The brother, a ruddy-faced man who resembled the classic image of Joseph Stalin, welcomed them all with glasses of home-made raki.

'We will be safe here,' Tokaj said, and raised a glass. 'Here's to the serpent who dispatched the Angel of Death.'

'And here's to us finding out who he is,' Gillard said, sinking his in one.

'Tomorrow we head off to the Accursed Mountains.'

'What was the name of that place that the waitress told you?'

'Haj. The x is silent.'

'What x?'

'The one at the front: X H A J.'

'Good grief,' Gillard said. 'That isn't a word, it's a car registration number. What a language!'

'It works for us, my friend.'

—

It was Monday, three days after Craig's warning, that Sam noticed she was being followed. It was nearly five, dull and overcast. She was in the little Ford Ka, with the rape alarm in the glove box. She had only got to the end of the close when an old black BMW that had been parked half on the pavement fell in behind her. The two youngish guys in it were wearing sunglasses, and one had a dark beard.

She was glad that she had changed her routine.

Normally she would run to the class, and that would have left her much more vulnerable. But Craig's warning on Friday evening had shocked her. Nothing is quite as frightening as realizing that the toughest and most capable person you know, who has looked after you and kept you away from danger, suddenly feels unequal to the task. So she had looked at the safety procedures Craig had put together for her in case her ex, Gary the stalker, should come back. There were things to do to indicate she wasn't alone at home even if she was. What to do if she was followed, a list of police colleagues based nearby who could check up on her if Craig was away, that kind of thing. She had changed her shopping routines too, she left a radio on low near the door when she was out, set the night-time security light, and stuck a 'Beware of the Dog' sticker on the front door, even though she hadn't got a dog.

Now, with her worst fears coming true, Sam again did what Craig had suggested, even though it wasn't really convenient. Instead of heading straight to the gym, she drove up the A23 to Purley. There was an ANPR camera in Coulsdon, and she noted the time she passed it, to make it easy for the police to find her and identify the car behind. Then she drove to the giant Tesco Extra and parked near the front, in the mother and baby section, within reach of the CCTV. Once inside she rang one of her old colleagues in the police. She didn't see either of the guys following her along the aisles. She slipped out without buying anything and drove off to the gym. She didn't see the men or the BMW for the rest of the evening, but when she got back home saw that some kind of symbol had been sprayed on the front door.

A triple-headed eagle, just like Craig had described.

—

Gillard was given a rustic bedroom above the stables where the brother's two horses and donkey were kept. There was a small brass-framed bed and a solidly built bedside table on which there sat a well-thumbed copy of the Koran. The brother brought the detective up a ewer of warm water, a rough grey towel and some soap. There was a hurricane lamp should the electricity fail, as he was told it sometimes did during the snow. The low-ceilinged room was certainly warm enough, and its hand-carved wooden shutters added a charm to the place. However, the stamping of the animals beneath, the jangling of harnesses and some early morning braying interrupted his sleep.

Breakfast was a big loaf of rustic bread, its gnarly crust a challenge to the teeth, with a chunk of creamy butter and a comb of honey suspended on cotton from the light shade over a lit candle. The three of them sat around a small rustic table, watching the honey drip out into the dish below, before scraping it onto their bread. It was delicious.

The brother, who spoke barely a word of English but had a gap-toothed smile for every eventuality, patted the British detective manfully on the shoulders and said: 'Good?' And it was, tasty and filling. The coffee was strong and dark, and Gillard was urged to sweeten it with honey if necessary.

'We have an important rendezvous today,' Tokaj said, checking his phone. 'We are going to meet our under-cover officer from the funeral. She apparently speaks good English, and now thinks she knows who killed the Angel of Death.'

Tuesday afternoon

Tokaj had arranged to meet the police spy in Shkoder, the mountain city which was the gateway to the Accursed Mountains. The woman, whose code name was Yeta, had suggested a rendezvous at the public library, half an hour before it was due to close at 4 p.m., giving plenty of time to get there in case the roads were blocked by snow. The old Golf did them proud, hauling itself noisily through one or two snowdrifts in exposed places and overtaking lines of trucks which were defeated by the icy slopes.

After defrosting themselves in a local bar in front of a roaring open fire, Gillard and the Albanian detective went next door to the library and waited as instructed at a large communal table in the reference section at the back. There was no one else in the place, except a male librarian who busied himself at the main desk in another room. A few minutes later a petite woman of about 60 with neatly coiffed grey hair and glasses entered through a rear door, shaking snow off her umbrella. She walked past, perusing a shelf of history books, then disappeared around the corner. A minute later the Albanian detective's phone vibrated, and he answered it. Gillard could hear her speaking from the other side of the shelf.

After hurried greetings, Yeta sat with them and began at a whisper. 'I have only ten minutes before I have to go back to Tirana,' she said. 'However I managed to secure some strong evidence, some video recorded by one of the other female mourners on her phone, and I was able to get a copy. Watch very carefully.'

She held up her Samsung. The recording began midway through the funeral liturgy. The viewer seemed to be opposite the bishop, about ten yards away. Nikolai Dragusha could be seen on the left of the image. Gillard would have been visible on the right of this frame, had he not been hiding behind a monument. At the bottom of the screen, a child pushed through the mourners. It was a back view, but the phone picked up the Dragusha emblem shaved into his hair and the teddy bear still clasped to his chest. There was no sign of the older girl whose hand he had been holding. The child passed out of the frame on the left, and another mourner, a short man with an ill-fitting jacket and dirty hair, seemed to get in the way. The man looked around, and seemed to feel for something in his jacket pocket. The image wavered slightly, and then there was the first pop. For a second the camera shook, and then there was an exclamation from the woman, then a second pop as Nikolai began to topple. The screaming of the crowd now dominated, and the image was too shaky to tell what was going on. Then it ended.

'I don't see anything useful,' Tokaj said. 'Maybe the scruffy guy, but I'm not sure.'

'Okay,' the woman said. 'Let's look at the second video and then go back.'

The second video was much shorter and showed a huge seething crowd, screaming, with some running away. There were more shaky images, and then a few seconds of clarity which showed one of the Dragusha henchmen, earpiece clearly visible, standing high on a monumental plinth aiming a weapon down towards the western gate. He shouted something in Albanian, which Tokaj helpfully translated.

'He's shouting "Everyone down so I can shoot the bastard",' he said.

A second later the video jerked left, in the direction the gunman was pointing, to show a scrum of suited men piling down the steps towards the gate. The first of them seemed to be crouching, and one even tried to squeeze underneath.

'You can't get under there,' Gillard laughed. 'I looked at it on the way in. The gap's less than a foot.'

A few seconds later, one of the taller henchmen helped an athletic guy onto his shoulders, who then attempted, initially unsuccessfully, to climb over the spiked railings at the top of the gate. The video then ended.

'This tells us something,' the woman said, taking off her glasses.

'I'm not sure what,' Gillard said.

'Assuming they were following the assailant, the initial attempt is to squeeze under the gate, rather than force it open,' she said.

'Perhaps they had shouted for the woman to open the gate, but had no reply,' Gillard said.

'Exactly so,' she said. 'Now let us go back to the last section of the previous video. I don't have great slo-mo on this phone, but HQ can take it apart frame by frame. Now watch.'

She restarted the video just where it was getting jerky just before the first shot. She hit pause, and then pointed with a propelling pencil to the bottom left-hand corner of the image. 'See the teddy bear.'

A sliver of the bear's golden-brown fur could be spotted between the dark trousers of two of the male mourners. 'That's the bear held by the boy with the symbol shaved in his head,' Gillard said. 'But where's the girl?'

'I don't know,' she said. 'I spent quite a while looking for her, until I realized that it's not the girl who is significant. Look,' she said, trying to move the video on in slo-mo. It took a few attempts, and then she showed it to the two detectives. 'Look. The boy is standing right behind Nikolai Dragusha. I cannot get a clear image for the moment of the first shot, but this I think is the second.' She played around with the screen a little more, and then turned it around to them as a still, using the pencil again to point out a detail.

'The bear's head jerks right back, and is that smoke?' Gillard asked.

'Yes, that's the gunshot,' Tokaj said. 'I think there was a silenced gun inside the bear.'

'So the child smuggled the gun in to someone?' Gillard asked.

Tokaj shook his head. 'No. That is unnecessary. Many adults would normally carry guns.'

'I believe the young boy was the assassin,' the woman said. 'He simply walked up behind the Angel of Death and fired at point-blank range.'

'There must have been a pocket inside the bear that he could reach into and fire the weapon,' Tokaj said.

'This child I think is less than ten years old,' the woman said. 'But amazingly, I have a picture of him from earlier, because I thought he was so sweet.' She pulled back her phone, worked the buttons for a few seconds and then turned it round again.

It was a lovely portrait of the girl in the severe dress holding the hand of the boy with the teddy bear. Gillard looked at the face of the boy, and his heart somersaulted.

'I don't believe it. That is little David Lund.'

Chapter 31

Tokaj looked at Gillard, his eyes wide. 'You know this child?'

'He's the adoptive son of Sophie and Dag Lund. He was the one kidnapped together with his sister Amber from the family home in Surrey. And to think all the time I've been worried about what might happen to him. It never occurred to me that I should have been more worried about what he might do to others.'

The woman looked at Gillard with a sympathetic expression. 'I'm sure in your country there are no precedents for this kind of behaviour. But here, if you are in a family feud, the obligation to protect the honour of the clan moves down from father to son, from elder brother to younger brother.'

A revelation exploded in Gillard's brain like a firework display. *David didn't just shoot Nikolai Dragusha. He also murdered Nikolai's younger brother, Pjetër. Pjetër Dragusha, Peter Young.* Finally the connections were all falling into place. David Lund was the last male in the Kreshniki line, the last chance for the honour of this dwindling crime family to be satisfied. His shooting of Pjetër Dragusha in Surrey, to avenge the death of his own birth parents, had reignited the vendetta, leading quickly to the death of

David's older brother Jetmire, and the threats against the Lund children.

Gillard had a hundred thoughts popping in his head, but he voiced just one: 'He could not have done this alone.'

Tokaj nodded. 'I agree. This was meticulously planned, even down to getting a Dragusha hairstyle to provide him with cover. There was the gun and silencer to provide, ammunition to procure, a teddy bear to hollow out. Someone brought him to the funeral, someone picked him up afterwards and whisked him away. While only a man can defend a family's honour, a woman could easily do any of these other things.'

'I'm pretty sure I know who must have organized this,' Gillard said. 'Zerina Moretti, the children's aunt. Of course, that's why she brought the kids back to Albania. They had a murder to commit! We have to find her, and soon.'

'Certainly before the Dragusha do,' Yeta said. 'And they already have the original of this recording, and perhaps other pictures too.'

Tokaj blew a long sigh. 'I bet they already have a good idea of where she and the children might be. Though undoubtedly the organization will be slowed down by this assassination, they have, as you have seen, much greater resources to bring to bear on it than we do. We have to make the most of our time.'

After the agent left, Tokaj stepped out into the car park to call his boss in Tirana.

Gillard remained seated in the library, his hands steepled either side of his nose. How on earth was he going to explain this to Sophie and Dag? Their quiet, introverted child an assassin? That made sense of another piece of evidence: the target practice near Colsham Manor, which was probably the aunt helping the boy to train. And of course with a silencer fitted to the weapon, no one would have heard a thing.

Tweedledum and Tweedledee had spent all their time combing the CCTV footage for a male adult on that bus. They should have been looking for a child.

-

Gillard rang the incident room in Guildford to let them know his discovery. Claire Mulholland was patched in to the call.

Mulholland listened in silence as Gillard described what had happened, and the overwhelming evidence of David Lund's responsibility.

'That's staggering,' she said. 'We assumed David and Amber were simply potential victims.'

'I'm afraid we've been caught by our own cosy preconceptions,' Gillard said. 'Gun use in Britain is confined to a few hardened criminals, and it was only adult perpetrators we were looking for. But look at YouTube. It's packed with videos of American five-year-olds being taught to shoot, sometimes with automatic weapons. Albanians might not make those videos, but gun possession is almost as common here.'

'So what's the next step?'

'I want Hodges and Hoskins to look again at the CCTV footage of the second bus, the one that passed the architects' window at the correct time. Amongst those posh little schoolboys on their way to St Cuthbert's, they might find a small, unassuming, dark-haired boy bent on murder.'

'I'll let Gabby Underwood know,' Mulholland said.

'Yes but keep it from the Lunds for now,' Gillard responded. 'Claire, I need you to ring round some schools: the girls' secondary school to see if any of the pupils remember a small boy sitting upstairs, St Cuthbert's to see if any of the regular boys who sit downstairs remember David, and the Lunds' own primary school to see if David was missing that day.'

'We're going to have to think about how we handle this with the press,' she said.

'Agreed. But it's the least of my problems now. Albania's most powerful mafia has been stirred up like a hornet's nest. Word will be out amongst the other crime families that a young child has humiliated the mighty Dragusha. You can't imagine a more profound blow to their honour. They are thirsting for blood. If they find David and Amber...'

'You've got to find them first, Craig.'

'Don't worry, I will.'

—

DI Claire Mulholland was having her own difficulties. Laura Diaz had finally admitted to receiving mysterious phone calls in the days after Peter's death. They were from withheld numbers, asking for permission for members of Peter's extended Albanian family to come to the funeral in Surrey.

'At first I said yes,' a tearful Diaz told the policewoman. 'But I asked for the names and details so I could arrange accommodation. They told me they weren't sure who was coming yet, and would make all the arrangements them-selves. I was very suspicious of this, because I had never heard from any of his family in all the years we'd been together. I obviously asked too many questions. Then this man said: "You will do what we say if you want your children to stay safe." I was told that I couldn't have the cremation that I wanted, that Peter was to be buried at a particular place they had reserved and paid for. He was to be prepared for an open casket. There were all sorts of demands. They said they would pay, money was no object. I really didn't feel I could refuse, and I certainly couldn't tell you. If they were stopped, they would kill my children.'

'Did you see any of them at the funeral?'

'I saw a few people I didn't recognise, but they stayed towards the back. Of course you can never be sure when there were so many mourners anyway: people who worked with him, passers-by who had read the papers. Anyway, it was only after the funeral reception, after all the guests had gone home that I went upstairs to my own room, our room, and there sitting on my bed was this very scary man with a face like a cherub.' She began to cry. 'He said terrible things to me, and he threatened the children if I ever spoke of having contact with him.'

Mulholland handed her a handkerchief.

'I had no idea that they would steal my Peter to take him back to Albania. What a cruel thing to do to me and the children, to take him away from us. It's as if we do not count for anything in his life.'

The detective kept her counsel. She had already informed Laura that the body had been taken to Albania, but had not provided any details. It seemed better to wait until Gillard was back with a fuller account of what happened.

—

When Mulholland got back to Mount Browne, she led an impromptu incident room meeting.

Carl Hoskins and Colin Hodges were already there, fast-forwarding through CCTV on a laptop. Rob Townsend, who had been working on trying to locate the aunt from her phone, was already in place. Michelle Tsu was on her way over from Colsham Manor and would arrive later.

The DI began by marking a minute's silence for Geoff Meadows. The unspoken fear amongst those present was what had happened to Geoff could easily happen to Craig Gillard.

On top of that there was a sense of stunned disbelief among the assembled detectives that one of the most vulnerable of the potential victims in the investigation, David Lund, could turn out to be the perpetrator.

'Look here,' said Colin Hodges. 'This is the bus CCTV of the stop before the one outside the architects' office. As you can see there is this great horde of schoolgirls piling off. There's two people trying to get on. You can see an elderly lady hanging back at the stop. And there's this child's head which you can just see. He's only just tall enough to get in the frame.' He froze the footage. There was a dark-haired boy, in a dark jacket with shirt and tie, a strap over one shoulder. He was only visible for a fraction of a second.

'We can't tell whether he went upstairs or down, can we?' Mulholland asked.

'No. And though it's possible he's David Lund, he could be somebody else. Carl and I ignored him because he didn't fit what we were looking for.'

Carl Hoskins took over: 'So what we're thinking now is that the lad bunked off school on the day in question, was dropped on Roosevelt Avenue by his aunt, caught the bus for a couple of stops, shot Peter Young through the window and was then picked up again. We know that the aunt was in Britain over Christmas until midway into January, covering the time when the murder of Peter Young took place. It's a question of the car she was driving.' He turned to look at Michelle.

She stood up and went to a pre-prepared flipchart covered in marker pen bullet points. 'I tracked down the details of the credit card that Zerina Moretti used when she took the ferry to France with the abducted children in February by cross-checking it with her passport. Using this card number I was able to cross-reference it for a deposit taken when she first went for a test drive at the Fiat garage a few days before, even though the dealership no longer had a record at their end. It also flagged up a B & B she stayed at in Haslemere, within easy reach of Colsham Manor, for the two days before the abduction of the kids.'

'What about the first hire car, back in January?' Hodges asked.

'I'm coming to that. I got a list of all the other transactions on it,' Michelle said. 'Going back to January, her first visit, there is a blue VW Polo hired at Gatwick airport. There is also a boy's jacket and trousers, some toys and a satchel, which we probably saw the strap of in the CCTV, all bought a week before Peter Young was murdered.'

Rob Townsend then took up the account. 'The blue Polo appeared on three occasions along Roosevelt Avenue, according to ANPR data. The first two captures preceded the murder by several days, and the last was on the same day, half an hour before the time Peter Young was shot. That must have been when she was giving the child a lift.'

'We can put the aunt in the vicinity at the time of the murder,' Mulholland said. 'David, of course, is below the age of criminal responsibility, but the aunt must have brought in the weapon, silencer and ammunition.'

'Through Gatwick, ma'am?' Hodges asked. 'It's possible in the hold, but it's a bit of a risk, innit?'

'Given she is connected to the Kreshnik gang, I suppose it's quite possible that weaponry was already available here,' Mulholland conceded. 'That's something I would have liked to ask Geoff Meadows.' She paused for a moment to reflect.

'One thing that gets me, ma'am,' Hoskins asked. 'Why get the kid involved? She's got the gun, she has done the recce, knows where Peter Young is, what time he gets to work, that he's in an office overlooked by the top deck of a bus. That's all the hard stuff. Why get that poor kid to pull the trigger, eh?'

Mulholland smiled. 'It's a very good question, and one I put to Craig when we last talked. He said that Albanian blood feuds require a male response. It would be a loss of honour to the family to have a woman defending them against a rival clan.'

'Poor kid,' Michelle said. 'What a responsibility to put on an eight-year-old.'

'Who said he didn't want it?' Mulholland said. 'If this child witnessed the execution of his parents, he might be more than happy to be involved. Sophie Lund said that he was withdrawn and had problems at school. No wonder. It's enough to make anyone a psychopath, surely.'

'What's the next stage?' Hodges asked.

'Finding him and his sister,' said Mulholland. 'Gillard texted us the name of the village. Well, hamlet really. Google Maps shows it as a tiny place. It's down to how soon he can get there. I hear they've had blizzards.'

-

Gillard answered the call from Mulholland while he was on the road with Tokaj. The Albanian was just overtaking a couple of heavy lorries on a steep blind bend on a mountain road, and the British detective's feet were unconsciously active on imagined clutch and accelerator as the car climbed laboriously, past the diesel-belching vehicles.

'We've got all the paperwork in place this end for extradition, for both Moretti and the kids,' Mulholland said. 'Once you find them.'

'It shouldn't be too hard, if we can get there,' Gillard told her. 'At least we're heading in the right direction. We're on our way north to a meeting of the police organized crime department in Tirana. I think there's going to be a big raid on the Dragusha soon.'

Tokaj turned to him, eyes wide and a finger on his lips. 'Shhh!'

'I will attempt to borrow my colleague for a trip to the Accursed Mountains,' Gillard added. 'Assuming the meeting doesn't last too long.'

'Be safe, Craig,' Mulholland said.

After he had hung up on the call, Craig looked at the liaison officer and wondered how much to tell him about the tracing of Zerina Moretti. Using David Lund to assassinate both Peter Young and Nikolai Dragusha may have been ingenious, but it was also an act of desperation by a crime family that had few resources left to defend itself. Tokaj had promised Gillard some time with one of his older colleagues at headquarters who knew the Kreshniki in their heyday, when they were a force to be reckoned with.

Gillard appreciated the offer, but felt that his first priority should be to find the aunt and the two children and get them out of the country. It was an extraordinary situation, because of the pivotal role of David Lund who was simultaneously an accomplished and coolheaded assassin, and a vulnerable, exploited and damaged child. Amber, his sister, was the only one of the three untainted by the crime spree. Teto Zerina, initially described to him by Sophie Lund as a jolly but rather unworldly matron, whose ideas were as out of date as her clothing, had now metamorphosed into something much more dangerous. She had inspired in her nephew a murderous spree, and at least initially covered her tracks and his very effectively. She was about as far away from the idea of a kindly aunt as could be imagined. She would undoubtedly resist any attempt to get the children from her and back to the UK. In Britain, Gillard had occasionally been present when children were taken into care, and it was often the most upsetting scene imaginable, the tearing apart of the bonds of motherhood. Mothers would resist with imprecations, pleading and tears. Zerina may only be an aunt, but Gillard didn't know whether she was going to be armed simply with Albanian persuasiveness or an AK-47 and grenades.

—

As soon as they arrived at police headquarters, Tokaj took Gillard to the records section in the basement. Here, working as an archivist, was Altin Hyka, a white-haired man in his late 50s, confined to a wheelchair. He spoke some English, and greeted Gillard warmly.

'I understand you were the first officer on the scene after Nikolai Dragusha and his thugs broke into the house of Armend Kreshnik three years ago.'

'I will never forget,' he said. 'The father had crawled to the front door to get help, blood was pouring from him. I left him to the paramedics and stepped over the bloodstained carpet into the lounge. There was the naked body of his eldest daughter...' His voice broke and he reached for a handkerchief. 'It was terrible.'

'Had she been raped?'

He nodded. 'Violated everywhere, and by every assailant. She was 13 years old. That was the age that the Angel of Death liked best.' He paused for a moment to gather himself. 'The mother had been shot in the head, and violated in the kitchen. She was already dead. But it was a few minutes later when we found the other children.'

'So there *were* more children?' Tokaj whispered.

'Yes. A little boy of five, Dretim, was found underneath the settee on which his older sister had been murdered. In his arms was his younger sister, Albana. Just two years old. He had kept a hand on her mouth during the whole ordeal to avoid giving their hiding place away.'

'David saved Amber's life.'

Hyka nodded. 'We all knew that their lives would be lived under a shadow if the Dragusha ever discovered that they had survived. So in the official police record there is no mention of these two surviving children.' He wheeled his chair around, and along a narrow aisle between two great floor-to-ceiling stacks of documents. 'I have the original case notes here.' There was a rail on top of the stacks with a kind of shuttle lift attached. Hyka was able to use a piece of dangling string to move the shuttle across to the correct location in the stack, then use a wheeled pulley system to lower the correct file down to where he could reach it. He came back to them with a box file open on his lap. 'Here is the official version, and here is the informal version.'

Tokaj flicked through the documents.

'This could only work because there was no court case,' Gillard said.

'Yes. There were no witnesses, not surprisingly. Though we had DNA evidence for the sexual assaults, we could not compel any of the Dragusha to give us samples for cross-checking. A senior judge, no doubt intimidated or bribed, ruled that it would be an invasion of their rights of privacy given that there was no other evidence to link them to the crimes.'

'So who looked after the children at that point?'

'There was an aunt who lived in Italy,' Hyka said.

'Teto Zerina,' Gillard said.

Hyka nodded. 'She came over with her husband, and though at that point the children's father was still alive, we suggested that the children should be adopted by her.

Otherwise they would have to go to an institution. But she refused.'

'Sophie always wondered why the aunt didn't take them,' Gillard said.

'She was afraid, I think, that they would attract attention and drag her back into the crosshairs of the Dragusha assassins. Having moved to Italy, got married and changed her name, she had escaped from Albania. She didn't want to go back to be part of that doomed family.'

'So they ended up in the orphanage,' Gillard said. 'Besin and I visited the Orphanage of the Blessed Saints in Shkoder where they were taken. The names were registered as Dretim and Albana Goga. The surname was obviously false, even though it had been attested by all the required signatories.'

'Yes. We facilitated the change of name, because obviously anyone with the name Kreshnik would be a potential target. Dretim and Albana didn't stay long at the orphanage, because we had already been tipped off there was a British couple looking for a boy and a girl to adopt. It seemed the perfect solution.'

Gillard stared at the man. 'Can I ask you why you stayed involved with these two children? It must have been beyond the remit of your police work.'

'Yes it was. I suppose I felt sorry for them. On the day I drove them to hospital in Fier, to say goodbye to their father, I remember how brave the little boy was. He was wearing a little woollen coat with bright brass buttons, and he was taken in to see a man whom no doubt he had once thought as invulnerable as the enfolding sky. But Armend Kreshnik's liver had been badly damaged by Dragusha bullets, and nothing could be done. At that point I left them and went out for a cigarette. I finished maybe three before they were ready for me. The aunt was crying, the little girl was inconsolable but Dretim had the same impassive face that he always had. The father had died as they watched, raging against their enemies.'

'What about Jetmire Kreshnik?' Gillard asked.

'Ah yes. The errant older son,' Hyka smiled. 'Another tragic Kreshnik tale. The problem with Jetmire was that from an early age it was clear he was a *bytheqir*, a faggot. Now you might think that Albania is a model of equality and liberalism based on the laws that we have passed in order to accede to the EU.' He chuckled. 'But there is a great shame in the traditional families to discover that a son is not a man. From what Armend told me in the hospital, Jetmire wanted nothing to do with the traditional Kreshniki criminal activities. He wanted to travel, and go places where he would be accepted. There was a rumour that he had a clandestine relationship with a boy from the Dragusha family.'

'A gay *Romeo and Juliet*,' observed Gillard.

'Yes and just as tragic. The Angel of Death dispatched Jetmire's boyfriend, and his name was never listed on the family vault. He was excommunicated after death by the bishop at the insistence of the head of the Dragusha family. No one knows where he is buried.'

'No wonder Jetmire wanted to come to London.'

'To nurse a broken heart.' Hyka nodded. 'He probably thought the tragedies of his life were over. But the Dragusha never give up.'

–

The Director for Serious and Organized Crime knew how to hold a meeting. Mr Zok had arranged for huge plates of food, brimming urns of coffee and a few discreet bottles of raki to be available for the more than 100 officers who were to be involved in the operation to take down the Dragusha. Gillard could just about follow the PowerPoint presentation, which described the strength of their enemy in almost military terms. The slide which showed the pyramid of power up to the Butcher of Fier was replaced by one which depicted a little explosion at the apex. There was a little nervous laughter at this across the room, with one officer raising a glass of raki in a toast that even Gillard could understand: 'Kreshniki!'

It gradually began to dawn on him that his Albanian colleagues were not particularly concerned with the murder of Nikolai Dragusha as a crime: it was simply an opportunity to achieve a knockout blow against a long-time enemy. It was, he gradually realized, seeing the posturing and boasting of senior police officers in front of their colleagues, a feud. And it was just as intense as those between crime families, and would probably be conducted in the same way: with blood, bullets and plenty of machismo.

That realization, and the inordinate length of the meeting, led Gillard to make a decision that he had been mulling for some hours. He was going to hire his own car, and go to the Accursed Mountains on his own.

–

An hour later, having sneaked out of the meeting, Detective Chief Inspector Craig Gillard had hired himself a four-wheel-drive Chrysler Jeep, in the requisite black of course, and had bought himself a complete set of Albanian-style winter clothing plus underwear, to replace the suitcase full of dirty washing he had left behind at Tokaj's brother's farm. Knowing that he would be hunted almost as doggedly as Teto Zerina and the children, he bought himself a new phone too. It wouldn't surprise him if Dragusha spies within the Tirana police were trying to track him. He still had with him Geoff Meadows's phone and the satnav from the hire car. He'd even splashed out on a pair of high-powered binoculars.

A delightful woman at a Tirana deli had made him an enormous multi-day picnic, full of pickled meat and fish; tough, dark mountain bread that would not go stale for days; and a variety of goat's cheeses. These, he was told, varied from the mild and creamy through to a particularly savage-sounding one from the Accursed Mountains which had been fermented for a year and rolled in boiled nettle leaves.

It was almost 3 p.m. when, under a crystalline-blue winter sky, the detective drove north out of the capital on the busy main coastal road north to Shkoder. A call from Tokaj came through an hour later while he was parked to refuel. 'Where did you go?' the Albanian asked. 'If you had waited another half an hour we would have been able to show you the first coordinated raids against the Dragusha's headquarters and businesses.'

'How's it going?' Gillard replied.

'Well, there have been 175 arrests. No shootouts, and the drugs and weapons seized will take months to catalogue. The one significant guy we are missing is Qendrim.'

'That's the guy who took us to Peter Young's funeral.'

'Exactly. The Dragusha's finance specialist. We really need to catch him, as he may end up the new leader.' The Albanian cleared his throat. 'So where exactly are you, Craig? I take it you're chasing up the Moretti woman.'

'Yes, that's part of what I came here to do. I've really got to bring her and the two children safely back to Britain. Both murders now look to be solved.' Gillard enquired about Leila and whether she felt safer now they were at Tokaj's uncle's farm.

'She is certainly happier, thank you. Hopefully this will only be a temporary measure and we can return to our home soon.'

The two policemen wished each other luck and ended the call. Gillard then tried to put himself in the shoes of Zerina Moretti. How confident could she be that the Dragusha had not got the details of her location? She probably did not know her sister had been murdered, and might, for now, feel safe in her ancestral lands. But what if she did know? Would she stay in the mountains or flee? And if so, where? He considered how much this middle-aged woman had achieved in her extended family's generation-long fight against the Dragusha. The two murders, superbly planned and clinically executed, would make any hit man proud. But he wondered whether she had even stopped to consider what would happen to David if he could ever be brought back to Britain. Put into care for a decade, surrounded by social workers and psychologists into adulthood and, once given a new identity, hunted for the rest of his life by the media who would inevitably find out who he was. For Dag and Sophie Lund, the dreams of a new family would be shattered, and who knows what effect all this would have upon little Amber.

That evening Gillard checked in at a roadside restaurant and B & B at Koplik, a sprawling agricultural village ten miles north of Shkoder. As everywhere in Albania, he was greeted warmly, and offered excellent food at extremely reasonable prices. The proprietor, a big man with grizzled grey hair, offered him free raki and a glass of the pungent local wine on the house. The detective bowed out at 11 before a serious drinking session got going, and stepped out into the moonlit but freezing-cold garden to make a call to his wife.

Sam picked up on the first ring, and it warmed Gillard to hear her voice. 'So everything is going okay?' he asked, not wanting to mention again his worries about the long arm of the Dragusha.

'Yes, basically fine,' she said.

'Basically?' He knew her well enough to know she was hiding something.

'Well, there was some eagle graffiti sprayed on Mum and Dad's garage in Keswick, and on our front door,' she said. 'And someone put this funny little doll thing on the shed door handle.'

'Our shed?'

'Yes, they also tried to force the back door. And I was followed to the gym by two guys in a black BMW.'

'Oh Christ. Did you let Claire Mulholland know?'

'Yes. I did what you suggested and went up to Purley. Claire got the car registration from the traffic camera thing, but it seems the car was stolen.'

'Not surprising, I suppose,' Craig said. He paused. 'I do worry about you, Sam. Are you following all the procedures?'

Sam listed everything she was doing and then added, 'Kelly from Caterham is driving past the house twice a day.'

'Glad to hear your old uniform colleagues are looking after you.'

'The kickboxing instructor was impressed with me too. He said my side kick would take the head off a gorilla.'

Craig allowed himself a laugh. 'Well, the good news is that the organized crime gang behind this is pretty much, as we speak, being raided by the Albanian police. The head of the clan died recently, and his right-hand man was assassinated at the funeral in front of about 1,500 goons and assorted hangers-on. It won't be the end of organized crime in Albania, not by a long chalk, but what's left of the Dragusha family should have plenty to worry about locally.' Even as he said it he wasn't completely convinced that a family famous for its feuding would ever forget a slight.

—

First thing next morning Gillard grabbed a quick but strong coffee for breakfast, and was out of the door before eight. The owner of the B & B had confirmed that the road to Xhaj was kept open throughout the winter months by the military who had bases further up in the mountains. He indicated that if the weather was good he should be able to get there in 90 minutes, but with this much snow, who knew.

Gillard set off under brilliant blue skies with barely a cloud to be seen. In the village every home, every parked car, every fence or wall was cloaked under a glittering mantle of snow. Children were throwing snowballs in the street, and thin wisps of woodsmoke curled lazily above white-capped roofs and slid into the car through the air vents. As he hit the mountain road, the scenery soon became spectacular. Peaks soared like rocky knuckles, too steep to hold the snow, while the shoulders and saddles between were softened by snow-girt coniferous forest. The road was clear and well gritted for the first 40 miles. There was very little traffic: just one or two empty timber trucks, an ancient army lorry and a few pick-ups.

Soon the weather started clouding up again, and a sharp wind began blasting powdered snow into the road. After another five miles, drifts were spreading like giant fingers across the carriageway, and small hard grains began to pepper the windscreen. Turning on the lights Gillard gunned the big vehicle over and through the spreading snow. The temperature gauge showed −2° C and a road sign marked a village at 1,000 metres altitude. The road from here on was marked by tall, red-topped, reflective poles to guide the snowploughs. Just as Gillard was beginning to believe that the road may become impassable, an old Soviet-style army truck with huge yellow headlamps came barrelling down towards him with a plough on the front. The car was half buried by what it threw up, but after he got out to clear the windscreen he was able to follow the narrow cleared channel uphill. It was only a few minutes later when he saw the sign: Xhaj.

There was nothing there but a few scattered stone-built farmhouses cloaked in deep drifts of snow, rustic fencing and drystone walls. Smoke rose from the chimneys of only three farmsteads of the dozen there. The first, on the left, had a long drive which clearly no vehicle had passed since the last heavy snow. It had a substantial barn whose open door was blocked by bales of straw. He drove past to the next where there had been many footprints and some tyre marks, now mostly filled in by fresh snow. There was clearly habitation here. He turned the Jeep up a steep and winding track until he came to a courtyard in which was parked a pick-up truck, vapour steaming off the bonnet. As he emerged from the vehicle, a large brindled dog with wolfish eyes came tearing out of the barn, barking furiously. The animal had its hackles raised, ready to bite, and Gillard was backed against the wing of the Jeep. An elderly woman, a big woollen scarf around her head and shoulders, emerged from the farmhouse and called the dog away. The detective felt annoyed that this mongrel should, at the sound of her voice, become a tail-wagging, friendly creature. It licked her hand as she rubbed its ears.

Gillard had considered all sorts of ways of trying to find Zerina Moretti, but had settled on the simplest one, which was to show on his phone a photograph of her and the two children to anyone he came across. When he did so here, a smile immediately lit up the woman's wizened features and she pointed back to the first farm which Gillard had passed. She then said a lot of things which he didn't understand, so he merely used his rote-learned Albanian thank you, and returned to the vehicle. It took only two minutes to drive down to the main road, retrace his route a hundred yards and then turn right again up the long snow-choked driveway to the first farm.

The detective eased the vehicle through the foot-deep snow, parking outside a two-storey building hewn of giant stones interspersed with ancient timbers. It had tiny windows and a roof tiled with rough-cut paving stone-sized slabs. A dog barked in the distance, but there was no other sound. Gillard waded through the drifts up to a pair of rough and sagging wooden doors, from which any paint had long ago peeled. The thick doors were chained and padlocked. There was no sign of any footprints apart from his own. Peeking into the gap between them, he saw a dark, wooden-vaulted undercroft, hung with ancient tools and containing a rusted baler. He knocked on the doors and on a small window next to them. No light was visible from within. He plodded around the left side of the building, the snow here overtopping his boots, and entered the barn by a side door. Dozens of murmuring sheep were crowded within, and eyed him nervously. A feeding trough still had pellets in it, and there was fresh hay on the stone floor.

Someone was clearly looking after these animals.

He edged his way through the ancient barn, looking up into the darkened timbers of the roof, where cooing pigeons gathered and shuffled on the rafters. A rear door, more modern than those at the front of the farm, gave a view over a small snow-covered kitchen garden and a rear extension of the farmhouse. He opened the door and immediately found himself facing both barrels of a shotgun.

The gun was being aimed by a ruddy, middle-aged man wearing a sheepskin coat and hat that looked like it had just been cut just that morning. The man bellowed something at Gillard, his breath pluming into the sky.

Gillard slowly raised his arms into the air and said: 'I'm looking for Zerina Moretti.'

In the next yell of interrogation, Gillard could pick out one now familiar word: 'Dragusha?' followed by the sound of a firing mechanism being cocked.

The detective shook his head, and then heard above a higher-pitched voice. A child. The farmer lowered his gun and looked up over Gillard's right shoulder. Turning to follow his gaze, he saw a rifle pointing from a high window in the back of the building. A boy's head poked out. 'Hello, David,' he said. 'I think you may have just saved my life.'

–

A few minutes later Craig Gillard was sitting in a comfortable chair in front of the fire holding a hot mug of some mysterious mountain tea. Opposite him was Teto Zerina dressed in russet woollens and stout boots. Amber Lund sat on her aunt's lap sucking a biscuit and staring at this mysterious but familiar policeman who had just emerged from the snow. David Lund stood wearing a rough leather coat and a matching sheepskin-lined cap. The eight-year-old's face looked serious, almost manly, though Gillard wasn't sure whether that was just the result of him projecting upon the child the adult acts that he knew he had committed. In the kitchen beyond, the farmer, who was introduced as Zerina's father, busied himself with the clatter and bang of crockery and pans.

'How did you find us?' Zerina asked.

'Your sister was a little indiscreet,' Gillard responded.

'Ach, I'd warned her. But she is such a big mouth.' She looked worried. 'I thought no one could find us here. I still worry about the Dragusha.' She eyed the children, and stroked Amber's hair.

'The Drash people are bad,' Amber said, chewing her biscuit thoughtfully.

'Dragusha,' her aunt corrected. 'They're not people, they are devils.'

Gillard looked at his watch. 'David, your parents are missing you and Amber very much. I think more than anything in the world your mother would love to talk to you both.'

'She will hate me for what I have done.' He folded his arms and met Gillard's gaze. His brown eyes were narrowed and shadowed by suspicion, innocence eroded.

'No, I think she will be upset, very much so. But I think her love for you will remain.'

Teto Zerina turned to David and said something in Albanian which sounded placatory and affectionate. She ruffled the boy's hair just as if she had encouraged him to do nothing more serious than pinching a pencil from school. Gillard had plans to deal with her later, but first he wanted to speak to Sophie. He got out his new phone.

'Be careful with the phone,' Zerina said. 'You can be traced. I'm keeping mine off.'

'It's okay,' Gillard responded. 'This is a new phone nobody knows is mine.' He tapped out the number for Colsham Manor. After a few rings, he heard Sophie's voice. 'Mrs Lund, it's Detective Chief Inspector Gillard, calling from Albania. I have some very good news.' He called David over and gave him the phone, and before the boy had started to speak he could hear the sobs of relief from the other end.

Chapter 32

While David and Amber spoke to their adoptive mother, Gillard asked to speak to Zerina in private. She led him into a formal dining room and closed the door. 'You cannot arrest me, or take them,' she said. 'You have no power in this country.'

Gillard smiled. 'That's not quite true. The European Arrest Warrant we have for you does not work here, but we are getting considerable cooperation from the Albanian police. Eventually, as you well understand, the Dragusha will kill you and the children if you stay here. But of course the moment you leave this country, we will be able to extradite you back to Britain for the murder of Peter Young. You will go to prison, but you will live.'

'No, this is my family and we will not surrender our honour to the Dragusha.'

Gillard shook his head at her obstinacy. 'When the weather improves, I can drive you over the border north to Montenegro. It is your family duty to save these children from a terrible fate.'

Zerina laughed. 'You don't have the first clue what our family has endured. Armend Kreshnik, the real father of David and Amber, was a peaceful man, a farmer. He didn't know that his older brother had begun this financial pyramid scheme. It appalled him. He did not know that

346

the wife of the Butcher of Fier had lost so much Dragusha money through her own greed. But blood is blood. The Dragusha began a feud with the Kreshniki and we had to respond. It is the way.'

'But to involve a child of eight…'

'David is actually nine, almost ten. It was easier to get him adopted with a year deducted from his actual age on the papers. He was always small, but he is a giant in his heart, and in his veins flows the blood of princes. When his father was dying in the hospital with five bullets in him, he sent word that he wanted to speak to his eldest son. But Jetmire would not come. This was a time of anguish for his father.' She shook her head. 'Jetmire stayed in London and would not be part of the feud, even though his sister had been raped and killed, even though his mother had been violated and murdered, even though our family had been humiliated by this attack. He turned his back on our family.'

'Someone has to stop the cycle of violence,' Gillard said. 'Someone has to forgive.'

'He didn't forgive, he was simply a coward. He was afraid. Those kind have no steel in their heart,' she said, fluttering her heavily ringed fingers dismissively. 'Jetmire's craven spinelessness did not save his life. The Dragusha needed revenge, and they had probably already tracked down where he lived long ago should killing him become a necessity. He was no loss to our family.'

'If you had not forced David to kill Peter Young, the Dragusha may not have retaliated against Jetmire.'

She laughed dismissively. 'Can you really imagine the Angel of Death deciding he had killed enough of our family? No, it's us or them. That is the way it has always been. That is the way it will always be.'

'That boy should be at school, he should be spending time with friends his own age, having a childhood, not being dragged into this pointless round of tit-for-tat killings.'

'It was not me but the Dragusha who stole his childhood from him.' The woman glowered at Gillard. 'I did not force David to kill. When Jetmire did not return home to see his dying father, Armend called for David. Armend was by then very weak, but he was still determined to save the family honour. I brought the child into his hospital room, and he cried when he saw how diminished his father was. "Do not cry for me," Armend said. "My time is past and yours is just beginning. You are young, but you are the head of our family, you inherit our honour. Lay your hand on my heart, and feel its faltering beat." David did so. "Now place your right hand over your own heart. Feel the life, feel the courage. Now swear to me on your life and on the soul of your dead mother and sister that you will take vengeance against the killers of our family and preserve our honour." The child swore that he would do so and I was so impressed at the man he had just become.'

'But who did the planning?'

'It was given to me. For the first year after Armend's murder, while Albana and Dretim were being prepared for adoption, I tried to work out a way to strike back at the Dragusha here in Albania. It was difficult, they were too well protected. But this is where Jetmire, for all that he was a pariah, helped us. Through his Dragusha boyfriend he learned that one of the Dragusha brothers lived in England, and was an architect. Once I heard this, I

348

spent the next few months trying to find him. Fortunately, I discovered him through an online article about some architectural award.'

'How did you get the weapon into the UK?'

'Simple. There are no significant border checks on the route we took. The gun and the ammunition were taken from Albania on the ferry to Italy, and driven by my husband to France. He passed them on to an associate on a tourist visa who took the Roscoff to Cork ferry, and crossed from the Irish Republic into Northern Ireland, where there is no border check at all. Then he took the ferry to Liverpool. We had originally planned the execution before Christmas, but I needed to train David with the weapon. Fortunately, we found somewhere quiet on the Colsham Estate, while Sophie Lund was at work. He was an enthusiastic pupil, and turned out to be an excellent shot.'

'The bus was a very clever idea.'

'Yes, it only came to me quite late, when I was watching the architect offices, that there seemed to be hardly anyone upstairs on the bus. I took the trip myself on a couple of occasions, in disguise, to check it would work.'

'But within a week, the Dragusha had struck back.'

'Ah, yes. I was surprised how quickly they found Jetmire. Still, I think he had been a little careless. The Albanian community in London is very close-knit, and there are many spies. I expect that when Nikolai Dragusha came to kill him personally, it was a statement of how seriously they took the eradication of my family. They took Jetmire hundreds of miles north to fool the police about who he was, and give themselves time to prepare for killing David and Amber before the heat got too intense. That was always Nikolai's way, to scare his victims, to feed off their terror.'

'So that is why you abducted David and Amber.'

'Abducted? I rescued them from certain death! The Lunds had no idea how close the children were to being murdered. Once David had rung me to tell me what had happened, I knew I had to act quickly.'

'When did you hear about the death of the Butcher?'

'The same day he died, when I was staying with my sister in Albania. We had already heard that he was failing, and I wanted to be back in Albania to be ready. I had long prepared David for killing Nikolai at this funeral in Fier. But the death of the Butcher came sooner than we expected.'

'What if David had been recognised?'

'The haircut was a good disguise. Besides, the Dragusha family is so big that a child joining the entourage attracts no attention. He feigned tears, and was taken under the wing of one the Butcher's granddaughters, who held his hand. The most difficult thing to get right was the escape route. For weeks, I had David training to run fast downstairs at Colsham Manor during games of hide and seek, and running down stairs wherever we found them. I reckoned he had less than a minute after the shots to run down those stone steps to the pedestrian exit before the Dragusha realized who had fired the shot.'

'That's the entrance I came in through,' Gillard said. 'So presumably the child squeezed under the locked gate?'

'Yes. We had practised that the evening before. But on the day, when I was waiting in a car outside, that was probably the most terrifying moment of my life.'

'What a terrible burden has been laid on that child.'

'We Albanians know that it is the weight of our burdens and how we shoulder them that turn boys into men, youths into warriors and princes into kings. Our country lies on the crossroads of history, and since the times of Alexander armies have beaten their way through our farms and our homes, looking for gold, for God and for glory. We have faced that, sinew against sinew, blood against blood. Meanwhile you English,' she sneered, 'you hide behind the waves that protect your shores.'

Gillard knew there would be no meeting of minds with this woman. He walked out of the room and into the cold hallway, where ancient home-made coats and cracked leather boots lined up against the walls like the corpses of history. He dug out his old phone and turned it on for the first time since leaving Tirana more than a day ago. There were half a dozen missed calls from Tokaj. Feeling a little guilty, he rang his liaison officer to ask how the raids against the Dragusha were going. The Albanian was a little cagey.

'Well, in terms of numbers it's pretty impressive. As I told you before lots of seizures of weapons, drugs and so on. But we also know that some of the senior family members have been tipped off, and they were not where we hoped they would be. We know they have spies both in the local police and here in headquarters. They may even have connections in the telecommunications company to trace your phone. We certainly do know that the unit that is tasked with wiping out the Kreshniki is still out there somewhere.'

Gillard told him about having found Zerina Moretti and the children.

'So were they in Xhaj?' Tokaj asked. The request was so casual, so natural, that Gillard almost answered it with a simple yes. But at the last moment a cautionary part of him intervened, and he said: 'No, by the time I got to them they had left and were actually in Shkoder.' He felt bad for lying and not trusting his Albanian colleague, but there was always the chance that his calls were being monitored. The fewer people who knew, the better.

—

Zerina's father prepared them an enormous lunch of grilled vegetables with goat's cheese and home-made pastries. Gillard returned to the car to contribute some of his own picnic, which he had not yet touched. The air was crisp and cold, and shafts of sunshine were piercing the cloud. Shielding his eyes against the dazzling light reflected off the snow, he opened the hatchback and lifted out the basket of goodies. As he slammed down the door, he eyed the road. There was a people carrier moving slowly up and past the farms. Against the sun he couldn't see how many people were in the dark vehicle, but he had a bad feeling. It went up the road and disappeared out of sight.

Going back in, he shared his misgivings with Zerina. Amber was being very chatty, and had pulled up a spare chair to the table for her favourite dolls. Among them was a small blue nylon kitten, about six inches high, on a neck strap. It said something in Albanian when you pressed its tummy. 'Kitty says "I'm hungry",' she said, offering it a piece of pastry from the table and mimicking the sound of eating.

'What a great little pussycat,' Gillard said, ruffling the little girl's hair. 'Did Teto Zerina buy it for you?'

The child shook her head. 'Mummy got it for me.' She continued to feed the cat, while Zerina's father continued to bring in dishes from the kitchen.

'Sophie Lund bought it for her. The Lunds shower the children with gifts,' Zerina said disapprovingly. 'They spoil them.'

Gillard choked back a retort about the real ruination of childhood. He looked again at the toy. 'May I?' he asked Amber, making to pick it up.

'As long as you hold her gently,' Amber said, passing the toy to the policeman. 'She's very little. I have her with me always.'

'Your mummy was very clever to get you a pussycat that speaks Albanian,' Gillard said. 'British shops don't usually have cats that speak Albanian.'

'My mummy speaks Albanian,' Amber said.

'No, darling, she doesn't,' chuckled Zerina, beginning to cut and serve out pastries. 'Just hello, goodbye and thank you. Her accent is awful, she sounds like a Serb with a cold.'

Suddenly Gillard stiffened as a realization came to him. He pressed the button on the toy's belly and heard the squeaky words that emerged from it. He turned the animal over and looked for the label. A small nylon tag showed the toy was made in China, but there were a few safety notes in tiny print in various languages and then, in red, shortened country codes. Among those codes he recognised Greece, Albania and Macedonia. He found a switch and turned it off. He also removed the batteries. 'I wonder if Sophie got this on eBay?' Gillard said.

'My mummy does speak Albanian,' Amber said. 'My mummy in heaven.'

'She can't have got you that kitten, Amber darling.' Zerina rolled her eyes at Gillard.

'It's from my *real* mummy!' the little girl shouted. 'She sent it to me. From heaven.'

'I don't think so, darling,' the aunt responded, pouring out wine for herself and offering a glass to Gillard. The detective said he would pass on wine, and continued to work his phone. The signal was very weak, and the Internet kept dropping off. He eventually found what he was looking for. It was an online toy shop serving the Balkans. 'Zerina, can you find Amber's toy on here? It doesn't offer a translation.'

Zerina tapped and swiped until she found the right page. 'There. Lost-Kitty-Find-Me. Phew, not so cheap. It's 3,200 lek,' she said, passing the phone back to Gillard. 'Do you have a grandchild to buy one for?'

'No, I haven't,' Gillard said. He then turned to Amber. 'Where did you find Kitty?' he asked.

'She was all wrapped up, waiting for me. She was late for Christmas.'

'But where?'

'In the boot room, Kitty was hiding in an old cupboard.'

'How did you know how to find her?'

The child's big soft eyes were wide with trust, and her little pink tongue worked at the corner of her mouth. She leant up towards Gillard and put her tiny hand around her mouth as if confiding the most delicate of secrets. 'The angel told me.'

They all gasped.

'What angel?' Gillard whispered.

'The angel who came in the night. He said it was a secret, so you mustn't tell anybody,' she breathed. 'Promise?'

'I promise,' Gillard replied.

Chapter 33

Gillard looked Zerina in the face. 'The Dragusha know exactly where Amber is. This toy has GPS. Lost-Kitty-Find-Me has a strap to be worn around the neck, designed for nervous parents to know where their children are. Nikolai Dragusha left it for her, with a spurious message from her birth mother. I bet it never leaves the child's side.'

The aunt buried her face in her hands. 'My God,' she said.

'We have to leave immediately – they could be here any time,' Gillard said. 'How often was the toy on?'

Teto Zerina looked heavenwards. 'All the damn time. "I'm a hungry Kitty, when is dinner?"' She mimicked. 'I told her to stop pressing the tummy button, which she eventually did, but I'm not sure she ever turned it off.'

Zerina explained the situation to her father who looked baffled and then angry. He strode up to Amber and snatched the kitten from her carefully arranged chair of toys, prompting an outraged squeal and then a piercing scream as she saw him head towards the blazing fire. He pulled his arm back to throw the kitten in, but Gillard seized his wrist and hand. 'No, we can use this to our advantage,' he said.

Zerina translated, and the old man shrugged and sat down.

'We have to leave here now. Where is your car?' Gillard asked Zerina.

'Under a tarpaulin in the back barn. It is my father's car, he came to collect us from my sister's flat in Fier. But we are not going.'

Gillard decided this was not the time to tell Zerina that her sister had been horribly murdered. His priority now had to be to save the lives that could be saved, not to lament those that had already been lost. 'Okay, I will take my car and the toy, to leave a false GPS trail further up the mountain. You should drive down towards Shkoder and we can rendezvous—'

David's shout cut him off. 'There are men getting out of two cars,' he yelled. The house erupted into shouting in Albanian between Zerina and her father. Gillard raced out to the front window by the side of the main doors and peered down the drive. A black minivan, the same one he'd spotted earlier, was parked at the end of the drive, the best part of 60 yards away, and there was another car behind. There were a half-dozen tough-looking men with sunglasses and big coats emerging. At least two of them had rifles with telescopic sights.

'And no plan B,' Gillard murmured. Zerina's father seemed to be upstairs, judging by the sound of creaking floorboards above. Turning around he saw David on the stairs, struggling to carry up a wicked-looking automatic weapon, while Zerina followed behind with a huge crate of ammunition clips. Amber, sucking her thumb and holding her kitten toy and a couple of other dolls, brought up the rear.

The detective realized that everybody here but him had long prepared for this siege. He grabbed his phone and dialled Besin Tokaj. He knew it was futile, given how long it would take anyone to get here, but he wanted the Albanian policeman to know what was about to happen, in case no one lived to tell the tale. Three of the Dragusha gunmen were wading up through the now knee-deep snow, while the two riflemen took cover behind a drystone wall.

The number was still ringing out when a thunderous cacophony of shooting on full automatic started from upstairs. The three approaching gunmen were instantly cut down in a blizzard of pink snow. An answering shot from the Dragusha blew out a window somewhere above. Gillard raced upstairs to see David in a front bedroom lying full length on a mattress on the floor. He was aiming the weapon through what appeared to be a purpose-built sniper's hole in the stonework. He fired a crisp second burst of less than two seconds. Looking to the right, he saw Zerina's father crouched on a chair at a window with a rifle and telescopic sight. One of the panes of the window had been blown out. At the far side of the window, Zerina looked to be loading another full-size weapon, one of half a dozen lying on the floor. Seeing him, she pointed at one of the assault rifles. 'Come on, it's loaded.'

Gillard looked around and saw Amber sitting at the back of the room wearing ear defenders. She was kneeling with her dolls and the kitten hidden behind a palisade of cushions. 'Pow!' she shouted, revealing a compact matt-black pistol pointing at him. She laughed at his horrified expression, and pointed at the safety catch to show it was on. Gillard felt trapped in some nightmare from which there was no awakening. 'Zerina,' he shouted, as another fusillade pounded the walls of the farmhouse. 'You can't win this. We should go out the back way.'

'We are not cowards. The Kreshniki will go down fighting,' she said, banging a fresh clip of ammunition into an automatic weapon, and sliding it onto David's mattress.

Gillard ran down the stairs and back through the kitchen. He needed to see how feasible it would be for them to escape through the back of the farm. The kitchen's rear was a long, low, rough-stone corridor ending with a solid timber back door, secured by a giant bolt. Left, on the hinge side, was a tiny glassless slit window, like something used by medieval archers. It gave a narrow view of a long stone building with a large timbered overhang, and beyond it a snow-covered meadow leading up to the pine-clad foothills of the Accursed Mountains. A figure in a dark quilted coat, just a few yards away, darted across his vision, carrying an automatic weapon. A moment later there was a thump and rattle as he reached the kitchen door. A shout in Albanian from just the other side was answered by someone further away. The detective retreated further into a stone alcove left of the door. He was now regretting not picking up one of the many proffered weapons upstairs. All he could see nearby was a shovel and some tins of paint. There was a solid kick at the door, which did not trouble the massive bolt, and then a few seconds later another, heavier one. Immediately after the third kick, Gillard reached across and slid back the bolt, before retreating again to his alcove. The next kick made the door fly open, closing off his alcove. He heard the crunch of boots and a breathless man pass along the corridor towards the kitchen. Gillard picked up the shovel, then kicked the door, which flew back to its original position. A dark-coated man, AK47 in hand, started to turn around. The detective thrust the shovel, the blade catching the man across the jaw, jerking his head backwards against the stone wall. As he fell, already losing consciousness, Gillard trod the barrel of the AK47 down. The gun coughed once, a deafening series of ricochets and chips of stone. Gillard grabbed the gun and retreated again into the alcove at the sound of another set of heavy footsteps crashing through the snow towards the kitchen door. The door flew open again, closing off the alcove, and there was an oath as the man spied his unconscious comrade. Judging the position of his enemy by the sound from the other side of the door, Gillard kicked at the solid wood and felt it crunch against something. There was just enough of a gap for Gillard to see the second gunman, on his hands and knees, entangled with the prone body of the first. Gillard pressed the tip of the AK47 into his back and said: 'Don't move.'

The man must have understood enough, because he clambered slowly to his knees so he could hold his hands up. This allowed Gillard enough space to emerge from the alcove and lead the captive at gunpoint to the kitchen. The man was short but broad, a shaven-headed bruiser, but he was scared. Gillard got him to pull the unconscious and bleeding body of his colleague and prop him in a kitchen chair. With one eye and the AK47 trained on the captives, Gillard rifled the kitchen drawers, looking for rope, and eventually found some sisal string, thin but tough. He got the bruiser to tie his colleague to the chair, supervising the knots to ensure they were tight enough. He then sat the remaining captive on a chair and tied him up.

The shooting from upstairs was desultory now, single shot rather than full automatic. The war had descended from full-on assault to sniping. Gillard guessed that the Dragusha, for all their urban power, would be feeling the cold as well as their losses in this rural guerrilla skirmish.

The bruiser thrust his chin at Gillard and asked: 'Kreshniki?' He was clearly dubious about Gillard's pale features. The detective shook his head. The words in the next statement he didn't understand, but from the bloodthirsty expression and withering tone it might have been along the lines of: 'You can kill me, but you can't win. We have numbers and we don't give up.'

There was another shot from upstairs and a wail, which Gillard immediately identified as Amber's. David came down the stairs at a run, a pistol in his hand, and called to the detective. 'Teto Zerina has been shot. Do you know first aid?'

'I do, but can you guard these two? I'm not sure string is quite man enough.'

The moment David came into view, the bruiser's eyes widened in hatred and he spat insults and threats at the little boy, rocking his chair in fury. David calmly raised his gun and blew his brains out all over the kitchen. He then shot the unconscious prisoner too. The entire room was splattered with blood.

'We Kreshniki don't take Dragusha prisoners,' he said to Gillard by way of explanation, and led the stunned detective up to the first floor.

Zerina was lying on the mattress with blood pouring from a leg wound, which had soaked through her skirt. She was barely conscious. Amber was stroking her face and whispering: 'Teto Zerina, please wake up.' There was no further sound of shooting. Zerina's father was keeping a lookout to the front of the farmhouse from his chair, with anxious looks over his shoulder to his daughter every few seconds.

Gillard hitched up the woman's skirt and saw that the bullet had narrowly missed the femoral artery. But it was still bad. 'She's lost a lot of blood already. David, call an ambulance. Use my phone,' he said, passing across his mobile. Gillard watched the boy's cool and emotionless face as he rang the number and spoke calmly to the operator.

The detective pressed down on the wound to staunch the bleeding, and mimed to her father to tear some bed sheets for a tourniquet. Eventually he got the idea, and Gillard was able to limit the loss of her blood. Once David got off the phone, he said that an ambulance from Shkoder was on its way, and the police too. 'Have the Dragusha gone?' Gillard asked. David and his grandfather had a brief conversation.

'Yes,' David said. 'The two cars have gone now, but my grandfather thinks they will be back tonight.' He looked wistfully out of the front window and said. 'We have killed six, maybe seven. But it is not enough.'

'David, it is more than enough,' Gillard said.

'I am head of the Kreshnik family now,' David said. 'I have to make a decision.'

'Surely, your grandfather here—'

'No, he married into the Kreshniki. He does not have our blood. It falls to me.'

'I think you should forget about blood, young man,' Gillard said.

'I have carried out my father's wishes, but I don't think I want to get sent to prison here. There are Dragusha everywhere.' His face started to lose its composure, and childish fears began to ripple through his cheeks and mouth. He was trying very hard not to cry.

Gillard took his hand. 'Let me take you to Britain, David. You will be put into the care system where there will be people to try to help you understand what you have done. Your sister, too, needs help to overcome the experiences she has had.'

David nodded, and sniffed. He spoke to his grandfather for a minute. 'We are going to cross the mountains into Montenegro. Grandpa says his tractor can tow a sledge with the rest of us on it. It will take a few hours, but now the snow has stopped it will be possible.'

'I must stay with Zerina until the ambulance comes,' Gillard said. 'I saw some skis and poles in the barn. I will catch you up.'

At that moment sirens could be heard in the distance, and Gillard urged David to leave. His last view, staring through the arrow slit of the kitchen, was of an ancient tractor towing a wooden door, fitted with skis. On that door, covered by a couple of huge old coats, were David and Amber Lund. David had his arm around his sister, but an automatic weapon lay on the wood between them as they chugged off into the snow, and the bitterly cold track into Montenegro.

Chapter 34

The military ambulance arrived first, an ancient green truck full of grizzled-looking medics well versed in dealing with gunshot wounds. They soon had Zerina Moretti in the vehicle, with a professional tourniquet and a saline drip. Besin Tokaj arrived ten minutes later, alone in his black Golf. 'I came as soon as I got your call. The others will be here in half an hour,' he said.

Gillard was relieved to see his Albanian colleague, who immediately realized this was a scene of carnage. A river of blood from the three dead Dragusha in the front drive had turned the snow flamingo pink all the way to the road. The kitchen was even worse. The two cops retreated to the barn and sat side by side on a bale of straw as the sheep, scenting the blood on Gillard, retreated to the far end. Only the cooing of pigeons above broke the silence.

'So you let them escape?' Tokaj asked. 'Over the hills to Montenegro.'

Gillard shook his head. 'They won't escape. I had wanted to get them out that way hours ago, but Moretti wouldn't hear of it. She wanted her death and glory moment, and she got it.'

'What about the children?'

The detective shook his head, struggling to convey what he had seen. 'I have seen a child of nine execute two grown men without a second thought. I didn't think it was possible.'

'In Albania, anything is possible,' Tokaj said.

'Even Amber, at five years old, knows how to use a gun.'

'Well, as the Dragusha might come for her too, it has its own crazy logic.' Tokaj broke open a packet of cigarettes, and offered one to him, with a box of matches.

'I haven't smoked since I was a teenager,' Gillard said, lighting up and taking a deep lungful.

'Neither have I,' Tokaj said, lighting his own. 'But it's either this or raki right now.'

Gillard pushed himself to his feet and squinted out towards the road.

'Everyone will want to interview you, Craig. The police from Elbasan over the missing evidence, my boss in Tirana because you might have tipped off the Dragusha when you ran off from the briefing, and not least Qendrim, the new head of the Dragusha. I'm quite confident that he would like to pull your toenails out while asking you some searching questions.'

Gillard nodded and retrieved the old wooden skis and poles from the rafters. He inspected the leather bindings, two loops designed to cinch over normal boots.

'I hope you don't mind, but I'm blaming everything on you,' Tokaj said. 'It makes Leila a bit happier if they aren't coming after me. It might rescue my career too.'

'You have to do what you have to do,' said Gillard. 'I'd best be going if I'm going to overtake that tractor.'

'I'll tell them that you had already gone by the time I arrived,' Tokaj said.

'I'd be grateful for that.' Gillard went back to his hire car, now a bullet-riddled wreck, and found that he could still use the fob to unlock the boot. He took the remains of his picnic and filled his brand new rucksack, which already sported a bullet hole, from the boot. He put on all his winter clothing, and took a fur hat from the hallway of the farmhouse. Finally, he laid out the long cross-country skis and did up the bindings.

'So you can ski?' Tokaj asked.

'Well, a few winter holidays' worth of lessons, so yes. But I've never used any skis as long as these.'

'Hold on a minute.' Tokaj finished his cigarette and dropped the end in the snow. He waded out to his car and opened the boot, and brought back something in a tennis-racket-sized package. 'These are my uncle's snow shoes. In case you have to go uphill. Take them.'

Gillard thanked him and strapped them onto the rucksack.

The sound of gunning engines carried up the hillside, and in the distance they could just make out dark vehicles carving their way up the road.

'Here come the police,' Tokaj said. 'Or possibly the next wave of Dragusha. Either way, I think it's time you hit the slopes.'

Gillard nodded and used the ski poles to lever himself uphill out of the kitchen-garden, and onto the hillside. Soon the soothing hiss of the runners and his own laboured breathing drowned out the approaching traffic, and he made his way across the meadow until he picked up the distinctive wide tracks left by the tractor and its sledge. Pulling up his hood against the cold and turning his back on the mayhem, Craig Gillard pushed hard, left then right, following the mark of tractor tyres along the old shepherds' path north into Montenegro.

It was an hour later, on the downhill section and when the light was already fading, that Craig Gillard saw the tractor, wheezing its way down the slopes towards Montenegro. As he caught up, he saw the dark furs on the sledge behind move, and two children, wrapped up against the cold, clamber to their knees. David had a snowball in his hand, which he threw towards him, but it fell short. The boy dusted off his gloves and smiled at Gillard as he approached. They waved to him, and he waved back. Just like you would with normal friendly, innocent children, playing happily in the snow.

Chapter 35

Once in Montenegro, David and Amber Lund went with Gillard to the capital, Podgorica, where they were met by consular officials, a senior social worker and two female police officers from Special Branch. They were taken back to the UK on a specially chartered flight to RAF Brize Norton in Oxfordshire. Amber played with the dolls brought over for her during the flight, while David lost himself in an Xbox. They again behaved like normal children, and were treated as such, despite everyone in their entourage being made aware of what had happened.

At the airport, Dag and Sophie Lund were waiting anxiously with liaison officer Gabby Underwood. The parents rushed out from the barrier the moment David and Amber came into view. A sobbing Sophie scooped up both children into her arms, holding them so tight they could hardly breathe. Tears ran freely down her face, while Amber's piercing wails of 'Mummy, I love you', echoed off the steel roof. The police, social workers and other officials held back, allowing the family some space to pretend that after this terrible scare, things would revert to normal.

Of course that could never be.

Later that afternoon both children were placed with temporary foster parents under a care order.

A week later, at Surrey Police headquarters in Guildford, DCI Craig Gillard and his team were wrapping up the Peter Young murder inquiry, under the watchful eye of Chief Constable Alison Rigby. The usual crew of DCs Hoskins and Hodges, DC Michelle Tsu and DI Claire Mulholland was there, along with Ciaran Rhys, an extradition specialist from the National Crime Agency, plus Gabby Underwood, the liaison officer.

Rigby spoke first. 'You should all by now be aware that the National Crime Agency and the Met Police have a joint operation with the Albanian police, codenamed Operation Talon, which they hope will roll up a large section of Balkan organized crime in major British cities.' She tapped at a document in front of her, then scanned the assembled detectives with a wry smile on her face. 'I'll believe that when I see it,' she added.

'Now, about those children. How did the Lunds take it, Gabby?' Rigby asked.

'Not well,' she replied. 'I think Sophie had braced herself, at some level, for the deaths of her adopted children, but this is a different kind of bereavement. David will be taken away from her. Poor, guiltless Amber is going to lose her brother just like she lost her birth parents. They are undeniably victims, even though one is a perpetrator too.'

'Death by social worker, that's what will happen,' Hoskins said.

'What about the aunt?' Hodges asked. 'She seems like the real villain.'

Rhys spoke up. 'Zerina Moretti is in the women's section of the prison hospital in Tirana. My information is that she is making a good recovery from her gunshot wound, and will be transferred to the women's remand wing in Tirana, where she will be kept under special protection until the trial over there begins. Our extradition will have to wait until she has served her sentence there.'

'As the last adult member of the Kreshnik family, her chances of surviving long enough to be extradited are pretty slim,' Gillard said. 'The Dragusha have no shortage of allies in prison.'

'Among both prisoners and staff,' added Rhys.

'Peter Young's widow is taking no chances,' Mulholland said. 'She's moving back to Peru with the kids. Somewhere even the Dragusha can't reach them.'

Gillard gave a wry smile. 'Maybe I should consider that too.'

Epilogue

Next day Alison Rigby convened a further meeting at Surrey Police headquarters to consider what to do about David Lund. They were using the largest of Mount Browne's meeting rooms to allow for the presence of senior lawyers from the CPS, a contingent of social workers, child protection specialists and two senior brass from the National Crime Agency. Gillard was almost surprised that he was thought qualified to be there himself. None of the others on his team had been invited.

'Craig, perhaps you could begin by filling us in on what you witnessed,' Rigby said.

Gillard described the siege in the Accursed Mountains, including the killing of the prisoners, and projected from his laptop the footage he'd been given by the Albanian police which showed David Lund's involvement in the killing of Nikolai Dragusha. When he finished, he looked around the room at the many shocked faces. 'So, in total, this child has committed four murders, albeit only one on UK soil. It's unprecedented in British criminal history for a boy his age.'

The Crown Prosecution Service came next. Its senior lawyer Hugh Gilchrist looked and sounded like a high court judge, and had a weighty pile of documents in front of him. 'I have here the report from the consultant paediatrician at Great Ormond Street Hospital. David Lund has not, in the opinion of Mr Medhurst, reached the age of criminal responsibility. There is no evidence of puberty, and his height, weight and general development are consistent with an age of nine years and four months, which matches that given by his aunt, and is exactly a year older than that recorded on the presumably forged birth certificate. Under the circumstances, we are not minded to contest these findings, in spite of some public interest consideration in favour of prosecution for such a high-profile homicide.'

Surrey's senior social worker, Barbara Harrington, concurred. 'The child protection considerations dovetail with that conclusion. The welfare of David Lund is best served by taking him into care, as he is clearly beyond the care and control of his adoptive family.'

'There will, no doubt, be howls of outrage in the media,' Rigby observed. 'That a young murderer is not being seen to be punished.'

'We should then steer them towards the extradition of the real culprit, Mrs Moretti,' Gilchrist responded.

'David is a victim, quite simply,' Harrington said. 'Our multi-agency strategy meeting showed that conclusively. I would point out, however, that Mr and Mrs Lund yesterday launched a High Court judicial review to over-turn our care order.'

She reached for a laptop projector in front of her. 'This is an edited version of an interview with David Lund and his sister.' She set the video running. It showed the two children in a comfortable lounge, full of toys, playing on the floor with two young women in casual clothing. 'This is the specialist interview suite for child crime victims,' Harrington said. 'The two women are senior family specialists Penny Jones and Harriet Skipworth, whom I believe a number of you know.'

The two women asked both children a number of questions while playing with them: Is it important to tell the truth? Is it wrong to hurt people? Do you feel safe now? Does anything make you worry? The answers were as expected: The truth is important, you can hurt people only to stop them hurting you. They both felt safer. Amber looked up and said: 'I'm scared of the night. Because that is when the *shtriga* comes.'

Neither interviewer knew what it was, and Gillard interrupted to explain it was an Albanian vampire.

David at one point asked if he was going to go to prison. Ms Skipworth replied: 'You might be sent to a special place where they can help you. But it's not a prison. They don't send children to prison.'

'So I could leave when I want?'

There was a pause. 'No, not until you are judged safe.'

'So it's a prison.'

'Not really. Your mummy and daddy could come and visit you, and sometimes you may be allowed to spend time at home.'

He nodded. 'Okay.'

Ms Jones was playing with Amber. She was holding the Lost-Kitty, and hiding it behind a cushion, until Amber squealed with dismay. 'Don't hide her, that's cruel.'

She apologized and gave the toy back. Amber cuddled the kitten and stroked its nylon fur. 'This was a present from my mummy.'

'Really?' said the social worker. 'That's nice of her.'

'Yes. My mummy in heaven.'

'Oh.' The woman shared a pouted 'so sweet' gesture with her colleague, who smiled back.

'An angel brought it down from heaven for me.' The child kissed the kitten on its furry nose. 'But the angel died.'

'Oh, how sad.'

Amber nodded. 'My brother shot him.'

Acknowledgements and Afterword

Please save this until you've read the book, as there are a few spoilers. I have taken a few liberties with the geography of Surrey and its public transport network, which will undoubtedly be noticed by those who live nearby. While Elmbridge is the real name of the council borough, there is no suburb bearing that name and of course Roosevelt Avenue, for all of its resemblance to many British high streets, is fictitious, as are the businesses therein.

I spent the best part of a month in Albania in 2017, and was treated with great hospitality. I was fortunate enough to witness a genuine mafia funeral, whose scale and power left a deep impression on me. Though some real crime families are mentioned in passing in the book, the Dragusha and Kreshniki are entirely my invention. Neither they nor their key personnel are based on any real organisation or people. Though, inevitably, a crime thriller throws a spotlight on the worst aspects of any society, I would emphasise that I was impressed by the vigour and aspiration of the Albanian people, striving to escape a troubled past. European readers who were taken aback by the revelation of the killer, and who doubt that such things are possible, may want to search YouTube for videos of automatic weapons being used by children as young as five. What is often proudly recorded in the U.S. is also true but less well-publicised in both Albania and Yemen.

On matters related to police and forensic procedure I would like to thank Kim Booth, Dr Stuart Hamilton, and Dr Jenny Ward. Neil Dowlman was kind enough to let me visit his architectural practice in Alford. I would also like to thank Kate Mitchell and Jess E. for their specialist insight and expertise, plus Sara Wescott for reading the draft. Any remaining errors are my own.

I would like to express particular thanks to Aless Thorbjorn for her excellent rendition of the Dragusha symbol and the map of Albania.

I would particularly like to thank Michael Bhaskar and his hard-working team at Canelo, who set me a tough deadline, and copy editor Séan Costello.

Above all, I owe everything to my wife Louise, always my first and most insightful reader.